The Other Side of the River

A Historical Novel

Betsy Ross Manning

VANTAGE PRESS
New York

For George, his family, and mine . . . pioneers all

FIRST EDITION

Published by Vantage Press, Inc.
516 West 34th Street, New York, New York 10001

Manufactured in the United States of America

ISBN: 0-533-13751-9

Library of Congress Catalog Card No.: 00-92235

0 9 8 7 6 5 4 3 2 1

Contents

The Other Side of the River

A Historical Novel

Part One

Chapter One
Nate

The Riley farm sat on deep rich bottom land in southwestern Tennessee about midway between the Hatchie and Mississippi Rivers. Three generations of Rileys had been faithful stewards of this place. The land and the family nourished each other.

One old timer with nothing better to do liked to sit on an old wooden Douglas chair tipped back to touch the wall of the small general store serving the simple needs of the Rileys and farmers like them. The store, the chair, and the old man were of the same vintage and when he was absent from his perch, customers inquired as to his health. The old man could take a joke but was at his best teasing strangers, particularly "uppity" ones, who asked him for directions.

When a gentleman mounted on a fine Tennessee walking horse stopped to ask directions to the Riley farm, the store's customers within earshot clenched their teeth to keep from smiling but strained to hear the old man's every word.

He pointed and said, "You go down this here road about four miles. You'll come to a sorry old rock wall. It marks the boundary of the farm of Riley's neighbor. The two of 'em never did get along. Now, Riley's place starts on the other side of that rock wall. Old man Riley and his sons don't build rock walls, never did. Riley plants his rocks. Only farmer I ever knew who could plant a rock and watch it sprout in less than a week. He taught his youngest boy, Nate, how to plant pebbles before their child could walk. Plants boulders by now, I reckon."

* * *

Nate Riley was born to farm. He could feel the changing seasons in his bones. Mother Earth whispered her secrets to him so he would know exactly which days were best for planting. He had the patience to wait for the autumn moon's announcement of the time for harvest. Even at his young age, Nate could predict the day rain would fall and seemed to know in advance when snow, a rarity in southern lowlands, would paint the landscape white.

This particular morning, Nate dressed quietly so as not to wake his brothers still asleep in the farmhouse loft. His clothes were not much different from those worn by children of other farm families. His shirt and undergarments were sewn of store-bought cloth and his trousers were made of homespun, the hardy fabric spun, woven, and hand sewn by his mother and sisters.

Nate was the last son to wear his present wardrobe. When he outgrew it, his mother would disassemble his garments, use the larger pieces of cloth to sew bodices for his sisters, and save the smaller pieces for quilting.

Nate was too big for a boy but not yet a man. Sometimes his voice was tenor and sometimes bass, neither of which could be anticipated. Scattered under his freckles, a few pimples waited to emerge. His sandy hair was crowned by a cowlick that refused to obey even when he slicked it down with grease. He was skinny and had a long stride, sometimes resembling a canter, and sometimes the gallop he used when his father called. The man's mood could be judged by the tone of his voice.

Mr. Riley was not a patient man and some found him rude and obnoxious. While his personality was wanting, as a farmer he had no peer. He tended his crops with the loving care he would not waste on his children. Strangely enough, the man had a shrewd eye that recognized the farmer's gift in others. He saw it in his youngest son. While his father's instructions were gruff, the knowledge he passed on to Nate was the greatest gift he could have given him. Nate drank it up like a thirsty mule at the water trough.

On this special morning, the boy was shaking, not from the chill, but from the excitement. It was his turn to go to town, something that happened only once a year for each of the eight Riley children. Farmers like Nate make plans a year in advance and only drought or fire or some other catastrophe can sway them from their orderly duties. Nate had planned all year for this day and envisioned what he could do when he arrived in town.

The boy had spent the past months in search of beaver. It took him nearly a year to trap the animals, skin and tan their hides. His older brothers teased him and said he couldn't do it. His father thought it was a waste of time. While his mother said nothing, the faint smile on her face was reward enough for his efforts. His sisters said they felt sorry for the beavers but they didn't hesitate to eat chicken when it was on the Sunday dinner table.

I'm going to make me some good money when I sell my pelts today, maybe enough to buy a young colt, he thought while splashing his face with water from the basin. Nate was surprised to find that he had to bend his knees so he could see his entire head in the mirror which hung on the wall above the wash stand. He smiled back at his own reflection. *I'm near as tall as Matthew,* he thought as he stretched on tiptoes. As usual, his cowlick stood at attention. The boy tried a little spit on it to no avail.

Nate reached for the storage place under his side of the bed in order to fetch the draw-string bag sewn by his mother and used to hold his precious beaver belts. His hand touched nothing but air. For a more thorough search, he slid under the bed on his belly. The bag was gone. He heard John snicker above him. The unexpected sound startled Nate who hit his head on the bedstead.

His four brothers, all fully dressed, threw off their bed covers and John grabbed Nate's feet and pulled him out from under the bed. Matthew jumped on his youngest brother's back while Ben and Caleb joined in the fun by pelting him with their pillows. John snatched the beaver bag from Matthew, the thief, who was twirling it over his head like a lasso. Caleb grabbed the bag from John, pulled it open, and laughed as he tossed the pelts, one by one, into the air. The brothers went after the flying furs as if they were trying to catch june bugs in the spring. Nate struggled to retrieve his hard-earned bounty and punched and shoved his brothers in the bargain. Sounds of the fracas rattled through the farmhouse.

"What the devil's goin' on up there!" bellowed their father.

Matthew, Ben, Caleb, and John, in that order and wearing their most innocent expressions, straightened their clothing, ran their fingers through their mussed hair, and calmly decended the stairs from their sleeping loft. They took their seats at the breakfast table and politely asked their mother to pass the grits, fried eggs, biscuits, sweet butter, honey, and the pitcher of milk. "Oh, yes, and the fried apples too, please."

They were half finished eating when Nate came down. His face was red and he looked as if he had been on the losing end of a fight, but he said nothing. He held his hat in one hand and the drawstring bag in the other.

"You're late!" yelled his father. He rose from the table and slapped his son across the face. "I've a mind to take Matthew with me today instead of you!"

"I'm sorry, sir," Nate said as he hung his head in shame.

"Mr. Riley," interjected his wife, "I do need Nate's help today with my herbs and medicines. He's the only other one in the family who really understands their curative powers and how to sort and store them."

Her husband thought for a moment. "Very well, Madam. He can come but without breakfast." Their father excused himself from the table and ordered his sons to follow, whether or not they had finished eating. "Time to load the wagons," he said.

Mrs. Riley and the girls had their own chores to finish. Even though it was not her job, Elizabeth climbed the stairs to the loft bedroom shared by her brothers. Because he was the eldest, Matthew got to sleep in a bed of his own. Ben and Caleb shared a bed, as did John and Nate.

Their sister shook her head as she surveyed the mess the boys had made. The wall mirror was crooked, the wash bowl dirty, and water had spilled on the floor. By some miracle, five towels were still hanging from pegs on the wall. Across the room, a few clothes still hung in place on wooden pegs but most clothing had fallen off and lay crumpled on the floor. Each brother kept small personal items in a basket stored under his side of the bed. Elizabeth found all baskets in their places except for Nate's.

The furniture had been scattered but was unbroken. Although three chairs had been tipped over, the small sturdy table remained upright. The two oil coal lamps were undamaged. While the chamber pot was upright against the north wall, nothing had spilled out of it. "Thank goodness!" sighed Elizabeth.

Even though she had heard the commotion, the mess her brothers had made of the room was greater than she had expected. Elizabeth, wise beyond her years, said nothing. *We'll never get to town if Papa sees this*! she thought. "Grace, Elle, come up this minute," she called down to her sisters. Elizabeth put her finger to her lips when the two girls appeared at the top of the stairs.

Elle and Grace gasped when they saw the disarray but joined their sister as the three of them quietly and quickly put the room in order. When they finished, Elizabeth whispered, "Papa won't know now. Hurry! We have to get our room done before he comes back!" The girls tip-toed down the stairs.

The sisters shared a bed in the small downstairs bedroom next to that of their parents. "I'll carry out the chamber pot if you two make up the bed," Elizabeth said. "Today the boys can empty their own after we leave. Theirs is too stinky." She put a cloth over the top of the open container so the liquid wouldn't slop out and carried it carefully out to the privy where she dumped the contents down the hole.

Unlike most families who simply threw the pot's contents out on the ground away from the house, Mrs. Riley insisted that all of the chamber pots in her house be emptied in the privy. And she, not her husband, was the one who chose the digging site each time the hole was full and the privy needed to be relocated. Mrs. Riley made absolutely sure their privy was 150 feet away and downhill from the water well.

While Elizabeth was tending to her chore, Grace and Elle finished smoothing the coverlet on their bed. "I'll be glad when Papa finishes the bed he is making for Elizabeth," Grace said.

"So will I," her little sister replied. "Elizabeth is getting too big and takes up most of the room. If she were a boy, she'd already have her own bed like Matthew. Papa likes boys better than girls."

"He does not!" answered Grace.

"Does so!"

"Does not!"

"Does so!"

"Does what?" asked Elizabeth who entered the room and pushed the chamber pot under the bed where it belonged.

"I said Papa likes boys better than girls and Grace says he doesn't, that's what!" Elle answered.

"Well, Papa likes Mama most of all, and she's a girl," countered Elizabeth.

"She is NOT a girl! Mama is a lady!"

With that, Grace and Elizabeth picked Elle up and threw her in the middle of the just-made bed.

"Girls! What are you doing?" chided their mother. "Finish your chores. Has everyone gone completely mad today?"

The sisters agreed that the morning had not gone well and promised to stop their arguing, at least until tomorrow. There was little left to be done in their own room. It was furnished much like the loft except for a bedspread and matching curtains at the single window. Each of their towels had the name of the owner embroidered on it so they would not be mixed up. The girls had done the needle work on their own as well as on the towels for the other members of the family.

All members of the household could quote from memory Mrs. Riley's familiar words, "You have enough weakness and sickness of your own so there's no need to borrow some from others." Their mother insisted each member of her household use only his or her towel. When her family members complained of their mother's fastidious ways, she merely quoted that part of the Bible, "writ large," she said, where the Good Book declared, "Cleanliness is next to Godliness." As far as Mrs. Riley was concerned, that was the end of the argument.

In addition to keeping a clean and orderly house, she also was known to examine the cleanliness of the barn from time to time. This was the one event he could not control and Mr. Riley dreaded the day his wife invaded his turf. He learned, however, how to read the signs portending the coming inspection and deemed himself fortunate indeed if he cleaned up the barn before his wife descended upon the place.

When he saw the bedding airing on the front porch railing and the rag rugs hanging from the clothesline while Caleb beat them with a fanned wire whip, Mr. Riley knew the time had come. He called to his other sons. "Matthew, shovel out the barn. Nate, bring some clean straw. Ben, make sure the milk pails are as clean as your mother wants. John, tidy up the chicken coop!" Under his breath, their father muttered, "Next thing you know, she'll be wantin' us to plant flowers in the pig sty!" With that, the master of the house put on his boots, grabbed a shovel, and headed out to the pig sty himself.

While he never complimented his wife on the care and energy she spent on her husband and family, Mr. Riley did notice that they all seemed to avoid the grippe and other maladies that sometimes were visited upon other farm folk and townspeople. *Maybe her ideas aren't all that crazy, at that,* he thought to himself. *But again, maybe they are.*

The Rileys making the trip to town finished their chores at about the same time. The wagons were loaded and Nate and his father hitched up the teams as Mrs. Riley carried the dishpan out to the end of the porch and threw the dishwater on her small kitchen garden. She went back inside the house to check things once more and fetch her bonnet, shawl, and satchel.

During her final check of the house, she smiled as she noted everything in order. The banked coals in the fireplace would last the day. The cooking pots, now clean, had been removed from their hanging hooks over the fireplace grate and stored beside the stone hearth. The table had been cleared except for a newly filled coal oil lamp placed in its center. The two long benches were pushed under the table as was Mr. Riley's chair at its head. Rag rugs, free of dust, were in place near the furniture in the parlor side of the large kitchen. A settee and four comfortable wooden chairs were arranged, as usual, in a semicircle facing the fireplace. It had taken Mrs. Riley a long time to train her family so household routines would become automatic. She knew her children, sons as well as daughters, would be able to care for themselves when they left their family home.

Mrs. Riley checked the girls' room and found it acceptable. The room she shared with her husband was neat and tidy, bed made, pillows fluffed, just as she had left it before she started breakfast. While some hats and clothing items hung on wall pegs, their best garments were kept in a beautiful and massive walnut wardrobe Mr. Riley had given her as a wedding present. It was the most romantic thing he had ever done.

"I reckoned you'd like the thing," he had shyly told her some twenty years ago.

"It's the most beautiful thing I have ever seen," she had replied as she kissed him softly on the cheek. She smiled at the memory and wondered if the children would ever see their father's loving side.

She quickly climbed the stairs to the loft bedroom and merely glanced inside as she heard her husband calling for her.

"Well now, I think we are ready to go," she said aloud as she carefully descended the stairs, walked through the kitchen, out the door, and down the porch steps. She smiled with pride, secure in the knowledge that the Riley home was as clean and tidy as any house in the county. Probably cleaner.

As Nate helped his mother up to her seat on the first wagon, they heard Mr. Riley giving final orders to the sons he was leaving behind. "Rest assured, Nate, the chores will be finished when we return home," his mother whispered.

"Load up!" Mr. Riley shouted as he climbed up to the seat of the yellow wagon and sat next to his wife. "Elizabeth, you go with Nate and make sure he stays two wagon lengths behind us. Grace, you and Elle come with your mother and me. I want no fightin' or fussin', understand?"

"Yes, sir," the girls replied in unison as each gave a courteous nod to her father. Those who dared show disrespect to Mr. Riley got whupped upside the head, something his three daughters, but not all of his sons, had avoided.

"Just look at him," said Mrs. Riley to her husband as they watched their youngest son take the reins to the mules pulling the older wagon. "He's never driven to town before. Are you sure he can manage the team?"

"He's been practicin' all week. He'll do fine or I'll take the strop to him." Mr. Riley, ramrod stiff and proud, clicked his tongue, snapped the reins, and felt the wheels turn as his splendid team of two matched black horses smoothly pulled the yellow wagon forward. It was fully loaded with the finest produce a farmer could grow.

The boys left with the chores hollered their good-byes as Nate followed two wagons lengths behind his father. He drove an older but sturdy wagon pulled by two cussed old mules. "Easy now, easy," he softly cautioned the team. He held the reins so tightly his fingernails left marks in the palm of his hands. Nate was fully aware of the value of his load and knew from first-hand experience the sting of the strop wielded by his father's heavy hand.

By the time the wagons had cleared the farm's fields, Nate began to relax. The steady rhythm of the mules' hooves complemented the more muffled sounds of the horses up ahead. Adding to the chorus were the rhythmic noise of the wagon's turning wheels and the comforting squeaks of board on board in an old wagon with a full load.

Nate was thankful talkative Elizabeth was quiet, probably because of the haste with which she completed her household chores. The only thing she said to him was, "Here," when she handed him three biscuits she had hidden in her skirt.

Nate gulped down this unexpected gift and hoped his father would not look back. He didn't. The young driver sighed with pleasure and surveyed his world. He looked up at the clear blue sky and noticed a flock of Canada geese flying south in a V formation. Now and then, Nate glanced into the woods and sighted splashes of yellow and red coloring the leaves of birch and maple trees. He wondered if there might be a beaver pond nearby.

"Look, Elizabeth, there's color already," he said as he held the reins in one hand and pointed with the other to the high golden leaf canopy an ancient oak had spread over the dirt road they traveled.

Nate was unprepared when a huge, five-point buck bolted out of the woods and darted between the two wagons. Mr. Riley kept his horse team under control, but the deer nearly ran over the mules pulling the second wagon.

The two startled mules reared but not in tandem. Each one bucked, snorted, reared and acted as an independent force with enough energy to break the harness, scatter the load, and injure or kill the driver and his passenger.

Nate reacted instinctively based on hours of practice. He was not aware that both hands grasped the reins tightly the instant he saw the deer out of the corner of his eye. He stood bracing himself against the seat and called out, "Whoa, now, whoa! Easy! Easy! Whoooaaaaaa. Whhhoooooaaaaaaaa," as he pulled back on the reins with all of the strength in his body. The tug-of-war seemed to last forever.

Gradually, the violent action lessened and when the mules finally stood still, their muscles continued to twitch. Nate, still standing and in shock, looked at his sister whose hands were still gripping the edge of the seat. Her face had lost its color and tears were rolling down her cheeks. Nate was too afraid to let go of the reins or to sit down to comfort her. He could not even speak but smiled weakly as if to signal that everything was all right now. The deer escaped without injury.

Still standing and shaking violently, Nate looked ahead to see the front wagon stopped and his family staring at him. His little sisters were crying. His mother waved her handkerchief. His father stood, reins in hand. He said nothing, but nodded slightly to Nate, turned around, sat down, and signaled his team to continue the journey.

Nate was afraid to get the mules moving again. "Let's go," Elizabeth urged. The boy, still shaking, sat down. He clutched the reins in both hands but did not move. It was not until Elizabeth moved over close, put her arms around him and gently rubbed his back that he was able to speak.

"I'm all right. I'm all right," he whispered over and over again. Nate breathed deeply in and out, in and out. It was not until he noticed that this father's wagon had disappeared from view that he was able to click his tongue and flip the reins. The mules started slowly as their driver held his breath.

By the time Nate and Elizabeth had traveled a quarter mile, they sighted the yellow wagon far ahead. It appeared to have stopped. Mr. Riley told his passengers he feared one of his horses had thrown a shoe. When Nate pulled up behind the yellow wagon stopped in the shade of a large poplar tree, their father was carefully checking the shoes on each of the horses' hooves. He patted the last horse on the rump.

"Teams seem thirsty," his father said to no one in particular. "Get water from that creek over there." He motioned as he handed Nate a bucket.

The boy dipped it in the water and tried unsuccessfully to steady his hands as he splashed water while carrying the bucket back and forth from the creek to the horses until all of the animals were watered. His hands became more steady with each trip.

As his father silently predicted, the chore he gave his son was a simple and repetitive task that relieved some of the tension the boy felt and allowed his mind to gain better control over his strained and aching muscles.

His mother took some peaches from a crate in the wagon, climbed down, and beckoned the girls to follow. "Grace, you and Elle wash these in the creek and we'll have ourselves a little picnic right here." Mrs. Riley spread a quilt on the ground, opened the basket she had packed with cold chicken and biscuits from breakfast, and served her family.

Nate was grateful for the food and the rest. He was waiting for the thrashing his father was sure to give him. Instead, when the last peach pit was thrown into the creek, Mr. Riley gave the usual command, "Load up!" Nate took a deep breath, climbed up into the seat and lent a hand to Elizabeth. The food and rest had restored his sister's voice.

"I thought Papa would whup you good. You almost lost our load! Why didn't he? Do you know why he didn't? I would have if I was him. At least, I think I would have." Her brother didn't answer. She didn't expect him to. She just liked to talk and kept up her chatter as the wagons rolled on without incident for another hour before horse and wagon traffic increased. Elizabeth grew more excited with each turn of the wagon's wheels.

Nate gave his full attention to driving and had tuned out his sister's chatter miles back. Her sudden silence, however, caught his attention. The quiet was broken as she made a sour face, gagged, held her nose, and whined, "What's that smell?"

"That's how towns smell!" her brother said dramatically as he grinned at her discomfort. He pointed out the slaughter house and the huge holding pens for hogs. "Some of those hogs are slaughtered right here, but most of them are loaded on those freight cars waiting on the railroad track. The pens are full. That means a locomotive must be coming soon to haul them off to a big market up north somewhere."

Elizabeth held her nose until they were past the stockyard and vowed not to breathe deeply again until they were back on their farm.

"You are a silly girl, Elizabeth. You should have stayed at home," chided Nate. "What's the good of coming to town if you act like a cross old woman. Why, I'll bet you faint when we drive past those saloons. The whiskey they sell is so strong the smell near knocks you down if you walk past the door. Then you'd miss the sweet-smelling stuff on that sweet-smelling Mr. Hall in that fancy barbershop he runs. I suppose you want me to turn around right here and take you home."

"No, I don't!" she said through clenched teeth. As if to prove she was serious, Elizabeth pointed to the first houses she had seen since leaving the farm. "Who lives there? The houses aren't very nice and they could use some whitewash."

"People who live there called themselves 'free blacks.' I think it means they were slaves once and now they're not. Matthew told me Mr. Sowell hired one to help in his store. The houses aren't much but their vegetable patches look pretty good," Nate answered.

"I smell a privy!" Elizabeth whispered as they drove past a larger section where the houses looked slightly different. Their board and batten siding may have seen whitewash at one time.

"That's where the poor dirt farmers live. They don't have any land to speak of. A man can hardly provide enough food to feed his family, much less have some left over to sell," offered Nate. "Folks in town call people like that 'white trash'."

"We're not 'white trash,' are we?" Elizabeth offered.

"I'm not, but you might be," Nate teased. She hit him.

His sister liked the houses in town much better than the ones they had passed earlier. Most of them were painted different colors and had white picket fences around their front yards. While she could glimpse small vegetable gardens in back, it was the flower gardens in the front yards that caught her eye.

"Why don't we plant more flowers at our house?" she asked.

"Papa says it's a waste of good dirt. Besides, there are all the wild flowers you could ever want in our meadows."

Nate followed his father's wagon up Main Street and was surprised at the changes in the business district. He pointed out a brick building under construction. "It must be another bank," he said, "or maybe a hotel. That must mean business is good. Papa says if business is good in town, it's good for us."

Elizabeth liked the two story buildings the best, especially the ones with balconies. Wooden plank sidewalks lined both sides of the street. She watched ladies walking on them as men tipped their hats while passing by.

Elizabeth smelled whiskey even before Nate drove past the tavern. She gagged dramatically. From the balcony above the establishment, painted ladies called down to Nate.

"Yoo hoo, farm boy!" the one in the silky red dress called out. "Farm boy, come up and let little old Lucille make a man of you!"

The other painted ladies laughed. Nate blushed and urged the mules to go faster.

Always wanting the last word, Elizabeth stood up, cupped her hands around her mouth and shouted back. "Lucille, you leave my brother alone! He's a near man already!"

"Hush, Elizabeth, hush!" Nate pulled on her skirt until she plopped unceremoniously onto the wagon seat. The entire scene was vastly entertaining to all within earshot. The boy was relieved to see Sowell's General Store in the block ahead.

Mr. Sowell was sweeping the board walk in front of his store when he saw the Riley wagons approaching. He gave one final sweep with the broom then smiled broadly, waved his arm, and called out a cheerful greeting. "Mr. and Mrs. Riley! Children! I've been expecting you! Do climb down and rest yourselves."

Chapter Two

Town Business

Nate liked Mr. Sowell. He was a friendly sort of man, about fifty and with greying hair slightly thinner than last year just after Mrs. Sowell died. Then her husband's sorrow showed in his face and in the slight shuffle present in his usual brisk walk. Nate thought the man looked much better this year and he was glad. The boy wished his father was more like the storekeeper.

As Mr. Sowell helped Mrs. Riley down from the wagon, she inquired as to the state of his health. "Are you well, Mr. Sowell? Eating properly? Getting enough rest? Have you stopped heavy lifting?" The woman stopped abruptly. "Forgive me. I didn't mean to be such a busy body."

"Not at all, Madam! Not at all! Mrs. Sowell, rest her soul, would be cheered at the thought of a lovely lady like yourself taking enough interest to nag and keep me on the straight and narrow. But I miss her. I've hired me a free black man, name of Ned, who does the heavy work. Sweeping the sidewalk is his job, but I did it this morning. Gave me an excuse to watch for you."

Mr. Sowell lifted Grace and Elle down from the yellow wagon as Mr. Riley jumped down from the driver's side and tied his team to a wooden post. Elizabeth jumped down by herself, and Nate slid off on the other side of the seat. *Thank you, Lord, for gettin' us here alive,* he prayed silently. *And please, God, help me stop shakin' and give my knees back their strength.* Then the boy smiled and shook the merchant's hand.

"I cherish my old friends like you," Mr. Sowell went on. "Ned cleaned out the boxes and barrels. We're ready to trade the empties for your full ones. I still say the best fruits and vegetables in the county come from the Riley farm."

Mr. Riley gave the storekeeper one of his rare smiles. *The man has a way with him,* the farmer thought. *He knows I'm the best farmer in the county and I know he runs the best general store within fifty miles in any direction. Have I really been bringing my harvests to this man's store for twenty years? In that time I've worn out two wagons, four teams, and had eight children!*

"Always glad to do business with you," were the only words Mr. Riley spoke aloud.

Ned came from the back room and started unloading the produce designated for his employer. Mr. Riley had an unspoken pledge to give the merchant first choice of his harvest. It was one of the reasons the storekeeper was among the most prosperous merchants in town.

Mr. Sowell was honest, his prices fair, and his unique practice of giving gifts to his suppliers and their families was the shrewd move that brought them first to his door. He gave the farmers pouches of fine tobacco and graciously allowed their wives to select a dress length of cloth from any bolt on the shelves. Each of the farm children was allowed to choose a baker's dozen pieces of candy from that enticing counter.

Before he drove off to call on his other customers, Mr. Riley directed, "You girls unload your mother's medicine baskets and carry them for her when she makes her rounds. Nate, when you finish here, get the mules fed and watered at the livery stable. Look for my wagon and if it's empty, do the same with my team. We should be finished in three, maybe four hours, and be on our way to get home before dark."

Nate, with Ned's help, filled the fruit barrels which were next to the windows and visible from the sidewalk. They handled the apples, pears, and peaches with care so the fruit would not bruise. Ned stacked the fresh corn against the south wall while Nate placed other yellow, green, and orange vegetables closer to the front of the store where they would attract a lady's eye. Their vivid colors accented the counter displaying sewing goods—ribbons, needles, thread, and bolts of fabric. There was a separate counter for items devoted to the rich—ostrich feathers, silk from Japan, French lace, tiny glass seed beads, and elegant brocades.

While Nate was arranging the vegetables, Mr. Sowell helped the three Riley sisters choose their candy. Then he went to assist Mrs. Riley as she selected her fabric. She chose a floral print of pastel colors. The lady smiled and said, "This will remind me of spring when I'm sewing this winter. I think I'll make a dress for myself. Thank you for your generosity, dear friend."

When his mother and sisters left carrying the medicine baskets and their gifts from Mr. Sowell, Nate and Ned were still unloading the farm wagon. Nate rolled barrels of cornmeal and wheat flour down a plank from the wagon to where Ned was waiting on the sidewalk. From there, both of them rolled the wooden containers through the store to the storage room and exchanged them for empty ones to be loaded back on the wagon. They made several more trips to unload sacks of potatoes, both sweet and white, and carefully stacked them to the far left of the wood stove.

Mr. Sowell was aware and approving of the careful work his hired hand and Nate were doing although not a word had passed between any of them since the unloading began. It was when the top of a cotton sack tore and a few sweet potatoes fell out on the floor that Nate spoke to his helper. "Do you like sweet taters?" he asked.

"Yas, suh, I likes 'em ash-cooked," Ned replied without looking up.

The two of them gathered up the potatoes, every one, and returned them to the bag from which they had fallen. Nate propped the bag next to the others so the potatoes wouldn't fall out again. Then he went out to his wagon and returned with three sweet potatoes in his hands. He looked to Mr. Sowell for permission and received a nod. The boy handed the sweet taters to Ned. "These are for you. Mr. Sowell hired himself a good hand," he said. Ned nodded his thanks and left to finish work in the store room.

The merchant gave Nate clean and empty lard buckets to fill with groundnuts which he placed beside the candy counter. His final task was to arrange the baskets of his mother's herbs on the counter next to the money drawer. The boy was surprised that more than an hour had passed since he began work. He was tired and went outside and sat down on the step to rest.

Mr. Sowell was pleased as he surveyed his well-stocked and inviting store. He got two glasses of cool sassafras tea, carried them out front and handed one to Nate as the storekeeper sat down beside him. "And here's some candy for you," he said as he took a bag out of the pocket of his big apron.

The boy, already grateful for the drink, nodded his head in thanks and smiled as he accepted the sweets. Because he had grown so tall in the past year, he had wondered if Mr. Sowell would offer him tobacco instead of candy. Nate liked candy best.

"Had you rather have tobacco?" the merchant asked.

"No, sir. Candy suits me fine. I'm mighty grateful."

"Do you smoke, Nate?"

"No, sir." Nate averted his eyes from Mr. Sowell's gaze. "Well, I did try it once with my brothers. It was on a Sunday after dinner when we were fishin'. All four of them were smokin' like chimneys in January. Matthew said I was a girl and would never be a man if I didn't at least try a pipeful.

"So I did, and it wasn't so bad. Matthew filled a corncob pipe with tobacco three times. I told him once was enough, but he paid me no mind. I kept on smokin' and fishin' and pretty soon I was feeling so woozy I couldn't even get the fish I caught off the hook. I walked back to the house and sprawled on my bed until my mother called us all for supper.

"I washed up and sat at my place at the table. When Mama passed me that fried fish, I just barely made it out the door and off the porch before . . . well, as my mother says, before the contents of my stomach came back up to greet me. I felt some better and went back inside. Matthew was laughin' so hard tears ran out of his eyes. Papa looked at me cross like but had a little smile slip out on his face.

"Mama was not happy. She was dishin' up the apple cobbler by that time. She called out, 'This one is for Mr. Riley, this bowl for myself, one for Elizabeth, this one for Grace, one for Elle, and this big serving is for Nate. I'll save it for him until he feels like eating. This surely is one of the best apple cobblers I have ever baked.'

"My brothers watched Mama dump their servings into the slop bucket going to the pigs. She gave Papa a look that almost dared him to complain about wasting food. Papa ate his cobbler without saying a word and my brothers just sat there watching everybody eat. They left me alone the rest of that day. I ate my cobbler for breakfast the next morning."

Mr. Sowell enjoyed Nate's story. It reminded him of his own youth. The man rose to his feet and started to go back inside his store when Nate took a deep breath and began. "Mr. Sowell, sir, I'd be obliged if you would look at some beaver pelts I have here."

He rose quickly and reached under the seat of the old wagon, took out the drawstring bag, and walked with the merchant back into the store. Nate took the pelts out of his bag and spread out the lustrous furs on the counter.

Mr. Sowell was surprised and pleased as he brushed the soft pelts with his hand and blew on the fur to test for quality and the animal and the skill of the tanner. "Did you trap and tan these yourself, Nate?" he asked.

"Yes, sir. I tanned them over the winter when farm work slows some. I'm hoping to sell pelts 'til I have enough money saved up to buy me a horse of my own."

"Good, good," Mr. Sowell said softly as he nodded his head. The man thought for a moment as Nate held his breath. "Will you take twenty-five dollars for the bunch?"

The boy's smile was his answer. The merchant opened the money drawer and counted out four fives and five one-dollar bills into Nate's hand. "Thank you, sir. I've never seen this much money at one time in my whole life."

Mr. Sowell laughed. "You have a good head on you, Nate, and you're not afraid of hard work. None of you Rileys are. I know your father is not an easy man, but he has taught his children well. He's honest and has a good business head. It's your mother, bless her heart, who has kept him human, although at times I don't know how she puts up with him.

"I can tell you for a fact how proud your father is of you, Nate. He sees himself in you. You have his gift of knowing the land and your mother's gift of a gentle soul. Would more people be so blessed." The storekeeper cleared his throat, embarrassed by his own flowery words.

Nate was silent and simply extended his hand to shake that of the storekeeper who had known him since he was born.

The boy untied the mules, climbed into the wagon, and headed up the dirt street to the livery stable. On the way he drove by the barbershop and waved back to his mother and sisters, who saw him pass. *Mr. Hall's barbershop smells a lot better than the livery stable where I'm headed,* he thought.

Mr. Hall was the third customer Mrs. Riley and her daughters had called upon that morning. The barber/dentist greeted them warmly. "News travels fast in our town, Mrs. Riley. I've been waiting for you. Do sit down and rest. I've made you some tea."

"How thoughtful, Mr. Hall," the lady replied. "Girls, put the baskets on the table and sit down." Elizabeth scrambled into the vacant barber chair, something she had always wanted to do. Her mother's withering glance directed her to get down from there and find one of the empty chairs in the shop. All of the Riley women properly thanked Mr. Hall who served them tea in china cups.

"My dear Mrs. Riley," he said when the tea party was over, "I am grateful to you for bringing to my most humble shop the finest medicinal plants in the county. What's more, you best anyone I know in your knowledge of the many ways to use them in treatment. I give you great praise, indeed! Now, let us look into your baskets and see what miracles you have brought to me today."

The three girls exchanged glances elicited by the barber's silly talk. It was not so silly, however, when he addressed them. "Young ladies, where are the little girls who came with their mother a year ago? Surely, they cannot be you. Wait. You must be Elizabeth, the oldest and now grown into a lovely young lady. And you, let me think—Grace! Yes, Grace with the beautiful smile. That leaves Elle. I've seen those dimples before, young lady. I do hope you three girls have been as blessed as your mother when it comes to her knowledge of medicines." Mr. Hall captured their hearts with well-chosen words. *Had Nate heard them, he would have gagged,* thought Elizabeth.

Mrs. Riley laughed. "The girls bake the best biscuits in the county, but Nate is the one who follows me into the woods to help search for plants that heal. It is a gift, you know. Now, sir, which of my 'miracles' as you call them, would you like to buy?"

Nate, at that moment, had his hands full. He found the yellow wagon empty which meant his father had finished his deliveries to all of his customers and had gone on to tend to other business in town. The boy unhitched and led the two cooperative horses to the livery stable where they took feed and water. The two old mules, true to their foolish ways, were so stubborn it took Nate nearly fifteen minutes to get one inside the barn and to the hay.

A stable hand enjoyed watching the entertaining tug-of-war. Since the man had nothing better to do, he said, "Can I give ya a hand with that other cussed mule?"

Even though he was embarrassed, Nate was grateful for the help. It took the two of them working together to lead, push, kick, and pull the second mule into the barn. When the beast finally gave up the struggle, it took the feed bag as if he were the most cooperative animal on God's green earth.

"Dumb mule! Dumb, stupid, dirty, worn out, stubborn, old mule fool!" Nate hissed as he kicked at the side of the barn with his boot. His preference was to kick the mule, but in such a contest there was no doubt who would win. After taking his frustration out on the side of the barn, he felt better.

The stable hand, accustomed to such scenes, asked, "Anything else you need?"

Nate thought for a moment. "Are there any horses for sale?"

"Reckon so. I'll get Mr. Barston for you." The stable hand disappeared into a nearby saloon and soon returned walking behind a heavy-set man who smiled at Nate and extended his hand.

"Young man, you are indeed fortunate to have come this very day. As it happens, I have a selection of fine horses from which to choose. What kind of a horse did you have in mind and how much money do you plan to spend?"

"I'm hoping for a fine riding horse, but gentle, one that my sisters might ride if it pleases them. I'm saving my money for one. How much do you get for your horses, sir?"

"Oh, from fifty to a hundred and sometimes more. Dollars, that is. Just how much money do you have, boy?" the man asked.

"Twenty-five dollars," Nate replied as he put his hand in his pocket to make sure the money was still there.

"Don't that beat all!" exclaimed Mr. Barston. "Just this morning a poor old farmer came in and sold me his fine horse for that very same sum. The man lost his crop to flood and needed the money to feed his family. I bought the steed out of the goodness of my heart. Feeding livestock, as you well know, is an expense. For that very reason, I will sell you that fine animal for what I paid for it, twenty-five dollars." Mr. Barston directed his employee to take Nate into the corral to see the fine steed.

Nate spoke softly to the horse as he slowly approached it and continued his one-sided conversation as he carefully but firmly opened the animal's mouth. The boy rubbed his finger's over the filly's teeth and inspected her tongue. He ran his hands over the withers and from top to bottom of each of her four legs. Nate picked up each foot to examine the hooves. He noted the lack of shine to her sorrel coat and darker mane and tail.

He asked for a bridle to see how the horse took the bit. Then, with little effort, he mounted the animal and galloped bareback more than a dozen times around the inside of the corral fence. When Nate dismounted, he listened to the wheeze coming from the horse's lungs. The boy whispered his thanks into the horse's ear, patted it gently on the nose, then walked away.

The two men were surprised by Nate's thorough examination of the animal. "Well, what do you think, young man?" asked Mr. Barston.

"I think you paid way too much for her, sir, but I'm sure the poor farmer appreciated your generosity. She's a gentle thing but not what I had in mind. I'll be back later with my father to get our teams and pay for the feed."

As Nate walked away, the stable hand ducked his head to hide the smile on his face. His cagey boss had been bested by a mere farm boy. Mr. Barston was speechless and his face turned red.

When Nate left the livery stable, he heard a loud commotion coming from the end of a street where he had never been before. Some boys ran past and he called to them, "What's happening?"

They yelled back, "Come see! They say he's the biggest slave in the world."

Although it made no sense to Nate, his business was finished and he was ready for some excitement. He fell in behind the running boys. When they got to their destination, there was such a crowd they couldn't see what was going on. Some dirt farmers were in the crowd, but most of the men were wearing fine clothes and riding sleek horses or driving fancy buggies. The few elegant women, clearly not happy to be present, remained in their carriages. They held nosegays of flowers in front of their noses to mask the odors of sweat, urine, vomit, and filth.

Unable to push through to the front of the crowd, Nate followed the boys who had climbed up on top of a nearby shed. They could see everything from there."What is it?" Nate asked a boy the others called William.

"A slave auction," he replied. "Haven't you ever seen one before?" Nate shook he head. William went on to explain, "The building over there is where the slave pens are. That man in the hat is the auctioneer and he has the slaves, one at a time or maybe a bunch of them, brought out from the pens and up onto that platform there. The auctioneer starts the sale when he is ready. Buyers bid or call out how much money they will pay. The one who bids the most money gets the slave. It's simple."

"Do you think we're too late, William?" one of the other boys asked.

"No, he'll be the last one out. That's why everybody is still waiting. I don't believe he really is the biggest slave in the world. They're just saying that to get a good crowd. We might as well settle down for a long wait."

The boys on the roof got as comfortable as they could on the sloping surface. Nate could not take his eyes off the activity. The sing-song cadence of the auctioneer was like music punctuated from time to time by a shake of a finger, nod of a head, or verbal offer made by the bidders.

Nate saw a dozen Negroes chained together with iron shackles like trout on a string. They were herded together up onto the platform. Some had irons holding their wrists together. One tall Negro wore a band of iron around his neck. Two thick iron spikes stuck out on either side of the band and there was a little bell at the end of each spike. It reminded Nate of the cowbells on their dairy cattle.

The auctioneer announced in a voice loud enough for all to hear, "These prime Negro slaves are offered for sale by the Estate of the late Honorable Mister Hugh Fitzlea of Perryville Plantation. It is my pleasure to auction them off one by one, after which I shall offer what has been called by some to be the biggest Negro in the world, followed by the sale of female and children slaves. Let us begin. What am I bid for this number one field hand? . . . "

The bidding continued until the lot was gone. William explained to Nate that prime field slaves go for close to a thousand dollars. Master craftsmen and blacksmiths cost more. Women sell for less unless they're lacemakers, children go for under two hundred, and babies a lot less. Nate was glad he had not bragged to these boys about his fortune of twenty-five dollars.

"You surely know a lot about it," Nate said with admiration.

William replied, "I want to learn a lot so when I buy me a slave, I'll get my money's worth."

The other boys agreed that William already knew a lot about buying and selling slaves and looked up to him as their leader in this and many other things.

The audience was growing restless waiting to see the prime attraction. A murmur swept through the crowd and the boys stood on the roof in anticipation. Mounting the sales platform was the biggest Negro any of them had ever seen. To Nate, he seemed to have arms as big around as the trunks of Loblolly pine trees and legs the size of apple barrels. His dark brownish-black skin was shining with sweat. His eyes, well, perhaps once they had been fierce but today the eyes were empty.

"Gentlemen. And ladies," the auctioneer announced with a slight nod to the women sitting in the carriages and buggies. "It is with great pleasure that McMasters and Brown Auctioneers offer this prime and unusual slave for bid. Once the property of Colonel Bradford Commager, this prime slave is a number one blacksmith. And in addition, he excells at hand-to-hand fighting and has never lost a match in thirty-seven fights. I have passed among you copies of an advertisement listing the dates and places of the matches, names of his opponents, and the total dollar amount of the thirty-seven purses won by his late owner whose coffers overflowed with money once belonging to fools who gambled against him."

That information drew a laugh from the spectators and a bit of quiet gossip among three ladies sitting under the canopy of an elegant buggy. "Too bad old Bradford never had the opportunity to spend his winnings. He died of pneumonia this past year," whispered one.

"I heard the three sons are still fighting each other over their inheritance," said the second lady.

"Penelope told me their father's will required the sons to equally divide the number of slaves and the rest of the estate. It was a slap at the oldest, who the old man never believed was his own. As the boys couldn't agree on which one would inherit the giant, they decided auction him off."

"Well, I heard the real reason is that the boys prefer cotillions to bloody fights," retorted the first as the three ladies giggled behind their fans.

"The only thing to do then was to sell the giant and divide the money equally," said the third, who was the most practical lady of them all. The others nodded in agreement.

Even experienced buyers are disappointed now and again and no one would be foolish enough to spend a large sum without a thorough examination of the product. Three men, whose wealth allowed them to compete for this prize, watched carefully as their overseers examined the Negro. They opened his mouth to inspect the teeth, tongue, and throat. They ran their hands over his torso, poking and prodding to reveal any broken bones, growths, or damaged organs. Finally, the Nego was directed to lift a heavy bale of hay from the ground up over his head ten times, after which the overseers listened for any wheeze that might come from the lungs.

The bidding was over in a few seconds. The aristocratic plantation owner paid the three thousand dollars in gold and directed his overseer to claim his purchase.

"Well done, Mr. Randolph, well done, sir," complimented the auctioneer. "You have a Hercules here, I think."

Everyone laughed. "Hercules it is, then," replied the slave's new owner as he prepared to leave.

The boys on the shed roof, except for Nate, jumped down and left after having seen the main attraction. Nate started to follow but stayed to watch as the women and children were herded onto the platform. Some female slaves had babies in their arms. Others had children by the hand.

One woman, a mulatto or a "bright Negro" as called by the auctioneer, was offered and sold first. The buyer did not want her child so the auctioneer's assistant pulled the screaming little girl from her mother's hand.

The sound captured the attention of the purchaser of Hercules. "Oh, no! I promised Evangeline I would bring her a special present, and I've no time to shop now if we're to be home by dark," he said to his overseer as he handed him some money.

"Speak to the auctioneer and get a good price for the girl. When she's cleaned up, I'll give her to Evangeline. My daughter has been complaining to me about the teasing rough play of her two brothers. A playmate near her own age should satisfy her. It should be less boring than playing with dolls."

He laughed as he looked down at his cordovan brown boot and said, "The slave child's skin matches the color of my boot. After a good scrubbing, she should blend in with the furniture. Mrs. Randolph would never forgive me if I brought home something that clashed with her color scheme."

Having completed his business, Master Randolph left the rest of the work to his men and turned his horse to leave. He had just enough time for one more stop if he expected to arrive at Fair Oaks Plantation before dark. Jubal, his body slave, also on horseback, followed close behind. "Look lak rain, Master Randolph," he offered.

The overseer chained Hercules between heavy items in the large wagon and said a silent prayer that the giant would remain where he was put. He lifted the crying slave child into the wagon and fastened her feet together with a strong rope. When she was empty of tears, the little girl became quiet and put her hand in the huge one of Hercules. He made no move to comfort her, but there was a slight glimmer in his dead eyes.

As he watched the slave wagon drive away, Nate heard a shrill whistle. It was the one his father used to call the family in from the fields. The boy jumped down from the roof of the shed and hightailed it back to the livery stable. The family had already gathered there and the stable hand was leading the horses to the yellow wagon.

"Where've you been, boy? We've been lookin' all over town for you," he father scolded.

"Sorry, sir!" Nate took some money from his pocket and paid the stable hand two dollar bills for the feed as his father looked on with interest.

"Sold your pelts then, did you?" his father asked.

"Mr. Sowell paid me twenty-five dollars for the bunch."

While Nate and the stable hand struggled to hitch up the cussed old mules, their father's wagon was already two blocks down the street. "Hurry up, hurry up!" urged Elizabeth who began a verbal and detailed account of the events of the day.

Finally, Nate settled himself in the wagon's seat and was ready to leave when the stable hand reached out to shake his hand as a salute to the boy who got the best of his boss. Neither spoke a word, but Nate took the courtesy as a sign of his approaching manhood and felt proud.

The sights, sounds, and smells of the southern town faded away about the same time Elizabeth began to wind down. She crawled back into the wagon bed, stretched out on a tarp, and went to sleep. Nate kept the yellow wagon in sight. It seemed unusually full of supplies while his own wagon carried only empty barrels and wooden boxes. The young and tired driver hoped the cussed mules would cause less trouble with the lighter load. He wondered if Papa was doing him a favor and was puzzled by his father's apparent good humor.

It seemed to Nate that the distance from town to the farm was twice as far as the other way around. He was so tired he barely noticed the landscape's rich, deep colors in the Indian summer dusk. The mules needed no human assistance to find the way back to the farm. Nate held the reins loosely in his tired hands and pondered the events of this day.

He felt a closer friendship to Mr. Sowell than he ever had before and wondered if it was because he himself was growing up. Or could it be that the storekeeper was getting older? The boy smiled at the memory of Mr. Barston's trickery and how flummoxed he was at its failure. He remembered the excitement of the slave auction and wondered if he would ever have enough money to buy a slave. *I should buy a horse first,* he thought. What surprised him most was the fact that his father failed to whup him upside the head. He never made the trip to town before without getting whupped upside the head at least once.

When they reached the eastern boundary of their farm, the travelers saw the long shadows cast on the ground by dry cornstalks in the fields as they drove past. Nate felt his prayers for a safe trip had been answered. "Wake up, Elizabeth. We're home." His sister stirred, sat up, but remained silent because her mouth was too dry to talk and she was still sleepy.

Both teams followed their natural routes to the barn and the drivers pulled their wagons to a stop. Nate and his father unhitched the tired and hungry animals and hung up the tack. When his son started to unload the wagons, Mr. Riley spoke up. "Leave that for tomorrow, boy."

He patted his son gently on the back. Nate liked the feel of it. *It's much better than a whup upside the head,* he thought.

The weary travelers walked slowly to the farmhouse. There was a light from the lamp in the kitchen. Smoke curled from the chimney. Mrs. Riley was pleased to find the table set and food warming on the hearth. *My sons knew how to take care of things,* she thought with great satisfaction.

Their mother knew her boys could be devils, at times, but they had so many good qualities, she could forgive them for almost anything and did so freely—after she punished them for any wrongdoing at which they were caught.

Too tired to talk, the family ate in silence and left the dishes to be washed the next morning. The girls were first in their bed. Nate was quiet as he climbed the stairs to the loft and slid in bed beside John. He fell asleep to the snoring of his brothers who had done all of the farm chores that day. Mrs. Riley turned down the wick of the lamp on the kitchen table before she joined her husband who was already asleep in their bed.

Mr. Riley's body clock woke him just before dawn regardless of the day or season. "It's God's way of creating farmers," he explained to his wife each time she urged him to sleep later on Sundays.

Today was Sunday. He did not begrudge his family their late sleep on this day of rest. The peaceful quiet gave him the opportunity to ponder things he had no time to think about during the busy week.

Mr. Riley solved the problems he found most vexing and made some of his most important decisions in the place on the farm where the chance of interruption was least likely, the privy. When not in use, its door with the moon-shaped cut-out usually was left slightly ajar.

This morning when the farmer entered the sanctuary, he closed the door tightly, dropped his trousers, sat down, placed his chin in his cupped hands, reviewed the events of the recent past, and made tentative plans for the near future.

As she was waking in their bedroom, Mrs. Riley stretched and extended her arm to the place in bed where her husband would be. The space was empty and the covers were cold. She was not surprised. The sun was up but low in the sky.

His wife was surprised, however, when she went into the kitchen and found the fire dying and an empty chair where her husband usually sat, filled coffee cup in hand, and waiting for her on Sunday mornings when the children were still sleeping. She stepped out onto the porch and listened. There were no sounds coming from the barn, the milk cows were still far out in the pasture, and the door to the privy was tightly closed.

She went back to the kitchen, added more logs to the fire, and fanned them to flame. She filled the coffee pot half full of water, spooned ground chickory into the vessel, and hung it from a hook over the fire. *A watched pot never boils,* she thought as she returned to the bedroom and threw a shawl over her nightgown.

Mrs. Riley returned to the kitchen to wait for her husband. She didn't mind the invigorating chill and taught her children to delight in autumn's chill, nature's way of reminding farmers to get ready for winter. She sat in a chair before the fireplace, closed her eyes and listened for the sounds of water when it begins to boil in the coffeepot. She heard the steam's hiss about the same time she heard the door open and her husband's footsteps.

"Are you asleep, Mrs. Riley?" he asked softly.

"I am not, Mr. Riley," she answered.

"I have been thinking," he said.

"I know," she replied with eyes still closed. "You were in there so long I began to wonder if you were ill."

"Not ill of the body. Worried of the mind."

His wife opened her eyes and looked intently at her husband. "What has caused you such distress?"

She waited for his answer while he grasped the coffee pot handle with a pot holder, filled two cups at the table and invited her to sit with him. They watched the steam rising from the cups.

"What worries you?" she repeated.

"I'll tell you, but first, we need to take stock of our trip yesterday. How was your business in town?" her husband inquired.

To pump him further would only make him more stubborn, she thought. *He will tell me in his own good time.* "My business was very good." His wife smiled. "We have a reputation, Mr. Riley, and our customers are always glad to spend the time of day while they buy our goods. Mr. Hall quite charmed the girls, and the cloth Mr. Sowell gave me is beautiful. Wait until you see me in the lovely dress I plan to make this winter. And your business?"

"The same," he answered, "except for the changes in the wind."

"What do you mean?"

"For the past two years, I've heard talk in town about those danged Northerners lookin' down their noses at us Southern folk. Some people, 'specially the planters, seem to think the South would be better off if the North tended to its own business and stopped interferin' in our affairs.''

''Interfering in our affairs? What exactly does that mean, Mr. Riley?''

''Those know-nothin', trouble-makin', so-called abolitionists want slavery stopped and think the government of the United States can do somethin' about it.''

''Calm yourself, Nathan. That has nothing to do with us. We don't even own a slave.''

''There's more.''

''How much more?''

''In town yesterday I heard talk of breakin' off and startin' a country of our own.''

''Impossible! That's just talk. It could never happen.''

''People are worried about a feller from Illinois named Lincoln. There's talk he might even run for president. If a Northerner like him gets elected president, anythin' could happen.'' Mr. Riley stopped before he explained to his wife that ''anythin' '' meant secession and even the possibility of war.

Instead, he pulled his wife to her feet and said, ''Come, Catherine, walk with me to the barn. I have a surprise for you.''

''But I'm not dressed, yet.''

''So much the better,'' her husband replied with a smile.

Matthew was awake and stretching when he looked out the window of the loft and saw his parents walking to the barn. His chore was to milk the cows Sunday morning but no one, not even the cows, seemed to be in a hurry. Matthew yawned, climbed back into his bed and went back to sleep.

As they walked toward the barn, Catherine thought how few people saw the many different sides of her husband's personality and was not sure she, herself, knew them all. She did know this quiet and brusque man believed it was better to listen than to talk and stored more information in his head than other people could ever imagine. She was not even sure herself of the full extent of his knowledge because they had become so adept at communicating with one another in silent ways.

The exception to this pattern came on the days after they had made their bi-annual business trips to town. Usually, they sat at the kitchen table and reviewed farm business for the year, made plans for the next growing season, considered long-range plans including possible acquisition of more land, and discussed the state of the family and their aspirations for their children.

As the couple walked to the barn, Nathan said, "When I heard the talk in town yesterday, it seemed best not to buy a slave as we planned. If the South secedes, and it might, we need to consider the possibility of a real fight with the North, maybe even one that turns into a war. I pray it won't happen, but if it does, many things will be in short supply. It could be good for us farmers with prices goin' up for food. Metal most likely will be scarce, gone to guns. If war comes, our sons . . . "

"Don't say it." Catherine put her fingers on his lips.

He changed the subject as they entered the barn. "I visited with the banker. We've done well, Catherine. I had some of our money changed to gold coins." He pulled out a leather bag from under the tarp still covering the bed of the yellow wagon. "We'll hide this behind a stone in the fireplace."

His wife listened, her hand at her throat. "There may come a time, God forbid, when gold won't buy food. We'll have to store food away, lots of it, and in many more places than we have now. We'll have to be better at it than the squirrels," Catherine said as they both laughed.

"I'll enlarge the root cellar under the barn. The boys can build another in the woods near the big oak tree at the edge of the swale. The bushes are thick there and a stranger would have trouble finding a well-hidden entrance. Matthew and Caleb can divert water from the creek and Nate, Ben, and John can build another springhouse." Nathan showed his wife sketches he had already drawn for the projects.

"Enough of this talk for now, Catherine. It is time for your surprise!" Her husband untied and threw off the tarp covering the wagon's load. Catherine gasped when she saw the cast iron cook stove with four round lids and a large oven. The front of the oven door was white enamel and had a fanciful design painted on it. The smaller firebox door repeated the same decoration.

"Look," said Nathan, "this is the stove pipe that slips in the back of the stove right here. This piece goes up out away from the wall, and this elbow piece attaches here and carries the smoke outside through a hole in the wall that I'll cut out tomorrow. Isn't it a beauty!"

Catherine was thrilled but somewhat apprehensive when she offered, "I'm going to have to learn to cook all over again."

Nathan ignored that remark, confident that his wife could cook on anything. He showed her the other unexpected purchases as a child might show off Christmas presents. In addition to the usual staples—table salt, lye, rope, sugar, burlap, gunpowder, shot, new blades for the plow, four galvanized pails, nails, and a half dozen salt blocks for the livestock—her husband took from the wagon five rifles, one for each son, and two pistols.

"You are so generous, Nathan. Did you get something wonderful for yourself?"

Catherine squealed with delight and hugged her husband with both arms when he unveiled the gleaming galvanized tin bathtub. Nathan playfully picked up his wife, twirled her around and put her gently into the tub. Giggling, she climbed out and chased her husband around the inside the barn until he caught her.

Matthew was still in bed when he heard the cowbells and the impatient lowing of the cattle as they walked in single file toward the barn. He dressed quickly, hurried down the stairs, and greeted his parents who were eating breakfast at the table.

"Here," his mother said as she handed her son a warm buttered biscuit and a steaming cup of coffee as Matthew went out the kitchen door.

He walked carefully so he would not spill his coffee and got to the barn just before the milk cows filed in. Matthew put down his coffee and half-eaten biscuit. He used the pitchfork to throw hay into the feed troughs, and when he swooped it up from the large pile, it looked as if someone had been rolling in the hay.

Chapter Three

Hercules

Thomas Randolph, Master of Fair Oaks Plantation, was elated over his successful bid for the slave now called Hercules. He left the slave auction and the remainder of his business there to his overseer, Mr. Bailey. "If you reach the plantation before I do, take Hercules and the girl to gunbarrel house number four. Not a word of this to Mistress Randolph," he said as he mounted his sleek Arabian stallion. "I may stop for a libation, but tell her other business took me longer than expected should the lady seek you out and inquire as to my absence."

When Randolph arrived at the Governor Arms Tavern, Jubal, his body slave, dismounted and took charge of both horses. The slave then sat down on the wooden sidewalk next to the hitching post to wait for his owner. Master Rudolph, he knew, was not loath to bragging and would enjoy lording it over his competitors in the bidding war for the expensive slave.

Upon entering the tavern, Randolph was disappointed to find them absent.

"Ah, Mr. Randolph, I hear congratulations are in order," the barkeeper exclaimed.

The other patrons clapped and cheered. The wealthy planter bowed slightly in acknowledgment of their applause even though he held these ordinary people in low esteem.

"What of my friends who had the courage to bid against me?" the plantation owner asked the barkeeper.

"They've come and gone, sir. With some disappointment, I might add. They spoke of a coming storm and their desire to get on the way to their homes before it broke. Or it could have been for the fact that you bested them so soundly they lacked the nerve to meet you face to face," he laughed as he polished a whiskey glass with a cotton towel.

"You may be right, and I hope they drown in the storm," the rich man answered in jest. "I must have sustenance for my own ride, damp or dry as it may turn out to be. Pour me a glass of Scuppernong." Randolph enjoyed the distinctive bouquet and sipped the wine with respect. "Barkeeper, did you know Scuppernong grapes must be squeezed gently like a pale and buxom woman in order for the wine to achieve this distinctive flavor?" He winked at the barman and left the price of the drink as well as a generous gratuity on the counter.

Randolph walked outside and took the reins offered to him by his body slave who had been waiting patiently at the hitching rail. The leather of both saddles was marked with a few small sprinkles of rain. Jubal, adept at hiding his feelings, gave no indication of his surprise at Master's brief visit to the tavern. He waited until Master Randolph was on his horse Hatchie, then mounted his own and followed respectfully behind his owner. The planter looked up at the sky and was startled to see dark and threatening clouds roll in to cover the late afternoon sun. The skittish animals seemed to sense the coming storm. After leaving the town's main street, the horses maintained a fast and steady pace without the sting of their riders' whips.

The first light sprinkles did little to slow them down, but by the time the two riders were half way home, rain poured down in sheets and made the road nearly invisible, slippery, and dangerous. The horses fought to keep their footing in the mud. Randolph cursed himself for refusing to have his mount shod anew when Noah, his blacksmith, suggested it be done before he made the trip to the slave auction.

Jubal shivered from the cold as they splashed through the driving rain. He figured his mount could see Master's horse ahead better than he could so he held on to the pommel and let his horse have its head.

Less than an hour later, the soaked riders saw the outbuildings of Fair Oaks Plantation. Thomas Randolph and Jubal were muddy and shivering when their exhausted horses finally splashed into the back courtyard of the big house. The groom, hearing the commotion, ran through the deluge to take the reins and lead the lathered horses into the barn.

Jubal had dismounted first, helped his master down from his horse, and half carried him to the waiting arms of Bessie, the cook, who stood at the open kitchen door.

"Who dat makin' a racket in da middle of da night! Master Randolph? Lordy! What you doin' tryin' to drown yourself, Master Randolph? Gabrel, come quick! Master's soaked hisself clear through to his bones. He gonna die of the 'monia iffen he don't get squeezed dry," Bessie called to her husband Gabrel, the head house slave.

Gabrel, wearing his nightshirt, carried a quilt as he came out of their room off the kitchen. He helped Jubal strip their master of his wet clothing 'til the man was naked as a jay bird. They wrapped Randolph in the quilt and sat him in Bessie's own rocking chair she had pulled from the slaves' room and placed close to the fireplace so Master could sit where it was warm.

Gabrel disappeared into the dining room and returned with a jigger of whiskey. Randolph accepted it but ordered his house slave to go bring back the bottle which Gabrel did immediately.

Randolph, sipping fine whiskey distilled on his own plantation, seemed unaware of Jubal, who knelt before him and rubbed the circulation back into his master's feet while Bessie put more logs on the fire.

Master Randolph, warmed inside and out, held the whiskey decanter in his lap and motioned his slaves away. "No need to wake Mistress," he said in an alcohol-softened voice. "I'm fine right here. Wake me in the morn . . . " His sentence ended in a languid snore.

Gabrel took his master at his word and went back to bed in the room he shared with his wife. Bessie, the head cook in the big plantation house, was not of a mind to leave her kitchen unattended when a drunk man was sleeping next to her fire. She spread a pallet so she could sleep on the floor and took it upon herself to dismiss Jubal. "You done all you can do, chile. Get yourself dry clothes and sleep 'til you hears yo' bell. We rings when Master needs you."

Identical call bells hung on a wall in the kitchen, in the house slave quarters attached to the barn, and outside at the back of the big house. Each bell had a particular tone when it rang. Each tone was matched to a particular slave so there would be no confusion as to who was summoned. The Randolph family accepted no excuse from any slave who did not come when called.

Jubal did not realize how exhausted he was until he ran through the rain, into the barn, and saw the groom rubbing down the horses. He waved to the slave as a compliment for his quick action when Master rode in. Too tired for conversation, Jubal quietly opened the door to the slave quarters attached to the barn.

He lived in the particular section that was home to the large number of slaves who were in attendance for each family member and their guests. These quarters were similar to the gunbarrel houses of the field, craft, and other workers. The big difference was the close proximity to the mansion. House slaves needed to be close to the big house, and their access to quarters was through the barn or from a door next to the kitchen garden.

Jubal entered his section of the men's sleeping room, removed his wet clothes, dropped them in a heap on the floor, and collapsed onto his bed. He felt a hand on his shoulder and opened his eyes to see a groom holding a small glass of whiskey. "Here, dis'll warm yo' insides," he said with a smile, and returned to the barn.

The groom was expert in the care of horses and took special care of these two animals. He continued to walk the horses until they were calm before he put them in their stalls. He would wait to feed them in the morning. The slave knew he would be punished if the horses took sick from their long wet and muddy ride and spent a fitful night next to the stall of Master's horse in case the animal showed signs of sickness or other distress. He assumed that Mr. Bailey, Caro, and the slaves with them had gone directly to the lower barn and corral where the freight wagons and mule teams were housed.

Both Master's and Jubal's horses were fit the next morning. The groom was relieved.

* * *

Bailey's party quietly arrived hours later. Everyone was exhausted and miserable. The overseer had expected Randolph to spend much more time in town and saw no need to hurry with his own business. Mr. Bailey was a trustworthy and deliberate man. He was proud Mr. Randolph recognized those traits in him and carefully kept the Randolph money separate from his own. After the overseer completed the purchase of the slave child and saw to it that the wagon's load was secure, he stopped at Sowell's General Store. Caro, Bailey's number one slave helper, and two other slaves were left outside to guard the newly purchased slaves, the wagon, and its contents.

While Mr. Sowell was collecting the items Mrs. Randolph had written on her shopping list, Mr. Bailey did some shopping of his own. He bought his wife a lovely rose-colored shawl with deep fringe on two sides and a yellow silk Japanese folding fan for his sixteen-year-old daughter, Patsy, as a surprise when she returned from school in Memphis. The girl was of courting age, and her father thought the fan seemed an appropriate gift. He never quite forgot a girl he once courted but did not marry. She had a Japanese fan and fluttered it in the most seductive way.

"Mrs. Randolph has fine taste," Mr. Sowell remarked as he carefully wrapped twenty-two yards of exquisite fabric, two dozen fancy sweet-smelling toilet soaps, and a small crystal bottle of French perfume. "Don't let these things get wet or we'll both get a lashing, tongue-lashing, that is, from the fine lady herself. Looks like it might rain before you get home."

Mr. Bailey nodded and smiled as he paid for her purchases out of Randolph money. "I've heavy tarps to protect the merchandise. As for the people, well, we don't melt!" he chuckled. He got out his own money to pay for his purchases.

"Your wife and daughter will be pleased with these gifts," Mr. Sowell offered. "You have fine taste yourself, Mr. Bailey. But what about your sons? Have they not earned a reward for their hard work?"

Mr. Bailey laughed. "I can be sure they work hard—in Texas. When they heard the women in Texas were more beautiful than the ones they courted here, every last brother of them upped and went off to Texas. The four of them married there and seem happy enough. We get letters from their wives about once each year. Our boys scribble a line or two at the bottom. At least, we know our sons are alive and that girls in Texas know how to read and write, something they can teach our grandchildren if they ever give us any."

"Grown, gone, and married! I can't believe it! I must be getting old," the storekeeper exclaimed as he shook his head. "They're Texas farmers, then?"

"My boys don't raise cotton; they raise cattle," Mr. Bailey replied.

"Cattle, eh?" Mr. Sowell said with some surprise. "Well, now that I think about it, there must be a good market for beef up north. How are they doing?"

"Business must be poor," Bailey answered with a wink. "Not one of 'em owns a single slave. Well, we'd best be getting along. I always like doing business with you, Mr. Sowell. I guess you heard about the excitement at the slave auction today. Mister Randolph is celebrating his victory at the tavern this very minute. I wouldn't be surprised if he stayed at a hotel in town tonight," the overseer said with a knowing grin.

A light rain started to fall as Mr. Bailey and his three slave helpers re-checked the tarps covering the items that could be water damaged. The load seemed secure and the overseer mounted his own horse and led off. The wagon followed close behind.

The rain stopped when they had traveled an hour, but the mud, caused by the earlier deluge, was deeper than before. The wagon got stuck in the mud two different times, and Hercules was drafted to help the other slaves push the vehicle out. Bailey had to remove the shackles from his ankles but left locked the ones on the slave's huge wrists.

When they traveled only another mile, they came to a creek running too high to ford, and the group lost another two hours waiting for the water to go down.

Caro led them to shelter beneath some trees. One of the other slaves scratched under a blanket of pine needles and found enough kindling to start a small fire, the only source of heat and light in the coming darkness. Caro left the horses hitched to the wagon but directed the other slave to get out the feed bags so the animals could eat.

Finally, a slave carried a torch made from a small dead tree limb and waded out across the creek to test the depth of the receding water. He kept his footing with some difficulty but made it to the far shore and motioned Mr. Bailey to come across.

The overseer gave the order to move out but found the wagon to be mired in the mud again even in that sheltered place. Bailey, hungry, soaking wet, and angry, joined the others, including the child, in the successful effort to release the wagon from the dark mud's hold.

"Caro, get more limbs for torches and lead us. Ride my horse. I'll drive the wagon myself. Everyone else has to walk across until we come up on the other side of the creek. Hercules can carry the girl across."

The crossing was slow and difficult. Caro held the torch so they could see what they were doing as the party aimed for the light held by the slave on the far side of the dark, rushing water. Another slave led the horses while the overseer used the whip on the frightened animals. Even Hercules struggled to retain his footing in the swirling water as the little girl held her arms tightly around his neck. Finally, they reached the other side of the swollen creek. Bailey counted the travelers as they came up out of the dark water and was satisfied none of them had been lost. A devout Baptist, the overseer was startled by the brief fragment of memory of his own river baptism by an itinerant preacher when he was twelve years old.

The pitiful procession, led through the night by Caro who replenished his torch as each one burned down, made no other stops. The storm was over, and stars filled the black sky. The only noise was the soft sucking sounds of the horses' hooves in mud, the muted rumble on the wagon's mud-encrusted wheels, the squeaking of wet board on board of the wagon's bed, and the faraway howl of a wolf.

The travelers arrived at Fair Oaks shortly before dawn. Mr. Bailey quietly drove the wagon into the lower barn. While the two slaves unhitched the horses, Caro checked the load and was grateful for the only good thing about the difficult trip. He found that the store purchases, carefully wrapped in the tarps, had remained bone dry.

"We'll unload in the morning," Mr. Bailey said in a hoarse and tired voice. He directed Caro to rub down the horses and motioned the two other slaves to accompany him as he took Hercules and the slave child to gunbarrel house number four. Before they started, the overseer got his rifle and was prepared to use it if any of the colored tried to escape.

Bailey walked behind the small party. The young slave child held on to the chain attached to the shackles binding Hercules's wrists. All of them were wet, muddy, and shivering with the cold. Even though he was exhausted, Mr. Bailey knew it was his personal responsibility to see to it that this new and expensive commodity be kept in the best of health and fighting form.

Not wanting to attract attention, the tired party walked quietly toward gunbarrel house number four where all of the slaves were asleep in the side rooms except for Luther. He was responsible for keeping the fire going in the large middle room which served as the house kitchen and the place for the slaves who lived there to eat and visit with one another when they weren't working.

Luther already had the water simmering in the large black kettle hanging from a hook over the flames in the huge open fireplace. He stirred the pot as he carefully shook cornmeal from a cloth bag into the steam. It was his method of cooking cornmeal mush the slaves would eat before going out to work in the fields at first light. Fried apples were sizzling in butter in a large pan sitting next to mounds of just-baked biscuits warming on the wide stone hearth.

"Um um!" the old cook said aloud. "Luther, you is da best cook in da whole county, I does believe." He chuckled at his own compliment.

He already had set for breakfast two of the three long tables. Pots of hot coffee were where he put them, resting on smooth rock slabs so as not to scorch the wooden tables. When the first diners arrived for breakfast, Luther would take a burning twig from the fire and light the candles he had placed at intervals on the tables.

The old cook heard an unexpected noise, frowned, and squinted as he looked in the direction of the sound. It took a few moments for Luther's eyes to adjust in the dim light when the newcomers opened the door and entered the room. When he was able to focus on Hercules, he dropped his stirring spoon on the floor.

Luther watched as Mr. Bailey chained the new slave to the heavy table and sat him on the bench. "Warm him, dry him, and feed him," the overseer ordered.

Luther picked up his spoon and cautiously approached his new responsibility to get a better view of who exactly he was supposed to warm, dry, and feed. The cook looked at the new slave's great bulk and felt a twinge of pity. In his imagination, the old man thought he saw in the room's shadows a tall and strong African leading his people into battle against an unseen enemy.

Mr. Bailey opened the door to the women's room and found old Clara still asleep. He shook her awake and she followed him into the kitchen.

"Take care of these two," he said as he pointed to Hercules and the child. "Master paid a passel of money for them, and if they die of the pneumonia, there'll be hell to pay and you'll pay it!" With that, the overseer dismissed the two wet and tired slaves with him, turned around, and left the slave quarters.

The overseer was as wet, muddy, and cold as the other travelers when he entered through the back door of his own large and comfortable home. He tracked mud across the kitchen floor as he walked to the large wooden rocking chair near the fireplace. He pulled the chair closer to the hearth, added kindling to the glowing embers and fanned them to flame. Before he sat in the rocker, the exhausted man took off his wet coat and let it slide to rest on the floor.

Mrs. Bailey heard him come in, slipped her wrapper over her nightgown, and hurried downstairs and into the kitchen. She was surprised to see the mess her husband had made. She bit her tongue, kept silent, and simply knelt and pulled off his dirty boots. She found it to be a difficult task. When she grasped each boot and pulled, the leather made a sucking sound as it separated from her husband's wet foot. Droplets of water sizzled on the hearth when she turned the boots upside down to dry.

Mrs. Bailey, known by her friends as a wise and practical woman, put the kettle on the fire after she poured him whiskey in a tumbler. As her husband stripped off his wet garments, she went upstairs to their bedroom and returned with dry towels, a quilt and his nightshirt.

Although curious about the outcome of the trip to the slave auction, she read the exhaustion in her husband's face and decided to save her questions for another time. Understanding his need to relax and reflect as he stared into the fire, she made sure he was comfortable, added two logs to the fire, poured hot tea in a cup, left the teapot on the table, and went back to bed. She was still awake and wondering when her husband slipped in beside her not long after the sun rose.

* * *

Old Clara felt she could have used more sleep. She rubbed her eyes before they focused on the giant chained to the table. She thought she must still be dreaming. "Who you?" she asked in a sleepy, hoarse voice. The giant did not answer, and Old Clara did not press the point.

Luther, at that moment, came out of the room on the other side of the kitchen. His arms were filled with quilts as there were no clothes to fit such a huge slave. *I cain't dress a man chained to a table anyway*, he thought.

It wasn't until Luther stripped the wet clothes from the slave as best he could and covered him with warm quilts that Old Clara noticed the shivering little girl still holding tight to the chain restraining the huge slave's wrists.

"What you doin', chile, sittin' there so quiet?" Old Clara took the little girl by the hand and led her to a bench near the fire. She picked up a rag doll that had been dropped the day before by one her young charges and put the doll in the child's hand.

"Don't be skeered, chile. You sit right here while Old Clara goes to get you some dry clothes. Den we'll fill your little belly wid good warm mush. Luther, here, he make good mush." The old slave was gone only a moment before she returned.

"Look, Old Clara has you a nice dry shirt an a quilt to get you warm." She put the quilt around the child's shoulders and deftly removed her dirty clothes.

Old Clara used a soft wet rag and warm towel to give the child a sponge bath that removed most of the mud from the little girl's skin. "Come mornin', we'll give ya a proper bath, Old Clara will, but dis lil spongin' will work jest fine.

"I's gonna put dis nice dry shirt over yo' head, easy like." As the shirt covered the child's face, Old Clara dramatically questioned. "Where dat child be? Luther, you see dat chile go? Where she done gone?" The old woman deftly pulled the shirt down to reveal the little girl's head and exclaimed with feigned surprise, "Der she is!"

The child smiled for the first time since she was dragged from her mother's side. She quickly pushed her hands through the sleeves, lifted her arms to Old Clara and felt the warmth of the old slave's embrace.

Luther led the little girl to the table where he had placed a bowl of hot cornmeal mush and a fresh-baked biscuit with butter and honey. The child ate quickly and hoped Luther would fill her empty bowl again. She smiled when he did so.

Old Clara refused the cook's offer of the same meal but accepted a big cup of coffee with a little sugar and a lot of cream. "My stomach still be sleepin' and not ready for more jest yet," she explained as she put her free arm around the shoulders of her newest charge.

As Luther set the coffee before Old Clara, he reassured the new slave still chained to the other table. "You is next." The cook ladled cornmeal mush from the cooking pot into a wooden bowl. He stirred and blew on the hot food so as not to feed the giant anything that might burn his mouth.

I sho don't wanna get on dat big old slave's bad side, he thought. *Course, I don't wanna feed him food dat's too cold either.* The old cook stuck his finger into the mush and smiled. "Jest right," he said aloud and smacked his lips.

Luther carefully approached the newcomer and was prepared to feed the giant whose wrists were shackled together. The slave pushed him away and used both hands to hold the bowl to his mouth as he devoured the cornmeal mush the old cook put before him. Then Luther brought a biscuit and fried apples which he had cooled to room temperature. He kept bringing food until the giant said, "No more," the first words he had spoken since the new slave had arrived.

After clearing the tables and stacking the dishes in a large pan, Luther looked around the room to see if anyone was watching. Then he slyly loosened a stone in the fireplace wall and removed a small bottle of whiskey he had hidden for himself.

He cautiously approached the giant and leaned over to whispered in the slave's big ear, "Dis be for you." The wrinkled old cook carefully uncorked the bottle and put it within reach of the giant's huge hands. Then Luther turned around and went on with his business of finishing breakfast and starting preparations for the mid-day meal to go out with the field slaves.

When the newcomers had finished eating, Old Clara returned to the women's room and brought back more quilts to make the giant, still shackled and chained to the table, as comfortable as possible. She folded one quilt like a pillow and put it on the table. The slave put his huge head on it and went to sleep. The old woman tucked the other quilts between and around the chains to relive some of the pressure on his body. She noticed the dried blood on his wrists where the tight iron shackles cut into his skin. *Mr. Bailey should have unlocked those awful things,* she thought.

Old Clara turned her attention to the child and led her by the hand into the women's room where she tucked the little girl into her own bed, still slightly warm from the old slave's body heat. The old slave sang softly to the little girl until the child fell asleep. Other women were waking and dressed quickly before going to the kitchen where many of the men were already eating.

Nursing mothers brought their babies with them and continued to nurse as they ate their own breakfasts at the tables. They visited quietly among themselves and enjoyed the only free time they would have until their long work day was over and they were too tired to talk.

One of the Negro boss men rang the large bell outside the gunbarrel house as the signal for the first group of slaves to get to their work.

The mothers put their babies back into their cribs in the women's room where Old Clara would be in charge of the babies and toddlers while their mothers worked in the fields. The women would return to the house in the early afternoon for the second feeding and then go back to work until the end of the day. No one, not even the Negro boss men, could disrupt the routine.

Everyone knew that Mistress Randolph was particular about the care of babies. Old Clara declared it the reason Mistress put Old Clara herself in charge of the nursery. The loyal old slave never tired of reminding all within hearing of how Mistress Randolph always said healthy babies grow up to be healthy, strong, and valuable workers.

It was a known fact that Mistress Randolph, herself, was the one who kept the breeding charts and decided how to match the men slaves with the women for better babies. Old Clara birthed twenty healthy babies herself in her breeding days. There was no question that Old Clara knew more about babies than just about anybody. Those of a different opinion were advised by the other women not to express it unless they wanted to end up on Old Clara's bad side.

The slaves ordered to clear the far field were the first to finish Luther's breakfast of cornmeal mush, eggs, frizzled fatback, biscuits, fried apples, butter, honey, milk, chickory coffee, sugar, and cream.

The wagon to carry them to their work was already out front and held the axes, saws and other tools used in clearing. For this job, the slaves rode in the wagon with the equipment. The field was four miles distant and if they had to walk and carry heavy tools as well, their time and energy would be wasted on just getting to the job.

They would work hard for a week or more to clear two acres of virgin land of trees so cotton could be planted there. Luther had already prepared and packed their mid-day meal in buckets and supervised the children who helped him load them on the wagon.

Luther was proud to be head cook in building four and often exchanged cooking tips with the head cooks in the other gunbarrel houses. All of the cooks had help from other slaves in their own buildings. They shelled peas, shucked corn, peeled potatoes, and chopped things like carrots and rhubarb as well as helped tend the vegetable gardens Master Randolph encouraged his slaves to keep behind their houses.

"Means Master, he don't have to give us so much food when he gives us da week's ration," Luther explained to his friends from other plantations and was disappointed when they told him their masters, just as smart as Luther's, did the same thing.

Although it was light outside, the sun had yet to rise and Luther had placed a few candles on the tables to supplement light from the flames in the fireplace and from the three windows in the room. Even so, the light was dim and the men and women coming in to eat barely noticed Hercules still asleep with his head on the table. It was a boy who first took notice, and his call to others to come and see the giant woke him. The boy exclaimed, "He bleedin' all over da table."

Luther quickly carried a candle close enough to see better and urged the boy to go for help. "Run quick to Bailey's house an tell 'em come quick!"

The boy did as he was told. As soon as Bailey got the message, the overseer's face turned white. *My God!* he thought. *Did I take off the wrist shackles?*

He rose from the breakfast table so quickly he knocked over his chair. Mrs. Bailey, holding the bowl of fried apples she was carrying to the table, jumped out of his way as her husband grabbed his keys and ran out of the house so fast he didn't hear the kitchen door slam behind him.

The overseer walked quickly to building four in the slave quarters. He feared he would attract too much attention if he ran as his instinct urged him to do. He disciplined himself to walk briskly but feared others would hear his pounding heart.

When Bailey burst into the room, Hercules was chained to the table exactly as the overseer had left him. Blood stained the tabletop where his hands rested, and the liquid had seeped on to the quilt that had pillowed his head. Wakened by the commotion, the slave was sitting up straight, and his arms were extended in front of him and resting on the bloody table. The giant's hands were discolored and swollen, and the iron bracelets, still locked, had cut deeply into the slave's skin.

Even after Bailey unlocked the shackles, he was unable to unhinge and remove them from around the slave's swollen wrists. Hardened blood and pus glued the iron into the deep cuts in the slave's dark skin. Luther brought a deep pan filled with cold water in which to soak Hercules's arms halfway up to his elbows. After a few minutes of this, Bailey lifted the slave's arms out of the water and placed them on a dish towel, furnished by Luther, on the table. The overseer took the tip of his pocket knife and carefully removed the softened material, bit by bit, from around the edges of the shackles. After each pass, he wiped the debris from his knife on the dish towel.

Luther felt nauseous and vowed to burn that towel when the ordeal was over. The old cook bit his lip to take his mind off thinking about the pain the huge slave surely was suffering.

Finally, Mr. Bailey took from its small case his own silver toothpick and used it to clean in and around the hinges of the wrist shackles. He put the toothpick on the table, then grasped the right handcuff with both hands and pulled it open. He heard the tearing of the slave's flesh and saw the flow of fresh red blood from around his wrist. Bailey quickly followed the same procedure with the left handcuff. When he finished, the towel was soaked with blood. Bailey's hands were shaking and spotted with blood.

Luther hurried to bring another pan of water so the overseer could clean his hands and some more dish towels which he used to wrap around Hercules's wrists. Bailey washed and dried his hands but was shaking so he couldn't pick up his toothpick from off the table. Luther did it for him.

Hercules tried to remain stoic even though he did grit his teeth and his eyes were moist, but the huge slave shuddered with pain when turpentine was poured over his raw flesh.

The others in the room had stopped talking and eating. Only the babies continued nursing at their mothers' breasts. Slaves were accustomed to witnessing torture and pain as punishment to those who defied their masters, although it was unusual to have it administered at the table during breakfast. What made this particular event different and caught the attention of those present in the room was the huge size of the new slave.

Outside, the Negro boss rang the bell signaling the first breakfast group to the fields. Overseer Bailey watched them clear the room then called out, "Old Clara, come here right now and take care of this big old slave Hercules!" The overseer used the sleeve of his shirt to wipe the sweat from his face.

Old Clara appeared with an infant in her arms. She handed the baby to another woman and replied, "Hercules? I didn't know da name of dat big ole slave."

She examined Hercules and shook her head. "Dis poor slave, he be hurt too bad. You best tell Mistress Randolph to get da doctor," Old Clara said. "Mister Bailey, you all right? You is shakin' like a leaf in a summer storm."

Bailey didn't answer but turned and quickly left the slave quarters. When he got outside, he leaned against a wagon wheel to steady himself and fought to keep from throwing up.

I'll never work here or on any other plantation if Randolph knows about this. How can I have been so stupid! It was the rain, the rain, and the long day, he thought. Instead of going to the big house for help, Bailey went back to his own so he would have time to think.

"What's wrong?" his wife asked as he almost stumbled through the kitchen door.

"Do you know a doctor or someone who can treat people with deep cuts and swollen hands?"

She poured his coffee as he sat down at the table. Mrs. Bailey sat across from him and waited for the man to better collect himself.

As he drank from the china cup, her husband struggled to find the words, began several times without success, and then finally managed to tell his wife what he had done to risk the usefulness, perhaps the life, of Randolph's three-thousand dollar slave.

Mrs. Bailey gasped. She was fully aware of the consequences of her husband's carelessness and put her hand over his in an effort to lend him a measure of hope. "There is a woman I have heard about, a farmer's wife who supplies Mr. Sowell and Mr. Hall with herbs and curatives. Her name is Mrs. Riley. People tell me she is as good as any doctor."

Bailey brightened. "Yesterday I was at Sowell's myself. Riley had been in that same morning and I saw his produce and herbs and medicines in the store. I'll ride back there now and have Sowell give me something for Hercules's wounds," her husband said.

"Do what you think is best. The secret, though, my dear husband, is what medicines go with what injuries. I myself know something about doctoring, but I have never had a patient worth that much money. You asked my advice, and I shall give it. It is my opinion that you have two choices. Either you tell Randolph to get a doctor or go and fetch the Riley woman yourself."

Bailey groaned. "If their farm is off the post road where I think it might be, to get there and bring her back would take almost a day."

"The day is not getting longer. What will you tell Randolph about the slave?" his wife asked.

"I don't know. I don't want to tell him anything. He'd probably order us off the plantation before nightfall. Perhaps I should go on about my business out in the clearing field. Randolph might think I have taken the slave with me." The overseer paused briefly. "What do you think of Caro going for the women?"

Mrs. Bailey nodded, called for Betty, her house slave, and instructed her to fetch Caro right away. She watched through the window as Betty ran to quarters that was home to slaves whose status was lower than that of house slaves but slightly higher than slaves engaged in crafts.

Betty rapped at the door of Caro's building located between the barn and the first gunbarrel house. Only male slaves lived there. Some of them were number one helpers and some of them were breeders. After a short time, Caro appeared at the door.

At Betty's direction, Caro ran to Bailey's house even though he had not eaten. The slave was surprised to learn he was being sent on a long errand so soon after yesterday's strenuous town trip, but he showed no emotion. He watched Mr. Bailey write out a pass for him to show to any patroller who stopped him. Without it, Caro would be taken for a runaway slave and be dealt with accordingly, something all slaves dreaded with good reason. Runaways could be whipped or hanged.

The overseer instructed him to take two fresh horses, one of them with a side saddle to be ridden by a farmer's wife he was to bring back in secret and without delay. "Her name is Mrs. Riley," Bailey said.

Against all custom, Mrs. Bailey handed Caro three biscuits, an apple, and a cup of coffee. The slave was startled by this breach of etiquette but gratefully ate the food when the overseer's wife nodded permission.

He waited as Bailey wrote a letter to the farmer's wife to explained the situation. He implored her to come quickly and offered a generous payment for her services. He also emphasized the need for confidentiality. As painful as it was for him to write, Bailey explained in detail the causes and nature of the slave's injuries.

The Baileys watched Caro ride out when the sun was still low in the sky. "It's best if you go about your regular routine," Mrs. Bailey told her husband. "There is nothing else you can do until Caro comes back with Mrs. Riley."

Slaves starting their day's work saw Mr. Bailey, on horseback as usual, following the wagon carrying the slaves to the clearing field. Bailey hated this job and would have left it to his boss slaves had he not wanted to be as far from the big house and Planter Randolph as he could get.

When they arrived at the clearing field, the men, women, and a few other children jumped down from the wagon and began to muck out undergrowth, cut down the smaller trees, and drag the debris out to cleared land. There they made piles of the stuff until the field looked like it was covered with small haystacks.

When the slaves stopped to eat their mid-day meal, the designated lighter went around to torch the older piles that were dry and easy to burn. Everyone in the vicinity was careful to stay upwind of the dense smoke which carried with it poisonous fumes and ash of wicked plants like poison ivy, poison oak, and other woodland plants even rabbits wouldn't eat.

Every slave knew the overseer always left such kinds of hard and dirty work to the direction of his well-trained boss slaves. Mr.

Bailey made motions as if he were in charge even though his mind was elsewhere.

In the afternoon, slaves used axes to girdle the trees too huge to fell. Deprived of nutrients rising sap brought to their leaves, the big trees, some of them hundreds of years old, would die slow and certain deaths.

On their trips out and back from clearing virgin land, slave wagons passed cultivated cotton fields dotted with the skeletons of huge dead trees still lifting their bare and craggy branches to the sky.

A few of the older slaves hid their eyes and refused to look at these ghosts of an ancient forest. None of the other slaves laughed at them when they performed their rituals.

Gunbarrel house number four was nearly empty of adult slaves, most of whom were at work throughout the plantation. Babies and children too young to work in the fields were left with Old Clara and the other old slaves who cared for them during the day. It was not all diaper changing and feeding.

Even the toddlers were taught to pick some vegetables and became expert pea shellers when they were a little older. Small hands could roll yarn into balls and weave simple pot holders out of old cloth scraps. Old Clara was skilled in turning work into games and quick to reward her small charges with compliments and some tidbits to eat.

She left the children in the care of another old nursemaid and returned to the kitchen in time to catch some of the craftsmen before they left for their work.

They didn't mind when Old Clara asked three of them to put two beds together in the men's room and help Hercules to the bed. The proud slave rebuffed their help and walked by himself, if a bit unsteadily, and slowly sat down on the side of the bed.

Old Clara gently and carefully rewrapped his wrists with strips of unbleached muslin she tore from a clean but old worn-out child's shirt.

Luther followed with a cup of soup and was prepared to feed Hercules, but thought better of it. Instead, he simply offered the cup to the injured slave who carefully took it in his swollen hands and drank it all. Luther and Old Clara helped him ease into the bed. The old woman put her hand on his hot forehead, sadly looked at Luther, and shook her head.

"I hopes Bailey done gone for da doctor," she whispered to Luther who nodded his head in agreement.

* * *

By the time breakfast trays had been delivered to all family members in the big house, Bessie knew everything that had happened in every single corner of Fair Oaks Plantation. She sent word to Old Clara that Master Randolph was still abed, exhausted from the wet ordeal of the day before. He said he was feeling poorly, either from the soaking or bad food he may have eaten in town.

"Uh-huh," Bessie said softly to herself when his tray came back, breakfast uneaten. "I does believe dis empty whiskey bottle might jest have somethin' to do wid it," she told Gabrel as she set the bountiful tray before her husband so the food would not be wasted.

Later in the day when Master ordered a light meal, Gabrel took up a tray of appetizing food. Even her husband did not know Bessie had laced his meal with ipecac, an emetic that would delay Master's recovery for another day or two and give Caro more time to complete his errand without Master's knowledge. Bessie wondered if the farmer's wife would return with him. The cook hated to think what would happen to them all if the woman refused to come.

Chapter Four
The Healer

When he was well out of sight of Fair Oaks Plantation, Caro was stopped by a patroller. The slave handed him the pass and waited for the man to read it.

"On a errand for Bailey, are you? Good man, Bailey. Takes no nonsense off any man, black or white," the patroller said to no one in particular. "You know the way to Riley's farm?"

"I knows it to be a far piece on da other side of da town," Caro answered.

"Uh-huh." The patroller took a pencil from his pocket and drew a map on the back of the pass. He signed his own name below it. "Here," he said as he handed the paper back to Caro. "Two other patrollers are working this section. Show 'em this and they'll know I've cleared you and won't need to waste their time. You might mention to Mr. Bailey that Patroller Gibson helped speed you on your way." The man turned his horse and rode back into the woods.

Gibson was right. Two more patrollers stopped Caro and quickly waved him through when they saw Gibson's signature on the back of Mr. Bailey's pass.

Shortly before noon, sun time, Caro came to a field of dried cornstalks, the first sign of the farm. When he drew closer, the slave saw a white boy chopping down the stalks with an ax.

The slave hailed him. "'Cuse me, sir. I be lookin' for da Riley farm."

"You found it!" Caleb hollered back. "If you let me ride your other horse there, I'll take you up to the house."

Caro reined in his horses. "Climb on den. I has a message here for a lady, Missus Riley, by name," the slave explained. "My name be Caro."

"I'm Caleb Riley. The lady you're looking for is my mother. It's only about a mile to the house."

The farm boy was surprised and a little embarrassed when he saw the side saddle. He considered walking instead but decided his brothers would tease him more if he walked when a horse was available than if he rode up to the house on a woman's saddle.

Caleb was even more embarrassed at the difficulty he had sitting the saddle and vowed never again to tease his sisters when they were up on such a devilish contraption. He took a deep breath, clicked his tongue, and held on the pommel as the horse started for the farm buildings. Caro, as customary, fell in behind him.

A short time later when they rounded a bend and came in sight of the house, the riders saw Matthew and John coming out of the woods. The two brothers were driving the two cussed mules pulling the old wagon loaded down with logs.

Ben was busy chopping wood for the small campfire between the house and the barn. He stopped when he saw the riders approaching and laid his ax on the ground before he walked out to meet them. He called over his shoulder to his sisters. "There's enough cut wood to finish your cooking."

A large copper pot, suspended by a metal frame over the fire pit, was filled with apples, and Elizabeth and Elle took turns stirring the apple butter with a long-handled wooden ladle. A large basket of apples sat on the porch beside Grace. Her job was to thoroughly wash the fruit in a large tub. When they were clean, she carried the apples into the kitchen where her mother peeled, cored and cut each fruit into four pieces. Grace was glad it was the last batch she carried out to her sisters who added them to the pot.

The apples mixed with spices were cooking down over the fire, and their delicious aroma mixed with the salty smoke coming from the smoke house where Mr. Riley was hanging up muslin-wrapped freshly salted hams by metal hooks onto crossbars. He arranged them by rows according to which year the meats were hung. A prime ham hung no less than three years before some southerners deemed it fit to eat. Nathan Riley felt a smoked ham was prime after hanging only a year.

As Caro approached the farm, he was surprised to see white folks doing slave work. *It do smell good 'round dis place,* he thought. *Apple butter, smokin' hams, de smells da same no matter in what place dey be.*

All members of the family stopped their work when they saw Caleb sitting side saddle and riding in on a strange horse. They were equally surprised by the sight of a colored man riding behind him.

Ben was the first to find his voice. "Look! Look! Here comes Caleb on a horse and there's a slave with him!"

By the time the two riders dismounted, the whole family had gathered near the barn except for Elizabeth and Elle who had been warned by their mother not to let the apple butter burn.

Caro removed his hat and said, "My name be Caro. I comes from Fair Oaks Plantation to find Missus Riley. Do you be her?"

"I'm Mrs. Riley," Catherine said and stepped forward.

Her husband put out his arm in front of her in a protective gesture. "What is this about?" he asked in a suspicious manner.

"I's to give her dis here letter an' wait for her to read it. Den, I's to bring her back wid me on dis here other horse." Caro handed the letter to Mr. Riley.

The children stood by quietly while their father read the letter. He finished and handed it to his wife. "Caleb, show the slave where to feed and water the horses. Then come inside."

Mr. Riley led his family back into the house. They sat around the kitchen table and discussed the contents of the letter. The apple butter was finished and the fire was out when Elizabeth and Elle joined the group.

"I don't like the sound of this," Nathan Riley said. "You owe the planter and his overseer nothing. We don't even know them. Let them call their own doctor if the slave is so sick and so valuable."

"I wonder how they heard of me," mused Mrs. Riley. "Perhaps it was in town. If the overseer did business at Sowell's or even with Mr. Hall, he may have purchased some of my medicine and heard my name."

"No matter. After his horses are fed and watered, we'll send their slave on his way," Mr. Riley announced.

"Papa," Nate said after some hesitation. "When you couldn't find me in town, I was watching the slave auction. I saw the planter, Mr. Randolph is his name, bid on the big slave and win him at the auction. His name is Hercules, and he cost three thousand dollars!"

Nate lowered his eyes and waited for a reprimand from his father. None came and the boy was relieved that it was no longer a secret from his family as to where he had been and what he had seen in town.

Instead, his mother announced, "I shall go. I may be able to help. And I have been offered a generous payment."

"I forbid it, absolutely forbid it, and . . . "

His wife's withering glance stopped Nathan Riley mid-sentence. "Forbid, Nathan?"

Catherine turned to her children and ordered, "Nate, get my basket of medicines. Caleb, go to the barn and tell the slave I will be ready to go with him very soon. Elizabeth, pack a change of clothing for me in the linen drawstring bag. Elle, get my bonnet and shawl. Ben, you and Matthew help the girls ladle the apple butter into the stoneware crocks and store them in the spring house until I return."

The children nodded and stood quietly waiting to see who the victor would be in this rare dispute between their parents.

Catherine stopped and bit her tongue. She could tell she had embarrassed her husband in front of the children, and she averted her eyes from his reddened face. "Come, walk with me," she said and took her husband's hand. She led him out the door, down the porch steps, and out to the orchard. They sat on the grass under the pear tree and talked for nearly half an hour.

Elizabeth, watching them from the kitchen window, announced to her siblings that their parents were on their way back.

When the parents entered the house, their father said, "Your mother and I have given careful thought to this matter. We have decided she would be more comfortable in the buggy than on horseback. Nate, you are to go with your mother, and I want you to stay with her every minute when she is away from here. I admit that I don't like the idea, not one bit. But I told your mother that I will not stand in her way if she truly has her mind set on this, well, this rather outrageous scheme." *And I know when I am licked,* Nathan Riley thought to himself.

"Thank you, Nathan," his wife said as she kissed him on the mouth, a display of affection something seldom seen by the children.

"We'll get the buggy ready and hitch up the horse. Come along, boys. Nate, pack yourself some clothes and meet me in the barn," their father ordered.

Caro was relieved when he saw their preparations for the trip. He was glad he did not have the sole responsibility to take a white woman back to the plantation and noted which boy was coming with them.

"Mister Nate, sir, let me show you how to get to Fair Oaks." The slave took a stick and drew a map in the dirt. "When we gets up close, I be da leader, if'n you don't mind, sir." Caro stood and helped load the buggy.

Elizabeth handed up a basket of food to her mother as they were ready to leave. Mr. Riley tied the spare horse to the back of the buggy, and Caro took his usual place on horseback at the rear. As the travelers waved good-bye, Nate felt excited at the prospect of seeing the huge slave again. The boy had never been on a plantation, much less a famous one like Fair Oaks, and wondered what it would look like. He glanced at his mother, and she smiled back at him.

The other members of the Riley family watched the small procession until it was out of sight. Their father led the children back into the house. He had them sit around the kitchen table and poured each of them a cup of coffee, something quite unusual.

Elizabeth said nothing but got up, poured half of Elle's portion back into the coffee pot, and refilled her youngest sister's cup with sweet milk. She returned to the table, gave the cup to Elle, resumed her own place, and waited for her father to speak.

"Well, your mother is a no-nonsense woman, and I expect she'll have that expensive slave up and healthy as a mule in no time at all. We'll have that apple butter put up by the time she and Nate get home." He paused to drink his coffee, and the children followed his lead. "You all know what your chores are. Get to them." Their father took the last swallow from his cup. "I hope your mother and Nate won't be away too long," he called after the children as they scattered to their chores. He put his cup on the drainboard and went back to the smoke house. Nathan Riley rearranged the hams on their hooks. He didn't trust himself to begin a different kind of chore until his churning stomach calmed down.

It was Elle's job to spread the still warm embers out from under the copper pot when the apple butter was done. She used a long-handled hoe and was careful not to throw an ember too close to where she stood. She moved back out of the way when Matthew carefully poured water from a bucket on what remained of any live ashes. He took the hoe from her and stirred the ashes to make sure the fire was dead.

John and Ben milked the cows. Caleb cleaned the round wooden lid used to cover the apple butter and keep the bees out of it while it cooled. Elizabeth prepared the evening meal. As she stood at the kitchen sink, she looked out the window and saw her father standing in the middle of the lane and gazing in the direction taken by Catherine, Nate, and the slave. The young girl shook her head at the rare sight of her father merely standing still.

I wonder what a big plantation looks like, Elizabeth thought, as she put the food she had prepared on the table. She was already lonesome for her mother when she went out on the porch and rang the dinner bell.

* * *

If his mother had a tinge of regret about her decision, she did not show it. There was little conversation between them as they drove past the far field and left the farm and family to do their chores. Nate was relieved to be driving the buggy instead of the wagon. His arms still ached from his battle with the mules on the town trip. Nevertheless, he had learned never to be surprised by anything that darted out of the woods.

Although the road was familiar to Nate at the beginning of their journey, once they passed the turn off to the town, everything looked different. He noticed that orchards and vegetable gardens gave way to huge cotton fields dotted with dozens of working slaves.

Other travelers on the road paid them scant attention. Nate didn't realize they were a common sight—a slave following his white owners at a respectful distance. Two patrollers saw the small caravan and waved them on. Nate stopped the buggy only once to allow the passengers a short rest to eat and the horses a drink of water. The men disappeared into the woods to relieve themselves before they resumed their journey.

They reached the outskirts of Fair Oaks Plantation late in the afternoon. Nate was impressed as he drove the buggy down the road lined with acres of fields of cotton. As it was near dusk, dozens of slaves had stopped their labor and were returning to their homes.

The ones who worked the farthest field rode in large flat-bed wagons, but most of the slaves were walking.

"Mama, have you ever seen anything like this in your whole life?" Nate asked, his voice filled with wonder.

Before she could reply, Caro rode up beside them and Nate reined in his horse. "Y'all is to follow me now, sir. We is gonna put your buggy an' horse in da lower barn. If you waits der, Mr. Bailey, he comes to git you right away."

"I don't like this," Nate said as Caro led their horse into the dark and musty barn. The smell of old leather tack caused the boy to sneeze.

"Y'all is to stay right here. We be back shortly. Dat other slave, he take care of your horse an' gear." Caro dismounted quickly, ran up a wide path, and knocked at the back door of the Bailey house. The slave explained the conditions of Mrs. Riley's arrival.

Within minutes, Mr. Bailey himself was in a small buggy on his way to the lower barn. Even though the sun was low in the sky and the barn getting darker, the Rileys had not been left alone long enough to be concerned. However, they were relieved when a white man drove up to get them.

"Mrs. Riley, young man, I'm Mr. Bailey. Please get into the buggy. I cannot tell you how grateful I am that you have come."

"I was surprised by your letter," Catherine Riley said as Nate helped her up to the seat next to the driver. This is my son Nate. He, too, is very good at doctoring, and we will do the best we can for your injured slave."

After a very short ride, Bailey pulled the buggy to a stop. "Forgive me for having you come in through our back door. You will understand, I think, that it is important for you not to be seen at this time.

"Tomorrow, if your presence is reported to Mr. Randolph, we shall say you are a cousin of my wife and are visiting us with your son for a few days' stay while on your way to see other relatives in Memphis. Our daughter is attending school in that city and anyone could surmise that she would be looking forward to seeing relatives, especially a comely one such as your son here." Although first annoyed by Nate's presence, Bailey realized the boy added credence to the story.

Mrs. Bailey came into the kitchen, greeted the visitors warmly, and took Mrs. Riley to her bedroom to refresh herself. "Thank you for coming. I know you must be weary from the trip. When you have finished here, I'll have supper waiting downstairs. You and your son must be starving. My husband will take you to the slave after we have finished."

"I'll hurry." Catherine drank in the pleasure of being in such a beautiful house but quickly took care of her needs and returned to the handsome dining room.

Nate, looking clean and less tired than he felt, was waiting, and the four of them sat down to a bountiful supper served by Betty, the house slave. Mr. and Mrs. Bailey were friendly and made small talk throughout the meal. Catherine Riley had hoped for more information.

When the meal was over, Mr. Bailey addressed her. "Mrs. Riley, if you will come with me, please. Your son will wait here where he will be more comfortable."

Nate spoke up for the first time. "I am to help my mother, if you don't mind. First, we must get her basket of medicines. We left them in our buggy as we didn't know where we were going."

"Caro can fetch them." Mr. Bailey nodded to his wife, rose from the table, and said to Nate. "Very well, you may come with your mother, if you must. I caution you both as to the importance of secrecy. I would have sent for a real doctor but for the sensitive nature of the situation."

Nate was ready to reply when his mother's glance warned him to keep his opinions to himself. "Of course," she replied sweetly.

It was just getting dark when the three of them walked down the wide path to the slave quarters. There were several long and narrow wooden frame houses in a row, and when they reached the fourth one, Caro, medicine basket in his hand, was already standing at the door. Mr. Bailey held the door open and motioned them inside.

Men and women were seated at long tables eating their evening meal. A number of candles illuminated the tables and other lit tapers placed in rough iron sconces on three walls provided adequate light. A large fireplace, similar to Catherine's own on the Riley farm, held cooking pots from which food was served.

Neither Nate nor his mother had been inside a slave cabin before. Catherine was surprised at how clean it was. The dirt floor was hard but swept clean, not unlike the floor of the Rileys' tiny cabin when they were first married.

Both of the outsiders felt uncomfortable, as if they were intruders in a place they should not be even though no one present had made a single action that would lead the farmers to that conclusion.

Catherine stepped back involuntarily when an old Negro woman approached her. "I's Old Clara. You come to doctor dat big ole slave, I reckon. Come 'long."

They obediently followed Old Clara, who led them through a door and into a large, dim room with more than two dozen beds.

"Get us more light," Bailey called back to those still eating in the kitchen.

Three slaves rose to carry candles from their table to where Hercules lay. No one complained that the order left their supper table in the dark.

Nate recognized Hercules at once. *He's dead already,* the boy thought. *All that money and the slave's dead!* Nate looked around in search of the little girl, but the only other person who had come into the room was an old slave who answered to the name of Luther.

Catherine sat down on a stool next to the bed. "Hold the light close," she said as she inspected the wounds around the slave's huge wrists. Although the skin was dark, she detected two short red streaks running up one arm, a sure sign of blood poisoning. His forehead was hot, and although the big slave stirred, he did not wake.

"Well?" asked Mr. Riley.

"Blood poisoning," she answered. "I shall do my best. I will stay here with him tonight. Get me a table for my medicines and more candles. Nate, find me a chair and one for yourself."

Mr. Bailey choked but insisted, "Madam, I cannot allow you to stay here in the slave quarters through the night."

Catherine paused, then sighed. "Very well. Prepare to bury him in the morning," the farm woman said as she rose to leave.

The overseer considered his future. "One moment please, Madam. Perhaps I have been too hasty. On second thought, I am sure you will be quite safe if I leave you in these capable hands." The overseer gestured toward the slaves standing by.

Mr. Bailey motioned them to follow him into the other room. "Old Clara, Luther, Caro, I hold you responsible for the safety of this white woman," he hissed. "If anything happens to her, I shall see you sold to the next slave speculator who comes by, but not before I myself tie you to the whipping tree and skin your black hides."

Mr. Bailey turned on his heel. He wiped the perspiration caused by fear, not heat, from his forehead as he approached the outside door.

Nate, who had overheard his threatening instructions to the slaves, doubled his fists and called after the overseer, "I can watch after my mother by myself, sir!"

The one-bed hospital was organized and functioning by the time Bailey reached the front door to his house. Mrs. Riley sat bedside in Old Clara's own rocking chair the slave carried in from the women's room. Luther furnished the small table he used to roll pie crust. He set a pan of hot water and the lady's basket of medicines on the smooth table top.

Caro found a stool for Nate to sit on and watched while the boy followed to the letter the instructions his mother gave him.

"Mix together equal amounts of powdered salt heliotrope root, capsicum, and honey. Use the big pewter spoon in the basket," she said. "Old Clara, can you bring me strips of clean cloth? We came in such haste, I forgot to replenish my basket."

The old woman was delighted to be given the task. She felt important when she returned with muslin strips torn from an old worn-out shirt. Nate had finished mixing the poltice, and Old Clara held a cloth strip taut as Mrs. Riley spread a thick coating of the medicine on the material. Catherine carefully and gently wrapped the bandage, poultice side down, around one of Hercules's wrists and followed the same procedure for the other one.

"I'll leave this on for seven hours," she told the slaves who were watching her. "The poultice will begin to draw the poison out. After that, we must change the poultice every three hours for at least six days even if the red streaks are gone before them. Who is the cook here?"

"I is," answered Luther.

"I have a job for you. Can you find chickweed?"

"Yes'm."

"It can be dried or fresh. I want you to put one tablespoon of dried or two tablespoons of chopped fresh chickweed into a pan with two cups of boiling water. Let it sit and steep for about twenty minutes. Then strain the water through a piece of cloth. Do you understand what I mean?"

"Yes'm."

"Good. When it is cool, give it to this slave to drink. He needs to drink all of it. Make him some three times every day until seven days after the red streaks up his arm are gone."

"Yes'm."

Forty minutes later, Luther returned with the liquid. The old cook and Nate held Hercules's head up high enough so he could drink it. "You done good," Luther said to his patient before returning to his kitchen.

Nate and his mother took turns catnapping during the night while one or the other kept vigil over the feverish slave. Old Clara, Luther, or Caro were always nearby and together the group kept Hercules's treatments on schedule.

The Rileys, overcome with exhaustion, slept atop the covers on the slave beds. They expected to be hosts for lice and were pleasantly surprised to find their clothing and bodies pest free when they woke. Mr. Bailey looked in from time to time but asked no questions and made no comment.

Mrs. Riley changed the slave's bandages and applied freshly mixed poultice for the first twenty-four hours. After that, Old Clara insisted that the Rileys get some fresh air from time to time. Luther fed the two of them their meals at a small table with chairs carried outside for that purpose. The furniture was placed behind some tall bushes and out of sight of anyone passing by gunbarrel house number four.

"Luther, you are a wonderful cook," Mrs. Riley told him. The old slave smiled in appreciation of the rare compliment.

"Is there any way we can look at Thomas Randolph's house? He's such a rich man, I think it must look like a palace. I've never seen a plantation house before," Nate said.

"Well," Luther answered confidentially, "if you is careful and lets nobody see you, you can peek out through da bushes right over here." The old slave pushed aside leaves on a crepe myrtle growing between the gunbarrel house and the vegetable garden. "You be careful, mind? Or ole Luther here gits his ole black skin stripped to his bones if'n anybody sees you."

Both Nate and his mother cautiously peeked out at the big house. Its splendor made them catch their breaths. It was three times as big as any church they had ever seen. In front of a veranda, longer and wider than an entire gunbarrel house, eight large white pillars soared to the top of the second story. Vines growing up the two center pillars reached as high as the balcony. The plantation's double front door was crowned by an etched glass fan light, and the windows on the first floor were wide and tall.

Luther whispered, "Somebody comin'," and they went inside.

By the evening of the sixth day, Mrs. Riley called Old Clara, Luther, and Caro to come and see for themselves. Nate held the candle close so the three slaves could carefully examine Hercules's wrists. They were surprised and relieved. Although the giant's wounds were ugly and still oozing some pus, the red streaks had disappeared.

Mrs. Riley felt the slave's forehead. "He's still warm, but I think his temperature is almost normal."

"Thank you, Lord," Old Clara whispered.

"Amen," the others sighed in unison.

Luther brought in a bowl of cornmeal mush and a tasty new drink made from mashed peaches, a splash of whiskey, well water, and secret ingredients given him by Mrs. Riley. "Dis be for you, big ole Hercules. Old Luther make it special jest for you."

The big slave struggled to sit up by himself. He saw a white boy standing in the room, a white woman sitting next to his bed, and three Negro slaves hovering over him.

Hercules shook his head to retrieve a shadowy memory, something from the time he had been out of his head. The vision cleared and a heavenly light shone down upon a white angel. He remembered how disappointed he was at the color of her skin. *I died,* he thought. *I's in the wrong heaven. Maybe I's in hell.*

When Luther spooned a little mush into the slave's mouth and held the liquid to his lips, Hercules clearly knew where he was, a slave on earth, and thought that he would have been better off in hell.

Nate knew his mother had bested death. He looked at her face as she let out a long, soft sigh and watched tears running down her cheeks.

Too overcome to speak, Catherine Riley, the farmer's wife who knew natural medicines as well as many doctors, merely touched each of the three loyal slaves lightly on their shoulders and nodded her thanks for their unstinting help in this victory over death.

Hercules, his eyes closed, but his mind alert and listening, pulled back his hand when she rested hers on his.

Mrs. Riley found her voice. "Caro, tell Mr. Bailey we'll be ready to leave in the morning. I'll come up to his house and give Mrs. Bailey instructions about Hercules's further care.

"All of you know what to do, although I am sure Bailey will not trust you to do it." Catherine regretted her words the moment she said them.

Early the next morning, Caro returned with the plantation's buggy and asked Mrs. Riley and Nate to ride inside so they would not be seen walking to the overseer's house.

Catherine had Nate prepare the medications Hercules would need for the next two weeks and left the medicine with Old Clara and Luther. Nate carried their medicine basket to the buggy and waited there for his mother.

Before she left the gunbarrel house, Catherine carefully examined the huge slave and was satisfied that he would live. He made no sound, but his eyes followed the white woman as she left the room.

Catherine climbed aboard the buggy then turned to ask Luther a question. "Why do you call it a gunbarrel house?"

" 'Cause da house be long an' narrow, jest like da barrel of a gun. Helps some to think of da women's room like da stock, da kitchen like da trigger, an da men's room like da barrel. If'n folks ax you, jest tell 'em you been livin' in da barrel of a gun." The old slave laughed and waved good-bye.

Mrs. Riley gave her report to the Baileys. "Hercules, that is his true name, isn't it?, has passed though the crisis period. That does not mean he is well. If the doctoring continues as I have instructed, he has a good chance of recovering. He should not be put to work for at least two more weeks."

Catherine went over the mixing of the medicines and how they should be used as she had done with the slaves. "I have given these same instructions to Old Clara, Luther, and Caro and, if you wish, the three of them can continue doctoring him. You should know, as well, that I would not have come had my son Nate not been present at the slave auction when your planter purchased the giant."

And if Papa had not forbidden her to do it, Nate thought to himself and smiled.

"You have my eternal gratitude, my dear lady, and that of Mrs. Bailey as well." The overseer handed Mrs. Riley a small leather pouch. "They are gold coins. I felt you would prefer them. Thanks to you also, young man. You are a great help to your mother." The overseer shook Nate's hand.

Mrs. Bailey brought out a lunch basket for their trip home and thanked the Rileys again for coming. The overseer's wife knew in her heart that it was her advice to her husband that saw a turn in their fortunes from what could have been disaster.

Of course, Mrs. Bailey thought, *the slave is not on his feet, as yet, but I will see that the lady's instructions are followed to the letter. God willing, he will be as fit and strong as the day Thomas Randolph bought him.*

When the Rileys walked to the lower barn, they found their horse and buggy were ready to go. Caro helped Mrs. Riley up to the seat and wished them a safe journey home. "You done a fine job, Missus Riley an' Mister Nate, sir. I's proud to brung you."

Mr. Bailey stood on the back porch of his house and watched until the buggy disappeared from sight. He felt a large weight lifting off his shoulders but knew prayer and luck would be needed if his own stupidity in the matter was ever discovered by Thomas Randolph.

Nate and his mother were quiet, drained of energy by the strain secrecy adds to a life or death event. Their horse, well-fed and rested, maintained a steady gait even though Nate held the reins loosely in his hands.

Finally, after the Rileys had cleared the vast lands of Fair Oaks Plantation, Catherine opened the pouch and exclaimed, "Nate, he paid us enough money to buy a slave!"

Part Two

Chapter Five
Conspiracy

Overseer Bailey did not know it, but members of the slave community on Fair Oaks Plantation had an interest in him keeping his job. Although they knew him to be fierce with a whip, he had hanged only three run-away slaves during the eight years he had been overseer. Any replacement could be ten times worse than Bailey. Even slaves whose bodies carried hideous scars received from the tips of Bailey's cat-o-nine tails dreaded the thought of a new overseer. True or not, they had heard the rumors circulated among the county's plantations about the cruelty of some newly hired overseers who wanted to impress planters by getting more work out of their slaves than the previous hires.

Luther was the first to pick up their concerns when he heard the boss slaves talking at breakfast. They had been trained by Bailey in his own ways and enjoyed the prestige of being in direct charge of many of the day-to-day operations of the plantation. Because of their positions, they received extra food rations, including corn whiskey, at Christmas and enjoyed a greater number of passes to town and to visit friends and relatives on other plantations. If Bailey left, they worried about what the new overseer would do with them.

Members of the slave population at Fair Oaks Plantation were allowed several passes a year to visit friends or go to town in order to shop with money earned by selling furs from animals they had trapped or vegetables from their own slave garden plots. Townspeople knew they were Fair Oaks Plantation slaves who enjoyed a certain status merely because they were the property of Thomas Randolph, the wealthy and successful planter who was held in high esteem by others of his social and economic class.

Of course, everyone also knew that much of the respect was passed on to him through the inheritance of his family name and the fortune that went with it. Even so, most people admired him because Randolph himself built Fair Oaks, and no one who knew him doubted that the man knew how to manage one of the most efficient and profitable plantations in the South.

Luther and Clara were two of the thirty-seven slaves willed to Thomas Randolph by his father who also left his son a large tract of virgin land. The young man had the knowledge and the money to purchase, mostly at auction, nearly two-hundred more slaves.

Luther and Clara were young then and proud when their young master made a brilliant marriage with Rebecca Beauregard, whose family pedigree matched his own. They were equally matched in ambition, as well, and it was not many years before their own slave population was self-sustaining due to the selective breeding program directed by Mistress Randolph herself.

Although they never really thought about it, much of the Randolph success could be credited to the slaves themselves, their individual skills, efficient labor, and the loosely-organized but quite stable community life in the slave quarters, the equivalent of a small town. There were leaders and followers, teachers and learners, young, middle aged, and old people. Each one of them had skills of marketable value. Many of them were expert in their work whether it was in the field, the craft shops, or as personal servants to the Master, his family, and guests.

Many of the slaves were related to one another but there were no feeble-minded among them due to Mistress Randolph's careful breeding. The large number of slaves on the plantation allowed Mistress to adhere to her rule of no copulating with anyone closer than a third cousin. Throughout her life, she had seen too many marriages of first cousins among prominent families and noted the number of their children who appeared to be "quite slow."

Among the Fair Oaks slave population there were, of course, some who were old and infirm as well as a number of men who were stove-up due to accidents. Slave bosses assigned them tasks that they were able to do like vegetable gardening, cleaning, handwork, sewing, helping the craftsman sharpen tools and carrying light weight raw materials to them when needed. Work was important for those "almost used up" slaves who were able to remain productive enough so they would not be sold. When they passed, they wanted to be buried in their home place among friends who had gone before.

Luther and Clara had grown old in service. Even though they were no longer officially designated as "slave bosses," they were recognized by their peers as still having the unofficial role. The younger slaves looked to them for guidance and were grateful for their wisdom.

"Cream always rises to the top," Old Clara often said to explain why a few of the children she cared for seemed to have a gift to watch out for and help the other children. This quality did not depend on the child's age but on the personality.

Old Clara, herself, had been one of these special children. Now ancient, she still had the power and recognized it as "cream."

Luther put it another way when the old woman convinced, rather, insisted that he add a pinch more cinnamon to his apple pie. "Woman, you is BOSSY!" he retorted as he added another pinch of cinnamon to his apple pie while Old Clara looked on.

Everyone in the slave community knew who was bossy or "cream" or a leader. They were the people who had good ideas, who the others looked up to, the ones others were willing to trust and to follow. Some people led, other people followed.

Once in a while, someone might challenge this order of things. A leader might even disappoint or betray them, but such a thing was rare. The Fair Oaks slave community trusted the courage, faithfulness, and collective wisdom of their natural leaders, their cream: Bessie, Old Clara, Luther, Jubal, Caro, and Noah, the blacksmith. Collectively, these six had current information on everything that happened on the plantation.

Luther carried squash from his own garden up to Bessie in the big house. Jubal was sitting on the kitchen porch steps and polishing Randolph's boots. Bessie came out of her kitchen to take the squash and to hear the day's gossip. It agreed with what she already knew. The slave community was worried about the injury to Master Randolph's expensive fighting slave and had very real concern that Overseer Bailey would be fired because of it.

"What if Master wants Hercules to fight next week?" Luther asked with concern.

"Dat'll never happen," Jubal answered with a smile. "Master too smart for dat. Hercules be a number-one blacksmith, an' Master, he not be a bettin' man. 'Cept he bet on gettin' one hundred dollars ever' day he rents out dat big ole blacksmith slave if he's of a mind to. Main reason Master buys 'em is to get the goat of his friends. Dey had fits when Master best dem at auction. Dey be so mad dey wouldn't even stay to drink wid Master. Jest the same, we needs to figure out what to do to keep Bailey here."

* * *

Bessie called the group together in her usual way. They had not met formally for nearly a year. After breakfast in the big house, Bessie, as usual, hung the damp dish towels out to dry on the small clothes line next to the kitchen porch. She hung three white towels in a row and then one green one. With that simple and routine act, the group knew to assemble in the lower barn one hour after sundown that same day.

Although Gabrel knew about the meeting, he was not a member and did not attend. " 'Tis for da safety of your own skin," Bessie explained.

The little group sat on hay bales and exchanged the information they had gathered that day. "Don't fix it if it ain't broken," summed up the general feeling among those living in the slave community. During the day, small groups had quietly discussed the plight of Overseer Bailey, whose carelessness caused the life-threatening injury to Master Randolph's new slave. Everyone, without exception, wanted Bailey to stay.

Compared to what they had learned from friends and gossip above slave life on other plantations, the Randolph slaves felt they were better off here under Bailey, the Negro boss men he had trained, and the present system under which they lived and worked.

The six leaders were in general agreement with the feelings and opinions of the community. Bessie and Jubal, who were intimately familiar with the personalities of the Randolph family members, knew the seriousness of the situation Bailey faced. What's more, when Master Randolph was on a tear, his anger spilled over onto innocent slaves who never knew why Master ordered them whipped severely.

At Jubal's suggestion, the group recalled some of their own advantages that were equal to or better than those of slaves on other plantations. Even though slave labor is hard and lasts from sun-up to sun-down, slaves at Fair Oak have some benefits. Master gives them permission to grow their own vegetable gardens on land behind their houses. Their crops supplement the weekly rations which Mr. Bailey passes out every Saturday morning.

Men and boys can trap animals and sell their hides in town on Saturday, and the woman and girls can sell their needlework there also. With passes, they can visit friends on the plantations on Saturday or Sunday afternoon. If two slaves of different plantations want to get married, Master Randolph usually will sell his slave to the other owner or buy his own slave's sweetheart so the two can live together as man and wife.

At Christmas, Mistress gives everyone two sets of new clothes and a new pair of shoes. Master gives double the week's food rations and a bottle of whiskey to the men. Field slaves and craftsmen don't have to work the week between Christmas and New Year's Day.

Throughout the year, Mistress Randolph makes every one of them bathe in the wash houses each Saturday so all of the Randolph slaves will be clean on Sunday.

Mistress takes twenty slaves at a time to her own church on the Lord's Day. They sit on benches in the balcony. Even though they find the preacher boring and the worship services duller than a potato masher, the Fair Oaks slaves enjoy visiting the slaves pressed into worship duty from other plantations at the church picnic following the service. It's a matter of pride to Mistress Randolph that her slaves bring better food to share than the other colored folks attending.

Those slaves left behind at Fair Oaks consider themselves fortunate to attend their own worship service held under the trees just beyond the cotton-bale barn. Both men and women lead the congregation in a ritual overflowing with emotional sermonizing and music so joyful the congregants know their black God and his angels up there in heaven clap their hands and tap their satin-shod feet right along with earth-bound saints and sinners.

Only yesterday at church meeting, the worshipers offered up prayers on the overseer's behalf and asked God's guidance in the matter. The oldest preacher called down to the front Bessie, Old Clara, Luther, Jubal, Caro, and Noah and asked God for a special blessing on the slave Hercules, to heal his wounds and make him whole once again.

The preacher asked for God's mercy on Mr. Bailey and forgiveness for the overseer's many sins. The service ended with the preacher's prayer for God to grant their leaders the wisdom and courage to get everybody out of the mess Mr. Bailey got them into.

With God on their side, and when all of the good things about life on the plantation were balanced with the bad as compared to the everyday lives of slaves on other plantations, there was no doubt that Mr. Bailey had to stay.

* * *

The next week after the plantation worship service ended and the Sunday picnic was over, the six leaders stayed behind. They settled themselves comfortably on the grass under the trees. The women were especially careful so as not to get grass stains on their Sunday best clothes. The meeting was brief. They expected the Randolphs and the twenty slaves with them to return from the white church within the hour.

Those in the little group recognized their problem was caused by Mr. Bailey's carelessness. Even though it was the overseer's fault, if fired, he would get off easy. The slaves knew it would be left to them to pay the price for Master's temper.

They agreed on a plan, inherently dangerous, to hide from Master Randolph the fact that Hercules had ever been injured. Randolph had to believe the slave was in the same perfect physical condition as he was on the day Master paid three thousand dollars for him.

Each of the six agreed to play a particular role in the risky plan they devised:

Bessie would fuel Master Randolph's "indigestion" as long as possible. When it looked as if Master or any family member was on the way to inspect the slave or his work, Bessie would signal using three white towels and one red checked one.

Old Clara and Luther would continue to nurse Hercules and follow the directions left them by Mrs. Riley. They would add to his diet purslane salad which is good for the blood. It would be their responsibility to get Hercules to the blacksmith shop when they saw Bessie's signal.

Caro would keep Mr. Bailey as far away from Hercules and gunpowder house number four as possible without arousing the overseer's suspicion. Caro could start a small fire in one of the far fields, if necessary, to divert his attention.

Jubal, with access to the fine clothing and accessories worn by Master Randolph, would carefully examine the owner's fine leather gloves and make a paper pattern for the tanner who, in turn, would stitch together a pair of gloves big enough for Hercules's huge hands and long enough to hide the wounds encircling his wrists.

Noah would forge new door hinges and partly finish a pair of saddle stirrups to be passed off as the work of Hercules if, and when, anyone from the big house came to see the new slave at work.

As the meeting ended, the six held hands, and bowed their heads. Bessie prayed, "Lord, you know our needs. Watch over your chilluns an' be wid us in dis risky business. In da name of Jesus who saves us from our sins an' who could save Bailey from his if'n he be a more careful man. Amen."

* * *

Overseer Bailey continued to be personally present even though he did not actually direct the slaves working in the farthest field, much to the consternation of his Negro bosses assigned the duty although they dared not show it.

They muttered among themselves until one of them suggested that Mr. Bailey was hiding from someone and guessed it to be Master Randolph himself. The boss slaves were relieved that the overseer most likely would not strip them of their rank because they had failed at their jobs. They watched Bailey with interest and made side bets as to the day Master Randolph would catch up with him.

Bailey, exhausted and dirty, returned to his home and looked forward to a bath and a shot of whiskey before supper. His body ached from the days he had spent sitting his horse in dusty fields doing a nasty job in which he had little interest and wasn't his to do in the first place. He was almost happy to hear his wife give him the expected news. "Jubal was here this morning. Randolph wants to see you in the big house at ten o'clock tomorrow morning."

At exactly ten o'clock, Overseer Bailey walked across the veranda of the big house. His throat felt constricted as he rang the bell and entered the front hall when Gabrel opened the massive door. "Master will see you in da library," he said with dignity.

"Bailey," Thomas Randolph said pleasantly as he rose from behind his desk to shake his employee's hand. "Please sit down."

"Good morning, sir. I'm glad to see you up and about. I trust you are feeling better," Bailey replied.

"Yes, yes, but remind me not to eat the food the next time we are in town. Is the slave child cleaned up and ready?" Randolph asked.

The unexpected question left Bailey's knees weak. "Yes, sir," he lied. "Old Clara has a way of cleaning up little slave children in a hurry."

"Excellent, excellent. Ask Bessie for some clothes and ribbon and find a big box somewhere. I want the box beautifully festooned, the child inside it, of course. Tell her to keep quiet in there. And see that she wears a pretty dress with bows and things that are on the dolls Santa Claus brings." He smiled. "Bessie can help you with that."

Bailey took a deep breath. "When and where do you want the box delivered?"

"Tomorrow afternoon, I think, and find someone to carry it up to Evangline's bedroom. I am on my daughter's wrong side, I fear. Can you imagine, here I've been near death for days, and all my daughter can think about is the present I promised to bring her from town. She's just like her mother," he said, more pleased than annoyed, it seemed to Bailey. "Go find Bessie. She knows what to do."

"Thank you, sir. I'll do my best," Bailey said with a slight bow as he left the library and gave a quick little prayer of thanks for spoiled and demanding Southern women. *His daughter's petulence may have given me another day or two before Randolph seeks out Hercules,* he thought as he walked into Bessie's kitchen. Although uninvited, he sat in a chair near the fireplace, an act that helped steady his weak knees.

The cook looked up and continued to roll out pie crust dough. "Bessie," he said, "Master Randolph wants the slave child dressed like a Christmas doll, put in a box wrapped like a present, and delivered to his daughter's room tomorrow afternoon."

Bessie kept on rolling the dough. "I knows. Got ribbons an' fancy clothes right over der." She pointed with a flour-dusted finger to the bulging pillowcase on a kitchen stool. "Best you carry 'em in da pillowcase so nobody sees 'em. I wants da pillowcase back. I gots da clothes. You needs to get da box.'' Bailey picked up the bundle and left by the kitchen door.

Bessie shook her head and smiled. *Dat Evangeline! She got her papa just where she wants him again,* she thought. As Bessie peeled, sliced, and added sugar and spices to the apples for her pies, she couldn't help but remember the time when the girl baby descended from heaven or escaped from hell, you takes your pick, to upset the serenity of Fair Oaks Plantation.

Gabrel came into the kitchen with the empty breakfast tray he had carried down from Mistress Randolph's sitting room. ''Mistress be worn to a frazzle from listenin' to da bellyachin' of da Master. Young Mistress Evangeline in wid her mama an' tryin to soothe her by readin' to her from a big book. Dey both will be takin' der dinner in dat room.''

''Hmm,'' Bessie said as she continued her baking. ''Dat's nice. Time da girl did somethin' for folks for a change instead of gettin' from folks all da time. She be a demandin' chile from da day she be born.''

Bessie dusted the flour from her hands, put the pies in the oven, poured herself a cup of coffee, and sat in her rocking chair to rest. The old cook thought back to the time of Evangeline's birth and the uproar it caused.

When Evangeline was born, she was like a dogwood tree in early spring. Everyone knew she would never be creamy white and buxom like a magnolia blossom which epitomized the graciousness of the South. Magnolia trees took their time to bloom and because of their lazy ways, their flowers were slower to attract attention. Many magnolia blossoms were shy and remained hidden among the large dark green and shiny leaves on stately trees.

Yellow forsythia usually won the race to spring, but it was only a shrub and didn't count. Dogwood trees are taller than forsythia and shorter than magnolias. They are asymmetrical with branches growing every which way as if they can't make up their minds. When green leaf buds begin to show, white dogwood blossoms burst open all at once as if to say, ''Here we are!'' Each flower has four petals brushed with strokes of purple near their centers. Dogwood and redbud trees often grow in tandem, and the latter's pink blooms complement the white and purple-splashed colors of the dogwood blossoms. Such color combinations shout for attention.

So it was with Evangeline. From the day of her birth, she demanded attention. She was a crying colicky baby who had to be walked and soothed day and night by a team of adults including her Grandmother Lee who had come up from Savannah and brought with her the Mammy who had raised Mistress Randolph.

Even Master, now and again, took a turn at walking and trying to soothe his infant daughter. His attention caused the baby's two older brothers to have much longer lasting deep feelings of resentment and jealousy than is usual for a family with a new baby in the house.

Bessie smiled as she remembered the first quiet day. It was soon after Mrs. Lee arrived with Mammy. The old Negro nurse simply made a sugar tit from a small piece of bread dipped in sugar and put in the center of a clean linen handkerchief. Mammy twisted the cloth to make a tit and put the business end of it into the newborn's tiny mouth. Evangeline quieted at once, sucked on her sugar tit, and eventually fell asleep. The adults breathed sighs of relief, tiptoed quietly from the nursery and retreated to their own beds for much needed sleep. Mammy napped in the rocking chair three feet away from the baby girl's cradle.

At the time, Gabrel told Bessie what Master did next. After his nap, the planter was refreshed and retired to the library to do some figuring. "You knows," Gabrel had said, "how much Master hates figurin'. He thinks it helps him if he figures out loud. I be tendin' to da fire in da library an' heard him figure."

"Even though Mammy is old, if we treat her well, and we surely will, she might live just long enough to raise Evangline, perhaps even to her wedding day.

"Now if the baby lives to age sixteen," Master said quietly to himself, "that would be sixteen years at one hundred dollars a year, a fair price for such an old slave. One thousand six-hundred dollars. I'll offer my mother-in-law fifteen hundred dollars for Mammy, probably more than the old thing is worth."

As far as Gabrel knew, Master said nothing about his idea until the end of the week. For every one of those seven days, Mammy had been the only one in the house with the magic to keep the infant Evangeline quiet and happy.

When Gabrel was serving breakfast in the dining room the day before Mrs. Lee was to return to Savannah, her son-in-law approached her with a business offer. "Mother, I wish you godspeed and a comfortable journey home. Give our love to the rest of the family. We can never express our thanks to you for coming all this way to be here for our precious Evangeline.

"Mammy has been a great help even at her advanced age. I wonder about the strain on her of making the long journey back to Savannah with you. I would be pleased to offer you fif—er, sixteen hundred dollars for her."

Mrs. Lee smiled in her graceful, genteel way. "How kind of you, my dear. Let us just say that Mammy is my gift to little Evangeline. It pleases me to know that she will take the same good care of my granddaughter as she did of my daughter."

Grandmother Lee kissed all of them good-bye, admonished her two grandsons to take good care of their baby sister, and directed her body slave to make sure none of her belongings were left behind. The elegant lady threw kisses as she waved from the carriage taking her to the dock where she would catch the paddle-wheeler for the first part of her journey.

Both Gabrel and Bessie rejoiced in Mammy's presence. They knew everyone's life would be better with the experienced old Mammy in charge of the nursery.

Although she had nursed her two sons, after this birth Mistress Randolph felt her milk to be bad and the cause of her baby daughter's early distress. She made the deliberate decision to go dry. She didn't tell her husband at the time, thinking he would object or find her less appealing as a woman.

Under Mammy's expert care, the baby continued to thrive. The old slave found several wet nurses among the plantation slaves. Mammy tried out three of them with Evangeline and chose the slave mother who best produced an amply supply of milk the newborn could digest, whose nipples were compatible in size with the infant's tiny mouth, who possessed what appeared to be a calm nature, and who handled Evangline with gentle loving care. The wet nurse produced an ample supply of milk to satisfy the needs of the white baby as well as her own colored infant.

When the serenity in the nursery brought smiles to all members of the household, with the possible exception of Raleigh and Alexander, Mistress Randolph told her husband of her decision not to nurse. He was not upset at all and proved it that night in their bed.

Bessie knew all about it although she refused to identify the particular source of her information. However, the slave's communication network seemed to be busier than usual.

The smell of burning pie crust jolted Bessie out of her reverie. She jumped up from her rocking chair, grabbed two pot holders, and quickly took her pies out of the oven. *When dey cools,* she thought, *I'll just scrape the burned part off wid a knife, an' nobody will know da difference.*

Chapter Six
The Present

Bessie was still thinking about Evangeline and her two rascal brothers as she scraped the burned crust from her pies. *Like I told Gabrel, three children in a family never be good. Two of 'em always gangs up on da one dat's left over.*

Lost in thought, she jumped when Caro came through the kitchen door. "Here's da pillowcase from Bailey," he said as he ran his finger around the empty bowl that once held the apple filling and licked his sweetened finger.

"Stop dat!" Bessie warned. "Men! Dey always acts like little boys when der's somepin' good in da kitchen. I'll give you a real piece of pie if'n you comes back in about an hour."

"I be back," Caro promised as he left and walked back down the lane to the overseer's house. He found no one there except Betty.

"Mistress Bailey done gone to check up on da big slave," she explained. "I sees her comin' back now. She checks on him two times ever' single day. Master Bailey said for you to come on down to da barn an' take his horse to da blacksmith for shoeing." As Caro was leaving, he held the door open for the overseer's wife.

Mrs. Bailey was satisfied with the care Old Clara and Luther were giving the huge slave. For all she could tell, they were faithfully following the instructions given to them by Mrs. Riley. In addition, and unknown to Mrs. Bailey, Old Clara was using a curative of her own.

Each day, Old Clara quietly took from under her bed a small basket which held a sacred talisman secretly passed down from generation to generation of the women assumed to be members of her scattered matriarchal family. The treasure was a narrow black and white feather tied with a leather thong to a six-inch hand-carved piece of the jaw bone of a tiger. The carved design could be an ancient alphabet or the simple doodles of a bored hunter. It made no difference to Old Clara.

She knew the oral tradition which told the story of how the talisman was stolen and carried to the New World's shores by an ancestor who was abducted from her family by a rival tribal chieftan and sold into slavery. The talisman was revered as the women's protection from disease and death during the hideous voyage on the slave ship. Of the three-hundred stolen Africans, Old Clara's unknown ancestor was among the seventy-five who survived the ship's ocean crossing only to be sold at a slave auction in Baltimore, or so the story went.

Old Clara hid the talisman in the folds of her skirt whenever she took it from the basket. She carried it that way into the room where Hercules lay. "Luther, ya best close yo' eyes if'n ya don' wanna go blind. I's gonna use my magic on dis big ole slave."

Luther, valuing his sight, clasped his hands over his eyes and turned his back on her for good measure. Old Clara extended the talisman in the air above Hercules and slowly moved it back and forth from his head to his feet three times. As she did so, the old woman chanted an incantation in an unknown tongue.

She was unaware that the new slave child had followed her into the room and was both curious and frightened as she watched Old Clara perform the ritual. When she saw the little girl standing in a dark corner, the old woman gasped, fearing she may have blinded her.

Hercules moaned and turned his head, the first time they had seen him move voluntarily. The child, unhurt, walked quietly up to where the huge slave lay, put her face up close to his, and gently touched his cheek with her small hand. She tip-toed to reach the slave's large ear and whispered in a tiny voice, "Don't die." Hercules heard her words and willed himself to live.

* * *

"Betty, I'd like tea," Mistress Bailey said as she walked through the kitchen and into the parlor. "I think the slave is getting better," she said to her husband who was standing and looking out the window.

"Where are we going to get a box?" he asked.

"My dear," she laughed, "if you ever went up to the attic, you would know." *Men!* she thought. *Whatever would they do without their wives!* "Sit down and have tea with me. After that, I'll take Betty to the attic and we'll find one for you, that is, unless you want to do it yourself," she teased.

After their refreshment, Bailey took the clothes to Old Clara and told her how to clean up and dress the child for the following afternoon.

The old slave sniffed, "She be CLEAN already," and grabbed the clothing out of the overseer's hands. The other women in the room looked up from their work and expected to hear a harsh reprimand for Old Clara's snippy ways and were surprised to see the overseer merely shrug his shoulders and walk away.

"Bringin' dat big ole slave and da chile here be makin' every'-body act crazy!" Old Clara said and didn't care if Bailey heard it.

When he got back to his house, no one was there so the overseer went into the dining room, took the bottle from the sideboard and poured himself a small whiskey. He didn't hear his wife and Betty rummaging in the attic.

"We need a box big enough to hold a little slave girl," Mistress Bailey explained as the two of them searched in the dim light coming in from the two gable windows.

"Over here, Mistress," Betty said. She was back in a corner where she found a wooden box sitting on top of a large trunk. It took both of them to lift the dusty box by its leather handles down to the floor. Mistress pulled while Betty pushed it over closer to a window for better light.

Mistress took off the muslin covering one of her winter dresses hanging from a peg and handed the cloth to her house slave. "Here, dust it with this." Even though she stepped back, both of them sneezed as Betty carefully removed years of dust and dirt coating their find. "It's a sea chest!" Mistress exclaimed.

Lifting together, they removed the heavy lid and put it on the floor. Mistress found the sea chest filled with yellowed and crumbling papers and what appeared to be log books. She carefully lifted out the contents and stacked them in a pile on the floor.

"What's that smell? Ummm, some exotic wood, I'd guess. Smell it, Betty; the fragrance is quite lovely." Mistress ran her fingers over the wood and said softly, "Perfect. Mr. Bailey will be pleased. Betty, go down to the kitchen and bring up some clean cloths and furniture oil."

The house slave did as she was told. Together, the two of them polished the sea chest until the wood glowed. Never before had Betty been assisted by her Mistress in doing any task, and the slave felt uncomfortable being so close to her.

Both of them were surprised as an image slowly appeared under their polishing cloths. "Look!" Mistress exclaimed. "It's a painting of a ship done by a sailor, I'm sure. This sea chest has been in my family for a very long time but I never paid it much attention because it was so dirty.

"I had a relative—an uncle or cousin or somebody—who was a sailor, or maybe an officer. . . . Yes, I'm certain he would have been an officer on a slave ship. And this must be a painting of it! A three-masted schooner! How beautiful it is! See how skillfully he painted the white seafoam made by the bow of the ship as it sliced through the water. It will make a wonderful box, the best kind imaginable, for Miss Evangeline's surprise. I'll get Mr. Bailey. You fetch Caro. It will take both of them to carry it downstairs."

Betty was silent and her face passive as she followed her happy and excited mistress down the attic stairs. The house slave's mind was not on the sea chest but on the ship that carried it and her ancestors into slavery. She imagined she could hear their cries and vowed never to touch the sea chest again.

While Betty was on her way to the barn to fetch Caro, Bailey followed his wife back up the stairs. She pointed with pride to the wooden sea chest. "Look what I found for you to use as the box." She retold the seafaring story with greater embellishment than before and when she was finished, the Southern belle radiated the charm born and bred into her since birth. She coyly asked her husband the question even though she knew his answer in advance. "Am I not wonderful?"

"Wonderful, indeed!" he said and took her in his arms.

* * *

Well before dawn the next morning, Bessie was up, dressed, and sipping her morning coffee as she stoked the fireplace and got ready to fix breakfast. She put her cup on the table, got out the ingredients for cornbread and whipped up a batch. She poured the batter into a flat pan and slipped it into her familiar old fireplace oven to bake.

Last year Master Randolph brought home a fancy cast-iron cook stove and had it installed in Bessie's kitchen. The old cook refused to have anything to do with the contraption and successfully carried out her threat not to make another meal until it was out of her sight.

Gabrel knew for sure that both of them would be sold to the next slave speculator who came by looking to buy slaves at a bargain price and selling them for a profit. The thought had crossed Master Randolph's mind until he learned that some of his planter friends were salivating to get the Fair Oaks Plantation head cook into their own kitchens.

When the cast-iron cook stove disappeared from Bessie's kitchen, feasts fit for kings appeared on the Randolph table, the old cook's way of defending her reputation. Some of the field hands put it another way: "Ole Bessie, she done rubbed his nose in it!"

Bessie didn't ask what had become of the contraption but had no reason not to believe the rumors circulating among the house slaves. They said the cast-iron cook stove ended up in the Compound kitchen. *Good riddance,* Bessie thought.

The Compound was about a half mile behind the big house and in a clearing in the woods. Everybody knew it was there, but nobody talked much about it. Bessie had never seen it herself but didn't doubt the stories others told. Master's colored mistresses and their children lived there. Master spent every other Sunday afternoon away from the big house on business, he said. Everybody knew Master wouldn't conduct business, ordinary business anyway, on the Lord's Day. Everybody said Mistress Randolph didn't know anything about Master Randolph's Sunday afternoon business, but Bessie knew better.

Bessie listened to their talk once when she served tea on a Sunday afternoon to four of Mistress Randolph's very best friends who were the wives of other wealthy planters. All of the ladies' husbands had Sunday business, and the ladies knew what the scalawags were up to. Bessie wasn't surprised that they talked freely in front of her 'cause rich folks don't think their slaves have ears.

"Don't ever let on that you know what he's doing," the lady in the peach-colored dress said.

"I don't WANT to know how many little mixed-blood bastards are running around back there, anyway," offered another.

"You're quite right," Mistress Randolph added. "If we don't know about them, we don't need to worry about any of them claiming the inheritance that rightly belongs to our own children. It's simply a matter of good business. All big planters have a place of one kind or another somewhere on their property."

Bessie stood by as Gabrel helped the ladies with their wraps when the tea party was over. They complimented Mistress Randolph on her lovely tea cakes. Bessie watched through the window as Gabrel helped each guest into her buggy and then stacked the dirty dishes on a tray.

Mistress Randolph followed Bessie into the kitchen, asked her for a wet cloth for her headache and retired to her bedroom to rest.

Bessie thought about the conversation she had heard. *Everybody, rich or poor, have der lil secrets.* Bessie remembered a secret of her own. She knew she had taken a terrible chance when she doctored Master's food and made him sick. She felt both guilt and pleasure over the success of her ploy that gave the new slave Hercules a few more days to heal.

Bessie couldn't remember her life before the Randolphs. She had dim memories of herself as a child picking cotton, then as cook's helper, and her pride at becoming head cook. She understood Master Randolph better than his wife did.

She knew Master Randolph, like most men she had known, turns into a child when he gets the slightest sniffles. Men like that demand attention from every member of the household, summon their wives and children to their bedsides, go over with them the terms of their wills, and give them the list of details for their funerals which they expect to be carried out after their deaths which would occur within the week.

When he was feeling poorly because of the doctored food, Bessie had felt empathy for Master in his discomfort and now was making his favorite meals as a way to make amends.

* * *

Bessie had finished cooking and Gabrel was ready to serve when

Mistress Randolph rang for breakfast. When Gabrel returned to the kitchen after serving the first course of sliced peaches with cream, he described the change in Evangeline's deportment at the table. "Da girl, she usually comes in wid her pouty face to remind her daddy dat he owed her a present. She won't look kindly on da poor man 'til she gets it. But dis mornin' she ain't poutin' but she ain't smilin' either."

"Dat Evangeline!" Bessie exclaimed. "Dat girl prob'ly looked at herself in da mirror an' saw a lot of little ole lines all 'round her lips from so much poutin' and decided poutin' is gonna make her ugly, an' dat's da truth!"

"I be glad when afternoon comes an' she gets her present! Den I hopes dis house gets back to normal," Gabrel said with a sigh and loaded up his arms with silver serving dishes filled with eggs, ham, grits, fried apples, potatoes, and cornbread. The coffee pot, milk pitcher, jellies, jams, honey, and sweet butter were already on the dining room sideboard.

Although not served with the same elegance, Luther's breakfast in the gunbarrel house was as hearty. Old Clara was overjoyed when Hercules sat up in bed even though she had to feed him. He did not speak, but his eyes followed the slaves leaving the room to get their breakfast.

"One thing about Master and Mistress, dey gives us good food and plenty of it," Luther said as Overseer Bailey watched the cook and his children helpers load their mid-day meals into the wagon with the slaves bound for the farthest field.

Bailey nodded in agreement. He thought of a planter he once worked for who didn't understand the connection between food and work. While not deliberately meaning to be cruel, the man half-starved his slaves and was surprised when his plantation failed.

He knew the Randolphs were smarter than that and understood that a generous table provided the food fueling their mighty "slave engine" to work efficiently and without complaining. It was their business sense that made them wealthy. Bailey admired them for that.

* * *

Overseer Bailey was too nervous to eat his dinner. He had instructed Caro to carry the sea chest and the slave child up to the big house in the buggy so she would not be seen. Old Clara was miffed that she couldn't go too, but Caro told her it would be unusual if she went and might arouse suspicion. "Bessie can tell you ever'thing that happened. You'll know all 'bout it before sundown. Now, go get da chile."

Caro didn't expect to see such a beautiful doll. She was dressed in a pale pink long sleeved dress trimmed in white lace. Frilly pantaloons peeked from beneath the small hooped skirt, and she wore long white stockings and black button shoes. Her bonnet matched her dress. She looked like the daughter of a wealthy planter except for one thing. Her face, hair, and small hands were that of a colored child. Caro lifted her up into the buggy, and Old Clara, still pouting, covered the little girl up with a lightweight quilt.

Both Bailey and his wife watched from their parlor window as the buggy drove past their house and then disappeared as it approached the big house. The overseer poured himself a small glass of whiskey and a glass of wine for his wife. Mrs. Bailey would have preferred whiskey but accepted the wine gracefully. If she had asked for whiskey, her husband would have known she was as nervous as he was.

Bessie, Gabrel, and Jubal were waiting for them on the porch. Caro carried the child into the kitchen while Jubal and Gabrel carried in the sea chest and put it on the floor.

"Dis lid on too tight for da chile to breathe," Gabrel said and disappeared into his room. He came out with a small carving knife and prepared to cut small holes through the wood. He studied the painting of the ship carefully then thrust his knife into the seafoam where the bow sliced through the water. "I thinks four holes be enuf," Gabrel said, wiped his knife clean on the side of his trousers and returned it to his room.

Bessie still had the child's hand in hers as they watched Gabrel work. "Don't be skeered, chile. I's Bessie, dis here's my man Gabrel, and dat's Jubal over der. Caro brings you up in da buggy. Sit right up here at da table an' I'm gonna get you a piece of apple pie. Den, you gets to ride in dis pretty box. You gonna be a present for Miss Evangeline." Bessie put her large apron around the child so no pie crumbs would dirty her dress.

The little girl ate quietly and watched the activity going on around her. A big slave woman came into the kitchen and said, "We's ready."

Bessie took off the apron, wiped the child's face and hands with a damp cloth, and helped her get into the sea chest. "Lay right down here an' be quiet as a lil mouse. You can see out da top when we goes up dem stairs, but when we gets to da room, we gotta put da lid on da box. Don't be skeered, but be very, very quiet. You gonna laugh when you sees da surprise on Miss Evangeline's pretty face. Caro an' Jubal, dey gonna carry you real careful like."

The child's face puckered as if she was going to cry, but she made no sound as the slaves slowly carried her up the stairs. They put the chest down on the hall floor just outside the bedroom door. Bessie patted the little girl on her shoulder and whispered, "Quiet, now," just before the men slowly lifted the box lid in place. Bessie tied it with a beautiful pink ribbon.

They strained to hear the conversation coming from inside the room. All members of the family had gathered there along with most of the household slaves, and Evangeline was not happy. "Why are all of you in my room?" she asked crossly. "I didn't invite you!"

"Now, darlin'," her father said, "we all just want to see your lovely face when you open your present." On cue, Jubal and Caro carried the beautiful box into the room and gently put it down on the floor. Thomas Randolph delighted in seeing his only daughter's pout change to a beautiful smile.

"Papa, what is it? It's so big! What did you bring me?" Evangeline exclaimed as she knelt beside the box and untied the ribbon. "Help me," she ordered when she couldn't lift the lid.

Jubal and Caro were quick to respond. Evangeline sat back on her heels and clapped for joy when she saw the beautiful big doll. She shrieked as she watched the doll begin to move slowly, laughed as it sat up, and was dumbfounded when the doll stood up and wobbled as it stepped out of the box. Everyone was so amazed, they didn't notice the terrified look on the little girl's face.

Evangeline took the child's hand as the people in the room clapped and oohed and aahed over the cleverness of Master Randolph. He had kept the secret from his wife and wondered if she would be put out with him.

"Forgive me?" he whispered to his wife.

"Of course, you clever man. However, I must say you could have saved us many unpleasant meals at the table if you had given Evangeline her present days ago."

Their daughter was carefully examining every part of her present much as girls examine their Christmas dolls. "I like her," she announced. "I'm going to name her Sissy because I don't have a sister, just two horrid brothers." She stuck her tongue out at Alexander and Raleigh who were making faces at their sister behind their parent's back.

The grown-ups laughed as Evangeline quickly grabbed the startled Sissy by her arm and pulled her out of the room. "I'm going to take Sissy outside to play," she called back to them.

Alexander and Raleigh were as surprised as their sister with their father's extravagant gift. They knew slaves cost more money than the pocket knives he had brought to them from town. "Father loves Evangeline more than us," Raleigh announced to his older brother as they followed their sister and her "present."

"You're right, but just you wait. We'll get even with her!" replied Alexander.

Sissy had never seen so many steps and held back as Evangeline led her down the curving staircase, through the kitchen, out the door, and to the play area on the kitchen side of the big house. Her brothers were close behind.

Alexander and Raleigh looked around to see if anyone was watching. They pushed each other out of the way and Alexander, as usual, got to be the first one to slide down the highly polished bannister. He slapped his young brother's behind as Raleigh reached the bottom and landed on his feet. They ran out through Bessie's kitchen but were careful not to let the door slam behind them and hid unseen behind a crepe myrtle.

The brothers watched as Evangeline led Sissy to the swing tied to a thick limb of an ancient oak tree. Their sister settled herself on the wide wooden seat, held on to the rope and called to her new playmate, "Push me, Sissy! Push me high!"

The young slave, never having seen such a contraption before, was hesitant and barely touched the back of her owner. "Harder! Harder!" Evangeline admonished. Sissy found the rhythm and the swing began to move.

"Higher! Higher!" she called as the swing sailed back and forth through the air. Sissy was caught up in the excitement of it and satisfied that she was pleasing the girl with the yellow hair. Neither of them noticed the brothers running up behind them.

Raleigh grabbed Sissy by her shoulders, pulled her away from the swing when it reached its highest arc, and pushed the slave down into the dirt, badly skinning her elbows and tearing the skirt of her beautiful dress. As she struggled to get up, Raleigh pushed her again, and his shirt sleeves brushed her arm.

When the swing arced back down, Alexander grabbed only one side of rope. Evangeline spilled forward to the ground, and blood gushed from her nose. She screamed as the boys ran away and hid out of sight.

Her parents, Mammy, and Gabrel came running. Evangeline screamed at Sissy, "You hurt me! You hurt me! You're not a doll at all; you're a terrible colored slave! Get away from me! Get away!"

Master Randolph quickly examined his daughter and determined she would live. He grabbed the startled Sissy, shook her like the "doll" he had intended, and slapped her face again and again.

Gabrel carefully intervened. "Master Randolph, sir," he said slowly, "dis here slave cares real good for de babies. Her lets five nursing mamas work in de fields 'cause she takes da best care of der babies."

"Take her from my sight, then!" *A bloody nose and torn dress are not worth the loss of the work by five field hands,* the planter thought to himself. He put his arm around his daughter, who was no longer crying. By the time they reached her bedroom, Evangeline's nose had stopped bleeding and she took her father's linen handkerchief away from her pouty face.

"Father, I don't like my present. You have to get me another one and I don't want to wait so long for it. Send Bailey to town and let Mr. Sowell choose something that I'll like."

"That is absolutely out of the question!" he replied. Although he would never admit it, Thomas Randolph, Master of Fair Oaks Plantation, knew in his heart of hearts that Southern belles, no matter their ages, are born with two non-fail techniques to get their way. The first one is the pouty face. The pouty face is replaced, sometime around puberty, by the hissyfit. If the man is a Southern gentleman, he doesn't stand a chance.

He kissed his daughter on the forehead and sent her to Mammy and Mistress Randolph who tended to Evangeline's other superficial wounds. Master returned to his accounts at his desk in the library and looked out the window to see Gabrel holding Sissy's hand as he led her to gunbarrel house number four.

Old Clara was surprised to see the child but knew better than to ask questions. Anyhow, she would hear everything from Bessie before the sun went down. "Come child, let Old Clara . . . "

"Her name be Sissy now. Dat's da name Young Mistress Evangeline done give her," Gabrel said as he left.

"Come, Sissy, let Old Clara doctor yo' poor ole skinned elbows. Den, I thinks Luther jest might have a bit of peach cobbler for you."

The little girl shook her head. "My tummy hurts. So do my feet." Old Clara took off her shoes, stripped down the white stockings, and untied her bonnet before she pulled the torn and dirty dress up over the Sissy's head. The old slave washed and put salve on the child's scraped elbows before she dressed her in a long cotton shirt like all slave children wore.

"Der, you be better now," Old Clara said as she hugged Sissy. "Now, I wants you to go find Luther and tell him Old Clara said to give you some peach cobbler."

Sissy left the women's room and instead of stopping in the kitchen, she walked straight into the men's room which was empty except for the huge slave. The child walked over to Hercules, found him to be sleeping, sat carefully on the side of his bed, and slowly put her small hand in his. He did not wake, but Sissy thought she felt him slightly squeeze her fingers.

Bessie had seen the entire swing episode from the kitchen porch steps where she had been sitting while stringing beans. She watched the two brothers, giggling with delight, enter the side door of the house. She finished her beans, threw the strings into her small herb garden next to the porch, and took the pan back into the kitchen where she washed the stringbeans until the water was clear and the beans free of any dirt.

A short time later, Bessie wasn't surprised when Alexander and Raleigh, clean and tidy in fresh clothes, came into her kitchen and asked for cookies. Bessie said nothing, but from her many years of having males of all ages in her kitchen, knew for certain that the thrill of getting away with doing something bad causes hunger in young boys. She nodded toward the crock filled to the brim with an assortment of her fresh-baked cookies.

The two boys watched her as they stuffed cookies into their mouths. She handed each of them a large glass of milk, turned her back, and went on with her preparation of the stringbeans. She heard them put their empty glasses on the drainboard and watched out of the corner of her eye as Alexander and Raleigh took as many cookies in their hands as they could carry and went out the kitchen door, letting it slam behind them. Bessie shook her head and smiled.

Evangeline's two brothers returned to the big oak tree and sat on the grass in its shade. The swing was motionless. There were a few drops of blood on the ground worn smooth by countless shoes of children pumping themselves up to the sky in a contraption made of rope and wood. The two boys giggled as they gazed at the scene of their crime. They congratulated each other on their derring-do and ate the last of Bessie's cookies.

Although it was not the regular day for it, Bessie gathered up the dirty laundry. While carrying it out to the wash house, she accidentally dropped two shirts stained with fresh blood directly in the path between the library and the parlor door.

Later that day, the serenity of the humid afternoon echoed with the sounds of a broad board meeting the backside of two young boys who were sent to their beds without their suppers. They weren't all that hungry, anyway. Bessie had not let them have all those cookies for no reason.

Chapter Seven

Ice Storm

Thomas Randolph, who was a light sleeper, knew what it was the instant he heard the crack and sound of splintering wood. *Damn! An ice storm!* he thought and fumbled for matches to light the lamp on his bedside table. As he quickly dressed, his wife stirred, "Go back to sleep, darlin'. I'm just going downstairs to check on something. No need for you to get up at this God-forsaken hour."

As he carried the lamp down the stairs, Randolph saw shadows cast by candlelight coming from the back of the house. When he got to the kitchen, Bessie and Gabrel, barefoot and wearing their nightshirts, were trying to cover up the table and chairs with quilts as the freezing rain tapped staccato sounds on the floor.

Randolph held his lamp high enough to see the shining ice-encrusted branches growing from the thick limb that had split off from the oak tree and crashed through the roof of the kitchen. The children's swing was tangled in the mess. Randolph couldn't tell the extent of the damage but was grateful the limb missed the dining room.

Gabrel rushed to open the front door when he heard the pounding. Jubal and other house slaves had been asleep in their own nearby building when they were awakened by the noise. They dressed and ran through the freezing rain as quickly as they could but were not able to get through the tangled branches or the opening left by the shattered kitchen door. Two of them carried lanterns and used large pieces of leather to shield the hot glass chimneys from the icy drops falling from the sky. The freezing rain frosted everything it touched with a heavy thick coating of ice that sparkled in their lamplight.

The house slaves removed their shoes and left them inside the front door. When they followed Gabrel back to the kitchen, they were stunned by the mess and damage. They were as surprised by the sight of Master sitting on a stool in the only dry corner in the kitchen with a cup of coffee in his hand.

Bessie, known by all of them as a cook who puts first things first, had made coffee. She added more logs to the fire, and its warmth was melting some of the ice on the intruding branches at the same time freezing rain coming through the roof added more. The cook offered the newcomers coffee from her boiling pot. She expected them to be working there for a spell. Bessie enjoyed the novelty of Master and his slaves drinking coffee out of the same pot at the same time in her kitchen without a roof over their heads.

"Well, nothing can be done until it stops raining and the ice melts. God knows how long that will take. Bessie, you and Gabrel take you pallets and sleep in the dining room. If your bedding's wet, find more somewhere. The rest of you, just go on back to your beds. I'll ring when I need you," Randolph said.

"In da mornin', I'll bring up breakfast from Luther," Bessie said to Master. "Next to me, he be the best cook in da place. Y'all take yo' coffee wid you," Bessie ordered. "I's goin' to sleep in da dinin' room."

Soon after daylight, everyone in the big house was wakened by the sounds of axes and saws as some of the house slaves and most of the field slaves from gunbarrel house number one, the slave quarters closest to the big house, struggled to clear the debris from the kitchen. There was minimum damage to Gabrel and Bessie's room although the floor was wet and icy. One of the Negro bosses was in charge of the clean-up.

Bessie and Gabrel dressed in the dining room, folded up their pallets and put their beds in a corner. As the door to the kitchen was closed, the rest of the house stayed warm, and Gabrel went about checking every fireplace and adding firewood, if necessary. He didn't enter any bedroom if the door was closed, and as he walked past Evangline's, he was nearly run over as Young Mistress flung open the door and stormed out into the hallway. "What in the world is going on? The noise is hurting my ears!" she complained.

At the other end of the hallway, Alexander and Raleigh had dressed and bounded down the stairs to see for themselves the cause of the disturbance. They whooped with glee when they saw the limb and branches nearly filling the space in the kitchen.

"Evangeline, come see!" Raleigh called up to her. "Bessie left a pumpkin seed in her pie, and it grew and filled up her whole kitchen! You don't get any breakfast today!"

"And your swing is broken, too!" Alexander added happily.

Their sister pulled her wrapper around herself and stepped delicately down the stairs in her slippers. She slowly and deliberately sashayed over to where her brothers were waiting. They opened the kitchen door and led her inside. When Evangeline saw the mess her mouth fell open in surprise, and she covered her ears because of the noise.

The working slaves averted their eyes. They knew they would be punished if they saw Young Mistress in her night clothes. Bessie walked past the door, grabbed her by the arm, and pulled her away from the kitchen and into the parlor. "Miss Evangeline! Do you be crazy! You has no business bein' down here in yo' night clothes. Yo' Papa would take a strap to you if'n he knowed. You gets yo' sweet self up dem stairs an' dress proper. An' don't you come near my kitchen again 'less I invites you!" she called up after the girl, who was ambling up the stairs and shaking her little behind on the way.

Raleigh was full of himself as he called after his sister, "I'm gonna tell! Nah . . . nah . . . nah, nah, nah." He stopped when Bessie turned her evil eye on him.

"You an' Alexander, gets yo' coats on." She disappeared into a small store room at the end of the hall and returned with two buckets and small shovels used to empty fireplace ashes. Bessie put on her own coat and handed each boy a coal bucket full of ashes and a shovel. "You is gonna shovel ashes on da ice so's we can walk all da way down to number four. Den you is gonna help me carry breakfast back up here to da big house if'n you 'spects to eat."

Alexander and Raleigh resented taking orders from a slave, even if she was the head cook. They looked upstairs and hoped their parents would come out of their room and save them from Bessie's wrath. "No need to look up der," she said. "Y'all be in more trouble if'n your pa don't get his breakfast!"

Overseer Bailey, unaware of the fallen limb and too far away from the big house to hear the commotion, had awakened earlier but went back to bed once he saw the ice-coated trees outside his bedroom window. He knew there would be no work in the fields today. Finally, he gave up trying to get back to sleep and quietly slipped out of bed so he wouldn't wake his wife. Bailey dressed, went downstairs, and found Betty already up and making coffee. He was having his first cup in the kitchen when he rubbed his eyes in wonder at what he saw out the window.

Alexander and Raleigh scattered ashes and made a path on the icy lane. Bessie walked carefully behind them on the newly spread gray ashes. When their buckets were empty, she stopped at the nearest gunbarrel house, knocked on the door, said something to the one who answered, and waited for a cook there to bring out dead ashes to fill their buckets again. The routine continued all the way to gunbarrel house number four. The two boys waited outside in the cold when Bessie went inside.

She hadn't been gone long before she came out leading Luther and two of his cook helpers. Alexander and Raleigh left their buckets and shovels outside by the door, and Luther took the food from his helpers and filled the boys' arms with baskets and pans holding breakfast.

Bailey called up to his wife to come quickly if she wanted to see the Randolph sons, arms filled with something, as they slowly and safely followed Bessie up the ashes path.

"I'd best find out what's going on in the big house!" Bailey said. He quickly put on his coat, took the bucket of dead ashes from in front of his kitchen fireplace, and went outside to spread ashes from his own porch and to connect with the path already made. He left his now empty bucket on the icy ground and slowly walked on ashes all the way up to the big house. Bailey arrived just as the Randolph family was sitting down to eat their breakfast.

When he saw him pass by in the hall, Master Randolph called, "Bailey, any ice damage down your way?"

"No, sir, none that I've seen so far."

"Good. We have enough up here. When the mess is cleared out of the kitchen, cover things up the best you can with tarps. We can't start repairs until the stuff melts, and that might take a day or two," Randolph said between bites of scrambled eggs.

As he left to inspect the damage in the kitchen, Bailey heard Mistress Randolph say, "Thank you, boys, for getting our breakfast. You had such a wonderful idea to make an ashes pathway. I'm sure Bessie appreciated your help."

As the overseer surveyed the damage done to that part of the house, he smiled when he thought that the two brothers would be helping Bessie a lot in the next several days if they expected to eat.

By mid-morning the freezing rain had stopped even though the sky remained overcast. The slaves had hauled most of the debris out of the kitchen and threw it in a messy pile on the ground next to the porch. Bailey told them not to bother with the small branches still on the floor and directed them to get the tarps up to protect as much of the kitchen as they could. Although Bessie and Gabrel's room suffered scant direct damage, their door was torn off its hinges and the ice-covered floor was very slippery.

"You all have plenty of work you can do inside the other buildings and barns. There'll be no field work today or until the ice melts," Bailey told them. "It may get to freezing tonight, but if it does and the ice doesn't melt today, the coating on any of the crops not yet picked should protect them from any frost damage."

He went to find Bessie, who was stacking dirty breakfast dishes in a large pan. "You'd best use the kitchen at my house to fix the Randolphs' meals," he offered. "It will be some days before yours is up and running again."

"What kind a stove you got?" Bessie asked.

"A new cast-iron cook stove," he said proudly. "It's a dandy. I ordered it from Stowell and he sent it out about three weeks ago."

"I 'preciates yo' offer, but I think I'll jest take da food down to Luther an' let him do da cookin' fo' us. Next to me, he be da best cook on da whole plantation. Now, if'n you 'cuse me, sir, I gotta take des dirty dishes out da wash house an' get 'em clean."

"Be careful and don't slip on the ice," Bailey warned.

"Oh, I be careful. I gots me some helpers who makes me a safe path out der wid dead ashes," Bessie answered and winked her eye.

Overseer Bailey nodded and covered his own smile with one hand. "Walk carefully," he advised.

Although the freezing rain had stopped by late afternoon, the night temperature got no higher than twenty-six degrees. Bailey was not surprised to find his thermometer still below the freezing mark by noon the next day. Ice storms, although rare in this part of the

South, wreaked havoc when they came, and there was nothing he or anyone else could do except wait it out.

By late afternoon, the plantation was marked by narrow pathways of dead ashes between all of the buildings. Even so, Bailey saw two slaves slip and fall in front of him as he walked to the barn to check for hard ice on the water trough.

The Randolph children, tired of being cooped up in the house, begged their mother to let them go outside and down to the barn to help feed the horses, something they seldom wanted to do. She finally relented and asked Mammy to make sure all three of them were warmly dressed.

Their parents and the house slaves were grateful for the quiet as soon as the bickering siblings went out the door. Gabrel shook his head in dismay as he watched after them. Instead of walking on the ashes paths they had so carefully made, Raleigh and Alexander had stepped off them and were sliding on the hard ice in the center of the lane.

Gabrel didn't hear them when they called to Evangeline to join them. He saw the girl put her hands on her hips and shake her head about the same time her brothers dashed toward her, grabbed their sister by the arm and pull her out onto the ice. He feet shot out from under her, and her backside slapped down on the hard surface.

Her brothers were half way to the barn by the time Old Clara, who heard Evangeline hollering, came to the door to see what the commotion was about. When the old slave came outside and helped the girl to her feet, the boys were already out of sight.

"Well now, Young Mistress, let Old Clara help you back to the big house an' we'll let Bessie have a look at you."

Evangeline had stopped crying until she entered the front hall. Then she began to wail as if she had been run over by a hay wagon. Her father burst out of his library, Mother still had her book in her hand as she ran down the staircase. The house slaves ran from everywhere to the front hall, and Mammy, who could not run anywhere, came out of Evangeline's room and looked down upon her charge from the second floor railing.

"Alexander and Raleigh! I hate them! They pushed me down on the ice and ran away! They never want to play with me!" Evangeline wailed as the crocodile tears flowed freely down her cheeks.

Her parents took their aggrieved daughter into the closest room, the library, and examined her for injury. Other than a torn coat and a tear in her stocking, they could find no damage done to her at all, not even a slight bruise on her body.

Her mother dried her tears and cradled Evangeline in her lap. "Calm down, dearest. It's all right. Let me take you upstairs, and you and Mammy can play a game or something."

"I don't want to play with Mammy. She's too old."

Her father scratched his head as dramatically as he could. "Well, darlin', Papa doesn't know what to do. Just yesterday I gave you Sissy for a playmate, and you wouldn't have her."

Evangeline thought for a moment. "I'll have her today."

Old Clara, who had come without a coat, was ordered by Master Randolph to bring Sissy back up to the big house. Bessie gave the old slave her own shawl to wear. Not long afterward, Old Clara returned it when she took Sissy up to Evangeline's bedroom. Sissy didn't want to go.

Knowing that Sissy was her last chance for a playmate that day, Young Mistress treated her like, well, like a sister, as an upstairs house slave described it to Bessie later that afternoon. "You shoulda seen her, jest like a little lady, shared her toys an' ever'thing. Young Mistress never got along wid her brothers near as well. Sent me down to ask you to make a tea party fo' 'em."

Bessie improvised a tea party from ingredients on the dining room sideboard. She used china cups and plates from the corner dish cabinet and put them on a silver tray. She poured a little cream in each cup and flavored it with a bit of strawberry jam. The cook cut in half and buttered a biscuit left over from breakfast and put a dab of honey in each center. She took two linen napkins with crochet edges from a drawer and a flower from the dried arrangement in the center of the dining table. Bessie put the flower in a crystal toothpick holder after she dumped the tookpicks into a saucer. When she arranged the portable party on a silver tray, the cook proudly and slowly carried it up the stairs.

When she quietly entered Evangeline's room, she saw Mammy sleeping soundly in the rocking chair. The two girls were sitting at Evangeline's play table. Young Mistress had a deck of cards and was patiently trying to explain something to Sissy.

"What y'all doing?" Bessie asked as she spread the tea party out on the table.

"I'm trying to teach Sissy how to play cards, but she doesn't know the names of the numbers. I don't think she knows how to count either," Evangeline patiently explained.

"Where you learn to play cards?" Bessie asked.

"Alexander taught me when he and Raleigh were mad at each other. He and Raleigh play cards all the time except when they have a fight. Then Alexander will play with me, but Raleigh never does."

"Do yo' papa an' mama know 'bout y'all playing cards?" the cook asked.

"No."

"You best not tell 'em," Bessie whispered as she turned to go.

"Bessie!" Evangeline called after her. "Thank you so very much for the lovely tea party. Sissy and I surely will enjoy it. The biscuit is quite exquisite." Bessie, surprised by the unexpected compliment from Young Mistress, nearly dropped her tray.

* * *

Even though it would cost him money, Thomas Randolph was almost grateful for the respite brought by the ice storm. He enjoyed the quiet, especially now with Evangeline calmed down and most likely bossing Sissy around upstairs. There was a hush over the whole plantation, and he hoped it would be at least another day before the weather warmed and melted the ice just enough for it to drop in sheets from the trees and roofs and shatter like glass when it hit the ground.

So much had gone on since his town trip, he hadn't had the time or felt well enough to give serious consideration to the discussion at the scheduled caucus meeting, the reason he had made the trip. He was almost sorry he had attended the slave auction. It had been an afterthought when he bid on the big slave to compete with his friends who really wanted to add Hercules to their stable. *They would have wasted the unique skills of a number-one blacksmith by fighting the slave anyway,* he thought. *Old Colonel Commager, God rest his soul, was a fool and could have made more money from his slave's skills than he ever made gambling on him. The Commager sons are as stupid as their father.*

Randolph lit his pipe, sat back in his chair, and reviewed the caucus deliberation in his mind. He was concerned that every planter, except himself, appeared to be in favor of seccession even though caucus members only discussed the matter and didn't bring it to a vote. He gave the men credit for listening seriously to his own opinion which was to wait on the outcome of the election.

"My personal opinion," he had told them, "is that Lincoln doesn't have a snowball's chance in hell of being elected President. I also believe Congress will continue to favor the South as it has always done."

Randolph remembered all caucus members agreed when he thanked God for those strong and mighty Southern congressmen we send to Washington year after year. The Yankees are bamboozled every time they try to pass a law harmful to our agriculture. Nearly half of the caucus members raised their hands when he had asked, "How many of you have had escaped slaves captured and returned? We can thank the Fugitive Slave Law for that," he had added.

Randolph smiled at the thought of his own name being bandied about as a possible candidate for high office if their own affectionately called "Old Senator Filibuster" dies in office before he has the good grace to retire. Everyone agreed that the man has done a world of good for the South, but like the land, he is wearing out.

Now to the business at hand, Randolph thought. Even though it was daylight, he lit the lamp on his desk and took one of his ledgers from a desk drawer. Although he disliked tedious work, Randolph knew he was far overdue in bringing his list of some of his assets up to date. He was current in listing each slave by name, age, and occupation on the plantation, but was almost a year behind in figuring the sum total amounts of their collective worth in dollars. Arithmetic had never been his favorite subject, and he usually put this task off as long as he could.

Even at that, Randolph enjoyed his general feeling of well being, He regarded the ice storm as a minor inconvenience. Like most people in this part of the state, he knew when ice storms hit the area, they usually are fairly wide spread, and he expected his planter friends to have felt the brunt of it, as well. He wondered if they were catching up on their paper work too.

If he made any major change at Fair Oaks, Randolph felt he would like to purchase more field slaves and reduce the number of house and body slaves. However, as the number of that group in personal service is considered to be a mark of status, he knew his wife would never agree. She would always insist that there be more house slaves tending to every need of the family members and of their guests than on any other nearby plantation.

He put down his pipe and put two more logs on the fire. Feeling the unusual quiet of this day would help him figure the numbers, he took out his pen and began to write.

Fair Oaks Plantation
Slave Inventory
November 10, 1859

Work Job	Average $ Value	Number	Total $ Value
#1 mason/bricklayer	$2,700*	3	$ 8,100
good " "	1,700	7	11,900
#1 blacksmith *	3,000*	1	3,000
good blacksmith	1,800	2	3,600
#1 field hand/laborer	1,600	75	120,000
good field hand	1,200	50	60,000
good laborers	1,000	50	50,000
#1 house slaves	1,800	2	3,600
#1 body slaves	2,000	2	4,000
good house/body slaves	1,500	36	54,000
#1 female craft *	1,800*	6	10,800
good female craft	1,000	10	10,000
good female nursery	1,000	12	12,000
slaves, unsound	100	10	1,000
children, age 2–11	450	36	16,200
infants	175	20	3,500
	Totals		
*for rent @ $25 to $100 per week		322	$371,700

Thomas Randolph got up from his desk and stretched. He noticed, for the first time, a small stack of mail that the post had delivered when he was away on his town visit. He quickly looked through the letters and put all of them down to be read later except for the fat envelope he had been expecting.

ELLIS & ELLIS, SURVEYORS
15 Broad Street
Brownsville, Texas
October 4, 1859

Dear Mr. Randolph,

I am pleased to enclose the deeds which have been recorded here and complete the transaction as ordered. You now are the owner of eight sections of virgin prime land some forty-five miles northwest of Brownsville. The southernmost boundry is the Rio Grande River, and your property is fed by several small streams that generally run all year.

Eight sections at 640 acres per section amount to 5,120 acres. Your cost at 50 cents per acre is $2,560. As per our agreement, our fee at ten percent of the purchase price is $256.00 We have been in receipt of your bank draft and your account has been closed.

Thank you for choosing our firm to be your agent in this transaction. We would be pleased to serve you in the future and would appreciate your good word on our behalf should any of your friends and acquaintances be interested in acquiring property in Texas.

My son and I look forward to meeting you in person at a later date.

Very best regards,
Eli Ellis, Esq.

Thomas Randolph was elated. He knew Fair Oaks Plantation land would never support the growth of cotton for another generation of planters. As his own father had made provisions for Thomas and his brother to continue growing cotton on their own virgin land, his purchase in Texas now assured his own sons the land ownership they needed to continue the Randolph dynasty as planters of the world's best short staple cotton. *And as for Evangeline, with her charms, my daughter will marry well,* he thought.

* * *

Evangeline called it "icicle rain" when the melting ice slid off the tree branches and roof tops and broke into pieces when it hit the ground. The plantation had remained in its icy grip for three days before the sun came out. The trees were stripped clean of ice by noon and the ice disappeared as cold water soaked the ground. Mud became the inconvenience, but things returned to normal by the morning of the next day.

It took four days for the kitchen to be cleaned up and the walls, doors, and destroyed roof section to be repaired by a small army of workers.

Bessie was the happiest cook in the county to be back in the comfort of her own kitchen. Bailey was grateful for the extra days for Hercules to heal before Randolph started looking for him. Thomas Randolph admired the new hinges and door knobs on the replaced doors. The metal work was perfect and he congratulated himself on the wisdom of his winning bid to acquire the number-one blacksmith. From the looks of his work, Hercules was indeed a master of the craft.

Mistress Randolph walked down to gunbarrel house number four to check on the babies and make sure none of them was sick due to the weather. She was pleased to see the little ones healthy and thriving under Old Clara's care and supervision of the other slaves caring for their future generation of workers.

Evangeline decided Sissy was a good playmate, after all, and made it a point to thank her father for the present, much to his surprise and pleasure.

Alexander and Raleigh were sorry to see the ice melt because it had afforded them so many opportunities to get into different kinds of trouble.

Chapter Eight
Sissy

After the confusion caused by the ice storm, Bessie was preoccupied with getting her kitchen running smoothly and had forgotten to get the latest information on the condition of Hercules. She felt her heart jump when she was serving breakfast and Master Randolph mentioned to his wife that it was time to take a better look at his new slave.

Bessie hurried back to her kitchen and hung out four dish towels to dry on her new clothesline just off the rebuilt kitchen porch. Three of the towels were white, and one was green.

By the time Master had finished his breakfast, put on his mud boots and coat, and started for the smithy, Hercules was already at work there. Earlier, Noah had put a new finely crafted pair of hunt spurs on a bench where anyone could see them. They were finished except for their leather straps. When Master arrived, he noticed them.

Hercules merely nodded his acknowledgment of his master's presence and continued to turn and strike with a small hammer a red-hot piece of metal on the anvil. The huge slave wore a pair of large leather gloves that came half-way up to his elbows. The rhythmic sounds of the hammer, one loud followed by two softer ones, tapped a pattern that was mesmerizing to anyone listening for more than a few minutes. The flexing of his arm muscles was in sync with the sound pattern made by his hammer. Randolph watched as the chunk of iron slowly took the form of an iron wall sconce that would hold not one, but two candles. Master had never seen one quite like it and knew his wife would be pleased. When Hercules thrust the red hot piece into a barrel of water, the steam that rose from it obscured him for a moment from Randolph's vision. He had seen enough and had other things to do.

The planter simply nodded his approval and walked away. As he returned to his home, he congratulated himself on his shrewd purchase. *The slave is, indeed, a number-one blacksmith with a touch of an artist in his hammer,* he thought, *though I shall keep this secret to myself for the time being.*

When Master Randolph was out of sight, Noah came out from behind some shelves where he had been hiding. He took the tools and wall sconce from Hercules, put them on a shelf, and walked with his charge back to number four. Old Clara met them and took the huge slave by the arm to guide him back to his bed.

"No," he said, gently removed her hand from his arm, and walked under his own power to the nearest bench and sat down at the table. He was breathing heavily but said, "Thank you, Noah, fo' yo' help."

Old Clara put a cup of chickweed tea in front of him. "When you done drink it, den Luther brings you some coffee." She sat down across the table from Hercules and studied his face. "You looks better, but you still has to take da medicines da lady left fo' you. Luther, you best bring coffee now fo' dis big ole blacksmith an' some fo' Noah an' me too. An' bring a cup fo' yourself. My knees be still shakin', and I 'spects yo' knees be shakin' too."

"Where da girl be?" Hercules asked.

"She up in da big house wid Young Mistress," Old Clara replied.

"She be all right?"

"Dey be playin' games an' things. I takes her up der myself. Miss Evangeline done name her Sissy."

That same day when Mammy was napping in her rocking chair, Evangeline asked Sissy to bring her a book from the bookcase in her room. "It's *Tales of the White Knight,*" she instructed, "third one from the right on the top shelf."

Sissy walked to the bookshelf, tentatively ran her fingers over the spines of the books, and looked to Evangeline for help.

Evangeline laughed. "Sissy, Sissy! How can you ever be my body servant if you can't even find the book I want to read! Why can't you learn to read like everybody else?" The planter's headstrong daughter stopped, gasped, and continued, "Because no one ever taught you, of course! Well, I'll take care of that!"

Young Mistress took Sissy by the hand, grabbed an alphabet book with the other, and led the way to her secret nook behind the wardrobe. "I'm going to be the teacher and you're going to be the pupil. That means you have to do everything I say. If you make a mistake, I get to hit your hands with a ruler," she said.

* * *

A few weeks later, Mammy had a gas pain that caused her to wake in the middle of her hap. She was stunned when she saw the slave Sissy reading a simple story from a small book while Evangeline proudly listened to her student. "That's good, Sissy," the young teacher said.

Mammy was horrified. "Evangeline! What you done, you naughty chile! You gonna be sent to da prison fo' teachin' a colored chile ta read! An' she can be tied to da whippin' tree and da life beat right out a her, and maybe me too! Never, never do dis again! An' never, never tell nobody what you done!"

Tears brightened Evangeline's eyes. She had never been spoken to like this before. Sissy, eyes shut tight and head bowed to her knees, was cowering in the corner of the room.

Evangeline promised Mammy that she would never teach anything to Sissy again as long as she lived. Sissy promised she would never learn anything else as long as she lived either.

* * *

Thomas Randolph, who knew nothing of Evangeline's propensity to become a school teacher, declared Sissy to be the best present he had ever brought home to his daughter. The quarrels between Evangeline and her brothers all but disappeared. Even though the floor of his daughter's room was strewn with toys, games, and picture books, Mammy made sure Sissy picked them up and put them away before she left in the afternoon.

Although she was Evangeline's playmate, Mammy had begun Sissy's training as a body servant, one who could anticipate and meet Evangeline's every need. The old slave, still possessive of her "baby," did not completely relinquish her own exclusive role, but she knew the years were upon her. She liked Sissy even though, at times, she felt a twinge of jealousy because of her youth and hours spent exclusively with Evangeline. Mammy was not always sorry to see Sissy leave when she dismissed her to the slave quarters each day. Sissy did not come to the big house when there were house guests and never on Sunday.

Old Clara was always grateful when Sissy's time was up at the big house and returned to help her in the slave nursery. The wise old woman saw to it that the young girl learned more than how to care for babies.

Sissy was a quick learner and grateful to the slave women who taught her how to spin yarn, weave cloth, and sew. The lacemaker even taught her to make simple patterns of lace.

Sissy helped in the slave vegetable gardens and learned ways to preserve food. Luther taught her cooking and even shared some of his secrets he had never passed on to anyone else.

When Sissy grew tired from days filled with so many different kinds of work, Old Clara reassured her, "Da mo' things you knows how ta do makes you mo' valuable if'n you be sold. Not only dat, dey makes you mo' valuable fo' Master ta keep."

Master and Mistress Randolph were only vaguely aware of the authority Evangeline's Mammy had taken for herself in directing Sissy's daily activities. When she was away from the big house, she took her orders from Old Clara. Neither of the powerful old women slaves was aware of what the other was doing.

Thomas Randolph didn't know of Raleigh's mischief nearly every day when Sissy walked back to gunbarrel house number four. The younger son disliked her and took every opportunity to bedevil her without his getting caught.

One afternoon Master Randolph was nearby but unseen when Sissy passed by on her way back to number four. The planter heard Raleigh's teasing sing-song refrain:

"Sissy's a freak! Sissy's a freak!
She's got two ugly, ugly feet!
She's got yellar boogers up her nose,
On her big left foot she's got six toes!"

Randolph stepped behind a building so he would not be seen and laughed softly. "What have I here? A son who's a poet?"

*   *   *

Two years after Randolph's successful bid for Hercules, the planter had recovered the cost of the slave and had made a tidy profit. The blacksmith's work, prominently displayed in the big house, started a run on his services. Every planter's wife who visited Fair Oaks yearned for the slave's elegant candle holders, lacy fire screens, and unusual door and window fittings.

Those among them who were able to sketch an item of their own design that could be fashioned of metal, bragged when the exclusive pieces appeared as if like magic under the hammer of Thomas Randolph's blacksmith. The demand was so great that Randolph upped the slave's rental price from one hundred to one hundred fifty dollars per week. Hercules was gone from Fair Oaks more than one hundred days a year. When he returned to the plantation, he never spoke of where he had been or what he had made.

Even though Bailey suggested that Hercules was needed at Fair Oaks, Randolph rented him out for two weeks to a the owner of a plantation near Nashville. The day of Hercules's return to Fair Oaks, he ran a fever. The whites of his eyes were red and he started to cough. "Open yo' mouth," Old Clara ordered. "Come over here to da window so's I can see better." She pursed her lips and shook her head when she saw the small white spots on the insides of his cheeks. "I thinks you gots da measles. Luther, you best get Bailey."

When Luther reported the bad news to the overseer, Bailey made the decision without even looking at the huge slave. "Put him in the pest house," he said. "I'll tell Randolph."

Bessie carried his bedding while Hercules followed her to the pest house, a small, self-contained, and very clean building a distance away from the other structures on the plantation. "Dis is da place da sick slaves go if'n dey be sick wid somepin' da other slaves might catch. We gots to get you somebody down here to nurse you," Old Clara said.

"I wants Sissy," Hercules replied without hesitation.

"Sissy? Why you wants dat sweet gal?"

"I wants Sissy," the huge slave repeated.

Old Clara shook her head and left him alone in the pest house. She took his request to Bailey.

When Bailey reported to Randolph, the planter honored Hercules's request over the loud objections of his daughter. "I'm sorry, darlin', but this is a matter of business. It's the money the blacksmith brings in that is paying for you and your sweet mama to go to England for a visit this summer. If Hercules gets sick and dies, you'll just have to stay here with all of us and the mosquitoes."

Evangeline sniffed her displeasure but made no further objections. She hugged Sissy and then watched out her window as her puzzled body servant followed Bailey down past the slave quarters and disappeared behind some far buildings. Evangeline wondered if Hercules asked for her body servant just for spite even though she could not imagine why.

"Evangeline," her father called, "come down to the library. I think it's time we had a little talk."

Something in the tone of her father's voice required the young girl to obey without complaining. She quietly walked into her father's library, gracefully sat in the wing chair facing his desk, and folded her hands in her lap.

"Darlin'," he began. "Perhaps your mama and I have been protecting you too much from the realities of this world. While it's important for Hercules to live, it's more important for the other slaves, and even us, to stay well and not come down with the measles, if that is what is making him sick. Old Clara says it is.

"When I was a boy, my papa lost a son, my younger brother, and seventy of his slaves to the measles. It spreads like a wildfire in dry grass. Hercules must have caught it at that plantation near Nashville, and I wouldn't be surprised if people are dying there at this very moment. It goes into pneumonia.

"I know you depend on Sissy, but if she can nurse him and stop the sickness at the door of the pest house, we will be fortunate, indeed. You aren't going to like this, but I'm going to send you to Memphis as a precaution. Mrs. Bailey has relatives there. In fact, her daughter is with them, and I'll have you go there until I can make arrangements to enroll you in a fine boarding school." He raised his hand. "No argument, my love."

Mistress Randolph was in total agreement with the decision her husband had made. "We can send Mammy with her," she said. By late afternoon, the women had finished packing and Randolph finished writing letters of introduction. He would trust no one but Jubal to drive Evangeline and Mammy in the carriage to town where they would catch the train to Memphis.

The next morning, Mammy failed to appear by the time the carriage was loaded. "I'll get her," Gabrel said and climbed the stairs to her room. He returned almost immediately. "Mammy, I fear she be dead still sittin' in da rockin' chair," he said in a quivering voice.

Evangeline was crying as her papa helped her into the carriage. "Don't worry, darlin'. We'll send your mama's body servant with you now until we make other arrangements."

Fifteen minutes later, a surprised Esther, a body servant, found herself on the way to Memphis with the daughter of her mistress. "It won't be long before we send for you," Mistress Randolph called after her own body servant. She buried her face in her hands. "She was my mammy, you know, before Evangeline's."

Randolph held his wife close. "I know, my dear. We'll bury her tomorrow," he said. They all waved their good-byes and watched the carriage until it turned the bend and disappeared from sight. *All things considered,* Randolph thought, *over the years Mammy gave the family good value for the money.*

The news of events in the big house had traveled via Bessie to Old Clara and then to every other part of the plantation by the time the carriage passed the far field. Sissy got the news along with the meals Luther delivered to the pest house.

All slaves had the day off for mourning and the burial even though most of them didn't really know Mammy. Hercules was too sick to care, but Sissy was heartbroken to hear of Mammy's death. She took some comfort in the fact that Mammy passed while sitting in the rocking chair, her favorite place. Sissy felt more grief for the loss of Evangeline and hoped that Master would send her to Memphis when Hercules got well.

She was ashamed of the anger she felt toward her patient but asked the question anyway: "Why did you ask for me?"

" 'Cause you done had da measles," he weakly replied.

"I don't believe you! How would you know?"

"I was der. You was little an' very, very sick. Yo' mama nursed you an' prayed to God to let you live. I know 'cause I's yo' pa." His deep breathing signaled that Hercules had drifted off to sleep.

Sissy sat stone still for a long time trying to unravel the information Hercules had given her. She searched her memory and saw shadow pictures of a beautiful light-skinned colored woman, her mother, she was sure now. The young girl had pushed the memories far away so as not to cause her more pain. There was another shadow and a voice coming from somewhere. The voice was deep but soft and sang a sweet song in a low, low voice before it faded away. Sissy bit her lip and looked at the sleeping slave. *Could this big, sick man be the one who sang that sweet song?* she wondered.

The patient began to stir, and Sissy took clean wet rags to sponge the feverish face and body of the man who had told her that he was her father. *He looks like a very sick man, not huge and fierce at all,* she thought. *I wonder if what he told me is the truth.* When Sissy sponged his feet, she discovered six toes on his left foot.

Even though Luther was always on time delivering their meals and would talk from a distance about the gossip of the day. Sissy was bored and restless now that Hercules seemed to be improving. She asked Luther to bring her sewing, but he refused saying she would have to burn it anyway 'cause it might carry the sickness. "You is gonna be here awhile even after da big slave gets well 'cause you gotta wait to makes sure you don't come down wid it yo'self," Luther said.

The next morning, Sissy pulled two chairs outside and left them in the sun but close to the door. "We needs some fresh air an' sunshine," she said as she took Hercules by the arm. He pulled away. "I can walk," he said and moved slowly out to a chair and sat down. He took a deep breath. "Feels good."

Sissy followed closely behind him, and when she sat down in the other chair, she noticed a covered basket sitting on the ground under a window. *Luther must have left it,* she thought. *I'll get it when we go back inside.*

They enjoyed their outing for nearly twenty minutes, and Hercules didn't quarrel when Sissy helped him back to his bed. She brought the chairs in and went back to get the basket. She put it down on the table and removed the napkin cover. Sissy stared at the contents and carefully removed the items one by one.

Hercules watched his daughter put three pencils, a sheaf of paper, and two thin books on the table. He broke the quiet in the room. "You reads an' writes?" he whispered.

Sissy's face was somber as she looked at him and nodded her head.

"Teach me," Hercules whispered.

* * *

Thomas Randolph had a pile of orders for decorative ironwork on his desk and his number one blacksmith in quarantine in the pest house. "I will say that I have learned a lesson," he said to his wife at supper. 'I'll not rent any more of our slaves out during sickness season. Hercules has earned me two times the amount of money that I paid for him. I think it best just to keep him working here at Fair Oaks. In another week or so, we can lift the quarantine and everything will be back to normal."

Raleigh couldn't wait for that day and accompanied Bailey to the pest house when the quarantine was up. Noah called for Hercules to come out. "I needs yo' help on a harness I be makin'," he said. As they walked to the smithy, Noah, who had expected to see a thinner slave, was relieved to note the usual bulk beneath Hercules's shirt and did not guess the bulk was not body fat or muscle but two thin books, paper, and pencils wrapped in a towel.

Bailey and Raleigh went into the room of the pest house and found Sissy opening the windows. She had already folded the bedding and had it ready to be washed. She had stacked the dishes from Luther's breakfast. The basket that had appeared mysteriously some days before sat on the middle of the table.

"Bailey, do you know what happens to slaves who can read and write?" Raleigh asked with a smirk.

"What kind of question is that?" Bailey replied curtly.

"I hear when a slave is caught with even a piece of paper, if it's not a signed pass, that slave gets whipped, sometimes even hung," the young man continued. He sauntered to the table, flipped off the cloth covering on the basket, and found it empty. Startled, he searched the room from under the bed to every cupboard looking for the pencils, paper, and books he had placed as bait outside the pest house in an attempt to catch Sissy in the illegal act of reading and writing. Raleigh was furious and swore using words even Bailey had not heard before.

Sissy, carrying dirty laundry, left the pest house during Raleigh's tirade and walked as quickly as she could to number four.

Old Clara and Luther were relieved to see her fit and well. Sissy washed and changed into fresh clothes before she hurried up to the big house.

No one else at Fair Oaks broke out with measles during the following three weeks, and Randolph decided there was less risk of catching the sickness now at home than in Memphis. He sent for Evangeline.

When Young Mistress arrived, Bessie cooked a special meal and Gabrel was relieved to serve it to a happy family at the Randolph table. The house slaves always ate later in the kitchen and enjoyed the gossip Esther brought back from Memphis. "Young Mistress Evangeline turned da heads of more boys dan I ever seed before. She pouted when her daddy sent fo' her, imagine dat!"

"Everbody in dis here house be happy now," Bessie announced with a smile. "Everbody 'septing Young Master Raleigh. I swear a wrinkled ole witch musta skeered that young-un when he be born. Raleigh is da kind a chile dat turns sweet cider to vinegar."

* * *

When they were isolated in the pest house, Sissy found Hercules to be an apt student. When he was released from the quarantine, he was surprised that he could decipher markings that before had no meaning to him. They were words like "cotton" and "Fair Oaks Plantation" marked on cotton bales. Every Sunday Sissy taught him near the creek. She used a stick to write words in the sand. Hercules copied them. One swipe of his hand in the sand erased the letters and kept their secret.

Chapter Nine

Secession

It was a Christmas gift Thomas Randolph did not want. Five days before on December 20, 1860, South Carolina, seceded from the United States of America. He voiced his disapproval to his wife who cautioned him to keep his opinions to himself. Even though he was one of the largest slaveholders and certainly one of the wealthiest planters in the South, Randolph considered himself to be a political moderate. He worried that South Carolina's rash move might entice other states to follow its lead. If that happened, established lines of commerce likely would be disrupted, and his business would suffer.

The planter's mood changed when he heard the shouts of the slaves announcing that Master Alexander was riding in. The family rushed out to the veranda and cheered at the sight of the dashing figure elegantly sitting his horse like a true Southern gentleman. Jeb, his body slave, followed on his own mount and led the pack horse carrying his master's luggage. Alexander had been away at University for nearly a year. When he dismounted, it looked to his family as if he had grown several inches and put on weight.

"My, but you have grown! And how handsome you are, my darling boy," gushed his mother, who ran up to kiss him.

Raleigh sauntered up to his brother and landed a brotherly punch to his stomach. "What did you put in there? An iron belt."

"Who is this beauty? Not Evangeline!" Alexander whispered in her ear as he lifted his sister off her feet and twirled her around.

Randolph was so overcome with the sight of the man his son had become that he was speechless. All he could do was hug him.

Their hearts were filled with joy, and as the family went back inside the house, their words began to flow all at once. The house servants had quickly gathered in the front hall and each one welcomed Young Master Alexander home. He recognized all of them except the slave at the end of the line.

She curtsied and said, "Welcome home, Master Alexander."

He stopped for a moment, looked carefully at the house slave, and said, "Sissy? It is Sissy all grown up and too big to tease, I see," he chuckled.

"I be Young Mistress Evangeline's body servant now," Sissy respectfully replied as she bowed her head.

The next morning after breakfast, Alexander reported, as requested, to his father's library. He dreaded the meeting but knew that if he did not tell his father he had failed most of his subjects in school, the news would be coming in a letter from the Headmaster. *It's better he hears it from me,* the young man thought. *He'll disown me if he doesn't kill me first. I can hear him now yelling that I'm the first Randolph male in more than a hundred years who couldn't gain admission to Oxford because he was too stupid even for an inferior American university.*

Alexander swallowed hard and began, "Father, there's something I must tell you . . . "

"Not now, Son. Tell me what they are saying in Nashville about South Carolina seceding from the Union?"

"People are divided," the young man lied. He searched his memory to recall what so many excited people were talking about at the tavern near the University, but he had been too busy at the poker table to pay much attention. What he remembered was the winning streak that filled his pockets with money.

"I think it is a mistake," he father offered. "Lincoln hasn't even been inaugurated yet, and who knows for certain what the man will do. We do know what lame-duck Buchanan will do. Nothing!

"Well, enough of that! More of my time is spent in Memphis these days on politics when I'm really needed here at home," Randolph continued. "It's time for you to take more of an interest and learn how to manage the plantation. I want to go over the books with you today, and tomorrow we'll ride out to see the improvements we have made since the last time you were home."

Alexander was very interested in the plantation books and was surprised to see how wealthy his family was. "I can take over the bookkeeping if that will help you, Father. I'm quite good at numbers," he said as he fingered the money in his pocket, an act which reinforced Alexander's belief in his superior skill as a gambler.

* * *

Overseer Bailey was surprised to find that he enjoyed working under Young Master Alexander. He no longer acted like the mischievous, spoiled, eldest son of a wealthy family and seemed to take a real interest in the day to day operations of the plantation. While Bailey credited Thomas Randolph's success to his unerring business sense, the man often was behind with his bookkeeping and resisted the idea of any help from an outsider. Alexander's interest in taking over the job would solve that problem, the overseer hoped.

What's more, Bailey was relieved that the young man "knew what he doesn't know," the overseer said to his wife. "He doesn't know much about planting, growing, and picking, but he does know how many slaves are needed to get a certain number of bales of cotton to market."

Alexander enjoyed his new responsibilities and completed his paper work each day before the sun went down. Randolph gave his son permission to take over his father's desk in the library. The chart on the wall behind the desk had less meaning to Alexander than it had to Thomas Randolph who kept the chart current. It read:

Secession of Southern States

South Carolina	December 20, 1860
Mississippi	January 9, 1861
Florida	January 10, 1861
Alabama	January 11, 1861
Georgia	January 19, 1861
Louisiana	January 26, 1861
Texas	February 1, 1861

February, 1861—Confederate States of America created in Montgomery, Alabama, the provisional capitol.

Delegates elect Jefferson Davis President of the Confederacy.

April 12, 1861—South Carolina fires on Fort Sumpter

Virginia	April 17, 1861
Arkansas	May 6, 1861
North Carolina	May 20, 1861

Thomas Randolph worried over his chart because of his reluctance to follow states that seceded from the Union. Kentucky, to the north, and Missouri, which shared a small portion of its eastern border with Tennessee, remained loyal to the Union. However, six other Southern states bordering Tennessee had joined the Confederate States of America.

Randolph had been relieved when an earlier popular vote rejected a secession proposal in his home state. Then he was fit to be tied when he received word that their governor, ignoring the wishes of the people, skillfully orchestrated Tennessee's secession from the Union, the last Southern state to do so.

Alexander was working at his desk when his father wrote the last entry on his chart.

Tennessee June 8, 1861

"This is a sad day for me, a sad day for Tennessee, and a sad day for us all. We are already at war, Alexander. As a Southerner, born and bred, it is my duty to uphold my family's sacred honor. As much as I abhor the thought, I shall do my part for family and for the South."

Alexander rose from his chair and put his arms around his father, something he hadn't done for a long time. He had heard the gossip of how his father and other moderates were almost shunned by the Southern society in which Thomas Randolph had been a social and business leader. Alexander vowed that he would never again speak to their former friends who now treated the Randolph family with disdain. *That will include Priscilla Arsenaux,* he thought sadly. *I shan't die of a broken heart even though she is a beauty. I could never marry into a family who shuns mine. Theirs would be a family of fools.*

* * *

When Overseer Bailey knocked at the front door of the big house, the caution he saw on Gabrel's face as the house slave opened the door caused Bailey to turn on his heel and hurry out to the fields. Mistress was throwing a hissy fit, the likes of which Gabrel had never heard before. As he hurried past the closed dining room door, he winced when he heard the sounds of breaking china.

"Lordy! What be da matter wid Mistress?" Bessie asked as her husband hurried into the kitchen.

"Not sure but I hears somethin' 'bout him goin' to da army and somethin' about her sayin' he done lost his mind."

"Hmmm," Bessie intoned as she quietly left the ham she was preparing in the kitchen and put her ear against the dining room door. She listened for a few minutes then returned to her task. Gabrel continued polishing the silver and waited for her report.

"Sounds like Master gone an' buyed hisself somethin' like a Colonel an' he has to get lots of soldiers for da army. Mistress is mad like an ole wet hen. I don't like da sound of it." Bessie shook her head, put the ham in the oven and started to peel the white potatoes.

"You are sitting there calmly and telling me that you bought a commission as a Colonel in the Tennessee Volunteer Army of the Confederacy and that you are obliged to recruit and supply a regiment of one thousand men and you expect me to take the news calmly!" Mistress screamed and threw another plate across the room.

Bessie heard Mistress storm out of the dining room and her footsteps pounding on the stairs as she ran up to her bedroom and slammed the door. The cook cracked the door just enough to see Master slowly follow. "Dey's both up da stairs now," the cook announced.

Gabrel opened the dining room door and found the room empty, as he expected. He went about the task of picking up the broken dishes and was careful not to cut himself. There were a few places on the wall where the flying china had chipped the paint. Gabrel would make sure the spots were re-painted and the room aired out before dinner.

Thomas Randolph stood in the hallway just outside of their bedroom. He understood that Rebecca's burst of emotion was only part rage and the other part was genuine fear of what might happen to him, their family, and their plantation if he was off fighting some war that he thought was a mistake to begin with. He knocked gently on the door. "Rebecca, may I come in?"

She didn't answer so he opened the door and found his wife crying on their bed. "Rebecca, come sit with me. We need to talk," Randolph said as he put his hand on her shoulder. When she slowly sat up, he took her hand and led her to a soft chair.

"I apologize for not telling you first," he began, "but it is better I go as an officer than a mere soldier."

"You have no military experience whatsoever," she countered and started to cry again.

"No, but you have always said that I'm a quick learner," he said in jest that drew no smile from his wife. "Look, Rebecca, many of our friends already consider me a Yankee-lover and might even boycott our business when the damn war is over. It can't possibly last long, and I should be home by the time the cotton crop is ready for harvest." He reached for her hand, and Rebecca didn't pull it away.

"How can we run the plantation without you?" she asked.

"My dear! Why do you think I married you when I could have had my choice of the fairest daughters of the South! I married you partly for your beauty and mostly for your brains, even though you thought you were being careful not to show them," he laughed and pulled his chair up closer to hers.

"We both know that you understand the workings of this plantation as well as I and much better than Bailey or any other hired hand I could bring in.

"Your father and my father understood the importance of the wife of a planter. We have been equal partners, as were our parents. We are blessed in that you followed your own mother's lead in her expert doctoring and careful breeding. That is why our stable of slaves has always been strong and healthy and much more productive than those belonging to any plantation owner boasting of a beautiful, vacuous, and disengaged wife. Have you noticed how many of those kinds of wives become a burden rather than an asset to their husbands?"

Rebecca smiled for the first time since their argument began. She daintily dried her eyes on her lace-bordered and embroidered linen handkerchief, and, as was the couple's custom, accepted the large handkerchief from her husband and used it to blow her nose.

Thomas turned the key to lock the door, concentrated on the movements of his awkward fingers which finally mastered the intracacies of unfastening his wife's hoop skirt, picked her up in his arms, and carried her to their bed. Quarreling was not uppermost in their minds. It was replaced by the tender love delighting them both as they lay beneath the French lace canopy of their marriage bed.

Gabrel was relieved the next morning when Master and Mistress were smiling when they came into breakfast. Raleigh, Alexander, and Evangeline arrived soon after them and if the siblings had heard their parents' loud quarrel, they made no mention of it.

After the blessing, Randolph discussed his future plans with the children. Gabrel, who went back and forth from the kitchen to serving the meal in the dining room, listened carefully to their conversation. He carried bits and pieces of the information to Bessie with each of his trips back to the kitchen.

When the meal was over and their family members left to go about their business, Bessie could hardly wait for Gabrel to clear away the breakfast dishes. She had two cups of coffee waiting when he finished. When he finally did, the two sat in their chairs before the fireplace and slowly sipped the brew.

"Well," Bessie demanded, "what else did Master say? I want you to tell me every word he done say."

"Master's gonna be a general or somebody. He gots to make men sign a paper to be in his army. Alexander's goin' wid his pa. Evangeline's gonna go to her gran'mammy in Savannah. Raleigh's gonna stay here wid his ma. Bailey's gonna run da plantation, an' da slaves, dey is jest gonna do what slaves always hafta do," Gabrel recited in a calm voice.

"Dat's all?" Bessie asked.

"Dat's all," Gabrel answered.

In less than half an hour, one of the house slaves carried the same information down to Old Clara.

After the slave had repeated Bessie's words, Old Clara asked her, "Is dat all?"

"Dat's all," she replied and went on back to her work up in the big house.

Old Clara carried the information to Luther who carried it to the cooks in the other gunbarrel houses. The nursing mothers who came in from the fields to nurse their babies at mid-day, carried the information back to the field slaves.

Overseer Bailey knew nothing about Master's plans until his wife told him what her house slave Betty learned from Caro.

Bailey asked his wife, "Is that all?"

She just shrugged her shoulders. "Would you like a cup of tea?" she asked. "Or maybe you'd like a wee bit of whiskey instead."

"Whiskey. And more than a wee bit, if you please."

*　*　*

Evangeline refused to be shipped off to Savannah. She surprised everyone by retiring her pout and acting like a grown-up woman as she contributed to the family's efforts to help prepare her father and brother for war. Although she had read stories about romantic knights and dashing pirates, she couldn't visualize what a real war would be like.

"Have Sissy sew the uniform for Papa and Alexander, because her work is the best," Evangeline suggested when she helped her mother figure the number of bolts of cloth they would need to order from Sowell's General Store.

Alexander kept ledgers, separate from those of the plantation, for their military effort. He listed each task with the estimated cost followed by the actual cost when the item or items were acquired. On another page, he listed the responsibilities of each family member. Alexander saw no reason to change Bailey's role because the overseer was very competent to supervise the day to day operations of the plantation and the work assignments of the slaves, his usual responsibilities.

1. Colonel Randolph: Purchase arms and field supplies, including food, to be paid for with Confederate money.
2. Recruit soldiers with the help of Alexander and Raleigh.
3. Rebecca Randolph: Procure uniforms, most to be made at Fair Oaks.
4. Alexander: Accompany Colonel as aide, receive commission as lieutenant, keep ledgers.
5. Raleigh: Assist with recruitment, oversee blacksmiths responsible for making tack and horseshoes, assist Mother, supervise house slaves (if requested by Bailey.)
6. Evangeline: Assist Mother, help oversee construction of uniforms, write to your father and brother often, remember not to pout.

When they were alone, Thomas and Rebecca made other plans they did not wish to share with their children at the present time. After the war expenses were paid, they decided to convert most of their remaining fortune into gold and hide it with the family jewels in the secret hollows of the four massive wooden posters of their marriage bed, a wedding gift from Rebecca's parents.

They sat quietly for a few minutes. Randolph spoke first. "I think it most unlikely that Union forces would ever come close enough to threaten Fair Oaks Plantation." He paused and cleared his throat. "If it should happen, it would seem prudent, I would think, if you took everything not nailed down and made your way to Texas. We have more than enough land to start over there. Alexander and I would know where to find you and head for Brownsville ourselves after the bluebellies have fled north with their tails between their legs."

"I don't think you're funny," Rebecca complained.

Chapter Ten
War

Overseer Bailey fretted with his wife. "The wrong Randolphs are away from the plantation and off to war. Who did they leave behind? Raleigh, who doesn't have a lick of sense! He struts around here like a proud peacock. I'm sure Rebecca Randolph doesn't know he's pulling off field workers to work in the smithy. Not only is the cotton crop suffering; the blacksmiths can't get their work done stumbling over the slaves who try to help but don't know anything but how to grow cotton! When Randolph gets back from signing up men for his very own little army, you know who he'll blame, don't you? Nobody but me!"

"I'm sure Mistress Randolph knows what's going on, but the poor woman is swamped trying to get the uniforms made. Betty told me that even the lady herself, Evangeline, and all of the house servants are busy sewing and the big house is showing dirt, the first time THAT ever happened," his wife said. "I don't need to tell you who is standing firm and doing only their own jobs," she added with a smile.

"Gabrel and Bessie," her husband answered with a sigh. "I think I'll become a cook."

Rebecca Randolph enjoyed her meals elegantly served in the dining room. It was the only time she could act as the Mistress of Fair Oaks Plantation. She felt like a slave when she herself had to oversee the construction of uniforms for men she had never met and were of a certainty far below her station in life. It was only out of love and her loyalty to her husband that she stooped to such low estate. Rebecca was surprised but pleased by Evangeline's enthusiasm and her skill with the needle. To embroider a sampler was one thing expected of all well-bred young ladies, but Rebecca never expected to see her daughter sewing buttons on uniforms for soldiers of the Confederate States of America!

Slaves did the heavy sewing in the slave quarters, but the final procedures—sewing on buttons, attaching badges, examining beltplates for flaws—were done in the front hall of the big house. Except for the kepis and wide-brimmed slouch hats which were obtained from a factory, the uniforms were complete when the last buttons were sewn and the clothing stacked in piles of twenty according to size. The stacks were placed in rows along the walls of the hall until their great number spilled over and became a maze, much like a garden maze of boxwood planted for the delight and entertainment of a planter's family and guests.

The slaves didn't come to help her one morning when Rebecca found herself, by accident, in the middle of the uniform stack maze. They giggled when they heard Mistress scream when someone grabbed her from behind. She turned to defend herself and saw her smiling husband who swept her off her feet. Evangeline, Sissy, and the other slaves continued sewing and finished several uniforms before Master and Mistress emerged from the "grey cloth forest."

Evangeline put her needle in the pin cushion and rushed up to hug her father. "Darlin'," he began, "I'm so proud to see you sewing and helping clothe the soldiers in our proud Army of West Tennessee. You and your precious mother have done more than I could imagine, more than the other women, our flowers of the South, I'm sure!"

"Just look at you," Rebecca said admiringly. She stood back with Evangeline and they admired the man wearing the regulation grey frock coat of a Confederate Light Artillery Officer. The gold rank-lacing on his cuffs and three braids on his kepi, which he had removed from his head, identified him as a Colonel. Three gold braids graced the light blue epaulets on his shoulders. The gilt buttons glistened on his coat. His trousers were light blue matching the color of the facing of his frock coat. A two-inch red stripe ran down the side of each trouser leg. Colonel Thomas Randolph wore a red silk sash under his waistbelt, another indication of his rank. When he walked, it seemed to the slaves as if his highly polished boots were as bright as a full moon.

"You are so handsome it takes my breath away," his wife said softly and put her hand to her throat.

Gabrel broke the spell when he made his way through the stacks of uniforms. "Welcome back, Master Randolph. Bessie says to tell y'all dat tea is served in da dining room if'n y'all follow me." He held the door open and Rebecca swept into the room like the wife of a Confederate Colonel. Evangeline followed. Raleigh was nowhere in sight, and Gabrel guessed he didn't know his father had come home and expected the boy to be put out for not being called for the occasion.

"Where be Young Master Alexander, sir?" Gabrel inquired of Colonel Randolph.

The Colonel directed his answer to his wife. "Darlin', your son is still recruiting and doing a fine job of it. We're near reaching our quota and already our brave men are training in the field."

"You've been gone two months," complained Rebecca. "I thought you and Alexander would be home by now."

Colonel Randolph laughed. "I fear you have been spoiled, my dear. Slaves can be trained quicker than hunting dogs, but farm boys . . . !" He sighed. "You can't even imagine! You see, darlin', military science dictates that armies must learn more than a hundred signals so they know which way to go and what to do when they get there. I do believe the drummer boys and buglers are smarter than the fighting men. They are the ones who drum or bugle the commands. The younger they are, the quicker they learn, it seems to me. The youngsters under my command have already mastered most of what they must know."

"Papa," Evangeline broke in, "you're a cotton planter. You don't know anything about, what did you call it, military science?"

"You're quite right, darlin', but your papa is learning fast, and I have good teachers. We have more and better generals who learned how to fight in the Mexican War than the Union Army has. It's a fact that most of them attended West Point together when they were young. Did you know, Evangeline, that General Robert E. Lee was offered the command of the Union Armies before he chose to go with the Confederacy? That alone should tell you the South will quickly vanquish our enemy!"

Evangeline made a face and sat back while Gabrel filled her tea cup again. Rebecca Randolph felt uncomfortable with the changes in her husband's attitude. She never expected him to be this enthusiastic about military service and wondered if he were being contaminated by close association with men some called war lovers.

"As I was saying, while a goodly number of my recruits can read and write a little, not every man who joined up knew his right foot from his left, if you can imagine that! It was a big problem. You have to remember that I, with the help of my headquarters staff, of course, will command three battalions of Confederate soldiers assigned to a dozen artillery batteries. In other words, more than a thousand men must learn to move all together at one time to accomplish a military maneuver, whether it be marching or fighting. Imagine the confusion of an army of men moving without knowing where they are going or what they should do it they ever get there! When the men get it right, it's a sight to see!

"Some of those old farmers are clever. I give them credit. Old Riley and his boys tied bundles of hay around the boots on the right feet and bundles of straw around the boots on the left feet of the men in their battery. Instead of trying to teach country boys to march left, right, left, right, we call out, 'Hay foot, straw foot, hay foot, straw foot.'

"It works. I made Nathan Riley a sergeant. Three of his boys joined up with him, and all of them can read and write. The man has two other sons at home, I understand. He wouldn't let them join because Riley doesn't want his farm to go fallow.

"We have many young soldiers, just boys really, but they catch on to things pretty fast. I can guarantee that the soldiers in Riley's battery now know their left feet from their right. Men in the other eleven batteries had better know it by the time I return or I'll make them march in their drawers and not give them the uniforms you have made. I know you're glad this is the last batch. If our fighting looks as good as the uniforms the men in my regiment wear, we'll be home before they get dirty!" Colonel said as he laughed.

"Papa," Evangeline said as she took him by the hand, "I want to show you how I sew buttons and badges on the uniforms. I don't put the belt-plates on the leather, though. Hercules does that at the smithy."

Colonel felt a lump in his throat as he watched his daughter, the fairest Southern belle in all of Tennessee, hold up a finished uniform. "See, everything's done," she said proudly. The brass rectangular belt-plate bore the letters *C.S.A.* The brass buttons were stamped with an *A* and *4* indicating the Fourth Artillery Regiment of the Army of West Tennessee.

Colonel Randolph put his arm around his daughter and kissed her on the cheek. "I want you and your sweet mother to give me silk scarves to carry with me wherever I go, not that I need to be reminded of you," he teased.

"Just like the Knights of the Round Table!" Evangeline exclaimed and left her father's embrace to run upstairs and return with a silk scarf that matched the color of her blue eyes. "This is my favorite," she said and handed it to her father who tucked it inside of his frock coat.

"And where is yours, darlin'?" he asked his wife.

"I'll give you mine tonight at bedtime," she replied ever so sweetly.

* * *

After such a tender and satisfying night together, Rebecca was surprised to find herself alone in bed later the next morning. She put on her silk wrapper and slipped her feet into soft Chinese house slippers and quietly went downstairs to look for her husband. She found him sitting in his favorite wing-back leather chair near the fireplace in the library. He was asleep and a book lay open in his lap. She carefully lifted it up, quietly put it on the desk, and noted its title, *Manual of Arms.* As her husband began to stir, Rebecca rang for Gabrel and ordered coffee when the houseman answered her call.

"When I awoke, you were gone," she said crossly. "What is of greater interest to you, some silly book or me?"

"Darlin', you surely know the answer to that question," her husband replied as he rose to his feet and embraced her. He pulled her into his lap as he sat again in the big chair. They remained there until Gabrel knocked softly at the library door then entered. He carried a silver tray and brought sweet rolls as well as coffee in a china pot and matching cups and saucers. He set up the refreshments on a small table nearby, poured two cups of coffee, one with sugar and cream, one without, and left the room as silently as he had entered.

When the door closed behind their head house slave, Rebecca took a small sip of her coffee before speaking.

"I thought you were against secession and very much against a war," she said. "You look to me as if you enjoy military life. What has happened to you, my sweet?"

Thomas shook his head. "You are correct on all counts, darlin'. At first, buying my commission was just about the same to me as out-bidding my friends, that is, my former friends, for the slave Hercules. It was simply another way to show them I was the best planter, the richest one, and the winner in another one of our silly little competitive games.

"I truly believe that most of the others in our little group were as much against secession as I was, but they were too cowardly to say so. Instead, all of them turned their backs on me because I was honest in my opinions. I wondered, too, if they turned their backs on me because of simple jealousy due to my success as a planter.

"Loss of their shallow friendship wouldn't have bothered me too much. I have always considered half of our so-called friends to be fools, anyway. What bothered me most was the way they and their wives shunned you and the children. I wanted, no, needed to punish them for that.

"The most public way I could get even with them was to become a Confederate Army Colonel. Not one of them has the courage or the money to do what I did. It must gall them to know that soldiers salute and call me, 'Colonel.' "

Rebecca filled their coffee cups. She looked at her husband as if he were a stranger but said nothing.

"Rebecca," he continued, "for the first time in my life, I am learning what I must do to command and take responsibility for a very large number of people. I never thought about it before, but even though I own hundreds of slaves, I have direct command over only one person.

"I command Bailey, just Bailey. He is the one who sees that my orders are carried out. I sit before you as husband, father, and master of one of the biggest and most wealthy plantations in the whole South. Yet, I have direct command of only one person. I don't even need to check to see if my orders have been carried out. If I don't hear from Bailey to the contrary, they have.

"This may seem paradoxical, and I would never talk like this to anyone other than you, but I am humbled and frightened to command and take responsibility for a thousand men. Of course, I have dozens of 'Baileys' who are my officers and serve to relay and carry out my orders, but often I am right there with them when they are implemented. My own responsibility is constant.

"Rebecca, if I rode Hatchie to the front of my regiment and yelled, 'Follow me!' a thousand men would do just that. The whole idea of it scares me but makes me feel fully alive at the same time.

"I would be lying if I didn't tell you that I fear death. My regiment has not even fired a shot in battle yet. There is a camaraderie among military men quite unlike anything I have experienced before. I am not a war lover, Rebecca, but I think I may be a lover of warriors. Please do not think less of me," her husband said as he took her hand.

"I love you all the more for your honesty. When you leave tomorrow with the uniforms, know that the love of your family will be with every man who wears one." Rebecca held tightly to her husband's hand.

* * *

Colonel Thomas Randolph had never before experienced such a heady feeling as on the day his battle-ready troops passed in review. He sat proudly on his horse, Hatchie, and his eldest son was by his side. Jubal, who stood some distance away, was overcome with pride to be the personal body servant of such an important planter-soldier. Although not as accomplished a cook as Bessie, the slave provided his Master and guests generous and satisfying meals from what seemed to be a bottomless larder.

That evening the senior officers gathered to drink a toast in celebration of recent news of the Confederate rout of the Federals at Bull Run in Virginia, only a half day's ride from Washington City, capitol of the United States of America.

"As I said to Mrs. Randolph, my lovely wife, it will be a short war," Colonel said. The other officers present agreed. "To the Confederacy!" he said and raised his glass. "To the Confederacy!" the others repeated.

* * *

The Brigadier General, sitting ramrod-stiff on his horse, was pleasantly surprised at the military bearing and spit and polish of the soldiers in Randolph's Regiment as it passed in review. When the parade was over, the Brigadier returned to his headquarters tent and sat outside in front of it where he met with a few of his staff officers who gathered there. They relaxed over mint juleps served by the Brigadier's body servant.

"Drink up, gentlemen. When I served in the Mexican War, this nectar of the Gods was only a memory. I swore that if I survived the fighting and was able to return to my beloved South, the sun would not set on any day until I had savored my julep."

"Hear! Hear!" the men said in unison. They discussed the benefits and pleasures of the drinks and then moved on to the business of war.

"I'll admit I never thought Randolph knew his eyebrows from his ass, but his regiment looked good on the parade ground. I hope it looks as good when the first Union shell bursts under the Colonel's feet," the Brigadier remarked.

"Once those farm boys could tell their left feet from their right, they learned mighty fast," an aide remarked with a smile.

"The good old boys who can shoot the eye out of a squirrel at five hundred feet nearly dropped their teeth when they saw the really big guns," the youngest officer remarked.

"Thank God they finally got here," the Brigadier added. "The train was so late, we have little time to practice in the field. I must say that the Nashville Foundry did itself proud. The guns are beautiful field pieces. Four six-pounder smooth-bore cannon and two twelve-pounder howitzers for each battery gives us enough fire power to attack the White House itself and win if only our Founding Fathers had seen fit to build the Capitol on the Tennessee River instead of the Potomac! The Potomac River is nothing but a creek. There's not enough water in it to drown that outlaw president, Lincoln!"

He knew his humor was not wasted on this small group of men, career soldiers all, who held him as their commander in the highest esteem. The Brigadier felt safe among them and continued his commentary.

"The country has been going to hell in a handbasket, and it's time we start afresh as a new nation here in the South. We should be better prepared for war than we are now, I think, even though I expect it to be a short one.

"I never liked the practice of men of wealth or political clout buying their commission in the army. Both the North and South allow it, and I will admit that a few of the golden boys develop a talent for war. Most of them, though, are an asset to the enemy!

"Knowing of his reputation as being against secession and more than a bit uppity in his own planter ruling class, I never expected Randolph to develop into anything like the military leader he may very well become. His officers and men seem to like him, and he hasn't made a disastrous mistake in training his troops so far. It's a good thing, because I wouldn't be surprised if we meet the enemy in battle before the month is out.

"The Colonel does need to get a better handle on the *Manual of Arms.* I imagine that before the sun goes down, this information will find its way to Colonel Randolph by some means." The Brigadier General winked at his staff officers.

Chapter Eleven
The Last Letter

"Are you feeling any better?" Alexander asked his father when he entered the Colonel's tent.

"Somewhat," Randolph answered. "Dysentery only lasts a few days. Some dastardly speculators are making their fortunes selling bad meat and wormy hard tack to the Army. They should be hung. Our slaves at Fair Oaks eat better than our troops. What do the surgeons say about the health of the men?"

"I overheard the head surgeon report to the Brigadier. He said there are about seventeen hundred men down with the measles, nearly two regiments. They're mostly country boys who've never even heard of measles much less been exposed to it before."

"God Almighty!"

"And that's the good news," Alexander said grimly. "Our Confederates have fallen at Mill Springs in Kentucky, and there is a rumor that Federal gunboat flotillas have been sighted on some of our rivers."

"Which rivers?"

Alexander paused. "Well, sir, you have to remember rumor is not the same as fact."

"Which rivers?" the Colonel asked again.

"The Mississippi, Tennessee, and Cumberland, sir."

Randolph doubled over with pain, and as he fled from his tent to the temporary officers' privy, he called back over his shoulder. "Wait there. I'll be back shortly."

Alexander took the opportunity to stretch out on his father's cot, much more comfortable than his own. He felt heartsick over the Southern war profiteers who cheated their own countrymen. The young lieutenant smiled when he remembered one of the soldiers telling his mates that mealy worms in the hard tack was a new meat and good for them. "Eat up," he had urged, "and you can feel the little buggers wiggling all the way down from your mouth until you grunts 'em out. The little buggers, still wiggling, will talk to each other about the ride of their sorry little lives. And that's a fact!"

Alexander wondered if the war profiteers would take their ill-gotten gains and run away to the North when the War Between the States was over. *I made my money honestly with cards,* he thought. *I have never, well, almost never, cheated, and what some call luck is really a skill. I can see in my mind's eye every card in a deck and remember who and when it was played. There is no such thing as luck.*

Alexander was getting concerned about the length of time his father was gone when the Colonel reappeared. His face had lost its color and he sat down quickly on his cot. "The Brigadier called us to his tent. He just received word that Fort Henry on the Tennessee River has fallen to Grant. Most of the garrison retreated to Fort Donelson on the Cumberland. Nashville is at risk," he said as he buried his head in his hands.

Alexander stood by and put his hand on his father's shoulder. The Colonel raised his head and said, "Alexander, please get my letter box. If we are ordered to Nashville, perhaps we will pass close enough to Fair Oaks to allow us a short visit. I must send Jubal with a letter to your mother, and I suggest that you write a few words to her, Raleigh, and Evangeline. They, I'm sure, are as anxious to hear from us as we are to hear from them."

Alexander put his father's wooden letter box in the Colonel's lap and made sure there was ample ink in the well and that the nib on the pen was not damaged. He watched as his father took out the paper, dipped the pen in the inkwell, and began to write before he left for his own tent which he shared with other junior officers. Alexander knew he would follow his father's orders to write to the family, but first he wanted to discuss the news with his friends, perhaps over a friendly game of cards.

February 10, 1862
Army of West Tennessee

My Sweetest Rebecca,

I am sending this letter to you by Jubal. I have written a pass for him. While I cannot tell you where our Brigade is at this moment, I can spare Jubal for the few days it will take him to carry this to you. I dearly hope he will bring letters from you and the children back to me. I miss you more than you could ever know during every day and dream about you every night. How I miss holding you in my arms and loving you.

It has been some months since I have heard from you. I would worry except for the fact that the other officers and men in my regiment haven't received any letters from their families either. Most of us blame, not our loved ones, but the railroads! The trains have not been running for some time, and somewhere a bored engineer must be entertaining himself reading all of the letters from wives and sweethearts to their gallant men fighting this damnable war.

The damn yankees keep blowing up our railroad bridges, but our skillful men can build them again as soon as the dust settles. Raleigh would be interested to know that our lads take every little sliver of wood left from the explosion and fasten them together like a puzzle to rebuild the structure. The replacement bridges are not handsome and some refer to them as "toothpick bridges." If Raleigh thinks building one is an easy task, he should try it with the toothpicks in our crystal holder on the dining room table!

I don't want him trying to make a "Yankee hairpin," though. Since our Southern boys were so clever at rebuilding bridges and relaying railroad tracks pulled up by the bluebellies, those damyankees took a lesson from the Devil himself. Now, after they have torn up a section of track, they pile the wooden ties high, place the track sections on top, and set the whole mess on fire. The metal rails become red hot, slowly lose their shapes, and bend over the pile of ties. When they finally cool, the rails are the shapes of giant hairpins and are absolutely worthless as railroad tracks. The Devil must keep a giant mistress with unruly hair down there in Hell!

You would be proud of your son, Lieutenant Alexander Randolph. The quartermaster complimented him on his records and told me that mine was one of the most well-run, or I should say, "most efficiently commanded," regiments in the Brigade.

The Brigadier, himself, complimented me last week on the accuracy of our artillery. We have been battle-tested and made some inroads in the enemy's position. Of course, there have been some casualties, sadly expected when fighting a war. However, to keep my mind in balance, I prefer to dwell on the most interesting aspects of military life instead of its difficulties.

The noise of battle ceases at sundown, except for the moans and cries of those wounded left on the field. Scouts search them out and there seems to be a gentleman's agreement, observed by South and North, that allows the wounded to be carried in safely at dusk.

Jubal keeps up with my laundry, but Alexander has told me that soldiers from both sides wash their clothes in the same creek and visit like neighbors when the fighting is done for the day. They trade goods, he said, and some recognize their kin from the other side and visit as if the hostilities didn't even exist.

In the early evening, I can see thousands of campfires where men and sometimes their wives and children cook the evening meal. It is a strange thing to see families travel with the Army, camp followers, they are called.

On some evenings, Alexander has even played cards with some Yankee officers who tell him they won't accept Confederate money when they win. That hasn't been a problem, he tells me, because he always wins!

A goodly number of our men have the measles, but Alexander and I are fine. Some of us do suffer, from time to time, with stomach upset. I do long for one of Bessie's fine meals. As I have said before, our slaves eat better at Fair Oaks than our soldiers here in the field.

Remember that I love you and expect that I shall see you not too many days hence. In the unlikely event that Nashville does fall into enemy hands, I think you should consider the plans we discussed relative to our land in Texas. Just in case, you understand.

Kiss the children for me. Tell Evangeline my troops look fine in their uniforms although they are getting to be a bit worn. I know Raleigh is a big help to you and trust he is learning much from Bailey as to how to run things at Fair Oaks.

Jubal will carry my love with this letter. He will leave early tomorrow morning and should deliver it in no more than three days. Alexander has acquired a horse for him to ride.

I remain your devoted husband,
Thomas

* * *

Jubal carried the letter in his saddle bag along with some hard tack and beef jerky that Alexander won from a Yankee in a card game. He had traveled without incident for two days and had not seen a patroller or anyone else even though he could hear people moving through the woods.

Colonel Randolph's body slave was a half-day's ride from Fair Oaks when four scruffy Confederate soldiers burst out of the woods.

"A runaway slave!" yelled one as the other three pulled Jubal from his horse. As he hit the ground, one of the animal's hooves grazed his head, and blood trickled down over his left eye.

Jubal struggled to sit up and shouted, "No,suh! I don't be no runaway! I's da slave of Master Colonel Thomas Randolph of Fair Oaks Plantation on my way to deliver a letter to Mistress Randolph. Here be my pass." Jubal fumbled in his pocket, grasped the letter, and handed his pass to the soldier who seemed to be the leader of the group.

None of the Confederates could read. They took a rope from the horse's saddle, made a noose, and hanged Jubal from a tree until he was dead. The four emptied the contents of the saddlebag on the ground and divided the food. The leader rode the horse, and the other three complained as they walked after him. The marauders left the letter on the ground. Late in the afternoon, a breeze came up and blew it away.

* * *

Colonel Randolph was disappointed when the Brigadier ordered the Army south. He had hoped to remain in their present location until Jubal returned from Fair Oaks. "Jubal will catch up with us," he told Alexander. "When a brigade moves, it leaves a wide trail. I had hoped we would be going the opposite direction and come close enough to Fair Oaks to allow us a short visit with the family."

"I'll send Jeb to help you, Father. He gathered my things and already has them on a packhorse," Alexander said.

* * *

Colonel Randolph lost track of the number of days his regiment was on the march and was relieved when their brigade met up with the other Southern forces, all told some forty-thousand Confederate soldiers. They were deployed quietly throughout the woods and were required to dig holes in which to build their fires so the enemy would not see the flames.

Alexander could not believe the Federals didn't know the Confederate Army was camped close enough to hear their buglers and smell their coffee boiling over their campfires. "I'm tempted to take two cups and go over to their lines to ask for some of that coffee myself," Alexander said to his fahter, still weak and not fully recovered from his bout of sickness although he did manage a slight smile at the idea of it.

"I talked with another young lieutenant who said the Yankees must be camped near Shiloh Chapel. It's a Methodist meeting house. His daddy used to be a circuit rider, and when the officer was just a boy, sometimes he went with his daddy when he preached there. As far as he knows, Methodists still gather there for worship," Alexander said. "Sleep well, Father. Tomorrow we attack."

In the middle of the moonless night, stomach cramps forced Colonel Randolph to seek relief in the woods behind his tent. He could barely see the white blur of his tent as he groped his way back to his quarters. His foot caught on the rope around a tent stake. When he pitched forward, his head struck another stake which pierced his skull, and he died on the spot.

At dawn Jeb found Colonel Randolph on the ground and quietly went to wake Young Master Alexander. "Come quick," the slave whispered. "Yo' pa, I think he be dead!"

Alexander was devastated when Jeb led him to his father's body. Finally, he found his voice. "Help me carry him into his tent. Don't say a word of this to anyone else. Do you understand?"

"Yes, suh," Jeb replied as he fought back his own tears.

They put Colonel Randolph on his cot, and Alexander sat beside him for a few minutes. Jeb uncovered his own head and held his hat in both hands as he stood by.

Finally, Alexander spoke. "Jeb, saddle Master's and my horses and bring them around to the front of the tent, then come in and help me dress him. Colonel Randolph is going to be riding among his troops and encouraging them to fire their cannons straight and true as he had always done."

Jeb wondered if Young Master Lieutenant Alexander was a might teched in his own head but followed his orders. He saddled the horses and tethered them in front of the tent. When the slave went inside, he found the Colonel nearly dressed in his uniform. Alexander directed him to make sure the Colonel's boots were polished before Jeb put them on his feet.

Although there was little bleeding from the wound, Alexander wrapped his father's head with a torn piece of sheeting and chose his slouch hat which he secured at a jaunty angle on the Colonel's head to hide the bandage. As he worked to prepare his father for battle, Alexander spoke aloud to him.

This strange one-way conversation spooked Jeb, who had never before been present when a live person was dressing a dead person and talking to him like he was a live person when he wasn't alive at all, just dead. "He be dead as a door nail," as Jeb remembered his mama sayin' when his own pa died after he got hisself caught in da cotton gin.

"Father," Alexander continued, "I'll see to it that you die with honor, a hero's death, something fitting for the best planter, the richest planter, the smartest planter in all of Tennessee. Generations will respect your memory, not hold you up to ridicule. I promise you that, as God is my witness."

The Brigadier did not miss Colonel Randolph at his final briefing. Just before dawn the buglers sounded the charge and cadence tapped by drummer boys joined the chorus of thousands of rebel yells as the woods came alive with charging greybacks who caught the Union forces unaware.

The officers marveled at the fierceness of their troops in the fighting that continued for twelve straight hours and left the surprised bluebellies confused and in disarray. Even though casualties were expected, his troops mourned the loss of Colonel Randolph and told of his bravery as the Colonel and his lieutenant rode through their ranks cheering on the gunners. They were stunned when the smoke cleared after a shuddering volley of fire and Colonel Randolph lay dead under his fallen horse, both killed by enemy fire. No one saw Alexander return his side arm to its holster. He cried for his father and for the gallant horse.

A cold rain started to fall and continued through the night as the Confederate General Staff planned how to continue their rout the next day. At dawn, the battle began again against a Union Army that had been reinforced during the night. Alexander led his late father's regiment because all higher-ranked officers were engaged with their own responsibilities. The fighting was even more fierce than on the previous day and by late afternoon, the Brigadier gave the order to retreat south to the town of Corinth.

Alexander used his knife to cut up his father's tent and had Jeb help him wrap the Colonel's body in the canvas. They tied it neatly with the tent ropes. Alexander thought it could pass as a side of beef and prayed no one would steal it. The two lifted the body, front down, over Jeb's horse and tied it to the saddle. Alexander mounted his own horse and rode slowly. Jeb held the reins to lead his horse and walked behind. They blended into the retreating Confederate Army.

At the end of the march, Alexander reported with the other officers to the Brigadier for instructions. "Lieutenant Randolph, my condolences for the loss of your father. I confess my early doubts about him as a planter-soldier, but he proved me wrong. You and your family can be proud of his service to our country and, though tragic, exult in his death as a hero.

"Our riders have brought information that the enemy forces are licking their wounds. Apparently, the Union Army is too exhausted for pursuit. Thank God, we Southeners have enough energy left to retreat!"

Alexander fell behind as the regiment continued its march to the south. By nightfall he had picked up a riderless horse for Jeb to ride. Gradually, they fell back from the group of soldiers and quietly disappeared into the woods. They were alone when they dismounted and lifted the body down from the horse and rested it flat on the ground. Alexander directed Jeb to make a small fire. He went back to a small creek they had forded and returned carrying six crayfish in his hat.

"Young Master Randolph, suh, where we be goin'?" Jeb asked while roasting supper on a thin stick he held over the fire.

"Home. We're taking the Colonel home."

* * *

Colonel Thomas Randolph returned to Fair Oaks Plantation. He was buried in the family graveyard alongside the tiny graves of his three other sons who died in infancy. Overseer Bailey granted the plantation slaves the day off for mourning.

Mistress Randolph was distraught with grief. Evangeline locked herself in her room for two days and wouldn't come out even to eat. Raleigh sat at his father's grave throughout the night and until hunger pains forced him in for breakfast.

Alexander was surprised to learn Jubal never arrived and assumed the slave had run away. When he became ill from eating too much food, Bessie put him on a diet of chickweed tea and chicken soup for three days and gradually added one meat and a small serving of a vegetable until his stomach adjusted to food.

Bessie fed the same food to Jeb but didn't let it be known that his body servant was eating the same as Young Master.

"You be wrong in callin' him dat," Gabrel chided. "Wid the Master dead, Alexander now be Master Randolph of Fair Oaks Plantation."

"Dat's so," Bessie agreed, "an' I hope he be up to da job."

Alexander didn't talk about the war. He told the family about his father's heroic death and how he was admired by the men in his regiment and how the Brigadier honored him. He would say nothing more even though Raleigh begged him for stories.

Jeb was mute. After going through what he did with Lieutenant Alexander, he did not want the new Master Randolph to have him hanged for telling stories.

Alexander spent most of his time going over numbers when he was at the desk in the library. His mother had shown him the deeds to the Texas land and briefly discussed the plans Thomas and she had made in the event things in the South took a turn for the worse, something neither of them really expected to happen.

"I don't think Father would have joined the Confederate Army if he had not believed that England would enter the war on the side of the South," Alexander said. "After all, the South supplied the cotton for the British mills turning out more cotton cloth than any other country in the world.

"Now our warehouses are overflowing with bales of cotton and we have no way to get them to market. The Union gunboats control our rivers, our trains don't run, and even if they did the North has blockaded our ports.

"Texas appears to be an out-of-the-way slave state and Brownsville lies near the Gulf. If we could go as civilians on packet ships still taking passengers down the Mississippi River to New Orleans, we might be able to catch a ship bound for Brownsville. Of course, it would cost a great deal of money, and I fear Confederate script is becoming worthless. What do you think about it, Mother?"

"Gold has held its value, has it not?" she answered. "I think your plan has merit. It will take great effort to prepare for the move and a generous amount of gold, I would imagine, to make arrangements for travel."

"How many of our slaves should we take? As no one seems to be buying at the moment, those we leave behind will be a total loss," Alexander said. "We also must consider the price of their passage for any slaves we might take with us."

Rebecca thought for a moment. "The breeders, certainly. We should take them, all of the sturdy children, and the babies young enough to travel for free. And probably all number-one craft slaves if they are younger than twenty, I would think. We should take our personal body servants but leave the house slaves. It will take some time to build a proper home and by that time, some of the children may be old enough to train."

"What about Bessie and Gabrel?" Alexander asked.

"They're much too old to go. We cannot afford to take any of the old slaves because there is not enough life in them to make it worth the money and trouble to move them. We'll just leave them here in charge of Fair Oaks, so to speak," she said.

* * *

Several months after the Randolph family, Overseer Bailey, his wife, and a large number of the Randolph slaves left for Texas, a dozen Union soldiers under the command of a recently promoted captain cautiously approached the big house. They walked across the veranda and stepped back when the door opened.

They were relieved when Gabrel formally greeted them and invited the men to come inside for dinner at a grand table set with more food than the soldiers had seen in some time. They ate in silence and without manners. At the end of the meal, they awkwardly thanked Bessie and Gabrel for their hospitality and then proceeded to search the house for valuables.

They found little they could carry. In frustration, one of them threw a vase and shattered a large gilt-framed mirror. Three others tore down all the window coverings in the house. One took his knife and slashed the canopy and satin bedding on a magnificent four poster bed.

Bessie and Gabrel followed the soldiers as they went outside to search the other buildings for booty. When they approached gunbarrel house number four, the two were stunned to see Hercules walk out the door. He was wearing the uniform of a Yankee soldier.

"Big old Hercules, is dat really you?" Gabrel asked.

"Da same!" he answered.

"You be in da U.S. Colored Troop Army?" Bessie inquired.

Hercules laughed. "I jest a colored blacksmith in a white cavalry 'cause I be da best blacksmith dey ever seen."

"Why you not let Bessie here make yo' dinner?" she teased with her hands on her hips.

" 'Cause I eat wid my friends Luther an' Old Clara. Dey feeds me good. 'Sides, next to you, Bessie, Luther be da best cook in da whole plantation. Where everybody else?" he asked.

"Dey takes demselves down to Texas," Gabrel answered.

"Sissy?" Hercules asked.

"Dey takes her, too," Bessie replied.

Other slaves cautiously came out of hiding to see Hercules and greeted him like the old friend that he was.

"Why so many of you still here?" he asked.

" 'Cause we's too old to waste Master Alexander Randolph's money on. Der be no market fo' slaves jest now," Luther added.

As the young Captain gave orders for his men to burn the plantation, Hercules took him aside. The giant looked down on the short blond officer and spoke a few words.

The Captain amended his order and his men set ablaze the big house, Bailey's house, all of the barns except the lower one, the hanging tree, and the fields planted in cotton. The Fair Oaks slaves watched the conflagration in silence and vowed to be better people now that they knew what hell looks like.

The Yankee soldiers, their haversacks filled with food, mounted their horses and rode away. Hercules followed them and didn't look back. They left intact and free of damage all of the gunbarrel houses, the vegetable gardens, a spring house full of food, three milk cows, two mules, six horses, a dozen chickens, a sow with three piglets, two ducks, and a big lazy dog.

Part Three

Chapter Twelve
Murder

Catherine Riley was exhausted. She and the children had been in the orchard picking fruit since early morning. Her hands were scratched and sticky. Her thumbs and every finger ached.

"Mama, you need a rest," Elizabeth said as she took her mother gently by the arm and led her to the house. Badog followed and continued to scratch at the kitchen door when he was denied entrance into the house. "I'm going to fix you a nice cup of tea, and I want you to sit in the rocking chair, put your feet up, and rest."

Catherine didn't object. She watched her daughter lift one of the stove lids and put another piece of wood in the fire box. Elizabeth went to the medicine cupboard, removed three sprigs of dried chickweed, crumpled them in a bowl, and poured warm water from the teakettle until the bowl was half full. She let it steep for a few minutes, tested the water temperature with a finger, and then put the bowl in her mother's lap. Catherine put both hands into the healing tincture, closed her eyes and listened to the muted sounds of water starting to boil in the teakettle. When she heard her daughter tapping on the tea tin, Catherine knew what Elizabeth was about to say.

"Mama, this is the last bit of China tea," she said as she poured the steaming water in the cup.

"I know. I don't think there is another tin of China tea in all of Tennessee. Soon we'll drink turnip tea, okra coffee, and other strange brews!" Both of them gagged.

When her daughter served Catherine what they agreed was the last cup of China tea in Tennessee, she kissed her mother on the forehead and said, "Sit and rest, Mama. We have one more row of pears to pick. I'll come get you to help us pick the apples. We're almost ready to start the apple butter. The cooking utensils are ready, and we'll wash and slice the apples tomorrow."

As Elizabeth went out the door, Badog slipped between her legs and plopped down on the floor near Catherine's feet. "Oh, all right! You can stay," she said, nodding to Elizabeth, who had stopped and stood with her hands on her hips. The animal knew he had won another contest and settled down for a nap. His mistress learned over, careful not to spill her tea, and patted the dog on his head. "Good dog," she said softly and settled back into the rocking chair.

She sipped her tea slowly and savored the precious liquid rolling on her tongue. When the cup was empty, she put it on the small table beside her and put her feet up on the gout rocker. The small piece of furniture was the last thing Nathan had given her. It was much like a foot stool, but under its flat quilted top were two wooden rockers that mimicked the motion of her rocking chair. Catherine had never before seen such a "contraption," as Nathan had called it. She stopped rocking and took a wrinkled letter from her bodice. It was the one she had wept over many times before. Tears filled her eyes again as she unfolded the paper. Just holding it in her hands gave Catherine some comfort. She knew the words by heart.

Encamped near Shiloh, Tennessee
April 9, 1862

My Darling Wife,

Today I saw a redbud tree and a sliver of color told me the buds were about to open. Soon pink flowers will crown the tree. I thought of the many times we walked together through the woods and how excited we were at the first sight of pink, knowing spring and white dogwood blooms would not be far behind. Redbud and dogwood trees grow together in harmony and the different colors they show are of equal beauty. Why can't people live together like trees in the woods?

Walk in the woods today and know I am beside you. When you see the first bloom starting to open, think of your dear husband so far away and missing you so much his spirit aches.

I miss Sunday. Sunday is the same as any other day when we are in battle. I miss Sunday morning at home. Remember how I always woke early, went into the kitchen, stoked the fire, and made coffee while I waited for you to open your beautiful eyes and walk barefoot in to meet me. Coffee never tasted so good as that we shared in front of the fireplace before I carried you back to our bed. I miss the feel of your smooth skin next to mine. You are the most beautiful thing in my life, Catherine.

I know Nate and John and the little girls are taking good care of you and of the farm too. I finally got the letter you wrote to me two months ago. One of Randolph's slaves brought a bag of mail but there were letters for no more than fifty men in the whole regiment. Of course, we are not a full regiment anymore. Many of our brave soldiers were killed or wounded these past months and we lost many more good men in battle here at Shiloh. Victory comes at high cost. That Yankee General Grant can fight, not like some damnyankee officers who turn tail and run at the very sight of grey and sound of a Rebel yell.

War is a terrible thing, Catherine. While our cause is just, the feeling in my bones tells me the price we pay is too high. But I feel I cannot shirk my duty as a Southerner, born and bred.

Catherine, I hesitate to tell you this, but it may be better for you to hear it from me rather than from some stranger. Three weeks ago, Ben and Caleb died on the same day from the measles. I will myself to think the two of them entered heaven hand in hand and that the Good Lord will keep them together in that peaceful place.

Matthew took it hard and has not been himself since it happened. He wanted to leave for home, but I kept him here forcibly, I confess. I told him there have never been any cowards in the Riley family and he didn't have the right to be the first one. He and I claimed the boys' bodies and we buried them here in the woods away from the killing fields. When this war is done, we'll come back for them and bring them home. They lie peaceful in a quiet stand of loblolly pine. We marked the trees with an "R" so we can find them again.

Tell Nate and John that I'm depending on them to get the crops in and expect a good harvest. The Riley farm always has a good harvest. Kiss Elizabeth, Grace and Elle for me. I surely do wish I had some of their fine apple butter on one of your biscuits, Catherine.

Remember that I love you. Tell the children I love them too and promise not to whup any of them upside the head ever again even if they deserve it.

I remain your loving husband,
Sgt. Nathan Riley
Tennessee Volunteers

Catherine sighed as she tucked the letter back into its place near her heart. *Nathan is more demonstrative on paper than he is in person,* she thought. *I can't remember him telling any of our children that he loves them. I suppose the man thinks that because he provides well for his family, that in itself is a sign of his love. I wonder if he will tell them that he loves them when he comes home.*

Catherine leaned back in the rocking chair and closed her eyes. The familiar squeak of the chair's wooden back kept cadence with the rocking rhythm, and the gentle back and forth movements soothed her sore and weary body. As she relaxed, her brief respite from hard farm labor allowed her time to think of the past and brought into clear focus many events of the last few years. Although the memories brought her both joy and sorrow, Catherine felt that by remembering her loved ones, the very act afforded her some comfort and them a measure of immortality.

It seems longer than two years since Nathan and the three boys left for war, she thought, *but the memory of it is so fresh I can see it in my mind's eye, every detail of it, right down to the colors of the leaves in early fall.*

That was the last year we had a truly bountiful harvest. We took two full wagon loads of crops to town. Elle and I rode with Nathan in the yellow wagon. Matthew had no trouble with the mules pulling the old one. Ben was with him, and his job was to sit in back and keep an eye on the sacks of flour and cornmeal piled high in the wagon bed. Late summer rains had washed out ruts in the road, and we didn't want to lose a sack when the wagon bounced over some of the deepest ruts. We left Nate and John to do the milking and barnyard chores. Elizabeth and Grace were responsible for chores in the house and had orders to have supper ready for us no matter what time we got back home.

We noticed changes as soon as we drove past the stockyards. They were empty. Not a single hog or any other animal awaited shipment by train. Usually, there were hundreds of them. Nathan pointed to stacks of what he recognized as military equipment and supplies near the railroad siding.

Horse and wagon traffic was heavier the closer we came to the main street of town. Confederate soldiers crowded the sidewalks and walked in the street, as well. I thought it strange that we saw no women walking alone to do their shopping.

Mr. Sowell was too busy to come out to greet us and when we went inside the building, he seemed excited and quite tense as he rushed about helping more customers than we had ever seen at one time in the store. Sowell called Ned out of the back room and he helped, as usual, with unloading our wagons.

Mr. Sowell forgot to offer us the little gifts as was his custom. Elle and I left the men to their business and walked through the crowd to Hall's barbershop. I carried my baskets of medicine in both hands and told Elle to hold tightly to my skirt with one hand and grasp her little basket with the other. I didn't want to lose her on the crowded street.

Mr. Hall was mannerly, as usual, but even he seemed hurried as he chose from my supply of herbs and medicines. It was the first time he did not offer me tea in all of our years of business dealings. I barely remember the notice nailed on the wall outside next to the door to his shop. I wish I had read it more carefully. It was some sort of recruiting poster.

When we met up after completing our business in town, I saw the gleam in Matthew's eye, that sparkle of the family tease, our trickster, the one who stopped just short of complete folly to avoid punishment. I was sure he was planning some outlandish trick to play, most likely on Nate, when we got home.

After we loaded our town purchases on the wagons, Matthew, aglow with pride, announced, "Colonel Randolph was at the livery stable. He's raising a regiment of Confederate Tennessee Volunteers, the best fighting men in the whole South, and I'm going to be one of them! Look!" He reached under the wagon seat and pulled out a gray uniform worn by privates in the now-forming regiment of Colonel Thomas Randolph.

"The Colonel will be coming over here himself to talk to you, Papa, and Caleb and Ben too. He says every farmer in the county knows that the Rileys are the best of the lot of them. Colonel says farmers make the best soldiers and most of them can shoot a squirrel dead in the eye from a hundred yards!"

Colonel Randolph was true to his word. We watched him, resplendent in his gold-braided grey uniform, ride down the street on a magnificent horse and tip his hat with a flourish to Elle and me.

"Gentlemen, and ladies," he said with a smile. "What a pleasure to meet Mr. Nathan Riley, at last. Matthew, a fine lad, tells me there are five stout young men in your family. My compliments to you, Mrs. Riley. The reputation of your skills with a rifle precedes you, sir. I've no doubt that your sons' dead aims are near equal to your own.

"You know, of course, that our South Carolina brothers broke those Yankee bluebellies like a twig on a dead tree when they attacked Fort Sumpter. South Carolina was midwife, so to speak, at the birth of the Confederate States of America. Pardon my language, ladies.

"It has caused me great pain that Tennessee came so late into the Confederacy, but now I celebrate our union with our ten Southern sister states. I, personally, have pledged my life and honor to defend our way of life and the new nation of the South. Any Southerner worthy of the name will do likewise. Gentlemen, will you do me the honor of accompanying me to my temporary headquarters."

Colonel Randolph rode on ahead. Nathan and his three sons followed. There were a dozen men there when Colonel spoke of one's duty to the Confederacy and convinced most of his listeners and the three other Rileys to sign their names on the military roster sitting on a table just inside the entrance to the livery stable.

Catherine shuddered at the memory of that day. *Later that same night, Nathan and I had the worst argument we ever had in all our years of marriage. He said that secession was something he thought would happen when the damned Illinois lawyer Lincoln was elected President. I'll never forget his exact words: "Catherine, I'm a Southerner, born and bred. My sons and I have a sacred duty to defend our land. Leave the North to their infernal machines that manufacture things and leave the South to men who plant the seed and reap the harvest as God intended." I argued, to no avail, of the hardship and danger to our family and reminded him that the Confederate Army has need of the food we grow.*

Tears filled Catherine's eyes as she thought of the day, four weeks after their town trip, when her husband and three oldest sons went off to war. They wore their uniforms proudly and put their haversacks next to those of five other recruits already aboard the wagon Colonel Randolph had sent to collect soldiers of his regiment.

Just before he jumped aboard, Matthew handed me a sack and said, "This is for you, Mama. He'll protect you when I'm gone. His name's Soldier." I held the wiggling bag closed as he had given it to me and watched until the wagon was out of sight.

Catherine stopped rocking, stretched, and let out a long sigh that woke Badog from his sleep. She learned over, put her face close to the dog's, scratched the animal behind his ears and said, "You, silly dog, is what Matthew gave me before he left. Can you imagine a man in uniform handing me a sack full of fluff and saying, "His name's Soldier'? Soldier, ha! A soldier is supposed to take orders. You were harder to train than my eight children put together!"

The dog looked into his owner's eyes as if he understood her every word. Catherine turned her head as he licked her face. "Bad dog!" she said and laughed aloud. She rose to her feet and carried the empty teacup to the drainboard. The dog followed at her heels.

"Poor Matthew," she said as her dog listened attentively. "He knew how upset I was at the thought of my husband and sons going off to war. The boy was so proud to be a soldier and truly believed he would come home a hero in less than six months after having chased the Yankees all the way back north of the Mason-Dixon Line.

"The generals had less trouble making soldiers out of farmers than I had breaking you of chewing on everything in sight!" she continued as she looked down at the animal. "I wore out a dish towel spanking your nose with it. 'Bad dog, Soldier! Bad dog, Soldier!' I said with every swat. Then, when you snuck into the house and chewed the rag rug by the fireplace, Elle said, 'Mama, save your breath and just call him Badog!' "

Catherine heard Elizabeth's steps on the porch. "Mama, did you have a good rest?" she asked as she entered the kitchen. "Nate says we have about two hours before sundown. He thinks we should sort and pack the fruit we already have in the barn instead of trying to pick the far orchard now. By the time we do that and milk the cows, it will be almost dark."

"That's a good idea." Catherine followed her daughter out onto the porch. "Look at all of this," she said as she spread her arms wide. "Our men marched off to war and left the six of us and one dog to work this whole place! Now, our farm's only bountiful harvest is the fruit in the orchard." She put her arms around Elizabeth. "Thank you, and bless you for working so hard. I love you, and Papa loves you too." The two of them held hands as they walked down the porch steps and headed toward the barn.

Badog followed them until he heard John's call: "Badog! Go get the cows! It's milking time! Go!" Badog ran off to fetch the cows in the far pasture. When he reached the grassy meadow, the dog barked, growled, and ran in a pattern that separated the milk cows from their nearby grown calves and the bull. Badog was too far away from the house to sense the danger.

The Rileys were out of sight and working in the barn when a scruffy-looking Confederate soldier came out of the woods behind the house. He cautiously approached, quietly entered the house through the kitchen door, and found the place empty of people. He emerged shortly thereafter and silently signaled to his three companions waiting in the woods. One by one, they joined him inside.

"Nobody's here," Tommy Boy said with a toothless smile, "but they must have been expecting us for supper." He pointed to the bread, jam, and peach cobbler Catherine had left out for the family's evening meal.

"I'll see what's in the cooler," Beau offered as he went back outside to examine the screen and wet burlap cooler box on the porch. *Farmers usually keep it full,* he thought, and smiled when he folded back the burlap flap and unlatched the screen door. As he had hoped, the cooler was full, and he called for Buddy to come help him carry in the large jug of milk, crock of sweet butter, half a smoked ham wrapped in muslin, and about a dozen white taters in a stoneware bowl.

They carried the bounty inside and put it on the kitchen table. Eustis already had chicory coffee boiling on the cast-iron stove. Buddy rummaged around in the cupboard and found dishes and utensils. He laughed in anticipation of sitting down at a real table and eating off plates with forks instead of fingers. "Jest like President Jefferson Davis, himself," he said proudly.

Beau snorted. "Since we're puttin' on airs, I jest think I'll be General Robert E. Lee comin' to supper with the President. How do you like that!"

While his companions were busy in the kitchen, Tommy Boy, the leader of the group, searched the house. He started upstairs in the loft bedroom. He took two shirts, a pair of trousers, and some long underwear from the wooden pegs on the wall. He found some boots he would have liked to have, but they were too small to fit his big feet. He took them any way, knowing he could trade them for something. Tommy Boy looked for something to carry his loot in and saw the tip of a basket under a bed. When he pulled it out, he was happy to find three pairs of stockings and a handsome hunting knife which he carefully secured in his belt.

He found nothing else of interest and went back downstairs. The girls' room yielded nothing he wanted, but when he entered the farmer's room, he stopped and caught his breath. Tommy Boy did not expect to see such an expensive walnut wardrobe in a farmer's house.

What a sly fox, he thought. *This farmer must be rich. I'll wager this is where he hides his money.* The intruder brandished the knife and went after the wardrobe like a hunter skinning a bear. He broke the lock with the blade of his newly-acquired hunting knife and opened the double doors. Two-thirds of the open space was given to hanging clothes, but the other third held three open shelves above three locked drawers.

He used the knife to pry open the drawers and threw their contents out on the floor as he searched for anything of value. The man was disappointed and angry to find in the bottom drawer only a small opal brooch and a gold watch on a chain. He searched the drawers once again but found no money, gold coins, or other jewelry.

He tapped the wooden surfaces of the furniture with the handle of his new knife and hoped to hear a hollow sound signaling a hidden compartment. There was none. Frustrated, he kicked the furniture and injured his big toe already sore from his ill-fitting shoes.

Tommy Boy put the brooch and watch in his pocket and then rummaged through the clothes hanging on the other side of the wardrobe. Most of what he found were women's things, winter quilts, and work clothes almost as worn as the clothes he wore. He smiled when he found one boot hidden under the hem of a long skirt and searched until he found its mate. He plopped down on the side of the bed, removed his own worn shoes, and put on the boots. He stood, walked around the room, and sighed with relief at the excellence of the fit.

Tommy Boy caught sight of himself in the wardrobe mirror hanging slightly askew but unbroken. He threw back his shoulders, cocked his kepi at a jaunty angle on his head, brushed the dust from his Confederate uniform, and saluted himself. "Tommy Boy, you are a handsome devil!" he said with enthusiasm.

In celebration of his good fortune, the soldier took a running jump and landed in the middle of the bed. He spread himself wide on the quilt and luxuriated in its feel and the clean, fresh smell of the bed linen. He couldn't remember the last time he had been in a real bed. Tommy Boy would have stayed there forever if not for the smell of chickory coffee and frying ham coming from the kitchen.

He followed the delicious smells, sat down at the table, and watched with amusement the antics of his three companions. Buddy had nearly finished setting the table, proper like, with real dishes and knives and forks and spoons. "Buddy," Tommy Boy asked sarcastically, "who are you 'spectin' for supper, General Robert E. Lee?"

Buddy just grinned and shook his head in the affirmative.

Eustis stood on a stool to reach the high cupboard shelves where a few extra dishes and food storage tins were kept. He searched each dish for money and finding none, threw them to the floor, and paid no attention to the shattering glass. All of the tins were empty except for three holding corn meal, wheat flour, and salt. He dumped the corn meal and salt on the drainboard and searched through the small piles with his fingers. The flour tin slipped out of his hands and the white contents spilled on Buddy's head when he walked past carrying a full cup of coffee.

In retaliation, Buddy kicked the stool out from under Eustis who crashed to the floor dusted with flour. He pushed himself up and picked the glass shards out of his skin as the others broke up with laughter at the sight of white flour covering a good part of the two men.

"I swear, you two look like cakes waitin' to be put in the oven!" Beau snickered and put down the knife he was using to cut the ham from the bone. "Let's put 'em in to bake! Somebody open the oven door!"

"Whoa! Just a dadburned minute!" Eustis hollered. "Why are we wrasslin" here when ole Tommy Boy's sittin' by himself over at that fancy table and eatin' all the dadburned food? He's such a big fat hog, there won't be none left for us!"

The banter and scuffling stopped as they raced to the table, sat down in real chairs, and "proper like" gorged themselves on more food than they had seen at one time in a year.

When he had eaten his fill, Eustis sighed. "I think I done died and gone to heaven."

"Saint Peter, hisself, woulda kicked your big ole behind clear to the bottom of Jacob's ladder where the ole Devil with a big, sharp pitchfork is waitin' for you," Beau said.

Buddy belched loudly, patted his chest, and said, "That ham was mighty good, smoked jest right. Reminds me of the night I sneaked real quiet like into a neighbor's smoke house and grabbed me a ham. My pa whupped me good and ate most of that ole ham hisself." He chuckled at the memory. "But this here ham . . . Well, I'd say this ole farmer, he knowed how to smoke ham! I declare I'm a mighty satisfied man!"

"Buddy, you always did think small. As for this ole boy, I'd jest say I'm only half-satisfied," their leader replied.

The others laughed. "Tommy Boy, don't you ever think 'bout nothin' else?" Beau teased.

"Well, now, you're as stupid as you act," Tommy Boy replied as he kicked Beau's behind. "No matter how good the meal, a woman for dessert is better than pecan pie." He smiled at the thought, then stopped and raised his finger for silence. "I do declare, am I hearin' the sounds of female voices comin' from somewhere?" he asked softly.

Eustis got up from the table and looked out the window over the sink. "You got good ears, Tommy Boy. Either that, or you washed them for a change," he snickered. "I reckon you jest might be in for a treat. Looks to me like four females are down there by the barn."

"Dessert." Tommy Boy said slowly, a toothless, lascivious smile breaking the caked dirt on his face. "And enough for all of us."

"John and I can finish up here," Nate said as he stacked apple crates against the barn wall. "We already chopped and stacked the wood by the fire pit. We'll get an early start on the apple butter in the morning. Grace and Elle washed the ladle and the big pot so we can start cooking right after breakfast. Mama, why don't you and the girls go on up to the house and get supper on the table. We'll be along shortly."

Catherine and the girls didn't argue and strolled leisurely up toward the house. They had prepared their evening meal earlier in the day, and all they had to do was heat and put the food on the table.

"Look, girls, it's Indian summer. See how much brighter the colors look before twilight this time of year," Catherine said. They stopped to admire the vivid hues of the leaves on the huge oak and poplar trees near the house. "This is my favorite time of year." Her daughters agreed.

The little group was walking by the fire pit when Catherine saw something out of order. The screen door on the porch cooler box was standing open, and the burlap flap had been flipped up on the top.

Before she could say a word, a group of men looking like a pack of grey wolves suddenly burst out through the open kitchen door. She and the girls started screaming as Catherine grabbed the long ladle from the cooking pot with one hand and pushed her daughters down behind the wood pile with the other. If they tried to run, she had no doubt but what the men would catch her girls before they could reach the woods or the barn. Their mother knew she had to fend off the attackers long enough for her sons to come to their aid.

Catherine stood her ground and swung the ladle like a sword. The sharp edge struck Eustis on the forehead and the spurt of blood clouded his vision. Tommy Boy enjoyed the game and parried Catherine's ladle tip with the hunting knife he had found in the house. Beau and Buddy circled back behind the wood pile and dodged the firewood thrown by the sisters.

John and Nate ran toward the house the instant they heard the first scream. "We're coming!" they yelled, but were too far away to prevent Beau and Buddy from storming the woodpile and snatching Elle and Grace from Elizabeth's arms. The men were so excited, they didn't feel the large bleeding scratches on their faces and arms as they pulled the girls away from the fire pit.

Tommy Boy became angry and tired of the game when Catherine landed a heavy blow on his shoulder. He grabbed the end of the long oar-shaped ladle and pushed it so hard that she fell backwards into the fire pit. He leaped in after her. The last thing Catherine saw before the hunting knife pierced her body was a flash of blue.

Nate and John, out of breath but ready to fight, reached the firepit and were startled by the sight. Amid a flurry of ashes, two soldiers were locked in battle. Nate saw the glint of a knife thrusting downward at the same time he heard the dull crack of breaking human bones. Ashes flew up as the grey-clad limp body hit the ground. Three more Confederate dead lay scattered about in unnatural positions, limbs askew like rag dolls dropped from a baby's cradle.

A huge figure wearing Yankee blue emerged from the churning dust. Nate whispered, "Hercules?" The word caught in his throat.

The huge man nodded, and tears ran down his face. "I didn't get here in time. I didn't know 'twas her 'til I seen her face. Poor woman's gone."

The stunned brothers ran to the fire pit and found their mother dead in the ashes. "Tend to her babies," Hercules said motioning to the three sobbing girls clustered amid the scattered firewood.

As their brothers slowly approached them, John said, "Grace, I'm going to carry you up to the house. Put your arms around my neck. It's all right now. Don't cry. It's all right. Nate's going to carry you, Elle." As the brothers lifted the two youngest sisters, Elizabeth stood alone.

Hercules, who had lifted Catherine into his arms, quietly spoke to the girl. "You can take hold of yo' mama's hand while we be walkin' up to da house." Elizabeth said nothing but gently held her mother's still-warm hand as the former slave led the sad little procession up to the house.

When they got inside, Hercules asked Elizabeth, "Where yo' mama's bed?" She led him into her parents' room and stepped over the clothing strewn on the floor. Hercules was about to lay Catherine on the bed.

"Wait," the girl said as she let go of her mother's hand. "Mama doesn't like a messy bed." Elizabeth smoothed out the wrinkled coverlet. "That's better. Now you can put her down." Hercules laid Catherine on the bed and spoke to Elizabeth. "I wants you to bring me a basin of water an' a towel. Den go back an' help da others clean up dat mess in da kitchen." While he was waiting for the water, Hercules quickly picked up the things on the floor and stuffed the clothing back into the wardrobe to hide the signs of destruction. Although the lock was broken, he stuffed a bit of cloth in the latch which was enough to hold the door closed.

Elizabeth returned with the basin of water and a towel. "This one is Mama's." She pointed to the embroidered name.

"Who did dis needlework?" the man asked.

Elizabeth smiled. "I did," she said proudly. "Everybody is the family has a towel with their own name."

"I declare, you does sew fine. Now, I wants you to go back in dat kitchen, clean it up, an' get some supper ready. Hear?"

Hercules didn't want her or any other member of the family to see what he had to do. He washed Catherine's body to prepare her for burial. Her skin was discolored around the wound made by the knife thrust deep into her left thigh. He doubted that was the intention of her attacker. Hercules did not want anyone to know that the woman died, not from the wound itself, but by bleeding to death. If given immediate help, there was a small chance she might have lived.

At least, the woman passed at home surrounded by her family, not like the poor souls passing amid the cries and moans of their comrades dying on the battlefield, he thought.

As Hercules went about the task, he put his mind to the strange twists that brought him to this place. He had learned to think of other things so he could deal with death automatically and without emotion. He believed it was the only way he could keep his mind from going crazy.

He found a winter dress with high neck and long sleeves in the wardrobe. He removed Catherine's bloody clothes, washed the last clots of blood from her body, and rolled her over so he could pull out the soiled coverlet on which she lay. Hercules folded the bloody things into a bundle and put it under the bed. He planned to take it outside later and burn it.

He dressed Catherine in clean clothes, spread a quilt, one-half at a time, on the bed. He lifted the corpse, placed it on the quilt's center, closed her eyes with his fingers, straightened her dress, smoothed her hair, and folded her hands together as if in prayer. He was familiar with the ritual.

When Hercules was conscripted for burial detail, he had been surprised that several of the dead Confederate soldiers were women. All of them had cut their hair, but there was no disguise in death. He hated the work but not as much as Mistress Randolph hated the Confederate officers who took her slaves for the war effort. The colored were not allowed to fight but worked as the slaves they were to build breastworks, bury the dead, and do the work of army mules when there were no more mules left alive.

Mistress had a hissy fit, Hercules remembered, when her number-one blacksmith was included in such a group. "You will be paid, of course," the young lieutenant assured Mistress Randolph. Both knew he was lying.

Hercules remembered the killing fields. The stench was so bad that strong men fainted. Dead bodies rotted in the sun. Some swelled with foul gasses to the point of bursting. Because of his size and strength, he was ordered to dig graves and help carry the bodies to their final resting places.

Hercules was at one end of a long stretcher that could carry up to three bodies, more if only body parts, at one time. The slave holding up the other end of the stretcher collapsed just before they reached the graves, and the bodies rolled onto the ground. Hercules looked around for someone to help him. There was no other living soul within a hundred feet. No Confederate soldier was in sight when he simply turned, walked through the littered battle field, ignored the cries of the wounded and dying, and disappeared into the woods. He never looked back.

Hercules's reminiscence was shattered by the frenzied barks of a dog. He opened the door to the kitchen and found the Rileys in an agitated state. "The cows! We forgot about the cows!" John exclaimed. "Get the lantern, Nate, and come with me. We won't finish milking 'til after dark."

The brothers were already out the door when Nate called back to the girls, "You take care of Badog!"

Hercules stepped out on the porch and watched. A middle-sized brown and white dog was barking and frantically scratching the ashes in the fire pit where Catherine had died. Elizabeth slowly approached the frenzied animal, bent down and extended her hand but kept her distance from the dog. Grace and Elle stood very still several feet behind their sister.

"Good dog, good dog," Elizabeth said softly. "Come on, come on, Badog," she coaxed. "Mama's in the house. Come." The dog stopped barking and slowly walked out of the fire pit. He shook the ashes from his fur and walked up close enough to Elizabeth so she could pet him. She continued to talk softly to him and coaxed Badog to follow her up to the house.

Hercules held the kitchen door open for them, and the dog went directly to the bedroom where Catherine lay. He sniffed around the room then sat on the floor beside her body, lifted his head, and howled. The mournful sound raised goose bumps on the skin of all who heard it.

"We have to eat," Elizabeth said and asked Hercules to go with Grace to the barn and fetch a sack of corn meal. By the time they came back with it, Elle had set the table with clean dishes and utensils, and Elizabeth was frying apples in the butter she found left in the crock. She had put a pot of water to boil on the stove and poured some of the cornmeal in it to make mush. "Thanks goodness Badog has stopped howling. He must be as tired as we are. I'm even too tired to chop white sugar off of the brick. Grace, please find the honey and put it on the table."

It was dark by the time the milkers returned from the barn. John carried a pail of warm milk into the kitchen. Although there were candles on the table, Nate left the lamp burning. The extra light added a warm glow to the room. John asked Hercules to say the blessing before the six of them devoured the fried apples and corn meal mush with fresh milk and honey.

When they finished eating, Elizabeth took a bowl of mush with milk but no honey in to Badog who was keeping vigil at the foot of her mother's bed. The girl gazed at Catherine and thought she looked pretty in her best winter dress. Elizabeth returned to the kitchen in time to hear John say, "Leave the dishes until tomorrow. It's way past time for bed. What about you, Hercules?" he asked.

"I still has work to do," the big man answered. "I got to find da horses da marauders stole from my outfit afor dey runs away. I needs to take care of my own horse an' put him in yo' barn, iffen you don't mind. I can sleep dere in my own bedroll. I'll stay wid y'all for da buryin'. Can I take yo' lantern wid me?"

Nate handed him the lantern. "There's a tin of coal oil in the barn if you need it," he called after Hercules as the big Yankee soldier walked out the door.

The children went together into their mother's bedroom. Except for Elizabeth, they had not seen her body since Hercules had prepared it for burial. Like Elizabeth, they thought she looked pretty and as if she were asleep. Each one kissed her on the forehead and all were about to leave the room for their own beds when Elle stopped them. "Mama sleeps with a pillow," she insisted and stood by while Grace got Catherine's pillow and, with Nate's help, put it under their mother's head.

By the time the harvest moon was high in the sky, five Riley children slept soundly in their beds. Badog remained quiet but on guard at the foot of his mistress's bed. Hercules slept comfortably in his Army-issue bedroll placed on a bed of straw. His horse was content in a barn stall. Before he went to bed, the big man had found the stolen horses picketed in the wood and secured them in the corral for the night.

The family slept later than usual, and when Nate came downstairs, he found Badog waiting patiently at the kitchen door. "Good dog. You don't want a swat on your nose with a dish towel, do you?" Nate said as he opened the door to let the dog out to do his business. The boy heard sounds coming from the barn and walked down there to discover Hercules already at work building a coffin.

"I built many of dese," he explained. "Sometimes we buried da dead in coffins; sometimes we jest put 'em in the graves as dey was. I found dis lumber in dat pile over der an' reckoned I could use it for you' mama's coffin."

Nate nodded his consent. "Can I help you?"

"I could use some more nails," Hercules answered. "You can start on da lid iffen you want."

As the two of them worked side by side, Nate asked the question that had bedeviled him since he saw the former slave in the uniform of a Union Army soldier: "What happened at Fair Oaks that got you turned into a Yankee soldier?"

"Massa Randolph, he goes off to war, and Confederates keep taking slaves off da plantation to work for the army. Mistress had hissy fits ever' time dey come, but cain't do nothin' 'bout it. I was one of da slaves dey took."

"My papa and brothers joined up with Randolph. I guess you wouldn't know them even if you saw them," Nate remarked.

"I didn't see much of live soldiers, jest dead ones. I had enough of dead ones an' one day, I jest ran away. Nobody stopped me. I was runnin' in da woods when I saw a young Yankee officer leadin' a lame horse. He was lost an' as skeered of me as I was skeered of him. We jest looked at each other for a bit an' den I told him his horse wasn't lame. It jest threw a shoe. He musta been a city boy not to figure dat out.

"Anyhow, I told the officer I could shoe his horse iffen I had a shoe. He got all excited 'bout me bein' a blacksmith an' said it was jest what his cavalry outfit needed.

"I knowed where da Confederate Army was, so da two of us led da horse an' walked in da other direction. Jest afore it got dark we saw da campfires of his outfit. I been wid it ever since. Who woulda thought ole Hercules woulda be wearin' a bluebelly uniform! All da soldiers brags dey got da best blacksmith in da army. I keeps da horses well shod an' doctors 'em iffen dey be wounded in da fightin'. Dey gets shot an' cut jest like soldiers. Four of my horses got stole three days ago. My sergeant, he says, 'Hercules, you track down dose sons-a-bitches horse thieves an' hang 'em by der balls.' I catched up wid em here."

"Why did Confederate soldiers do such a terrible thing to our family?" Nate asked. "We're Southerners too."

Hercules spat on the ground. "Dey no soldiers. Dey be marauders. Dey steal an' hurt an' kill for da fun of it. Both sides has 'em. Dey should be hung, no matter da color of der uniforms!"

"Where are their bodies? I didn't see them when I walked down?" Nate said.

"I left dem lay where dey fell last night an' went lookin' for da horses. Found 'em. Dey be in da corral now. Dis mornin' at first light, I stacked da four debils like firewood, then tied 'em on two horses an' took 'em back to a clearin' in da woods I passed through when trackin' 'em. Der be bear tracks all about. I reckon some bears be fat an' happy when dey goes into der caves an' sleeps all winter," Hercules said with a grin.

Nate hammered the last nail in the lid of his mother's coffin. He and Hercules returned to the house and ate the breakfast the girls had prepared. As they sat at the table, John suggested that their mother be buried under the biggest pear tree, her favorite of all the fruit trees in the orchard. Hercules offered to dig the grave, but John wanted to do it by himself. It seemed fair to the others because Nate had helped build her coffin.

Each one of them went about the assigned task deliberately and with great care. Elizabeth, Grace, and Elle selected the quilt in which to wrap their mother's body. It was one Catherine had pieced together from scraps of clothing all of the Rileys, even the parents, had once worn. Badog was underfoot and would have been banished to outdoors under other circumstances. "Just let him be," John said. "He loved Mama as much as we did."

The sun was setting by the time everything was ready. Nate and Hercules carried the coffin up to the house. Together, the five children carefully wrapped their mother's body in the quilt, and John lifted her up off the bed and lovingly placed her in the coffin. Together, they put the coffin's lid in place and each one took a turn to hammer in the nails to secure it.

All of them helped carry the coffin to the orchard. Badog followed. Sunset turned the sky a rosy pink, and Elle said that meant the angels were waiting to carry Mama up to God's heaven.

Hercules stood on one side of the open grave, the five children on the other. They lowered the ropes guiding the coffin to its resting place. Each one took a turn shoveling in the loose dirt as the coffin disappeared from sight and settled at rest deep into the fertile land Catherine loved so well.

Elizabeth reached up into the pear tree, snapped off a small branch, and placed it on the grave. "We'll make a cross tomorrow," Nate reassured them. The children stood in a circle around the mound of rich farm earth and held hands. Together they recited the Twenty-third Psalm learned years before at their mother's knee.

" 'The Lord is my Shepherd, I shall not want. He maketh me to lie down in green pastures. He leadeth me beside the still waters. He restoreth my soul. He leadeth me in the paths of righteousness for his name's sake. Yea, though I walk through the valley of the shadow of death, I will fear no evil for thou art with me; thy rod and thy staff they comfort me. Thou preparest a table before me in the presence of mine enemies; thou anointest my head with oil; my cup runneth over. Surely goodness and mercy shall follow me all the days of my life and I will dwell in the house of the Lord forever.' "

The young mourners felt as if the earth stood still. There were no sounds coming from the creatures of the forest, no noises from the cattle or horses or mules or hogs or chickens.

The hush was broken by a low, sweet voice that melted into the sky as their huge black savior lifted his head to the heavens and softly sang:

"Was you der when dey crucified my Lord?
Was you der when dey nailed him to da cross?
Ohhhhhhhh, ohhhhhhhh, ohhhhhhhh.
It causes me to tremble, tremble, tremble!
Was you der when de crucified my Lord?
Was you der when da sun refused to shine?
Was you der when dey laid him in de tomb?
Ohhhhhhhh, ohhhhhhhh, ohhhhhhhh.
It causes me to tremble, tremble, tremble!
Was you der when dey crucified my Lord?"

All of the Riley children cried until they felt as if they were empty of tears. Elle held her arms up to Hercules who lifted her up and carried her back into the house. Elizabeth and Grace held one another's hand, and John put his arm around Nate's shoulder. Badog settled himself for the night on the new grave.

They were too spent and tired to eat. "Thank you, Hercules. Sleep well, and we'll see you in the morning," Nate said as he started for the loft stairs.

The next morning when Nate went to the barn, Hercules and his horses were gone.

Chapter Thirteen
Homecoming

No one in the family objected when Elizabeth suggest that they allow Badog to sleep in the house in front of the fireplace at night now that the nights were getting colder. The dog's presence was a comfort, especially to the girls. Whoever was up first in the morning would open the kitchen door to let Badog out, and the animal would run around a little before he settled himself on Catherine's grave. He spent less and less time there as the weeks went by and took up his farm dog duties again. He would bring in the cows for milking, retrieve game birds shot by Nate or John, and had learned from painful experience to keep out of a porcupine's path after Nate had to use pliers to pull the quills from his tender nose.

Elizabeth usually fixed breakfast and cleaned up the kitchen after everyone had finished eating and left the table to go about their chores. This morning, she called Badog up to the porch to eat his bowl of food scraps and then went back inside to sweep the kitchen floor with a well-worn broom. She swept the dirt out the door, around Badog, across the porch to its edge, and over the side. She watched the dirt change to particles of dust as it fell to the ground below and knew her mother would have scolded her for such sloppy work.

"Anything worth doing is worth doing well," was only one of the many truisms their mother had etched on the collective conscience of her children. Elizabeth propped the broom next to the kitchen door, stepped over Badog, and sat down on the top porch step. She began to cry. The dog, who had emptied his bowl, came over to her and put his head in her lap.

She petted him absentmindedly and thought, *Mama, why did you die? Don't you know how much we need you? I'm trying my best, but I'm not a mother like you. I try to comfort my sisters and brothers, but I can't do it like you did for us when Jeb and Caleb died. I need someone who can comfort* me. *Am I being too selfish?*

Grace and Elle think I'm bossy, but I only want them to help more than they do. Only five of us are left, only five, and we're supposed to run the farm! John and Nate work all the time and can't get everything done that needs doing. To be fair, I guess Grace and Elle do as much as they can. Sometimes I forget they are the youngest in the family. But Grace is older than Elle, and Grace isn't doing her part.

It wasn't fair when Papa and Matthew and Caleb and Ben left us to go and fight a war someplace. Then you died. I don't think that's fair at all! Why did God let that happen to us? Is He punishing us for being bad? I don't think we're bad. I think we've always tried to do the best that we could.

Elizabeth pushed Badog's head out of her lap and stood up. She wiped her wet eyes on the hem of her dress and brushed her hair from her forehead as she looked down the lane. John was helping his two youngest sisters learn how to milk the cows. "I hope they get better at it. I hate milking cows!" Elizabeth said to Badog. She pointed to the pear tree, "Go, Badog, go tell Mama good morning." The dog sped off to his post, a slight depression in the grave's mound where he had spent so many hours.

Elizabeth squinted both eyes and raised her hand to shade them as she scanned the fields looking for Nate. She saw him driving the wagon with a load of corn stalks into the barn. The boys would chop them into smaller pieces and throw them into the silo where fermentation would change the stalks into silage to feed the stock next year. She felt guilty at not going down to help her brothers unload the wagon but petulantly decided to go back into the house. *Out of sight, out of mind,* she thought.

Then Elizabeth caught sight of something moving far down the lane and wondered what it could be. She skipped down the stairs and broke into an easy run to get a closer look. She made out the figures of two people, one walking and one on horseback. "Grace! Nate! John! Elle! Somebody's coming!" Elizabeth called to them as she ran faster past the barn.

John looked out the wide barn door. "I declare, it does look like somebody might be coming! Let's all take the wagon and see who it is."

Nate turned the wagon around and stopped to let Grace scramble aboard. John lifted Elle up into the wagon bed and sat himself on the seat beside his brother Nate. The horses moved out quickly. Even so, Elizabeth was far ahead of them, and the brothers feared for her safety at the hands of strangers. They saw her stop abruptly and expected her to run back to them for protection. Instead, Elizabeth screamed, "It's Matthew! And Papa's with him!"

She slowed her pace as she came closer to the travelers. Had she not recognized his walk from a distance. Elizabeth would not have known her brother Matthew. His tattered uniform hung loosely on his thin frame. His hair was long and matted, and there were sores around his mouth. She bit her lip and walked up to hug him, filthy clothes and all. "Matthew, we've missed you," she said quietly.

Matthew did not speak. Tears ran down his face as he gently touched his sister's cheek.

"Is the war over?" Elizabeth asked.

"No. I brought Papa home," Matthew answered, his voice choking with emotion and fatigue.

Then she noticed that it was her brother who held the horse's reins in his hand. She slowly approached the animal and put her hand on the rider's knee. "Papa, it's me, Elizabeth."

Her papa's body bent over the saddle. His left hand clutched the pommel. His right arm, crushed and blood-caked, hung limply at his side. "Elizabeth," he answered weakly and slipped out of the saddle just as Nate and John arrived to catch him before he hit the ground.

When they gently lifted their father into the wagon bed, Grace and Elle drew back at the sight of the gruesome stranger. The youngest girl started to cry out of fear and was not comforted when Nate said, "It's Papa, Elle; don't cry. He's hurt. Don't cry, Elle. It's Papa."

Nonetheless, Elle climbed out of the wagon and ran back alone toward the house. Grace scrambled out of the wagon bed and up to the seat where she sat and drew her skirt tightly around her legs.

"Elizabeth, climb up here and stay with Papa while we help Matthew," John directed. He took the horse's reins from his brother's hand and tied them to the back of the wagon. Nate helped John lift Matthew into the wagon bed. Nate sat down next to his oldest brother and gently held him while Elizabeth cradled their father in her arms.

"I'll drive," John said and took his place on the seat beside Grace. He drove the wagon slowly and carefully toward the house. They overtook Elle and stopped to offer her a ride. She refused and continued to walk even though the wagon drove on ahead of her.

Their father was still unconscious as they neared the barn. Matthew had his wits about him and warned the others not to go to the house. "We're full of lice and Mama won't let us in the door like this," he said with a wan smile. "Stop by the fire pit first and de-louse us. Papa's lived this long. He's not likely to die in the next hour."

John would have ignored his brother's warning had he not started to scratch his own head. He stopped the wagon at the fire pit and turned to see his passengers scratching themselves, as well. "Leave Papa and Matthew in the wagon for now," he said. "Nate, get some logs and start a fire while I unhitch the horses and stable them in the barn. Matthew, I'll take your horse to the corral. We have feed and water in the troughs there. Elizabeth, you stay in the wagon with Papa and Matthew. Grace, come with me and we'll bring back buckets from the barn. We're going to need lots of hot water and plenty of soap."

John carried the wash kettle in one hand and two buckets in the other. Grace followed him with two buckets and put them down by the pump where Nate, who had the fire burning, started the pump. When the buckets were full, all three of them carried the water and poured it into the wash kettle that sat on a grate near the firewood just beginning to burn. The three of them returned to the well, pumped their buckets full of water again and set them around the edge of the fire pit close enough for the flames to warm the water.

Grace ran back to the barn to get the pan of soap, held it carefully in both hands, and walked slowly back to where her brothers were working. "Look," she said as she wiggled the flat pan. "The soap's not set up yet 'cause it wiggles like jelly."

Nate carefully took the pan from her. "You're right, Grace. We won't use this on ourselves. The lye would burn our skin, but I think we can wash our clothes with this if we rinse them well." He poured about one-fourth of the glop into the wash kettle. It made suds good enough for killing vermin while cleaning clothes.

John dipped cool water from a clean bucket and gave the dipper to Elizabeth who held it up to the lips of Papa and then passed it to Matthew. She couldn't tell if Papa swallowed any water but when Matthew gave it back to her, the dipper was empty. The water in the other buckets was warm enough for sponge baths and washing hair when Elle came out of the house and cautiously approached the group.

"Elle," John called to his little sister, "I want you to stop right where you are. This is a game, and you can't take another step until I say, 'Go, Elle.' Do you understand?"

She nodded. It was the urgency in his tone of voice that caused Elle to do exactly what her brother said, not the promise of learning a new game. Much of the time, she was deliberately slow to follow directions and took advantage of being the spoiled youngest child, especially since their mother's death.

John walked toward her but stopped ten feet away. "That's good, Elle," he said as his sister stood as still as a fence post. "The next part of the game is very important. You are the only one in the whole family who gets to play this part of the game. None of the rest of us can go inside the house because we have a lot of little bugs in our hair and on our clothes. We're going to have to take our clothes off and boil them in water to get rid of those little bugs."

"Do you have to get your hair boiled too?" Elle asked.

"No, but we have to wash all over ourselves very well before we can come in the house or even give you a hug for doing such a good job," John continued.

"Are all of you going to take off your clothes?" she asked.

"Yes, but you don't need to look at us if you don't want to. Have you ever seen a naked man before?"

'No, but I did peek in Mama's room once and saw Papa. He didn't have any clothes on."

John took a deep breath.

"Boys are different from girls, aren't they, John?" Elle said.

"Yes. Now, Elle, I want you to listen carefully and do what I tell you. First, I want you to go to Mama's medicine cupboard and find the sassafras oil. *Sassafras* starts with an *s* and I think it's in the big jug with a flower painted in blue on the side of it. Then I want you to get the jar of cloves. Do you know what they are?"

"Yes. Mama put cloves in pumpkin pie."

"Good. Then get two bars of hard soap. You'd better find a basket to put everything in. Carry the basket with the sassafras oil, cloves, and hard soap very carefully and bring it out to me. I'm going to draw a line in the dirt right here, and I want you to put the basket right on top of that line. I don't want you to get any closer to us than that. You are the only one of us who doesn't have little bugs. Do you understand?"

"Yes. Are the little bugs spiders?"

"No. They are lice and fleas and maybe some other kinds whose names I don't know right now," her brother answered. "Ready, set, go, Elle!"

The little girl ran quickly up to the house and was out of sight for what seemed to John an hour. Then he saw the door opened slowly as Elle, holding the basket handle with both hands, came out of the house, walked very deliberately across the porch, and wabbled slightly as she balanced her heavy load while walking down the stairs, one step at a time. John had to smile as he watched Elle's serious face when she carefully carried her precious cargo and put it on the line her brother had drawn.

"You did just fine! Now, are you ready for the next part?" She nodded as he continued. "Bring the lantern hanging on the kitchen wall and Mama's scissors. They should be in her sewing basket. Go, Elle!"

"And carry the scissors points down!" Elizabeth called after her.

Elle enjoyed playing the game and waited for the next command after she put the scissors and lantern on the line. "I'm ready!" she said.

"You're going to like the next part," John said. "Now, you get to rest for a little while. I want you to go back inside the house and eat your supper at the table. Call Badog to go with you and remember to feed him too. We're going to clean up Papa and Matthew. When you finish in the kitchen, bring back a jug of sweet apple cider and some cups. You know where to put them."

"On the line!" Elle said with enthusiasm. She called to Badog and the two of them went into the house together.

John returned to the barn and brought back the tarp used to cover the wagon and a half-dozen empty feed sacks. He spread the tarp on the ground near enough to the fire pit to keep them warm. Nate and John helped Matthew from the wagon and sat him down on the tarp where he watched his brothers lift Papa out of the wagon bed and carefully lay him on the tarp.

"Elizabeth," John said, "you're good with scissors. I want you to pretend you're Mr. Hall and cut Papa's hair and beard. Cut as close to his skin as you can without cutting him and then throw the hair into the fire. When you finish with Papa, do the same for Matthew."

Elizabeth did as she was told but gritted her teeth as the vermin crawled on her hands. When she threw locks of human hair into the fire, she shook the lice and fleas from her own hands and shuddered when the hair and insects sizzled as they burned. When she finished the job, she was shaking. John poured a small amount of sassafras oil into the palms of her hands to rub on the scalps and faces of her father and her brother and her own skin.

Elizabeth had tears in her eyes when she asked John the questions. "Do I have to cut off all of my hair?"

"No," John replied. "When we finish with everything here, you can wash your hair with hard soap. Then when it's almost dry, rub a little sassafras oil in it and on your scalp too. Nate and I'll do the same. We'll have to watch each other for nits, the little eggs lice lay in hair. They look like tiny white buds on a pussy willow stalk. If we see any, I'll help you comb nits out of your hair before they hatch. You can do the same for Nate and me. That's what Mama did when Matthew got lice from wearing another boy's cap at school. That was before you were born."

"What about Grace? Will she get lice too?" she asked.

"She wasn't as close to the bugs as we were, but she'll need to wash her hair and take a bath anyway. We'll watch for nits in her hair too. You and Grace go up by the porch and wash your hair." He handed each girl a bucket of warm water. "You can share the soap. Don't go inside the house just yet, but you can sit on the porch steps until I call you. I'll need you to fill up your buckets again at the pump and bring the water back to us here by the fire pit. And don't forget to bring the hard soap back with you.,"

After the girls left, John took out his knife, cut off the metal buttons on Papa's and Matthew's ragged uniforms, and put them in his pocket. Nate helped him strip the vermin-infested clothes from the soldiers and throw them into the sizzling fire. Nate brought back two buckets of water warmed by the fire while John covered the private parts of the men with feed sacks. He called the girls to bring the soap and put the newly-filled buckets near the fire pit to warm the water.

Elizabeth and Grace averted their eyes after their first glances at the emaciated bodies of their kin. "Come on, Grace," Elizabeth said as she took her sister's hand. "Let's go to the barn and see if the horses have enough hay."

John and Nate carefully washed the filth of war from the bodies of their father and their brother, men whom they loved dearly and desperately needed to make their family partly whole again. They patted them dry with the feed sacks and then rubbed sassfras oil on every part of their bodies except for Papa's still-bandaged arm.

"Elle," John called. "Come out. We need you for our game again."

Their youngest sister still stood on a stool in front of the kitchen window where she had seen everything that happened at the fire pit. Elle, eager to be part of the group again, jumped down from her perch, ran outside, and put her feet next to the line in the dirt. She stopped and listened to her brothers talking among themselves. Elle heard Matthew ask them a question: "Where's Mama?"

When Nate and John didn't answer him, Elle thought they were not being polite. "Mama's under the pear tree," she offered. "A bad man killed her."

Matthew gasped in disbelief. His head dropped forward, and he slumped over as if the life had gone out of his body.

Nate grabbed him by the shoulders and shook him. "Matthew! Matthew! You can't die too! Matthew!"

The oldest brother raised his head and looked Nate squarely in the eye. "Then it's up to you! You'll have to do it now that Mama's gone!" Matthew put his face in his hands and wept.

His two brothers fought their own tears. John was the first to regain his composure. He called to Elizabeth and Grace who were coming up from the barn. "We need you now. Grace, go back to the house with Elle and help her bring out some clean clothes for us. Matthew has grown as big as Papa, so bring two of Papa's shirts and trousers if you can find them. Nate and I are going to wash ourselves, so we need clean clothes and some towels too. Elizabeth, you need to take your clothes off here and throw them in the wash kettle. Rub sassafras oil all over your skin, then cover yourself with a feed sack. I think you can bathe in the bathtub inside. Don't worry; we won't watch."

Elizabeth picked up a feed sack, went behind the privy where no one could see her, and emerged holding the feed sack around her body and carrying her clothes on the end of a long stick. She dumped them in the sudsy hot water in the wash kettle.

Grace and Elle walked carefully down from the house, their arms filled with clothes and towels. They stacked them neatly on a clean spot on the tarp. "You look funny!" Elle smirked as she pointed to Elizabeth. "You don't have any clothes on, just a feed sack. That's not clothes!"

"Elle, hush!" Elizabeth admonished as she grabbed her little sister's arm with one hand and held tightly to the covering feed sack with the other. "We're going in the house and get in the bathtub. I'm going to scrub you good with soap, and I might use a little of it to wash out your mouth."

Elle turned and called back to her brothers, "I get to take my bath in the bathtub, but Matthew and Papa didn't. You took off all of their clothes and . . ." Elizabeth pulled her through the kitchen door.

The brothers laughed. John and Nate stripped off their clothes and tossed them into the hot soapy wash water. They scrubbed themselves from head to toe and rubbed sassafras oil in their scalp and over their bodies. While Nate finished dressing, John poured sweet cider in the cups and held one to Papa's lips. He didn't respond to drink. Matthew drank his cider quickly and Papa's portion, as well. Nate and John emptied their cups, and the sweet cider gave them energy.

As they finished their brief respite from the grueling day, Matthew said quietly, "Mama's gone, so you'll have to do it, Nate. You'll have to cut off Papa's arm. When the cannonball hit him, I knew I had to bring him home to Mama. He would have died for sure if those army surgeons touched him. They are butchers, and the hospital is like a slaughterhouse. Arms and legs stack up like firewood when they're chopped off. At night, I still hear the screams of those pitiful brave soldiers. Some of them pray to God to die because they suffer so. I tore off part of a tent to wrap Papa's arm. The canvas was dirty but not as filthy as hospital bandages. They are in such short supply, the doctors take bandages off dead men and use them again on the wounded."

He stopped talking when Elizabeth, wearing clean clothes, came out of the kitchen. She carried a pot of stew. Grace followed with bowls and spoons. They were quiet as they served the food to their brothers. Elle was not far behind them but stopped at the line and put down the quilt her sisters asked her to bring. Papa was breathing. His eyes were closed, but Nate was encouraged when he forced a half-teaspoon of stew gravy between his lips and Papa swallowed it.

After some discussion, the brothers devised a plan. They did not dress Papa but wrapped him in the quilt. John guessed the wagon was alive with lice, so he carried his father to the barn. Nate helped support Matthew as they walked slowly behind them. The three girls walked on ahead and prepared a bed of straw for their father. John thanked his sisters for their help and told them to go back to the house and stay there. "The barn's too far away to see much from the kitchen window," he said with a smile and put Papa down on the straw.

Matthew and John sat on a hay bale and watched Nate get ready to remove the improvised bandage from Papa's arm. He soaked the stiff and bloody tent canvas until it was pliable. When he unwrapped it, the brothers gagged from the putrid stench of gangrene.

Papa's right hand was completely gone. The bones as far up as his elbow were shattered and their sharp pieces pierced his discolored, blotched skin.

Nate rose to his feet and turned his head. "I can't do this."

John grasped his brother's shoulders with more strength in his hands than he knew he had. "Nate, Mama's dead. She said you were as good at doctoring as she was. I believed her. If you don't do this, you make Mama out to be a liar!"

Nate nodded his head but said nothing.

"I have the meat saw ready. It's clean," John said.

Matthew spoke in a stronger voice. "I'll stay right here with you and show you where to cut. I watched when the stumps of men's arms or legs were dipped in hot tar to stop the bleeding. Mama wouldn't have done that. What would you have done, Nate?"

Nate took a deep breath and said, "Capsicum stops bleeding. I'd have a pan of capsicum and put the arm in it until the bleeding stopped. I'd not move it for about an hour. Then I'd make a poultice out of dried heliotrope root, some more capsicum, and honey. That's what Mama used when we doctored a big old slave once." Nate decided he wouldn't tell Matthew the particulars of Mama's death just now.

"Do you have the medicines you need?" Matthew asked.

"Yes. You stay here with Papa. I'll go to the house and get everything. John, will you get two lanterns? If we're going to do this, it has to be tonight. I'll need you both when I cut off Papa's arm. I don't think he'll live until morning."

Matthew sat beside his father as his two brothers left to complete their tasks. Soon Nate, carrying a large basket of medicines and herbs, walked out the kitchen door and started toward the barn. He was followed by Elizabeth who carried two quilts. Grace carried pans and knives, points down, and Elle carried Mama's sewing basket. The little girl picked up the scissors John had left by the fire pit and put them, points down, in the sewing basket. When the procession arrived at the barn, Nate thanked his sisters again for their help and ordered them to bed.

The brothers lifted their father on to a makeshift table they devised. It was made of three wide pieces of lumber tied together with rope and placed on three barrels, one at each end and one in the middle.

Nate washed Papa's upper arm with a cool chickweed brew. Matthew pointed three inches above the elbow to indicate the spot where Nate was to sever Papa's right arm. Nate forced his mind to remember how to butcher a cow. He took the clean sharp hunting knife John handed him and sliced through the skin and muscles. When he felt the knife stop, he spread the flesh apart and saw the ghostly white bone. Nate exchanged the knife for the saw and quickly separated the upper arm bone. He switched back to the knife to complete the disection. The body part fell to the dirt floor as John held clean cloths against their father's raw flesh to stem the blood flow.

Matthew pinched the artery walls while Nate quickly stitched them together with needle and thread he took from the sewing basket. Then Nate thrust the bloody stump into a pan of capsicum. The blood mingled with the ground red chili peppers. The brothers watched the flow of blood change the powder to a darker hue which spread almost to the sides of the pan and then stopped.

Matthew looked up at Nate, whose face was ashen, and smiled. "The bleeding has stopped," he said with awe.

Nate began to shake, but he found his voice. "Don't move anything for an hour." He moved away from the makeshift table, washed most of the blood from his hands and arms, and splashed water on his face.

John, who could not speak, washed the knife and saw, put them on a hay bale to dry, and disappeared. After he vomited outside away from the barn, John saw the things Elizabeth had left for them near the fire pit. He was grateful to her as he lifted the handle of the hot coffee pot with a folded-up feed sack and balanced the three cups in his other hand. He was careful not to spill the precious chicory coffee. When he got back to the barn and filled the cups with the fragrant dark liquid, the three brothers raised their cups in salute to each other. All three held their cups with shaking hands.

They took turns standing watch over Papa during the night. When the sun came up, Nate lifted his father's stump of an arm out of the pan and was relieved to find the blood well coagulated and his father still breathing. He placed his hand gently on his patient's forehead and felt fever. Nate mixed a poultice from some of the contents of his medicine basket, spread it on a clean piece of muslim and wrapped his father's stump. He poured a small amount of chickweed tea he had made during the night into his coffee cup and spooned the liquid into his father's mouth. While some ran out the sides of his mouth and onto his chin, Papa swallowed most of it.

Matthew woke and went to his father's side. He rejoiced to see the man still alive, clean, and with a poltice neatly tied to what was left of the man's arm. "Papa's going to be all right, Nate," he said and put his arm around his young brother. "Go up to the house and get some breakfast. I'll stay with Papa and clean up the mess while you're gone."

Nate did not need a second invitation. As he ate breakfast, he reported Papa's condition to his sisters and almost as an aside, mentioned that Papa now had a good one-half of his right arm. Elizabeth and Grace understood what he meant and exchanged knowing glances.

When Nate got up from the table to relieve his brothers so they could come to breakfast. Elizabeth said, "We want to bury Papa's arm by Mama under the pear tree."

Her sisters nodded in agreement. "And we want to wrap it in this," Grace added. She held out a quilted pillow top. "This was supposed to go with Mama's quilt, the one we wrapped her in, but she never got it finished before she died."

Nate took the pillow top in both hands and examined the tiny stitches. He remembered the hours his mother had spent in quilting and how much it had pleasured her. "It's beautiful," he said and carried it back with him to the barn.

When Nate was in the house, John dug a deep hole far back in the woods and helped Matthew bury the shattered arm and other bloody residue from Nate's surgery. John filled the hole and spread brush and leaves on top so the spot would go undetected. He doubted any animal with a keen smell would bother it.

Although the brothers had shoveled out the bloody dirt floor and replaced it with clean hard ground, the putrid smell still lingered. It made the horses nervous, and John had already taken them out and let them loose in the field. He was suspicious of the army horse in the corral and wanted to examine the animal for disease and vermin before it had contact with any of the Riley livestock.

Nate showed his brothers the quilted pillow top and explained the sisters' wishes.

"Wrap a piece of wood in it and make a wooden box to fit," Matthew said. "We won't tell the girls the difference. As far as they'll know, Papa's arm will be buried next to Mama."

Nate walked over to the straw bed and put his hand on Papa's forehead. He still had a fever, but Nate was pleased that his breathing was steady and no sign of blood darkened the poultice bandage. He bent over to sniff the stump of the arm and detected no smell of gangrene.

He told Matthew and John to go to breakfast. While they were gone, Nate found some rough cedar lumber and planed it down to make a small and simple coffin, an "arm coffin," he thought wryly. He brushed up the cedar shavings and spread them around on the barn floor in the hope that their pleasant odor would mask any lingering odors from the surgery.

Grace sent down strong chickweed and gingeroot tea which Nate spooned into Papa's mouth every two hours. By early afternoon, his father could sip from a cup when Nate slightly elevated his head. Papa opened his eyes a few times but made no sound.

While Matthew carved a small cross out of a cedar wood scrap, John scoured out the wagon bed until he was sure there were no fleas, lice, or any other living thing on board. Even though there were no visible pests on their bodies, all of the Rileys were generous with their continued use of sassafras oil. Before nightfall, Nate decided Papa could tolerate a trip to the the house if they were careful when they lifted him in and out of the wagon.

When the wagon slowly stopped in front of the porch steps, the girls held the doors open as John carefully carried their father into the house, to his bedroom, and gently laid him on the immaculate bed. Although he was too weak to speak, Papa did open his eyes and his children wanted to believe that he knew he was back in his own bed.

John worked out a schedule so that one of them would be with Papa at all times. Nate asked to be on first watch so he could be alert to any signs of deterioration in Papa's condition that may have been caused by the move from the barn to the house.

Grace brought supper to Nate sitting in the bedroom. He heard his family talking at the supper table and the comforting ordinary sounds they made as they cleaned up from supper and prepared for bed. Elizabeth was in her nightgown when she brought a small bowl of chicken soup.

"I made this for Papa," she said. "I wrung the chicken's neck myself. Elle cried when the chicken was jumping all over, but she did help me pluck the feathers. I told her she had to if she wanted to see what a naked chicken looked like."

"My story made you smile," she said to her brother, "but it really is true."

"I believe you," he answered. "I wish I had seen it myself. You always ran and hid your eyes when any of us killed a chicken. I wish Papa had seen it. He'll never believe it when I tell him how this soup came to be. Thank you, Elizabeth. I'll feed him right away."

Elizabeth kissed her brother on his forehead and went to her own bed. Nate held Papa's head up and carefully lifted the bowl to his lips. His father slowly swallowed half the soup. Nate thought he saw a slight smile as he eased Papa's head back onto the pillow. Nate reconsidered and decided the change in Papa's facial expression was caused by gas pains, not pleasure.

Around midnight, John took Nate's place at Papa's bedside.

"If he wakes, try to get him to swallow some of this chickweed and gingeroot tea," Nate whispered as he pointed out the pitcher on the table. He hadn't realized how spent he was until he climbed the stairs and crawled, still fully clothed, into his bed. He had a start as he saw a shape in Matthew's bed until he realized that his oldest brother really was home again.

Nate was still asleep when Grace shook him awake. "Matthew says to come down now. He's watching Papa."

Nate was barefooted when he flew down the stairs and into Papa's room. "I think his fever broke," Matthew said. "The bedding's damp, but Papa feels cool to me." Nate felt his skin and nodded in agreement.

As his son caressed his face, Papa opened his eyes. "Am I dead?" he whispered.

"No, Papa," Matthew whispered back, "you're home. Both of us are home."

"I don't hear the gunfire," Papa said.

"That's because you're home in your own bed. The war is over for you and me, Papa." He gently held his father's thin hand in his own. "Let's get you something to eat."

Nate left the room, went to the kitchen, and told the girls their father was awake. "Don't go in just yet," he cautioned. "Papa's not himself, but he is hungry. Elizabeth?"

His sister knew what he wanted and handed him a bowl of chicken soup. Nate thanked her and asked her to brew some more medicinal tea. "I'm going to change the poultice on Papa's arm and I'll be back to mix it," he said. "Let John sleep as long as he wants. It's been a long night. Matthew will soon be ready for his breakfast."

Nate applied his fresh poultice to Papa's stump and rewrapped it while Matthew ate in the kitchen. As a soldier, he was not accustomed to keeping regular hours and didn't feel the need for sleep. He complimented his sisters on his breakfast of eggs, fatback, fried apples, biscuits, and even the dried okra coffee.

Elizabeth explained that they saved the chickory blend for emergencies and asked her brother why he took such small servings of food. "Don't you like my cooking?" she said defensively.

"Your cooking is almost as good as Mama's. It's so good my poor old stomach, used to mealy hard tack and rancid salt pork, would throw up good food until it got used to small amounts at one time," Matthew replied only half in jest.

He invited his sisters to sit at the table with him even though they had eaten long before. "Tell me," he said slowly, "about the bad man that killed Mama."

Elle started to talk, but Elizabeth put her hand over her little sister's mouth. "We can't tell you. You need to ask John or Nate," Elizabeth said as she took her hand away from Elle's lips.

"But a big black soldier helped us!" Elle blurted before she scampered away from the table.

"That part's true," Grace added, "but you still had better ask Nate or John."

"Ask me what?" John said as he entered the kitchen, poured himself some coffee, and sat at the table. He served himself from the plates of food on the table.

"I want to know how Mama died," Matthew said. "And what is this about a big black soldier?"

John drank from his coffee cup. "Grace, it's time for you and Elle to milk the cows. Elizabeth, you could help us a lot if you made up our beds. We didn't get much sleep last night."

When the sisters had left to do their chores, John told Matthew everything about the day Mama was killed and the general story again of how Mama had saved the life of the slave called Hercules. "Nate was there, and he can tell you more about him than I can. One thing I can tell you is that all of us would be dead if that Yankee soldier hadn't come along."

Matthew was silent when he poured himself half a cup of coffee and filled the rest of the cup with cream. "I needed to know everything that happened, and I'm grateful to you, John, for being honest about it. I thought I was accustomed to death. Papa and I have seen so much of it these past years. But I never thought it would be Mama. Come to think of it, Mama died because of the war." He paused, drained his cup, and started for the kitchen door. "When

Papa's better, I want to be the one to tell him. Now, let's wrap that 'arm' in the pillow top and nail the coffin's lid on tight."

John followed Matthew and picked up a thin, short piece of firewood. He wrapped it in the quilted piece, placed it in the arm coffin and spread straw around it so the "arm" wouldn't rattle. Matthew held the lid in place while John hammered it closed. He knew his sisters would be disappointed if they didn't get to hammer, so he held out three nails, one for each of them, and carried the hammer and a shovel with him to Mama's grave under the pear tree. Matthew followed with the small coffin in his arms.

While John dug the hole at the foot of Mama's grave, Badog sniffed at the small coffin. It was of no interest to him, and the dog ran to the house when he heard Elizabeth call him to the full bowl of food scraps on the porch.

Matthew followed Badog, went into the house, and told his sisters the time had come to bury Papa's arm. He stuck his head in the bedroom and asked Nate to come out. The brothers agreed that Papa, who was sleeping, could be left for the short time the arm funeral was expected to take.

It was a solemn event. Each sister hammered a nail in the coffin's lid. Elle insisted on choosing the song this time. They sang three verses of "Yankee Doodle" as Nate and John, on their stomachs, lowered the coffin into the ground. John shoveled the dirt back in as Badog howled. The family members held hands and recited the "Lord's Prayer." Elle patted Mama's grave and whispered that Papa could rub her back like he always used to do. All of them, except Matthew, remembered their other family funeral and Hercules's song.

* * *

Papa grew stronger every day. By week's end, he sat up to eat and struggled to feed himself with his left hand without spilling any food. He seemed to be aware of what was going on around him but said little and asked no questions. By the end of the second week since the loss of his arm, Nate was relieved to see a sturdy scab covering the raw flesh at the end of the stump of his arm. John and Nate helped him out of bed and held his good arm as he walked around the room.

Before long, Papa was walking with their help into the kitchen where he sat in the rocking chair and exercised his muscles by pushing the chair to rock back and forth.

The following week, Nathan Riley walked by himself, much to the consternation of his daughters, from the rocking chair to the table and sat down. Elle brought him a cup of chicory coffee which he sipped while Elizabeth finished making supper.

"Elle," her sister said, "you can ring the dinner bell tonight." The little girl stepped out on the porch and rang the bell with gusto until Elizabeth opened the kitchen door and yelled. "That's enough, Elle! Enough! Enough!"

The other Rileys walked up to the house, covered their ears with their hands, and laughed as they teased their little sister. Elle hid behind Papa's chair. Elizabeth smiled and felt grateful for their little joke. *There aren't many smiles around here like there used to be,* she thought.

The family members were surprised and delighted to see Papa sitting in his place at the table. They greeted him warmly. "I get to eat Elle's supper," Nate announced, a remark that quickly brought her out of hiding and into her chair.

After the blessing and before Elizabeth started passing the food, Papa spoke in a strong voice. "Thank you, Matthew, for my life. Thank you, Nate. Your mother taught you well. I would be lying next to her but for you, John, and Elizabeth and Grace and you, Elle."

"But your arm is, anyway," Elle offered. Grace kicked her under the table.

"Matthew told me everything, and I'm grateful to know how it all happened. But I like Elle's story too."

There was a moment of silence at the table. Then Elizabeth asked, "What, exactly did Elle tell you, Papa?"

"She said you were going to make apple butter and the Devil doesn't like apple butter so he sent some of his devil helpers to spank everybody and then there was a big fight and Mama got killed and the angels came from heaven and told us not to cry 'cause Mama likes heaven and watches us just the same and that God has a black face."

Matthew cleared his throat and said, "It could happen."

Elle said, "Please pass the biscuits."

The mid-morning sun banished the chill from the air as his sons loaded the rocking chair into the wagon and helped their father up to the wagon seat. Nate and Matthew sat behind and held Papa so he wouldn't fall. John drove slowly to the orchard where they unloaded the rocking chair by their mother's grave and helped Papa down. "Leave me," he said softly as he settled into the chair. "Your mother and I have a lot to talk about."

Chapter Fourteen
Elizabeth

When Nate, still in bed, felt the heat from the rays of the low winter sun spilling in through the loft's window and onto his face, he pulled the quilt up over his head. The act held the sunlight at bay but failed to shield him from the morning sounds on the Riley farm.

He heard someone fixing breakfast in the kitchen and someone, probably John, chopping wood outside. Two of his sisters were arguing. He could hear the tone of their voices but few of their words. *If I don't open my eyes,* he thought, *I won't have to get up.*

He was unaware of his youngest sister's stealthy climb up the stairs. Nate instinctively pulled his knees up when he felt her tickles on his feet. Elle laughed as her small hands searched again under the quilt for his toes. "Elizabeth said to tell you she's going to feed your breakfast to the hogs if you're not in the kitchen in one minute."

"Grrrrr! I'm a big brown bear sleeping in my cave, and you, little human girl, woke me up. I'm going to eat YOU for breakfast!" Nate yelled as he threw off the covers, grabbed his little sister, and tickled her until she laughed so hard she cried. He released his grip and Elle escaped. He heard her still laughing all the way down the stairs.

The floor was cold on his bare feet as Nate, reluctantly, got out of bed and quickly gathered his clothes hanging from the wooden pegs on the wall. There were never enough pegs for their clothes when five brothers shared the room. Nate gently touched the pegs now left empty in memory of the ones who died. *Empty wooden pegs are sorry tombstones for Ben and Caleb,* he thought. *We need to bring them home. Mama won't lie peaceful in her grave 'til then, and Matthew might remember how to laugh again.*

Nate dressed quickly and sat down on the sun-warmed spot on his bed to put on his shoes and stockings. He wondered how long

John and Matthew had been up and hoped he was not in for a tongue-lashing from Papa for being lazy. He poured icy water from the pitcher into the wash basin and cupped his hands to splash it on his face. He dried his hands on his hair to slick it down and carelessly ran his fingers instead of a comb through the damp strands. So tall, he had to bend over to glance in the mirror for a self-check of his speedy grooming. The image reflected was that of a careless young man's strained and sorrowful face crowned by a shock of unkempt sandy red hair.

Nate gasped and stepped out of the mirror's view. *If I came downstairs looking like this, Mama wouldn't let me sit at the table. She'd make me eat out in the pen with the hogs,* he thought. *It doesn't matter now.* He sat again on the side of his bed. Tears welled up in his eyes as he looked at the two empty beds still made up as if Caleb and Jeb were coming home tomorrow. *Well, Mama,* he thought, *maybe you're all up there together in heaven.*

Nate returned to the mirror, carefully combed his damp hair, and tucked his shirt in his trousers. He hung his nightshirt on a peg and carefully smoothed the covers of his bed the way their mother had taught her sons as well as her daughters. The task was automatic and as Nate worked, he spoke aloud to his mother as if she were standing in the room and checking on his work.

"Mama, did you hear Elle laugh when I tickled her? There hasn't been much laughter in this room for a long time. We used to laugh all the time. Matthew was always playing jokes on us. It's not the same Matthew who lives here now. It's a different person. John and I try to play tricks and joke with him, but it's not much use. He seems filled up with sadness. We tell him the war and the killing and the dying aren't his fault. We tell him that he's a hero for bringing Papa home alive. I don't know what we would do without Matthew and Papa.

"You know about Papa, don't you? Mama, the hardest thing I ever did in my life was cut off the bad part of his arm. I told Matthew I couldn't do it, but he said I had to or Papa would die for sure. He said, next to you, I was the best doctor he knew and a hell of a lot—excuse me, Mama—better than those butchers in the army hospital. Matthew told me to think about everything you taught me, Mama, to quiet myself down and if I listened, I would hear you whisper to me and I would know just what to do so Papa would not die. Mama, I couldn't see you, but I could feel you standing right there beside me and guiding my hands when I cut and sawed and sewed up what was left of my own father's arm.

"Thank you, Mama. Papa's alive. He never was a talkative man, still isn't, but you should see him. Maybe you do. Even though he has only one good arm and a stump for the other, he can outwork any man with two. When he catches one of us doing something he thinks is wrong, he bellows just as loud as he always did. He doesn't take the strop to us boys or whup us upside the head anymore. He's easier on the girls like he has always been. He misses you so much, Mama. He misses Jeb and Caleb too. Every night after supper, he goes down to the orchard and sits by your grave under the pear tree just to visit, I guess.

"Papa probably told you the harvest is way down. The main reason is we've not been able to get hold of much seed. You remember we bought most of our seed from Mr. Sowell. Who would have thought seed for planting would be hard to come by in Tennessee! Well, it is and so is just about everything else in the whole South.

"We delivered only half a wagonload of fruit to Mr. Sowell this fall. His store was almost empty, but the town was full of people. Some of them were stuck there waiting for the train. Seems like the Yankees pulled up and bent the tracks up the line someplace, and no one knows when the train will run again.

"I saw a lot of soldiers milling about trying to act like they know what's going on. I swear it makes my eyes tear up to see so many men who once were soldiers just doing the best they can with crutches for legs and stumps for arms. I think Papa is doing better than any of them, and he knows it too. Maybe I shouldn't tell you this, but we're losing the war, Mama. No one says it, but everyone knows it deep down inside.

"Papa told us you said that someday food would be more valuable than gold. You were right. The extra root cellars and the other spring house we built before the war started still hold a goodly supply of food. You'll be glad to know that your family still eats well. We could even feed another family, if it comes to that, I think.

"We still have a dozen chickens and a breeding pair of hogs. We're down to only four cows and the bull. At least, we know the thieves were smart enough not to tangle with that mean old bull. All of the other cattle were stolen. We don't know if the thieves were marauders, soldiers, or our neighbors. It wasn't Mr. Morris, who never got along with Papa. He died last year of the pneumonia and anyway, most of the thieving didn't start until after that.

"We keep the horses in the corral during the day when we're not working them and bring them into the barn at night. One of us takes a gun and sleeps in the barn. We take turns so there is always somebody watching out for things. Papa thinks Elizabeth is old enough to take her turn on watch because we are short two brothers, and he is having John teach her how to shoot a rifle. She's not too happy about it, but he tells me she's getting to be a pretty good shot.

"Come to think of it, she's not too happy about anything these days. Mama, I wish I knew more about girls and women. Elizabeth used to drive me near crazy with her talking. The only time she was quiet was when she was asleep. But Grace told me that Elizabeth even talks in her sleep! Can you imagine that! Well, Elizabeth doesn't talk much now. If I say something to her, instead of snapping back with a fifteen-minute speech, she just starts to cry, runs into her room, and slams the door! Grace says she doesn't talk in her sleep anymore, but she does groan a lot and makes a funny sound like she's grinding her teeth and . . ."

"Nate Riley! You lazy thing!" Elizabeth screamed up from the bottom of the stairs, "Grace is carrying your breakfast out to the hog pen!"

Nate skipped stairs on his way down through the kitchen and out the door, but he was too late. He reached the hog pen as Grace was throwing his breakfast into the slop trough. "Grace! Why did you do that?" he shouted as he shook his finger in his sister's face.

She shoved the empty bowl into Nate's hand. "Here! You take it back! Elizabeth is the boss around here! You have to do what she says or she'll scream at you!" Grace started to cry.

Nate put the bowl on the ground, knelt down, and put his arm around his sister. "I'm sorry, Grace. I shouldn't have yelled at you. It's not your fault."

"You don't have your coat on," Grace sobbed and whispered into his shoulder. "You'll catch your death." She slipped two cold biscuits into her brother's hand and ran back to the house. She said nothing to her sisters and walked straight to the fireplace. She turned her back to the flames and lifted her skirt. The heat banished the goosebumps on her skin and as her young backside warmed, Grace sighed and thanked God that she was a girl who wore dresses and not a boy.

As the family members went about their routine tasks, the ill will of the morning events evaporated in the sunshine of a cloudless winter's day. At Elizabeth's request, Nate went to one of the hidden root cellars and brought back apples for the cobbler she wanted to bake for supper. As the oldest sister, she planned the meals but had help with the cooking. Although the Riley men could cook, clean-up after meals fell to the women. Elizabeth and her sisters felt it fair and preferred doing the dishes to mucking out the barn.

Elizabeth hummed to herself as she cored and pared the apples. After rolling out the pie crust, she used a table knife to scrape the un-needed flour from the board into a small bowl. She added a little water, stirred it with her finger, and gave the bowl of flour paste to Elle who sat with Grace at the kitchen table.

Her youngest sister smeared a bit of paste on her pointer finger, spread it on a triangular piece of blue cloth, and carefully pressed the paste side down on a wide, flat strip of bark. "I'm making something pretty for Nate," Elle explained, "because it's my fault he didn't get any breakfast. I should have held his hand and made him come downstairs with me." She reached into the basket for another piece of cloth among the scraps left over from sewing. "I wish Mama taught me how to sew before she died," Elle sighed.

"Mama taught me, and I'll teach you," Elizabeth offered as she pushed the cobbler into the oven. *It's so much easier to bake on Mama's stove than in the fireplace,* she thought.

"Mama taught us lots of things," Grace added as she continued to practice writing numbers and alphabet letters on a well-worn slate. "Do you know something, Elle? Elizabeth and I are going to be your teachers just like Mama was our teacher when we were little like you. Then when you're bigger like us, you can ride the horse to school with us. All three of us can fit on Brownie's back, I think. What do you think, Elizabeth?"

Elizabeth looked stricken but nodded her head. "Watch my cobbler," she said as she put on her coat and walked out the kitchen door. She passed Matthew who was splitting logs at the wood pile and headed straight for the barn. There she found Nate sitting on a milk stool and mending tack. John was greasing wagon wheels, and Papa, using one hand, was mucking dirty straw out of the stalls.

Elizabeth ran directly to her father and shouted, "Papa, you are a liar, a liar! You said you would always take care of us and you went away! Mama is a liar! She said she would take care of us and she died! I am a liar, a liar! I said I would take care of us and I can't!"

His oldest daughter pushed her startled father so hard, he fell backwards into the dirty straw. Elizabeth, tears streaming down her face, turned and ran from the barn. She passed Matthew and ran into the privy and slammed the door.

"What's the matter?" John asked as he and Nate helped the father up out of the straw and to his feet. "Are you all right?"

"I'm not hurt, but what's the matter with Elizabeth? She's never acted this crazy! Is she sick! Have you two done anything to her?" Papa demanded.

"No. I don't know what's wrong with her," answered Nate. "It's been impossible to get along with her lately. We used to be good friends and now she treats me like her biggest enemy."

Matthew, out of breath, came running into the barn. "What happened? What's wrong with Elizabeth?"

"We don't know," answered John. "Did you see where she went, Matthew?"

"She ran past me to the privy, went inside, and slammed the door. Do you think she's sick?"

"I don't know. I'd better see if I can talk to her." When Nate sprinted from the barn he saw Grace on the porch.

She called to him, "Where's Elizabeth? I think the cobbler might be done. She'd better look at it or tell me what she wants me to do."

"You'd best take it out of the oven, Grace. Be careful and don't burn yourself. No, don't do that. Wait a minute." Nate called back to John still in the barn, "John, get yourself to the kitchen. Grace needs help. We don't need a raw cobbler for supper or a burned one spilled on the kitchen floor."

As he got closer to the privy, Nate slowed down, breathed deeply to catch his breath and calm himself, and walked slowly up to the privy door. "Elizabeth, Grace thinks the apple cobbler is about done. What do you want her to do next?" he asked.

No answer came from the privy.

"Elizabeth, are you all right?"

Still no answer.

"Elizabeth, have I done something to hurt your feelings?"

"No."

"Has anyone done something to make you feel bad?"

"No."

"Elizabeth, are you sick?"

Nate heard his sister sobbing. "Elizabeth?"

He strained to hear her whispered answer.

"I'm dying."

"You're WHAT?"

"Dying."

"Why do you say that? What makes you think so?"

"I'm bleeding to death," she said between sobs.

"Elizabeth, open the door and come out. I'm a good doctor. You know that. Come out and let me help you. We need to talk about this," Nate implored.

"No. I just want you to go away," she answered.

"It's not like you to be a silly girl, Elizabeth. I want you to open that door and come out this very minute!" her brother demanded.

"I'm staying right here 'til I die. You can't do anything about it. Now go away and leave me alone."

Nate sighed. "All right. I'll go if you promise me one thing."

"What?"

"That you won't kill yourself by sticking your head down the hole." Nate gagged as he said it.

Elizabeth paused and thought for a moment. "All right. I'll promise if you'll promise to bury me under the pear tree next to Mama."

"Promise." Nate turned and walked away to meet Papa and Matthew coming up from the barn.

The three Riley men spoke for a few minutes and decided to leave Elizabeth alone. Papa went back to the house and into the girls' bedroom. Elizabeth slept alone in her own bed now, and what he saw on her quilt confirmed his suspicions. He went back into the kitchen and called out the door to Matthew and Nate, "Hitch up the buggy."

Their father returned to his bedroom and washed up. He put on clean clothes and his best coat and hat. When he returned to the kitchen, he told John, Grace, and Elle not to wait supper. "I'll be back before sundown. Your sister is in the privy and won't come out. Leave her alone. You all can use the woods if nature calls." Without another word, he went outside, climbed into the buggy his sons had brought up to the house, and left his children wondering what their father was going to do. They watched the buggy until it disappeared around a bend in the lane.

"The apple cobbler is done. John took it out of the oven for me," Grace announced.

Matthew took charge of supper, something he had not done since cooking as a soldier in the field. He warmed over the turkey Nate has killed earlier in the week and served up cornbread dressing, gravy, pickled beets, black beans and rice, biscuits with butter and blackberry jam and apple cobbler still warm from the oven.

There was little suppertime conversation, partly because of fatigue from hard physical labor and partly due to worry. No one knew what had gotten into Elizabeth. About every half hour, one of them quietly went up to the privy door and listened for sounds of Elizabeth's breathing, crying, or any little noise that would assure them she was still alive. Papa ordered them to leave her alone, and they did.

About a half hour before sundown, the children saw Papa returning. There was a woman beside him in the buggy and as they grew closer, Nate said, "I think she might be the Widow Morris." They watched Papa stop the buggy by the privy and help the woman down. She carried a large carpet bag and simply stood there while Papa got back in the buggy and drove up to the house.

"Nate, get the rocking chair and carry it out to the Widow Morris so the lady can sit down. Matthew, take care of the buggy and the horse. John, light a lamp and carry it out to her before it gets dark. Sit it on the ground and make sure it's level so the lamp won't turn over. Grace, do you and Elle have my supper ready? I hear you helped Elizabeth bake a fine apple cobbler."

"Which one are you?" the Widow Morris asked as he came out carrying a rocking chair.

"I'm Nate, Ma'am. Where would you like me to put this?"

"Nate! You've grown to a man! Put the chair here." She motioned to a level spot of ground.

"And I'm John, the one born before Nate. Papa thought you might need a lantern. I'll put it right here on level ground. Anything else I can get for you, Ma'am?"

"You might bring another shawl, if there is one. I haven't seen you children since you were small. I can't get over how you've grown. I'm so sorry about your mother. We were best friends when we were young. I know she wept over the passing of Ben and Caleb. Matthew is home now, isn't he?"

"Yes'um. I'll be back with a shawl," John called over his shoulder as he headed back toward the house.

Nate whispered and made motions to alert the lady as to Elizabeth's situation, and the Widow Morris motioned back to let him know Papa had already told her about it and that she was here to help resolve the impasse.

"Thank you, John," she said as she accepted the shawl when he returned. "I'll be very comfortable. I'll call if I need anything else. I brought my knitting and I'll sit right here in the rocker—it's a beautiful chair, built by your father, I would guess—and knit until it gets dark. Don't worry. I'll be just fine."

As the boys reluctantly returned to the house, they heard the Widow Morris singing a familiar tune, one their mother often sang to them.

"Lost my partner, what'll I do?
Lost my partner, what'll I do?
Lost my partner, what'll I do?
Skip to my Lou, my darling.
Lou, Lou, skip to my Lou.
Lou, Lou, skip to my Lou.
Lou, Lou, skip to my Lou.
Skip to my Lou, my darling."

A soft voice coming from inside the privy joined in singing the second verse.

"I'll get another one prettier than you.
I'll get another one prettier than you.
I'll get another one. . . ."

The Widow Morris laughed. "Oh, my. Elizabeth, you sing like your mother! Catherine and I loved that game and sang the song over and over when we were young. It drove the boys crazy, and we loved to tease them.

"I'm sure you miss her. So do I. There weren't so many people out here when we were first married. The men were gone most of the time hunting and farming, and farm women got so lonely. We might go months before seeing another woman's face.

"Your mother and I worked out something we called 'chop talk.' It was so quiet, we could hear the ax when it fell on wood even at the distance between our farms.

"If your mother chopped twice, she told me she was going to church on Sunday. Three chops meant Nathan was passing by in the wagon and would drop her off to visit me on his way down the road. One chop meant someone was sick and needed help. We always answered each other with the same number of chops. If one of us didn't get an answer, we knew something was wrong and sent our husbands to find out about it or we went ourselves.

"I remember when she borned you, Elizabeth. I'm a midwife and when I took hold of that tiny red head and eased you out of your mama's belly, she was the happiest woman in the world. After having five boys, she wished and prayed for a girl, and there you were. Of course, she had two more, but her first girl baby was special."

"I didn't know that," Elizabeth said softly through the privy door.

"I delivered many babies, but never had one of my own."

"Did it make you sad?" asked Elizabeth.

"Yes. And angry with God. It didn't seem fair for your mother to have so many children and I had none. She was busy with all of you and didn't need me anymore. Then your daddy and Mr. Morris had a falling out. It was an argument over a horse, I think, that caused such bad blood between them."

"I'm angry with God, myself," Elizabeth volunteered.

"Why?"

"Because I'm a young girl and I'm going to die. I don't think it's fair. I haven't been bad, at least, not very bad."

"Women don't need to be very bad. Eve was very bad for us. She disobeyed God and ate an apple when He ordered her not to.

God punished her and all the women coming after her. God put the curse on all of us forever and ever. But God rewarded us in a peculiar way. For all of the pain, He gives us a gift of a newborn baby."

"Is God so mad at you that He won't give you a baby?" the girl asked.

"Oh, I hope not. Even barren women put up with the curse," the lady answered.

"What's the curse?" asked Elizabeth.

"I'm sure your mother meant to tell you. Women are a little bashful about it. When a little girl starts to grow into a woman, her body changes. Every month something happens to her body so she'll know she's a woman. Blood flows from her private parts for about five days and then stops. Some people call it 'flowing,' but most women I know call it 'The Curse,' " the older woman explained.

"Does the curse kill you?" Elizabeth asked in a soft and solemn whisper.

"No, but sometimes it can hurt and you might wish it would."

"Widow Morris . . ." Elizabeth began.

"Call me Emma. You mother called me Emma."

"Widow . . . Emma, I'm bleeding. Do I have the curse?"

"I don't know. If you'd like to take me to your house, we can go into your bedroom and can see about it."

Elizabeth slowly opened the privy door and stepped out. Her eyes were puffy from crying and she looked like a worn rag doll.

"If you carry the lamp, I'll just put my knitting in my bag and bring it with us to the house. Nate can come back and get the rocking chair."

It was dusk as the two women, one older and one just beginning to blossom, walked back to the house. They said nothing to the silent family members gathered in front of fireplace. Elizabeth entered the girls' bedroom and put the lamp on the small table. Emma followed and closed the door behind her.

Grace and Elle were thrilled when Papa told them to sleep in his and Mama's big bed and to stay out of their own room until Elizabeth felt better. He ordered the boys to their room and followed them to the loft where he readied himself to sleep in Caleb's bed.

When the family gathered in the kitchen the next morning, they saw evidence of someone having eaten a late meal. Only crumbs were left in the cobbler pan, and two of Mama's best tea cups had been used. Laundry was soaking in the wash tub on the front porch. When Grace, with Nate's help, began to fix breakfast, they heard voices coming through the bedroom door. Elizabeth and the Widow Morris were singing "Skip to My Lou."

The two of them joined the family for breakfast, and Nate was careful to direct their guest to the chair usually occupied by his middle sister. "Grace, you sit in Mama's place."

She glanced up at him to confirm his order. No one had sat in Mama's place at the table since she died. The look in Nate's eyes left no room for doubt. "As soon as I get the food on the table," Grace replied.

The Rileys and their guest were quiet during the meal. The confusion of the previous day left them spent of energy and with uneasy feelings, the cause of which was hard to identify. Elizabeth was the only one who seemed relaxed, and Nate felt angry with her for upsetting the familiar rhythm of their family life. He failed to notice the change in her mood.

The Widow Morris broke the silence. "Thank you for the wonderful breakfast. I can tell your mother taught her children how to cook. Elizabeth and I had a good talk last evening. Nathan, I'd like to have her come home with me for a few days and ask your permission."

"Elizabeth has a tongue. She can ask herself, if she's of a mind," Papa snapped.

"Of course," the woman answered as her face turned pink.

The children caught their breaths at the display of Papa's bad manners.

"I'll go another time. I've lots of work here to catch up with now that I know I'm not dying," Elizabeth said with a bashful smile. "Thank you for coming, Emma. Now, may I be excused please, Papa?"

He nodded. "We're all finished, I think. John, get the buggy ready and I'll take the Widow Morris home. We all appreciate your help with Elizabeth. And, Matthew, gather some fruit and vegetables in a sack for the lady to take with her."

"That isn't necessary, thank you. You may have forgotten that I brought Elizabeth into this world," the lady said with a wan smile.

"I haven't forgotten," he answered.

Just before Papa drove off, he spoke to his children who had gathered by the buggy to see the Widow Morris off. "I'm going on into town and won't be back until late. Mr. Sowell and I have some business to discuss. I expect the chores to be done by the time I get back."

"Watch out for marauders, Papa," Nate cautioned as the horses pulled forward.

When Papa and his passenger were out of hearing distance, Matthew called his siblings back into the house. "I know what Papa's up to," he said. "A farmer can't farm when there's no seed. Mr. Sowell can't sell when his store is empty. Those two men are as close as brothers and I'll wager they're planning to to get out of this dying place."

"Leave? Papa would never leave this farm!" Nate protested.

"It's leave or die," Matthew countered.

"Where would we go?" John asked.

"Far away from here. We'd head west, I imagine, maybe to Texas. But we won't go today," Matthew said as he laughed. "Let's get to our chores!" He wondered if he had said too much.

The day went well, and Elizabeth's return to almost normal was one of the reasons. The children did their chores quickly and well and had time enough to read and play checkers before supper. They didn't begin to worry until well after dark and wondered if they should ride out with lanterns to look for their father.

Chapter Fifteen

Emma

Nathan Riley was befuddled and the feeling left him in the kind of uneasy state he had not experienced since he was a young man. The presence of Emma Morris sitting next to him on the buggy seat caused him great discomfort. Not a word had passed between them since they left the Riley farm. As they approached the outlying fields of the Morris land, sentences began to take shape in Nathan's mind, but his lips refused to say them.

He remembered the times long ago when the two young farm couples had been friends. Gradually, the Morrises displayed a coolness that ripened into downright hostility toward the Rileys and broke off their relationship. Nathan and Catherine never understood the reasons why, but Catherine once told her husband that she suspected their neighbors' apparent inability to have children might have caused them to be jealous of the Rileys who had so many.

Yesterday, when Nathan went for Emma's help, he noticed the signs of deterioration on the Morris farm, once as tidy and productive as his own. The fields were fallow, fences were in need of mending, and the barn door hung askew on broken hinges. Even though he had heard of the farmer's death, the sight of the dying farm startled him.

As he approached the farm house, not a living thing had come out to meet him, not a dog, a chicken, a goose, or even a cat. The only sounds he had heard were made by his horse and buggy until Emma stepped out of the house and called his name. She did not invite him in but agreed to come with him when he explained the situation with Elizabeth. He remembered that she went inside the house and came out almost immediately with her hat, shawl,and carpetbag. They barely talked to one another on the trip back to the Riley farm where he dropped Emma off at the privy where Elizabeth had barricaded herself.

Her father did not know what went on that night between his daughter and their neighbor, nor did he care to know the details. When his other children questioned him about the visitor to the privy, Nathan frowned and answered, "I got the Widow Morris to talk to your sister about female things."

The next morning when their visitor and Elizabeth came in to the kitchen to join the family for breakfast, Nathan had been surprised at the ease with which the girl seemed to have accepted Emma. His daughter appeared to be happier and more relaxed at breakfast than he had seen her in months. The other children had been less than polite to the woman. Nathan felt ashamed of them and more ashamed of himself for the rude way in which he spoke to her. He silently scolded himself, *Nathan Riley, you are a fool to start a new day like an ignorant, ungrateful, grumpy old man!*

Now, the horse and buggy was nearing the outlying field of the Morris farm when Emma broke the silence. "Nathan, I would be obliged if you would let me come with you to town. I have business myself with Mr. Sowell."

"Fine with me," he replied and wondered if the woman had money to shop at Sowell's. Instead of turning off on the lane to the Morris farm house, Nathan kept to the road leading to town. The two of them engaged in idle chatter about the weather until they approached the spot on the road where Nate had been surprised years ago by the huge buck darting in front of the wagon the first time he drove to town. Nathan relished telling the tale to a fresh audience. Emma's appreciation of the story and the humor of it seemed to relax them both.

Little more was said during the next hour. Nathan drove past the spot where the family usually stopped to eat and rest but reined in the horse a few minutes later in a similar area. "Grace packed dinner," he said as he climbed down from the buggy and lifted out the food basket from behind the seat. He had intended to help Emma down, but she jumped to the ground before he got around to her side.

Nathan carefully examined an old log for chiggers, deemed it safe enough to sit on, and they relaxed there to eat in silence. There was enough food for two, and when they finished the simple meal of roast pork, biscuits, and apples, Nathan cleared his throat. "Emma," he said, "I'm sorry I snapped at you back at the house.

I have a worrisome mind. Here I am, a one-armed widower farmer with three living sons and three daughters growing up without their mother. That's bad enough, but this sorry war has ruined the South and everything in it. A man hardly knows where to turn."

"It's a hard time for us all," Emma said. "Elizabeth, bless her heart, is changing into a woman at the very time her family and the world, as she knows it, are falling apart."

"She's been a handful," Nathan went on, "but she seems to have taken a liking to you."

Emma smiled. "It isn't easy to be living in a place where the men outnumber the women. When I was there, it made the numbers even and more fair, to Elizabeth's way of thinking. She told me how very much she loved and misses her mother. I'm not surprised. Catherine was a special person. I know all of you miss her."

Nathan Riley took a deep breath and blurted, "Emma, will you marry me?"

"What did you say?"

"I asked you to marry me." He went on before the startled woman could reply. "I'm a practical man, Emma. I have girls who need a mother. I have a stash of food hidden away, almost enough to feed a company of soldiers for a month. You are a widow with a tumble-down farm, no animals, and a bare cupboard, I'll wager. We got along fine with each other once, and we could again. Catherine always loved you and would approve, I do believe. Elizabeth would be happy and so would her sisters or she'd whip the tar out of them," he said with a wry smile."

"If I accept your offer, when would we be married?" asked Emma, who was surprised by the words coming out of her own mouth.

"Today, if there's a preacher left in town," he answered.

Emma frowned. "That's much too soon."

"If it's going to be, it has to be now," Nathan replied. "Sowell and I have been planning something for months and waiting for the right time to do it. We have to get away from this place, even though it's been good to us both. The South is scorched by fire, and the ground is red with the blood of our sons and brothers." Nathan Riley sighed, "And there is no seed for planting.

"If Sowell agrees, now is the time for us to pack up what we can carry and head west. We're not likely to get caught in the fighting. Both armies are far to the south of the route we've planned.

We're armed and ready to take on any marauders who haven't been shot or caught and hung by now."

"I see," Emma said softly. "Let me think about it, and I'll give you my answer when we reach the General Store."

Nathan Riley nodded, put the empty food basket behind the seat and helped Emma up into the buggy. They were silent the rest of the trip, each one with his or her own thoughts, until they drove through the near-deserted street leading to Sowell's General Store.

"What has happened?" Emma whispered as she gazed at the quiet streets and boarded-up buildings.

"War," Nathan answered and pulled to a stop in front of the General Store. He tied the horse to the hitching post and helped Emma down from the buggy. They entered through the door and found the store empty.

Sowell and Ned were in the back room when they heard footsteps and and looked out to see who had entered the store. The morning light was behind Nathan and Emma and when Sowell saw their silhouettes, he gasped. "Catherine?" The storekeeper walked to meet them, and the facial features of the travelers became clear. "Emma Morris! For a minute there, you gave me a start! Nathan, it's good to see you!"

The farmer wasted no time and got down to business. "I drove in today because I think it's time, Sowell. Emma is coming with us. We're going to marry, if she agrees. Is there a preacher still in town?"

Sowell was flabbergasted. He caught his breath, ignored Nathan, took Emma by the arm, and guided her to the store counter. "Emma, put the things you brought me right here on the counter, then look around the store and pick out whatever you need. Ned, you mind the store while Mr. Riley and I take a walk up the street. We won't be gone long. Come along, Nathan."

The two men left the store and when they were well out of hearing distance, Sowell turned to his friend. "Nathan, have you lost your mind? When did all of this happen?"

"Well, yesterday I went to get Emma because I needed help with Elizabeth. She's the only woman I know within half a day's ride who could help me. Elizabeth was having a hissy fit and locked herself in the privy and wouldn't come out."

Nathan paused, and Sowell looked solemnly at his friend.

"And?" the storekeeper queried.

Nathan continued, "Well, it seems that things worked out just fine between the two of them. Elizabeth, fussy and bossy as that girl is, seems to have taken a shine to the lady. This morning when I was driving Emma back home, it just seemed right that the two of us got married, her without a husband and me without a wife. So I asked her, but she hasn't agreed yet."

Sowell shook his head in wonder. In all the years he had known Nathan Riley, he never once heard the man say that many words at one time. "Well, it may not be as crazy as it sounds. Since her husband died, Emma has been bringing in her belongings to me to trade for food. I took most of her furniture and was able to sell it. Now, the poor soul has been bringing me beautiful little doilies and dresser scarves to trade. She makes them out of pieces of her wedding dress. It was the best cloth she had, and the rich plantation women have been eager to buy the doo-dads, not knowing where they came from."

Nathan was silent. He felt guilty knowing that a neighbor was starving when the Rileys had an abundance of food. He took a breath and went on, "I told her if she agreed, we would have to marry right away, and she knows the reason why. I told her we planned to leave here."

Sowell put his hand on Nathan's shoulder. "Old friend, I agree that now is the time for us to leave this place. I hate the thought of it. Preacher Pruitt is in the Methodist church down the street. Ask him to come back with you, and I'll speak to Emma. She is a wise but desperate woman, and I know what her answer will be."

He turned and went back to his store while Nathan continued down the street to the Methodist church. "Emma, what beautiful things have you brought me today?" Sowell said as he opened her carpetbag and took out two knitted caps and three beautiful silk brocade doilies with crocheted lace edging, the last remnants of her wedding dress.

Emma had chosen a small bag of flour, a package of sugar, two sweet potatoes, and a box of wooden matches which she had placed beside her handiwork on the counter. "I'd like to trade for these," she said in the most business-like voice she could muster.

Sowell took both of her hands in his. "Dear lady, the food is yours, but please keep your handiwork as a wedding gift from me.

Nathan has told me of his proposal of marriage, and I am delighted. Taking your place in that family will not be nearly as hazardous as the dangerous journey we are about to attempt. Nathan has told you about our plan?" he asked.

"Briefly," Emma answered. "I know I would not want to be left behind in this place. My world is as topsy-turvy as Elizabeth thinks her world is. Nathan pleases me, but we had not spoken for years until yesterday."

"You will say 'yes,' won't you, Emma? I urge you to accept his proposal. Nathan Riley is a quiet man, sometimes gruff, but as honest as the day is long. He's the best farmer in the county, and I have never known him to raise his hand in anger to any woman."

Emma had no time to reply. Nathan Riley, with the Methodist Preacher Pruitt in tow, walked through the door of the General Store. The storekeeper took a pink silk rose from a counter, cut a piece of white ribbon from a spool, and tied it around the flower which he gallantly presented to Emma. Then Sowell took a silk cravat from the same counter and tied it around Nathan's neck. It masked the collar of the farmer's rough shirt.

The storekeeper motioned Ned to come out of the back room, and his free black employee hummed a beautiful melody as Preacher Pruitt led the couple in their wedding vows. Sowell paid the preacher with a sack of flour and a bag of roasted coffee, something too rare for money to buy. The preacher left smiling.

"Come," Sowell said to the newlyweds. "We must make our final plans now if we expect to leave before the week is out." He locked the front door of the store, pulled the shade down behind it, and led the way to the back room.

By the time Nathan and Sowell finalized their plans, the sun was low in the sky. Emma grew tired listening to the men talk. Her hands, unaccustomed to being still, held knitting needles and yarn as she completed another woolen cap. *Have I been sleeping?* she thought. *Have I really married that man bending over maps at the table? It must have been a dream. I have no ring on my finger.* She took a ball of yarn from her carpetbag and starting a new row for a knitted neck scarf.

Ned listened to the conversation as he busied himself packing store items in wooden crates. After Sowell called him over and whispered something in his employee's ear, Ned went behind the counter at the front of the store, took a ring hidden at the back of the cash drawer, and put the it in the hand Sowell held behind his back.

"Nathan," the storekeeper said, as he brought the ring into view and twirled the gold band between his thumb and forefinger, "I'll trade you this ring for a horse."

Nathan was puzzled by the strange offer and was about to question the wisdom of such a trade when Sowell kicked his friend under the table and whispered an order.

"Ouch! Uh, fine." Nathan accepted the ring and walked slowly to where his new wife was sitting. "If you put those needles down, I'll slip this ring on your finger, Emma."

Emma smiled and followed his direction. She gazed at the ring on her hand and said, "We must be married. There's a ring on my finger."

"Kiss her, you fool!" Sowell hissed.

Nathan kissed his bride on her mouth. Both of them found it to be sweet. They kissed once again as Sowell smiled.

"We best be on our way. We stayed longer that we should have," Nathan said. Sowell helped Emma into the buggy and waved until the pair was out of sight.

"Well, Ned, I never thought I'd live to see such a day as this. We have two weeks' worth of work to do in a few days. Are your wife and boy ready to go?"

"Yes, suh. Dey be a mite nervous 'bout leavin', but we's ready an' grateful to y'all for takin' us along."

It was dark by the time Nathan and Emma reached the outlying fields of his farm. He could not see the road but knew the horse would go to the barn if he loosened his grip on the reins. Even so, the farmer was relieved to see a bobbing light in the distance.

Soon Nate, holding a lantern, rode up on his horse. "You said you'd be home before sundown," the boy scolded. "You worried us, and we've been out looking for you, and . . . Oh, beg your pardon, Widow Morris; I didn't see you there." Nate looked quizzically at his father but received no response from the man. "Anyway, I'm glad I found you. Follow my light home, Papa."

As they approached the farm house, Nate hollered the news of their Papa's arrival. His daughters spilled out of the house and his sons came running from different directions. All of them met in the barn to greet him. The father was pleased with their greeting but gave no outward show of his feelings. Matthew unhitched the horse, and Nate led it away with his own mount.

"We were worried about you, Papa, and thought a marauder might have jumped you," Matthew said. He was surprised to see the Widow Morris but nodded his head in greeting to the lady.

"My business at Sowell's took longer than I expected. We're all tired now and need clear heads for tomorrow. I'll tell you everything in the morning," Papa answered. He picked up Emma's carpetbag as the two of them walked up to the house. The weary Riley children followed. The girls automatically went to the beds assigned to them the night before.

Emma shyly looked up at her new husband and whispered, "You said you'd tell them everything tomorrow." She took her carpetbag from him and slipped into the girls' room. Elizabeth was already asleep.

John was first to wake the next morning. As it was his turn to milk, his ear was tuned to the bell around the neck of their single milk cow that walked alone into her stall and waited to be milked. John wondered if she missed the herd. *Cows don't have feelings!* He scolded himself for having such a silly thought as he crawled out of bed, dressed, and quietly left the house so as not to wake the others.

Nate and Emma woke up next and met each other in the kitchen. He replenished the logs in the fireplace to warm the room on the chilly morning before he built a fire in his mother's cast-iron stove.

"Is there coffee?" Emma asked. Nate pointed to the pot and a tin container on a shelf over the drainboard. She took down the coffee pot, filled it half way up with water, and spooned the grounds in the basket. The *blup, blup, blup* of the coffee boiling in the pot filled the kitchen with the sound and smell of breakfast in the making.

Elizabeth, Grace, and Elle came into the kitchen. Elle set the table and had to go back for another place setting because she forgot they had a guest. Elizabeth cut the bread she had baked the day before, then sliced apples, spread the pieces out in the pan, and slowly fried them in butter. Grace, not yet expert at frying eggs, scrambled two dozen of them. Breakfast was ready by the time Papa and Matthew came down from the loft. They waited to say the blessing until John came in from the barn, washed his hands at the sink, and sat in his place at the table.

As they passed the food around, Nate nearly dropped the platter of scrambled eggs when Papa said, "Pass the apples. Emma and I got married yesterday. Sowell agrees it's time to go."

Matthew was the first to find his voice. "Where are we going, Papa?"

"West," he answered, "and Sowell will meet us here on Sunday. He's bringing Ned and his wife and boy and two loaded wagons. We have a pile of work to finish before then. I'll have some more coffee, Elizabeth."

"I'll get it," Emma said as she rose from her chair and took the coffee pot from the stove top. "Your father was kind enough to ask me to marry him. He felt it his duty to provide a mother for his children, especially you girls. Of course, I'm not your real mother. Catherine was, and I loved her almost as much as you did. It would pleasure me if you called me 'Emma' as your mother did." She finished freshening the coffee of those who wanted it, returned the pot to the stove, and sat in her chair.

Elizabeth rose from the table and bent over to kiss Emma on the cheek. "I'm glad you're part of our family now. Aren't we?" the girl said as she looked at her siblings in such a way they dared not fail to endorse their sister's acceptance of their new stepmother.

Nathan said nothing, but when he caught Emma's eye, he smiled slightly and nodded his head in approval of his new wife's behavior and the children's positive response to it.

Emma and the girls quickly cleared the table as Papa got out his hand-drawn map and written lists of the work to be done in the next few days. All of them gathered around and wrote down their specific jobs as Papa assigned them. "When you finish the job, check it off your list and show it to me," he ordered.

Nate had known all year that something unusual was going to happen because Papa ordered them to do things on the farm that they had never been done before. The announcement that the family would be leaving the Riley Farm came as no surprise. What Nate didn't anticipate was Papa's marriage to the Widow Morris. *Papa is a wise man,* he thought. *The girls need a grown woman around.*

Papa called his name. "Nate, I want you and John to take the two mules to Emma's barn. Put some tools in the old wagon, hitch up the horses, and take the woman with you. It's a pretty good wagon, as I remember, but she told me it has a broken spoke on one of the rear wheels. I think you can fix it. We can use another wagon.

"Emma, get what you want to take with us out of your house. Bring only what you really need. We want most of our load to be food. I hope it's better than money when we're on the trail.

"John, you and I'll keep working on the false bottoms we're building for the wagons. We'll hide most of our food under them and put the furniture, bedding, a few crates, and the like on top so we'll look like the other travelers.

"Elizabeth, I hope you've calmed down enough to help your sisters sort through your clothes and pack just what you need. Pack just enough dishes—tin or enamelware is best—for our family and pots, pans, and eating utensils. And don't forget the coffee pot!

"Elle, you're old enough now to help Grace gather up the quilts for bed rolls. Most likely, we'll sleep on the ground.

"After these little jobs are done, we'll all have a hand in packing the food. Oh, yes, and I'll need something to carry our gold coins."

Emma spoke up. "The girls and I can take care of that. We'll make vests for you men to wear and sew the coins in the lining."

Papa nodded his approval, but Nate said, "That's a very good idea, Emma."

"Thank you," she answered. *That's the only compliment I have received from any Riley man,* she thought. She turned to the sisters. "I know your mama taught you how to sew. What we need is strong cloth, linen if you have it. For the lining, we need something softer, like muslin. Don't forget the thread. It must be strong even though we'll sew it double."

The girls scattered in every direction and quickly came back with the linen coverlet taken from their parents' bed and the dress-length of cloth Mr. Sowell had given their mother.

Grace felt sad when she handed the pastel flowered cloth to Emma. "Mama was going to make herself a dress out of this, but she died."

"I know," Emma answered softly. Elle handed her mama's sewing basket holding scissors, needles and strong thread.

Emma felt it best if she sent Elizabeth to measure the men for their vests even though the garments would not be constructed to fit tightly. Elizabeth was delighted with the task and drafted Grace to write down the number of inches from the top of the spine to the waist and clear around the chest of each male in her family. She knew her father and Nate were ticklish and made a special effort to make them giggle when she put the measuring tape around them.

Elizabeth and her sisters were even sillier and howling with laughter when Emma told them the vests would be shaped more like women's corsets because they would be worn under the men's shirts and next to their skin.

Emma became serious. "You have an important job. Put the coins, one at a time, between the linen and the lining. Use tiny stitches so the coin won't fall out. You must sew each gold piece separately. That way, if your papa needs to spend some money, he can take one or two coins and the rest of them won't fall out. The most important thing is that you never tell anyone where the gold coins are. Do you understand?"

The girls nodded and solemnly went about their important task. Papa brought out his stash of gold from behind a stone in the fireplace. As Elle was not very good at sewing, her job was to count out the coins in groups of ten, and tally them with a mark on the paper when her sisters sewed the coins, one by one, into the vests.

Emma sewed with them until they heard John call to tell her they soon would be ready to leave for her farm. "You're in charge, Elizabeth," she said. The girl was an efficient task master and doctored their finger blisters with ointment when the job was done.

As Nate gathered the tools they would need for the repair and went to the corral to rope the mules, he thought of the months of hard work by everyone in the family. *If I hadn't seen it myself, I wouldn't believe it.*

In the fall, instead of making apple butter, the girls took the apples and other fruits from the orchard and spent hours cutting the fruit into thin slices. They spread the pieces on clean cloth or woven wooden screens to dry in the sun. They packed the dried fruit in small cloth bags which they stored in a root cellar.

Both of the root cellars were nearly full. Layers of sweet and white potatoes, turnips, carrots, and a few other root vegetables were separated by layers of soil. Strips of beef jerky hung on strings like clothes drying on a clothes line.

Water flowing through the spring houses kept the food cool. Loaves of sweet butter and cheese wrapped in muslin sat on shelves lining the walls of the enclosure. One large milk pail sat in the shallow running water. Matthew had stacked sausages, hogs' heads, pigs' feet, and cuts of beef on shelves opposite the others.

Papa had kept only one milk cow and calf. They butchered three cattle and traded the rest of them for four horses and two mules. The men had slaughtered all of the hogs and filled the smoke house with hams, ribs, and fatback. They would wrap the meat in heavy tarps to prevent the enticing smell from giving away their secret freight.

When he hitched up the horses to the wagon, Nate counted three sacks of wheat flour, a dozen sacks of cornmeal, and six large bags of sugar. "John, I think Papa is right. We do have enough food to feed a company of soldiers for a month. Let's just hope it's enough to trade for what we need to get us to wherever we're going."

John shrugged. "We'll find out if Mama was right. She said food might be worth more than gold someday." He paused, then went on, "Nate, I don't like the Widow Morris coming in to take Mama's place."

"I'm not keen on it myself," Nate answered, "but Mama would want us to be fair. Matthew told me he remembered they were good friends once. He was little then, and you and I hadn't even been born." Emma walked to meet them. She declined their offer to sit on the seat beside Nate and sat instead in the wagon bed.

The boys were as shocked as their father had been at the sight of such a dilapidated farm. Emma stayed inside the house while they worked for nearly two hours on the wagon's repair. When they finally hitched it up to the two mules, they called to Emma, who came out the door carrying a large carpetbag and dragging a small trunk behind her. John ran up to help her and lifted her meager belongings into the wagon bed. "It's your turn to ride up front," he said and climbed in back and sat down between her trunk and their own tools.

Papa's new wife took Nate's hand as he helped her climb up to sit beside him on the wagon seat. Emma smiled her thanks. On their way back to the Riley Farm, he slyly glanced at her out of the corner of his eye. Nate liked what he saw but knew the woman could never replace his mother.

Chapter Sixteen
Westward

Before dawn Sunday morning, Sowell drove his loaded wagon for the last time down the main street of his home town. Ned and his family followed in a smaller wagon. Both of their loads were covered with tarps secured with rope. The street was deserted. . . . *A small blessing,* Sowell thought. *If I saw an old friend, I just might not have the courage to leave.*

They drove past the empty hog pens next to the railroad tracks at the edge of town. Sowell couldn't remember the last time a train had rolled into the loading dock.

Ned was careful to keep close to the lead wagon and the white man's protection. Even though his was a family of free blacks, he was sure their oldest son had been kidnapped by speculators and sold into slavery more than a year ago. It was a common occurence, and free blacks could never relax their guard, especially if they were alone in the country, or even in some parts of town.

The small party did not stop to eat or rest and arrived at the Riley Farm well before noon. Emma and the girls had prepared a hearty meal for everyone. She insisted that Ned, his wife Birdy, and their son Will come into the kitchen and eat with Sowell and the Riley family.

Birdy stayed to help clean up the kitchen. She joined Emma and the sisters as they packed up household items and carried them out to the barn where the men were loading all five wagons—three, including Emma's, belonging to the Rileys; Sowell's, which was the largest of them all; and Ned's small one. The buggy was of no use on the journey and would be left behind.

Nate wondered whether strangers would discover the deserted farm and rejoice in their good fortune. *It's more likely soldiers will strip it of everything they can carry off and then burn the place to the ground,* he thought.

Badog was suspicious of strangers and ran about sniffing the newcomers. Nate clapped his hands and called to the animal, "Here, Badog, here! Come here, boy!" He knelt down and scruffed the dog's neck and tried to dodge the animal's wet tongue. "There's a lot going on, I know, but you just settle down. Come on; let's go see if Elle has some scraps for you." The dog followed him toward the house. About the same time that they reached the porch, Elle came out carrying a bowl of leavings from their meal. "See? Everything's fine. Eat up, Badog. We have a long trip ahead of us, and you're coming along."

Nathan Riley, in charge of the loading, was as organized and precise with the freight as he was with planning and planting his crops. He listed every item and its place in the particular wagon load. Things to be used by the people en route were packed for easy access. While most of their food was hidden underneath the wagons' false bottoms, food for their own needs was accessible if hidden from casual sight.

Over Emma's objection, relayed to her husband in private, Nathan insisted they prepare their supper, eat and sleep outside in the farmyard as if they were on the trail. "That way, we'll know if we forgot something important," he reasoned.

"And maybe we'll be more comfortable spending the night in familiar surroundings. It might help us get a little more used to camping before we have to stop in strange places," added Emma without looking at her husband.

Elizabeth wished she could cook the beef stew on her mother's cook stove in the kitchen instead of over the open camp fire. She was sorry they were leaving the stove behind, but when they had to choose between bringing the stove and her mother's repaired wardrobe, all of the children agreed they should take the wardrobe in their limited space. Nathan Riley, practical as ever, would have preferred the stove but gave way to his offsprings' wishes. The children were surprised.

The group of travelers sat on the grass to eat their evening meal, and Sowell urged Ned and his family to join them instead of eating off by themselves. "We'll all be traveling together for a long time," he reasoned, "and each one of us needs to carry equal loads, so we might as well eat together. Seems fair to me." No one objected.

Birdy and Grace washed the dishes in creek water while the others spread the bed rolls on the ground. Since there was no hint of wind and the sky was clear. Ned carefully banked the fire and left enough live coals to start up a fire to boil coffee the next morning. Everybody finished chores by twilight, and all of them crawled into their bedrolls before dark.

Nate, who slept in his clothes like the others, woke just before sun-up the next morning. He had slept more soundly than he had anticipated, but his body felt stiff and sore from the first night on the hard ground. *Guess I'll have to get used to it,* he thought. He got up quietly, rolled up his bed, and walked as quietly as he could to the orchard. As Nate approached the pear tree, he heard Matthew speaking softly at their mother's grave. Nate stepped back into the trees and felt a slight pang of guilt as he listened to his brother's words.

"Papa says we can't take you with us. We're not going back to get Caleb and Ben, either. I guess I always knew they would always sleep under the pine trees where we buried them," Matthew said, his voice cracking with emotion.

"War changes men, Mama. It makes them do things they would never even thought of doing before. Doing something terrible leaves them with guilt and sorrow afterwards. I knew I had to get Papa home when his arm was half blowed off. After Papa was hit, another shell hit an officer on his horse right next to us. The man was all bloody and hollering for help. Instead of helping him, I grabbed his boot out the stirrup, pulled the man right out of his saddle, and left him bleeding on the ground. I don't know, to this day, if the man lived or died, but I know I stole his horse right out from under him, Mama. I never told Papa that he came home on a stolen horse, one I stole from a Confederate officer, and a wounded one at that. I feel guilty, Mama, and hope the Lord forgives me. I know Papa won't if he ever learns the truth."

Nate watched his brother pause to bow his head. Then Matthew looked up into the pear tree, broke off a small twig, and put it in his pocket. "Good-bye, Mama," Matthew said and walked back to where the horses were tethered. Badog, sleeping in his usual place atop Catherine's grave at night, was alert and listening to Matthew's familiar voice.

Nate made sure he was alone before he walked to where his older brother had stood. Badog yawned and sat up as Nate knelt at the grave of his mother and spoke softly to her. "Mama, Papa would have died and left us orphans if Matthew hadn't done what he did. Papa was near dead when they got home, and Matthew made me cut off half his arm when I didn't think I could do it. He said I had to or Papa would die, for sure." Tears welled in his eyes at the memory of it.

"All of us hate to leave you here alone, Mama, but Papa says we have to go. Papa's taking us to some place west of here to get away from the war. I don't think he knows exactly where, himself. He says the war has ruined the South and our farm along with it. Mr. Sowell is going with us and so is Ned, the free black man, with his wife and son.

"Papa got married to Emma. She says she was your friend once. I guess she's nice. The girls like her a lot but not as much as you, Mama. We're taking your wardrobe with us but not your iron stove. Papa made room in the yellow wagon for all of our medicines and herbs. He says I'm the best one of us at doctoring. If Papa says it, I guess it's true. You know he's pretty stingy with compliments. I've got to go now, Mama. They're calling me to come get my hot coffee. It's real coffee. Mr. Sowell brought it. We'll eat last night's leftovers and cold biscuits for breakfast, then be on our way. Watch over the Riley Farm for us, Mama." Her youngest son leaned over and kissed her grave, wet from his tears. He walked away quickly and joined the others as they made final preparations before heading out.

Papa told Nate to check the load on the yellow wagon and that he was to drive it. The boy was surprised. Papa usually drove that one but chose to drive Emma's wagon "to see if you fixed that broken wheel," he had explained. As Nate checked his load and found it secure, he noticed that each member of his family went separately to Mama's grave to tell her good-bye. The last person to go was Emma. She knelt down and stayed for quite a while. Nate wondered what she said. He watched Emma get up, lean over and scratch Badogs under his chin. She walked away, then stopped and turned to motion the dog to come. He stood, shook himself, and lay on the grave again. By the time Emma had walked half way back to thc camp, Badog left the spot of his vigil and trotted along beside her.

Nathan Riley made the day to day decisions as to the livestock, wagons, and where to stop for the night, but it was Sowell who had arranged the overall plan. As a business man, he had contacts with many people in other towns and cities. He felt it important to keep secret the details until the others had the need to know them. While Nathan did not place his complete trust in many people, he did in Sowell.

The small caravan had moved steadily but cautiously on the Memphis road for two days. They followed the routine set that first night on the farm except for meals. Emma had suggested they needed a hearty breakfast and dinner to get them through the rigors of the day and a cold supper of food left over from the two big meals. Nate, John, and Will fed Badog, who followed Emma around as a pup followed its mother, and the livestock when the travelers stopped for the day. Usually forage was available, and the boys watched while the animals grazed and erected a simple rope corral for the animals at night. One of the three young men stood guard, and if Nathan Riley caught him sleeping on duty, the boy got no breakfast.

Matthew was scout and rode about a quarter mile ahead of the wagons. It was a job he knew well, having done it many times when he served in the Confederate Army. He was alert to any sign of danger waiting for them on the road or hidden in the woods bordering the road. They passed through many open areas that bore scars, debris, and lingering smells of battles once fought there. Those were the times Matthew broke out in a sweat and thought he could hear the roar of cannon and the screams of men dying. He was glad he was scouting alone and no one could see him shaking in his saddle.

Matthew had spotted several people walking, a few of them wearing ragged uniforms, but none of them appeared to pose a threat to his family and friends. Shortly before he had planned to return to his group for the mid-day meal, he heard the sounds of wheels and animals indicative of a very large group up ahead. He left the road and went up into the trees where he could approach without being seen. Matthew caught up with the wagons and reined in his horse where it was unlikely he would be seen.

He caught his breath. It looked like an army on the march. *There are at least thirty wagons,* he thought, *and way over a hundred men marching behind them. But there's no army left with thirty wagons in this part of Tennessee.* He reached for the binoculars, still in the saddlebag of the stolen horse he rode. Matthew raised the glasses to his eyes and gasped when he saw the enlarged images of dozens of slaves. "It looks like an entire plantation all packed up and going somewhere!" he said in wonder.

Matthew arrived back in camp when dinner was cooking on the campfire. He reported the activity he had seen to his father and the storekeeper. "You say it looked like a whole plantation on the march?" Sowell inquired. "How many slaves were walking?"

"It looked like maybe a hundred, but that's too many, I guess," Matthew answered.

"No. No. And you said about thirty wagons," Sowell said softly almost to himself. "That makes sense. If there were two slaves to each wagon and about a hundred more walking, that would make about a hundred and sixty slaves. And whites, how many whites did you see on horseback?"

"I don't know. I was so surprised; I didn't look for white men on horseback," Matthew answered.

"No matter," Sowell assured him. "There would have been white men on horseback, but the women, and maybe their body slaves, would be riding in wagons, I would guess." He took a deep breath. "Well, my friends, there can be no doubt about it. With that many slaves, it has to be Fair Oaks Plantation on the way to some other place, and I have no idea where!"

Nate was dumbfounded when he heard the news, and the images of Fair Oaks and his time there with his mother surged through his memory. He wished he had asked Hercules more about the slaves who had helped when the two Rileys nursed him back to health, but the grief of his mother's death had overwhelmed all of them, and the former slave was gone before they knew it.

Sowell's next words broke his reverie: "Ned, I don't want you and your family to be seen when we are on the road. I wouldn't want you to be mixed up with any plantation slaves," he said, trying to make light of his words.

Emma spoke up. "Nathan can drive Ned's wagon, and the family can ride with me. After all, it's my wagon and I have driven it many times. We carry the bed rolls, and if anyone approaches, they can burrow under them to hide. Sowell, we need covered wagons," she said as an afterthought.

"And we shall have them, dear lady, tomorrow or the next day," Sowell replied. "That's when we should arrive at the lumber mill on Slurry Creek. I've supplied the lumbermen with canvas since the Gold Rush days. They make as much money converting farm wagons to prairie wagons as they make felling trees or digging coal, and it's a lot less dangerous. You'll have a roof over your head if it rains and you can sleep under canvas when you've grown weary of looking at the stars at night."

As promised, the travelers arrived at Slurry Creek about noon the second day. They were surprised so see about fifty wagons camped in an area that had been cleared of trees years before. Some of the wagons, like theirs, were waiting for the conversion with canvas and wooden staves, but many appeared finished although the drivers gave no indication of leaving any time soon. Other wagons had stopped among the trees surrounding the clearing and it looked as if the families with them had been camped there for some time.

Sowell left his wagon in Ned's hands and walked up to the lumberman who seemed to be in charge. After a brief conversation, he returned and spoke quietly to Nathan. "Five hams, one for each wagon, a bushel of dried fruit, one sack of flour, two dozen pigs' feet, half a side of beef. I told him it was fresh butchered. We're to camp by ourselves over there in the woods. He'll bring up a wagon after dark and we'll load it for him. It would be nice if Emma has a jar of honey to slip in as a special treat, you know, like the treats I gave my good customers at the store."

Nathan Riley understood. "I have a question," he said. "When are we leaving this place?"

"In about a week. In the next day or two, more wagons will be coming in. We're all going west together, about seventy-five wagons and over two hundred people, at last count. The larger the number, the safer the travel, or so I'm told," Sowell answered. "We'll have a guide, a good one. Name's Raines, been to California and back three times. Folks in the other wagons are going to feed him on the trip, but I promised you and I would pay him in gold before we leave. It's the same price for one wagon or a hundred. I just thought we'd get our money's worth and invite other folks to come along with us. I didn't know that safety in numbers was so expensive!"

Sowell laughed at his joke and wasn't offended that his longtime friend didn't get it.

The carpenters arrived at the Sowell/Riley camp the next morning not long after the sun was up. The four of them were happy and satisfied. It had been a long time since they had eaten such a substantial breakfast and with honey on their biscuits, at that! By noon, the carpenters had the staves in place on all five wagons and promised to return the next morning to sew the canvas coverings over the rainbow-shaped supports.

Five days later, all preparation had been completed, and the travelers were eager to get on their way. The guide had not yet arrived, and Sowell heard grumbling among some of the people in the group. His plea for patience fell on deaf ears, and by noon the following day, drivers of two dozen wagons gathered their families and livestock and started off in a caravan of their own. One of the loudest complainers vowed he could lead the way, having personally talked to many men who had made the trip all the way to Texas or who had known someone who did.

The morning of the seventh day, Sowell was getting a little concerned himself. He heard other families making preparations to leave and then a shout. "Somebody's coming! Looks like a mountain man!"

Sowell, with the Riley men close behind, ran to meet the stranger. "Raines?" Sowell called out and saw the man wave his hat as he dismounted.

"I'm sorry to be late. I led a party into Memphis and put them on three packet boats bound for New Orleans. Some packets are still running even though they can't keep their regular schedules. The Yankees have control of the Mississippi, but they keep close watch for Rebels and haven't paid much mind to the boats carrying civilian passengers. There's not enough cargo on this side of the river to fill a rowboat, anyway.

"When she hired me, I didn't know the woman was going to bring her whole plantation, slaves and all. There must have been near two hundred slaves. I lost count of the wagons." He took out his bandana and wiped his brow.

"If you can give me a cup of coffee and a biscuit, I'm ready to start now. When we stop tonight, I'll gather y'all after supper and go over with you what we're going to do and how to stay alive on the trip. It isn't easy, but if you know what you're doing, and the Good Lord's willing, I'll get you to where you want to go."

Sowell and Nathan Riley liked the man and both shook his hand. Sowell went to find Emma, who brought Raines a cup of real coffee and three ham biscuits. Nathan climbed into his wagon where he wouldn't be seen, took off his shirt, then his money vest, and used his knife carefully to cut the stitches around the agreed number of gold coins. He put them in a leather pouch and took it to Raines, who was sitting on a wagon tongue with a smile on his face.

"I do appreciate it," the guide said with a smile, "but I think I can appreciate these ham biscuits every bit as much. Tell your boys to get on their horses and alert everybody else who's coming with us. It's time to round 'em up and move 'em out!"

Twenty minutes after they left on their errand, the brothers reported back to Raines. "Two families changed their minds and aren't coming," Nate said.

"The same with three other wagons," John offered, "but the others I told are hitching up their mules and are nearly ready to go."

Matthew came in last. "I tried to get them to change their minds, but four other wagons won't be coming, either. Someone is sick in every one of them."

Sowell started to ask for the names, but Raines interrupted. "No need to do that now. We can get the names, the count, and the number of wagons and livestock when we stop for the night. There's a five-hour trip in front of us and we'd best get a move on." He motioned Sowell to lead off with his large wagon.

Emma, carrying Ned and his family in her wagon, came next followed by Mr. Riley driving Ned's wagon, then John with the old Riley wagon, and finally Nate driving the yellow wagon.

Raines noted Matthew's skill as a rider and had learned of the young man's military experience from Sowell. "Matthew!" he called. "I'd be obliged if you would direct the other wagons to fall in behind the wagons in any order. Once we are organized, each wagon will have a given number and the driver will keep its place in the train, but we'll take care of that after supper."

"Yes, sir!" Matthew answered smartly and turned his horse to direct the other drivers to move their wagons forward in an orderly line. Although he was not asked to do so, Matthew counted forty-two wagons, including his own party, in the wagon train. *I hope we get along with each other,* he thought.

* * *

Raines was glad some of the wagons dropped out before the trip began although he did not say so. He knew from experience that most timid or faint-hearted travelers could not cope with the rigors of the trip. Their presence would slow the train down before the poor souls eventually would drop out and often die on the trail. Although they were no longer his responsibility, Raines shuddered and remembered them every time he passed an empty abandoned wagon or, worse, scattered human bones bleached white by the unforgiving western sun.

Raines turned his horse and rode back several times to check on the progress of the train. The animals, as well as the wagons' drivers, appeared to be nervous. He knew the tension in the air, while not welcome, was normal for a train composed of people, most of whom had not seen one another before. The travelers he had guided years ago were excited and full of hope seeking riches and opportunity. *But lately,* he thought, *the travelers are different, even reluctant, because many feel forced to leave their homes and head out for unknown destinations feeling it to be the only way to escape the desolate aftermath and horror of war.*

Raines was pleased with his selection of Matthew to "ride herd on the people," a favorite expression he used only in the presence of others in his line of work. "You're doing a good job, Matthew," Raines said as he rode by.

"Thank you, sir," the young man replied, "but I can tell you that not many of these farm boys have been in the Army. Few of them know their left from their right." He smiled and wondered if Raines understood his little joke.

"Because we're running late and I want to get to our campground well before dark, you need to keep the wagons and the stock moving right along, Matthew. Get everyone on foot into the wagons. It will be their last ride for a while. When we get on the trail, only the drivers ride the wagons. Everyone else not on horseback walks to save the animals from wearing out too soon from the heavy loads they're pulling.

"Even those on horseback will need to ride about twenty minutes, then get off and lead their mounts for the same amount of time, and so on. If you've been around cavalry, you already know how the troops can keep going forward that way for days on end. But don't worry. This isn't an army. We're just a wagon train, a neutral one, at that. If anyone asks if you favor the North or the South, my advice is simply to answer, 'Yes,' and let it go at that." Raines waved to Matthew and rode up to take his place at the head of the train.

* * *

All members of the wagon train, without exception, were relieved when they reached their destination, a large clearing about five hundred yards from a cliff. Raines warned everyone to stay in camp and not wander off. "We're near a cliff," he explained. "Fix yourselves an early supper. After that, we'll meet by that large oak tree over there to elect a captain of the wagon train, draw up rules and regulations, and adopt the ones we want to govern our expedition. We will need to agree on a name of your wagon train, and as for who will be the wagon master, I strongly suggest that you vote for me," he said with a chuckle.

"I chose this campsite for the plentiful grass. The stock will graze here without wandering off. The animals are tired anyway, and I don't expect we'll have any trouble rounding them up in the morning. Gather wood for your fires, but keep them small, just enough burning to make your supper. Be sure your fires are out before bed. A night breeze is common this close to the river. One hour from now, about when the sun touches the top of that oak tree there, we'll meet together over by Sowell's wagon."

Before Raines joined the family he would eat with, he met briefly with Mr. Sowell and Mr. Riley. "It would save time if we could make a list of names of those in the train," he said. "Who can read and write?"

"Everyone in my family reads and writes," Riley answered to Raines's surprise, "and Sowell, here, of course."

"Matthew," Riley called, "I want you to give every wagon a number, starting with the Sowell/Riley wagons, and then some of you need to get the names of all the people with that wagon. Do you understand what I mean?"

Emma spoke up. "I'll take Elle with me and Elizabeth can take Grace with her. Nate, you can go by yourself, and, John, you can too. Matthew, didn't you say there were forty-two wagons, all told? Elizabeth and Grace, get the names of people on wagons numbered one through ten; John, eleven through twenty; Nate, twenty-one through thirty; and Elle and I will get the rest. There will be twelve wagons for us, Elle. Do you know another name for twelve, like in twelve eggs?'' Emma asked.

''Yes. One dozen,'' Elle answered proudly.

Raines hid his smile with his hand and appeared to cough. *This is going to be an organized wagon train,* he thought.

* * *

Members of the wagon train hoped the meting would not take too long when they gathered near the Sowell wagon. Riley began to speak even though some stragglers were still coming. ''If all goes well, we will be traveling together for about three months before we reach the Lone Elm, the rendezvous tree where the trails split. It's the only tree on the prairie for miles around, and it has been a landmark for travelers since the early days. Some of you will meet up there with other trains heading northwest to meet the Oregon Trail. Some of you will stay with me and head west before dropping down south to Texas. We'll follow the route of the Butterfield Overland Mail, which cuts across the tip of Indian Territory.

''I'm asking you to think like people who live in one small town. We are like a small town of one hundred and twelve people traveling in forty-two wagons. In our small town are two single women and six single men, each driving his or her own wagon. Fifteen of your children are under age twelve, and thirteen of them are between thirteen and sixteen years of age. Thirty-two married couples are parents of those children as well as seven unmarried sons and four unmarried daughters scattered among them. I wouldn't be surprised if we might have a wedding or two before we reach Lone Elm.'' The young people snickered, and a few of their parents nodded their heads in agreement.

Raines continued. ''Like all towns, large or small, it is necessary to have some sort of government with laws or rules, as we call them on the trail. Everyone has a certain responsibility to his neighbor even though our homes may be bedrolls or wagons. You will elect someone like a town mayor, who is the captain of a wagon train, as well as a wagon master, who is the guide.

"Every man can do at least one thing better than most, and we will make use of those special skills. Women and children also are expected to help on the trail. It's normal to have a falling-out once in a while, and we will look to the most sensible people among us to settle quarrels. I expect you to use your bullets to shoot game, not each other. It will take all of your energy just to get through every day on the trail. I'll stop talking now and let you visit among yourselves before you decide on rules and the government for the Sowell Tennessee Train, if that name is agreeable to all of you and to Mr. Sowell, as well."

*   *   *

The sun was setting when Raines dismissed the meeting. 'Thank y'all for a good job. Mrs. Riley and her girls will make copies of your rules tomorrow when we're waiting to cross the river by ferry. Our crossing may take three or four days with this many wagons. Sleep well. I'll wake camp by ringing my cowbell at dawn, and we'll be on our way exactly one hour later. Mr. Hughes, you and your boy have first watch over the stock tonight. Mr. Riley, you and John relieve them at midnight."

Raines picked up his bedroll and found a level spot on the ground for it away from the wagons which were scattered about in no sort of order. He felt tired and welcomed the quiet and solitude as he walked slowly to the cliff which fell straight down twenty-five feet to the muddy shore of the Mississippi River. He was not sure if the sound he heard of a riverboat's horn was real or imagined, but the voice behind him was real. He looked back and saw Nate, one of Riley's sons.

"I never saw a river this big," Nate said in awe. "It shines like the satin ribbon that used to be on my mother's best dress." Though uninvited, he sat on the ground beside Riley.

The man was intrigued by the boy's description of the river's reflection of the setting sun. "She's beautiful tonight," he agreed, "but like any other woman, the old girl has her moods. I've seen the river spread out over her banks 'til she's more than three miles wide. At flood stage, she'll wash away anything not hanging tight by its deep roots that must reach half-way to China." He glanced at Nate out of the corner of his eye and noted the quizzical look on the boy's face.

"The Hatchie River never floods like that, but the fishing is good," Nate replied.

"Do you like to fish?"

"Yes, but I like trapping beaver better. Mr. Sowell used to buy all I had and . . ." Nate's voice broke off.

"What are you planning to do when you get to Texas?" Raines asked.

"Don't know just yet," Nate answered. "I'll have to be patient, wait, and listen for the land to speak. It will tell me what to do. I was born on our farm back home, and I grew up thinking of the land as just another member of our family—my brother, not my sister. I seemed to know how to treat it and use it, and the land returned the favor." Nate paused, then chuckled. "There must be Indian blood in me. I guess I think of land as the Earth Mother too. But now that we've left, I don't expect to see the farm ever again. I don't even know what's on the other side of this here river," Nate said so softly that Raines had to strain to hear him.

"Every river has two sides, the side you are on and the other side," Raines answered as he struggled to make sense of what he wanted to say to this homesick and uncertain young man.

"Take this river here, the Mississippi. She's the biggest river that I know of and she slices the land in two halves. This river cuts the Confederacy in two just like a knife gutting a deer. Folks talk about being east of the Mississippi or west of the Mississippi. That means, I guess, that tonight you are east of the Mississippi and tomorrow, after you ride the ferry across, you'll be west of the Mississippi. When you're in the middle of the river, you'll have one foot in each of the two halves of the Confederate States of America." Raines stopped talking and felt like a fool.

Both of them were silent for a few minutes before Nate asked, "What is REALLY on the other side of the river?"

Raines intertwined his fingers, lay back on the grass, and rested his head on the palms of his clasped hands. He closed his eyes and described the places from memory. "On the other side of the river, the trees grow shorter and the sky becomes bigger and bluer. After a while, the trees are no higher than a bean stalk, and some have scaly bark or thorns. Then trees disappear. There are no trees at all on a vast plain where the grass grows so tall newborn calves get lost in it and drovers can't find them. There are mountains so high their summits are white with snow year 'round, and gorges so deep that settlers have to lower their animals by ropes one at a time and do the same with their wagons.

"On the other side of the river, there are good people and bad people, but enough land for everyone willing to work hard at ranching or farming or mining or even fighting Indians. And those things are only some of what's waiting for you on the other side of the river." Raines said no more, got to his feet, and walked back to where he had spread his bedroll. The guide was asleep by the time the evening star appeared in the sky.

Nate continued to sit quietly until he heard the sound of some animal he couldn't identify. He quickly got to his feet, returned to the wagon, and pulled out his bedroll. He saw the other members of his family already asleep on the ground. When he snuggled into the comfort of his own bed, Nate was not sure he really wanted to cross over to the other side of the river.

Exactly one hour after Raines rang his wake-up cowbell, Sowell snapped his whip in the air to start the horses pulling the lead wagon down the zig-zag trail leading to the eastern bank of the Mississippi and two ferryboats waiting to take them across to the other side of the river.

Matthew was careful to start each wagon in the proper numerical order, but the travelers in wagon number 27 were still eating breakfast. He had anticipated the tardiness of the family and had asked Raines what he should do.

"Nothing. When a party is late for no other reason than their own convenience, the wagon train never waits. If any driver starts late, the wagon goes to the end of the line. The only exception to this rule is if the wagon breaks down, their horses or oxen drop dead, or the woman is in the middle of birthing a baby even though we prefer her to drop it Indian-style while we're traveling," Raines said and shook his finger for emphasis.

The wagon master galloped on ahead, and Matthew kept watch on wagon 27 so the driver would not try to cut in line. When he tried to do so, Matthew told him the wagon had lost its place and would have to go to the end of the line. Matthew felt it was not necessary to list the exceptions, at least, not today.

Matthew was pleased to see the caravan moving along at a fast pace and was relieved the wagons were driven and owned by ordinary people. He hoped he would never see a long line of army wagons ever again if he lived to be a hundred.

* * *

Raines was the first to reach the dock and dismounted at the same time Sowell noticed a group of wagons stopped some distance away. It wasn't until he got closer to the ferryboats that Sowell recognized the group as the impatient ones who left Slurry Creek in a huff while the others waited for Raines to arrive.

"Ahoy, Captain!" Raines called out from the dock. "Are you ready for boarding?"

"Always ready for you, Mr. Raines!" the Captain called down in reply. "Come aboard, sir, and bring your train's captain with you. We'll sort out our business quicker than an osprey can lay an egg. Yankee gunboats are thicker than mosquitoes on this river. They've not bothered us yet, but let's not tarry."

Raines and Sowell hurried up the wide gangplank and were greeted by Captain Agnew who escorted them into the wheelhouse. Sowell liked the man immediately and noted the leathered and lined face of a man who plied the waters for a living. He could not guess the Captain's age and was surprised when the waterman introduced the other men waiting for them.

"This is my son Jackson Agnew, who is captain of the other ferryboat, and the young man taller than either of the two of us is my grandson, Willie Agnew. The boy will make a better captain than his pa or me, but we don't tell him," his grandfather said proudly while Willie blushed. "How many wagons in your train?" Captain Agnew asked. "And what is the livestock count?

"Forty-two wagons," Sowell answered. "We have one hundred and twelve people, eleven milk cows, six calves, thirty pack mules, twenty-three saddle horses, eighty-eight draft horses, and twenty oxen."

"Those people waiting down beyond the lower dock are not in your wagon train, are they?" Captain Agnew asked.

"Not anymore," Sowell replied. "They wouldn't wait for Raines and started off alone even though I advised against it."

"Good riddance, I'd say," Captain replied. "They've done nothing but argue since they have been there. I told them I already had a wagon train scheduled to cross. I gave my word that our boats would be here for Raines and his party.

"We can take two wagons at a time with their draft animals on each sternwheeler. When all of the wagons are across, and it will take three, maybe four days, some of the men will have to come back and help us load the rest of your livestock.

"The driver of each wagon will pay for his own outfit's passage. The amount is based on the number of people and the number of animals carried across. Willie figures the amount and collects the fare. We'll take gold or silver, but no Confederate money. Knowing that good money is scarce, we'll also barter for things people brought along, and we're always glad to accept food. On some days, it's even better than gold."

Raines and Sowell took the information back to the Rileys, who spread out according to the numbers they had given the wagons the day before and informed the members of the train what the procedures would be and how each party could pay for passage.

Nate watched, fascinated, as Mr. Sowell and his father drove their wagons, one after the other, up the wide gangplank jutting out from the bow of the ferryboat and resting on the dock. Deckhands appeared from nowhere, or so it seemed to the boy, and held the horses' bridles so they would not rear from fright when the noisy boat started to move.

Nate saw Captain Agnew high in the wheelhouse and heard two sharp blasts of a shrill whistle as the Captain started the engine and the boat backed smoothly away from the dock. Nate watched two boatmen work the winch that slowly raised the heavy gangplank up from the dock and into the air where it clanked to a stop. Nate thought the gangplank looked like the finger of a huge giant pointing to an eagles' nest high atop a tree nearby.

The two smokestacks continued to belch black smoke as the sternwheeler turned around, its bow pointed toward the far shore. Nate was still watching the paddle wheel propelling the ferryboat smoothly through the water when he heard Raines call his name.

"Nate, get a move on, boy! Mrs. Riley has her wagon on the second ferry already, and you're just standing there with your teeth in your mouth!"

Nate felt the blood rush to his face and quickly climbed into the wagon seat, carefully drove his team up the gangplank, and stopped behind Emma's wagon.

Elizabeth yelled, "Wait for me!" as she ran after him and climbed up on the seat beside her brother just before they heard the metallic noise as the gangplank rose from the dock.

When the gangplank was secure, one of the deckhands approached the passengers. "No need to stay in your wagons. We have blocks for the wheels to secure them and we can handle your horses. They're mighty fine, not like some of the mangy stock we see once in a while.

"The Captain says to invite you up to the wheelhouse. You'll never see a river like this again where you're going. Folks tell me a lot of rivers in the west have water in 'em about once or twice a year. The rest of the time, they're nothing but sand." He grinned.

Captain Jackson Agnew pointed out landmarks and answered Emma's questions about the birds they saw. He told stories of the gigantic fish reeled in from the river, and Nate guessed him to be telling nothing more than tall tales.

Elizabeth felt a bit woozy and asked to be excused from the group. She descended the ladder to the main deck and stood at the rail near the bow where the wind in her face gave her some relief. She fastened her gaze on what appeared to be a small town on the far shore and watched as each building gradually took on its own distinctive silhouette. Elizabeth was disappointed that the small cluster of weathered shacks were not much of a town at all. Whatever it was, she couldn't wait to get off the rocking boat and put her feet on solid ground.

The first sternwheeler was already on its way back for two more wagons when Captain Jack, as the crew called him, was docking. Two deckhands jumped off the ferryboat and secured the lines. Two men worked the winch to lower the gangplank while three others removed the blocks from the wagon wheels. When the lowered gangplank was secure, Emma and Nate tightly held the reins of their teams while deckhands slowly guided the horses down the gangplank and onto dry land. Elizabeth jumped from the boat to the ground first, got out of the way of the horses, and threw up. She bent over walking to a large tree nearby and sat on the ground with her back against its trunk. She closed her eyes and welcomed the slight breeze caressing her pale face. Elizabeth prayed that her stomach would settle before the next ferry arrived.

* * *

The two captains continued the same routines during daylight hours, and the entire Sowell Tennessee Wagon Train made the river crossing in three days. During that time, the Riley men and Mr. Sowell helped young tall Willie Agnew collect and store the items the travelers, and others gone before them, had paid for their passage across the river.

Nate had never been inside a cotton warehouse before and was impressed by its large size although he didn't like its musty smell. The warehouse was empty now except for the neat stacks of items collected as fare but destined to be sold by the Agnews in New Orleans when the war was over. He recognized some of the food packages his own family had prepared for the trip and guessed that Mr. Sowell paid his fare with gold. Nate noted that the Agnews were as shipshape on land as on water and had carefully organized and stacked the items with care.

With his storekeeper mind's eye, Sowell inspected the items and automatically figured the prices some of the pieces should bring in New Orleans if and when they ever got there. He wiped a tear from his eye as he examined a treadle sewing machine similar to the one so prized by his late wife and wondered who the woman was who gave up the machine to the Mississippi River. "What a morbid thought," he said aloud and hoped no one had heard him.

When Emma went inside the warehouse to call the men still working there to supper, she noted a dozen or so baby cradles carefully placed side by side, the largest one first, the smallest last. Each one was different, carefully crafted, she guessed, by fathers and most likely used by all of the babies born to the parents. She gave one a small push with her open hand and watched the cradle rock back and forth until it stopped still. Emma wished one of the cradles had been her own.

* * *

Raines called a short meeting after supper to see if everyone who had made the passage intended to continue the overland journey. No one spoke up, and he ended the meeting by going over the rules once again: "The Riley women have written the rules on paper, which is scarce. We have a few copies to pass around for you to read, and we'll post them each night on the side of Captain Sowell's wagon. I'm going to read them to you right now. If you object to any of them, now's the time to speak up. If I don't hear an argument, all rules will be enforced.

" 'One: All children, except babies, will gather grass when it's plentiful to feed the stock when there is no forage. The older ones will tie the grass into bundles and each wagon will carry enough bundles to keep their own stock alive, if need be.

" 'Two: Healthy men will take the night watch here in the wagon camp and out with the livestock. Two men will be on each shift at each site, the first shift from sundown to midnight; the second shift from midnight to dawn.

" 'Three: The best shots with a gun are designated game hunters.

" 'Four: Four men will be designated scouts to ride ahead and locate the next suitable campsite. Two will wait at that location, two will return and guide the train in.

" 'Five: Two scouts, or outriders, will look for any danger that might come from men, animals, or nature.

" 'Six: When we must ford a river or a stream, the strongest swimmer will first check the depth and swiftness of the water.

" 'Seven: Cooking and laundry will be done by the women and girls. Men traveling alone will do their own. We encourage sharing work and generosity toward others.

" 'Eight: Each wagon is responsible for collecting its own firewood and donating one log when there is a group fire in the evening.

" 'Nine: Everyone not driving a wagon or riding a horse is to walk with the exception of babies and the sick. Riders will alternate riding and leading their horses cavalry style.

" Ten: Those of you with special skills—doctor, carpenter, wheelwright, ferrier, butcher, bullet maker, and so on—are asked to inform the Captain, Mr. Sowell. Don't be modest about your abilities.

" 'Eleven: The wagon master, myself, will choose the route and, if necessary, divide the train into two groups if the feed for the stock becomes so scarce there is danger of their loss by starvation. I don't expect that to happen, but I retain the right. The wagon master has final say as to the stopping place for the night and the configuration of the wagons for defense.

" 'Twelve: Remember that the safety and success of the wagon train to reach its destination depends on the people, not only on the horses, oxen, and mules.'

"Any questions? No? Then, I'll wish you all a good night. We'll be on our way one hour after you hear my cow bell." *I know one wagon that will be in its place in line,* Raines thought as he rolled out his bed under a tree and went to sleep.

Other members of the train followed his lead. They had extinguished all fires, and the four men on watch were in their assigned places.

Nate could not sleep. The events of the day kept replaying in his mind. He crawled out of his bed roll, waved to the watch, and walked back to the bank of the river where he stood quietly listening to the sound of water lapping against the shore. The river was bathed in moonlight, the same as the night before, and Nate was disappointed that both sides of the river looked the same to him.

He wondered how it looked farther downstream and thought about the boats they had seen going all the way to New Orleans and then to the sea. If it really was Fair Oaks people whom Matthew saw several days ago, Nate believed that they must be all the way down river by now.

Nate thought about the time he was with his mother when they nursed Hercules. He remembered how well Old Clara and Luther had taken care of them and thought about Mr. Bailey and Caro and the little girl slave. They must have been on those packet boats. I wonder where they're going.

Nate didn't know how long he stood there alone and jumped when he felt a hand on his shoulder. "It's midnight, boy. You need sleep." He turned and saw his father. "I'm on watch 'til dawn. You be sure to have the coffee ready when I'm done."

Part Four

Chapter Seventeen

Downriver

Nate had seen many different kinds of boats going up and down the river during the three days the wagons were crossing. He guessed that the three packet boats carrying the inhabitants of Fair Oaks Plantation were far down river from where the Sowell Tennessee Wagon Train had camped for the night. Finally, he went back to the comfort of his bed and went to sleep.

* * *

Many miles downriver, Evangeline, on board the second packet boat, was miserable. Not only was her cabin tiny, the food horrible, and the packet boat crowded with unsavory people, Young Mistress was angry because no one would pay a mind to her complaints. She had tried her pouty face on the Captain, but he scowled at her and actually ordered her to stay out of the way and get back to her cabin.

She remembered his exact words and repeated them to Sissy. " 'Madam,' he said to me, 'a packet boat is not the front veranda of a plantation house. You may not have heard that a war is in progress and has disrupted many lives other than your own. I have been forced by circumstances to crowd you and many of your slaves onto a boat built for vastly fewer passengers and cargo. While your family paid in gold, it is barely enough for putting up with you. As Captain of this ship, I order you to your cabin, and I do not wish to see your face again until you disbark at New Orleans. And what's more, I pity the Captain of the steamship waiting for you there!'

"Have you heard anything like this in your whole life, Sissy? The next time the boats stop to take on more wood, I'm going straight to Alexander and tell him what that horrid man said to me.

I will not step foot on this miserable boat again. Mama will let me stay with her when she hears about it."

When Evangeline flung herself on to the small bunk, her feet stuck out over the edge. Sissy gently put a wet cloth on the forehead of her agitated Mistress. "I'll leave you be for a spell so you can rest," she said quietly, walked the few steps to the cabin's door, opened it, and closed it quietly behind her.

Sissy walked carefully through the throng of passengers, many of whom slept at night on the deck, and found an open spot on the railing. Although she had never seen an ocean, the air smelled salty and she guessed the Gulf of Mexico could not be too far away. At least, that's what she heard some of the other passengers say. While she enjoyed the adventure, Sissy sorely missed Old Clara and Luther and the other old slaves she loved as if they were her own family. *They really are my family,* she thought, then banished the memory from her head for fear of weeping for those left behind at Fair Oaks.

The first packet boat's shrill whistle startled her and she watched as it changed course to dock at the western shore where she saw stacks of wood piled high. Sissy, in the second boat, returned to the cabin and carefully woke Evangeline. "It looks like we be stopping for wood soon," she said.

Evangeline woke up slowly. "Mama and Raleigh are on the first boat," she mumbled. "Gather up my things, Sissy. We're leaving this awful place. Is the third boat stopping too?"

"Far's I know," Sissy answered. "Master Alexander, he on dat one. Just think, all dat's left of Fair Oaks Plantation fits on three little boats on da biggest river in da world."

"Hush, Sissy! Just get my things and come on."

The Captain was busy giving orders to the dockworkers replenishing the wood for his paddlewheeler. He longed for the old days when passengers traveled in style, the dining salon was elegant, the smoking and card rooms turned a tidy profit for the gamblers who gave him a percentage of their winnings, and transporting cargo was secondary to the passenger trade.

The Captain and crew were too busy to see Evangeline Randolph disembark the boat and hurry toward the boat ahead where Mrs. Randolph and son Raleigh were quartered. Sissy, loaded down with baggage, followed her. The dock was crowded with workers and passengers who had gotten off to walk around while the three packet boats were docked for refueling.

Evangeline, with Sissy in tow, pushed her way up the gangplank of her mother's boat as passengers were disembarking to stretch their legs on solid ground and enjoy more space than was afforded them on the over-crowded packet boat. Evangeline wasn't looking at faces when she strongly shoved aside one man coming down the gangplank.

"Ouch! What do you think you're doing!" he said and shoved her back. She looked up in surprise and saw Raleigh.

"I'm looking for Mama," she said crossly. "I'm going to stay with her for the rest of this miserable trip."

"Mama's gone back to find Alexander, her favorite son," Raleigh said sarcastically. "He's on the last boat and so are the Baileys. If you want to see Mama, you'd better hurry back there. Her cabin door is locked and you can't get in. Besides, this crowd probably would push you overboard. We're overcrowded as it is." Raleigh didn't wait for his sister's reply and pushed his way down to the dock where he disappeared in the crowd.

Evangeline groaned. "Come on, Sissy." They turned, fought their way back down the gangplank, and started toward the third packet boat waiting for its supply of wood from the dwindling pile. They didn't even see the two scruffy men who slipped up behind them and quickly lifted them up off their feet. The men pushed both of them into a small tool shed nearby, slammed the door shut, and pushed a strong stick through the eyelet protruding through the hasp to lock the door from the outside. The noises on the dock and boats masked the young women's screams.

Raleigh stepped out from behind the shed, surreptitiously paid the two men with Confederate money, and stepped back into the crowd beginning to reboard the boat. He grinned as he thought of the clever way he had just gotten even with Evangeline for being their father's favorite child. He knew she would get herself to the steamship or, if not, find another way to Brownsville. His sister had always charmed men who went out of their way to take care of her and fulfill her every wish. As for Sissy, he hoped she would drown before she got to Texas. *I hated that little colored "present" the minute I saw her. I can't prove it, but I think Evangeline taught that uppity slave to read,* he thought.

When Raleigh was back on board, he stood by the boat's rail and watched for his mother who had stopped on the dock and seemed to be arguing with Alexander and Bailey. When the shrill whistle sounded on the first boat, Mistress Rebecca Randolph turned and hurried to board just before the deckhands hauled up the gangplank.

"Have you seen Evangeline?" she asked when she approached Raleigh still standing by the rail.

"No. I don't think she got off the boat. Seasick, I would imagine. Evangeline never did like the water. Is everything all right, Mother?" he answered.

"Quite all right," she answered and left him standing where he was as she turned her back on her youngest son and returned to her cabin.

* * *

Alexander and Bailey continued their conversation on the dock. Mrs. Bailey stood at the boat rail looking down at the two men and wondering about the nature of their conversation. She knew her husband had misgivings about the whole enterprise and had complained to her about the folly of leaving behind all of the leading Fair Oaks slaves who kept their own tightly-knit black community functioning smoothly and efficiently.

He felt that some of the younger slaves the Randolphs had brought showed promise, but without the guidance of the leaders left behind, the slaves they chose to bring were restless and unhappy, especially since they were cooped up in the hold where cotton and other cargo normally was stacked. Bailey told Alexander that he could not identify any one slave who seemed to have the trust and confidence of the others, something the overseer felt was necessary for leadership. He was discouraged when he believed in his heart that the eldest Randolph son had no idea what he was talking about and wondered if Master Alexander thought Bailey himself to be ignorant.

"We'll be in New Orleans tomorrow," Alexander countered. "There will be more room, and, hopefully, more food on the ocean-going steamer. If we let them off these packet boats, some slaves might try to escape and head north. I understand the Yankees now are refusing to recognize the Fugitive Slave Law and return escaped slaves to their rightful owners as they have done before. Some fool Union general at Fortress Monroe in Virginia declared slaves to be contraband of war now that the Confederate States of America is considered to be a foreign country and, therefore, the law no longer applies.'' Alexander spit in disgust. ''Have a little patience, Bailey. Things will be better when we reach Texas.''

Alexander reboarded the boat and went to his cabin. He shared it with no one, saying he needed all the space for his record books. To pass the time, he got out his playing cards, practiced sleight of hand moves, and fondly remembered the hours he had spent at university practicing the tricks of a gambler's trade with several of his classmates who were doing the same.

Bailey stood at the rail and watched the final loading of firewood then joined his wife in their tiny cabin. She had a glass of whiskey waiting for him.

* * *

The Captain of the oceangoing steamer *Texas Star,* at anchor near New Orleans, did not mind the wait. Ellis & Ellis, Surveyors of Brownsville, Texas, had paid his company handsomely in gold to transport the Fair Oaks Plantation party, slaves and all, from New Orleans to Port Isobel, not far from Brownsville. The Captain looked forward to the generous bonus they had promised him if the precious cargo was delivered without loss and in good order.

''My dear Mrs. Randolph,'' Captain Cunningham greeted her as Rebecca walked up the gangplank on the arm of her eldeset son.

''I hope your accommodations outshine those on packet boats,'' she said wryly before introducing her sons. ''Captain Cunningham, may I present my sons, Alexander and Raleigh Randolph. My daughter Evangeline will be coming shortly. She suffers from seasickness, I fear.''

''On the river?'' the Captain asked. ''Then we shall have our medical man take a look at her. I'm sure he has a cure for whatever may be causing her distress. She will be escorted to stateroom number four when she arrives.''

Several orderlies guided their passengers to their respective staterooms which were, indeed, elegant in comparison to those they had just left behind. Mrs. Bailey went alone to their assigned cabin on a lower deck and waited for her husband who was supervising the loading of their cargo and the herding of the slaves into the hold along with crates of provisions.

Bailey said nothing, but he thought it unwise for the dockworkers and ship's crew to store the Randolph food crates in the hold along with their slaves. The overseer felt tired, unappreciated, and angry about what he considered to be unwise decisions Mistress Randolph and Alexander had made to effect the move from Tennessee to Texas. He believed staying at Fair Oaks, regardless of the war, would have been a better choice than the folly of this difficult move. Bailey felt certain a goodly number of crates stored with the slaves would be empty of food by the time the Randolph party left the ship at Port Isobel, and the thought gave him a feeling of perverse pleasure.

The feeling grew stronger when he arrived at his cabin and found it to be quite substandard, nothing like he was led to believe by Alexander Randolph. "I suppose the Randolphs are having fits again," he said to his wife.

"Not at all. From what the ship's purser told me, the family's staterooms on the upper deck are quite luxurious," his wife said. "But look. Here's a bowl of fresh fruit, there are clean sheets on the beds, and the bathroom is just down the gangway. You might even find it a relief to be as far away from the Randolphs as possible for a few days. I doubt any of them will lower themselves to come down here looking for you." She put her arms around her husband and kissed him soundly. "There. This isn't so bad, is it?"

* * *

The *Texas Star* was two days at sea before the doctor informed the Captain that he had not been able to treat Mrs. Randolph's daughter because he hadn't been able to find her. Not only that, the orderly said the beds in the young lady's stateroom appeared not to have been slept in.

The Captain quietly initiated a search of the ship from bow to stern and top to bottom. Either the young lady had never boarded or she had jumped overboard without being seen. With great reluctance, he informed Mrs. Randolph and her two sons of the situation.

Mrs. Randolph promptly fainted when she heard the news. Randolph rushed to his mother's side, and waited for the doctor to bring the smelling salts. Alexander, not taking the Captain's word, got Bailey and a dozen of the slaves to search the ship again.

The chosen slaves were delighted with the task. When their unsuccessful search was over and the slaves returned to the hold, they regaled the others with stories of the magnificent ship, the luxurious staterooms, the noisy and frightening engine room, the amazing galley, and the strange-looking uniforms the sailors wore. They briefly considered mutiny, but since few of the slaves could swim, they decided against it. They entertained themselves for the rest of the day by making up stories of what had happened to Young Mistress Evangeline. "And don't forget Sissy," one of the woman said, "Wherever Mistress Evangeline be, for sure, Sissy be der too."

Alexander, Bailey, Mrs. Bailey, Mrs. Randolph, Raleigh, and the ship's purser spent the rest of the day again questioning everyone who had been on the packet boats as to whether or not they had seen Evangeline and Sissy the last day.

None of the slaves had seen them. Raleigh, also assigned to the first packet boat, said that he had seen them several times throughout the trip down the river. After jogging his memory, he added that he thought he saw them get off at the last stop to take on wood. He seemed to recall that Evangeline wanted to speak to their mother and he just assumed his sister had found her then returned to her own assigned boat and continued the journey. "Of course," he added, "I thought Sissy would watch and protect Evangeline. That IS the duty of a body slave."

"Somehow, they missed boarding the *Texas Star*," Alexander finally announced grimly. "Don't faint again, Mother. After we disembark at Port Isobel, I'll return with the *Texas Star* to New Orleans and find my sister and her body servant. Evangeline is not as fragile as she looks. I'm sure she is safe wherever she may be. Mother, she has money, has she not?"

"A good deal of it, gold coins sewn into her petticoat," his mother answered.

"It's settled, then. Raleigh will take care of things here with you. The Ellis brothers are meeting the boat and will look forward to helping you in any way, I have no doubt. Don't worry, Mother. Evangeline and I shall be back here before you've even had time to miss us,'' Alexander reassured his mother while Raleigh looked on. Then he approached the captain of the ship. ''Captain, will you be returning to New Orleans soon?''

''Indeed,'' he replied, expecting an additional bonus. ''It will take us the rest of the day to unload and then take on cargo from here. We shall do our best to work as quickly as possible and set our course for New Orleans in the morning.''

* * *

Mr. Mallory, the owner of the company supplying wood to Mississippi river boats, seldom visited his wharves. Curiosity brought him to the wharf this day. He wanted to see the entire population of Fair Oaks Plantation going en masse down the Mississippi, something of a rarity even in these peculiar times.

After visiting with the captains, he went searching for his manager and found him in the office going over the books. ''Mr. Mallory, sir, how good to see you. You have made a fine amount of money—in gold—today, but our wood supply has been depleted, and I'm getting the cutters ready to go out again tomorrow.''

''I saw the Fair Oaks Plantation group and talked to the packet boat captains,'' Mr. Mallory said. ''All three seemed pleased with the money but were anxious to be rid of the group. I suspect travel with that many slaves on board made them edgy.

''Yes, sir. I don't doubt it. Things were pretty busy here for a while, but we had help from some of the slaves on board. I think they were glad to be off the boat to do the work. We think there were over a hundred of them, but most of the slaves were kept on the ships.

''The Randolph family got off and walked the docks some. To tell the truth, even I was glad to see them go. The packet boat captains said they were pretty demanding, and captains usually are closemouthed about their passengers.''

Mr. Mallory laughed. ''Maybe so, but I'd imagine those same captains are counting their money right about now. The captain of the *Texas Star* will be the one with the headache and the money before too long. You might as well close up and send the dockworkers home. It's nearly dark. No more boats will be coming in today and you say we don't have enough wood to supply them even if they did.''

Mr. Mallory absentmindedly whistled "Dixie" as he walked the distance to his carriage. He jumped when he heard banging on the tool shed door. The noise was interspersed with female cries for help. The door was simple to open. He merely pulled out the stick, swung back the hasp, and pulled on the door. His mouth fell open as he gazed in amazement at a beautiful Southern belle and her colored maid.

"Thank God!" Evangeline exclaimed as the threw her arms around the startled man. "Where is everyone? Where is my mother? And my brothers?" She collapsed weeping.

"Mistress, Mistress," Sissy comforted. "Everything be fine now, thanks to dis kind man."

"Are you part of the Fair Oaks group?" Mallory asked.

Sissy nodded her head. "Looks like Mistress Evangeline and me be left behind. Da rest be gone to Brownsville, Texas."

Mallory regained his composure. "It would be my pleasure, and the pleasure of my wife, I'm sure, if you would do me the honor of accompanying me to my home. I can help you catch up with your party tomorrow. Until then, please allow me to take you to my carriage. We shall be at my home within the hour." He helped Evangeline up to the seat and took his place beside her. Sissy climbed up by herself to sit next the colored driver. He nodded a welcome to her, cracked his whip, and the handsome horses broke into a smooth gait as the carriage traveled down the road. Sissy liked the rocking motion of the carriage and the sounds of turning wheels on dry land better than boat noises.

After an hour, Sissy found the carriage ride to be only slightly better than the boat ride, and she welcomed the sight of a house up ahead. It was dusk and she saw lights in the downstairs windows but the upstairs remained dark. The driver stopped the carriage at the front door and quickly hopped out to assist Evangeline and Mr. Mallory.

Evangeline let out a loud scream and exclaimed, "Sissy!' You left my things back in that horrid shed! I've a mind to have you whipped!"

"I'm so sorry, Mistress! If dis kind driver take me back, I gets dem," Sissy answered.

Mr. Mallory broke in, "My dear young lady, I do hope nothing of great value was left behind. I fear the scoundrels who frequent the docks at night will have absconded with your things by now. Let me accompany you into the house. I'm sure we have everything to meet your needs."

Evangeline took his arm and smiled her sweetest smile while the carriage driver helped Sissy down to the ground. The driver whispered, "Take care. Da master has a way wid female people. If 'n ya needs me, I be in dat room next to da kitchen." He turned to lead the horses to the barn and left Sissy standing at the foot of the porch steps.

Sissy climbed up to the porch and followed Evangeline and Mr. Mallory into the spacious front hall where a young mulatto servant took her master's hat and coat. Sissy guessed the girl to be no more than twelve years old and in the family way. There was no doubt about it, and by the look of her belly Sissy feared the birth would come at any minute, and she hoped she and Evangeline would be gone before then.

"What's that you say, Biddy? Mrs. Mallory was called away to nurse her mother who fell down the porch stairs? What a shame that you won't be able to meet my lovely wife, Miss Evangeline. I know she will be crushed not to have met you. Oh, I see that Mrs. Mallory left me a note on the hall table explaining her absence. Biddy, take Miss Evangeline up to the guest room. On second thought, I'll escort her there myself," Mr. Mallory said as he took Evangeline by the arm and led her up the stairs.

Biddy turned to Sissy. "You waits here an' I makes you a bed in da pantry room."

There was something in the pregnant girl's manner that gave Sissy an uneasy feeling. *It's because I'm so tired,* she thought, and walked over to sit in one of the brocade upholstered chairs at each end of the narrow hall table. As she sat down, her arm brushed against a paper on the table and it fell to the floor. Sissy quickly picked it up and as she returned it to the table top, she couldn't help but see the large script. It was a letter and she felt compelled to read it.

Mister Mallory,

You have broken my heart many times, but I shall not allow you to do it again. After my many demands to know the father of Biddy's baby and my threat to turn her out of my house if she continued to keep silent, the child has told me that my own husband is the father. How could you do this to me? And under my very own roof, you cad!

Have I not simply ignored the common gossip of your assignations with women of every class both here and in New Orleans? Have I not furnished you with a prosperous business left to me by my father? Have I not been a loving, faithful, and forgiving wife?

When your sexual appetite invades the sanctity of my own home, when you abuse the loyal slave who is mine alone, having inherited Biddy from my own dear Aunt Arabella (may God rest her soul), when you have betrayed my own trust and love, you leave me no choice.

I have gone to New Orleans to see my solicitor and to file for a divorce, the Church be damned. God will forgive me for leaving a wretch like you, my husband in name only, who has given me no children but with other women—white, black, and brown—has increased the population of the entire parish!

At my instructions, my solicitor will erase your name from my will and send his man to evict you from my property including the house, the lumber company, the farm land, and in addition, reclaim the gold watch and chain I gave you as a wedding present.

[Signed] Your Former Wife

P.S. Do not ever speak my name again in what's left of your miserable life!

Sissy, wide-eyed, returned the letter to its place on the table. She thought how foolish Mr. Mallory had been not to read the letter when he came in, but then, he could not have been expected to know that he had left alone a slave who could read.

Biddy came back and motioned Sissy to come to where the slave had prepared her bed. Sissy shook her head. "Biddy, be very quiet and go get the carriage driver, quickly now."

Biddy returned with the driver who was still dressed. Sissy told them the contents of the letter as Biddy wept softly.

"My name is Ezra and Biddy be my chile," the driver said and put his arm around her just as her contractions began.

"Help me take her to your bed," Sissy said, "then go quickly to find Miss Evangeline and bring her to us. And be quiet."

Sissy had the water heating on the stove by the time Ezra returned alone. "Master, he lock da girl's door, but I hears him singin' and getting hisself ready in da other room. I comes down for da keys." He quickly grabbed a ring of keys hanging from a nail on the kitchen wall and disappeared.

Within minutes he was back pulling Evangeline behind him. "What is the meaning of this! How dare you . . ." The look from Sissy stopped her mid-sentence.

"Thank this man for saving you, you ungrateful girl! That charming Mr. Mallory was about to deflower you as he did to the young girl in pain and ready to deliver his baby in the next room!" Sissy shouted in anger.

Astounded, Evangeline began, "Sissy, you have never . . ."

"Hush, girl! Carry this water into that room and then heat some more in that pan over there. Ezra, I need clean cloths." Sissy followed the sounds of the girl's pain and disappeared into Ezra's room. Although she had never delivered a baby by herself, she had been present at many births at Fair Oaks Plantation and called on the spirit of Old Clara to be with her and guide her hands through this one.

As it traversed the birth canal and pushed its tiny head into the world for all to see, they could tell that the baby was white. "Too much white blood in the mama and not enough black blood in the papa for it to be any other way," Sissy said.

Both Ezra and Evangeline were mesmerized. Even though she gagged, Evangeline didn't object when Sissy told her how to clean up the newborn. Sissy was surprised by the serene, almost prayerful look on her Young Mistress's face when she laid the baby girl next to its mother. Sissy guessed it to be the first time in Evangeline's entire life when she had participated in something that was truly real with no bows and pretty paper to mask the emotions and significance of the event.

After Sissy had cleaned up after the birth and both mother and baby were sleeping soundly, she went into the kitchen and was surprised to find Evangeline and Ezra sitting at the same table and drinking coffee from simple cups. She knew Ezra had brewed it because Evangeline had trouble heating the water.

"Sit yourself," he said as he got another plain pottery cup and poured some for Sissy. "Thank you fo' bringing da baby into da world. Da baby be white, I sees. I 'spects Mistress take it as her own, her wantin' a baby so bad."

Sissy nodded. "I think you right. Ezra, will you please get da letter I told you about on da table. Mistress Evangeline needs to read it."

Evangeline turned white as she read the woman's letter. "What a terrible man!" she exclaimed. "We must get away from here immediately!"

"No need, Mistress. I done locked Master in da room. Der be no way he get out afore da man comes from da so-li-ci-tor. Mistress, she left three days ago. Da letter be der all da time, but Biddy an me, we don't know what it says. We cain't read."

* * *

The next day when the man from the solicitor's office arrived, Evangeline explained in great detail the events from the time Mr. Mallory "rescued" her and Sissy from the tool shed up to the present time. She gave him the letter. He read it, found it hard to keep from smiling, then went upstairs and slipped it under the door for Mr. Mallory, the intended recipient, to read.

The solicitor's representative returned to the kitchen and formally introduced himself as Mr. Jenkins. When he first arrived, he had deemed it odd to find the obviously wealthy and beautiful young woman sitting in the kitchen with slaves and stranger still to find her with a newborn white baby in her arms when he came downstairs after "delivering" the letter to Mr. Mallory.

"If someone will give me the key to the man's room, I'll bring my assistants in to take him away. To be fair, his wife, rather the lady who is divorcing Mr. Mallory, will allow him to take his clothing and personal effects and any cases he may need in which to pack them. I, personally, have been instructed to reclaim the gold watch and chain."

Ezra took the proper key from the ring and gave it to Mr. Jenkins. The representative opened the front door and called to the two burly men with him. The three of them went upstairs. About thirty minutes later, those in the kitchen heard Mr. Mallory protesting loudly all the way down the stairs, through the front hall, and clear out to the wagon waiting to carry him to an unknown destination.

Shortly thereafter, the owner of the home entered the front door. "Biddy," she called, "where are you?"

Ezra walked out to meet his mistress in the front hall. ''Biddy be in my room. Da baby be born. A girl. Come see, Mistress Mallory.'' He paused, embarrassed. ''What do I call you now?''

''Mistress Dupre, my maiden name, will be fine.''

''Two new folks be here. One slave an' her mistress. Da slave bring da baby an' Biddy be fine.''

Mistress Dupre simply nodded to Evangeline as she went through the kitchen to Ezra's room. When she saw the tiny white infant next to the mother-child, tears filled her eyes. She held Biddy's hand and sat on the side of the clean but worn bed.

Sissy had followed the woman into the room and stood back watching. Biddy, still weak, spoke to Sissy with her eyes and the slave who could read walked to the bed, gently lifted the baby and placed her in Mistress Dupre's arms.

* * *

Late in the afternoon Ezra served tea in the parlor. Sissy had never taken tea in a parlor before and expected Mistress Evangeline to disallow it. Mistress Dupre personally invited Sissy to join Evangeline and her and questioned them as to how it came about that Sissy was at her home when the baby came.

Evangeline related the story, leaving out no detail, while Sissy sat quietly sipping her tea and enjoying the luxury of it.

''And was it you, my dear, who taught your slave to read?'' Mistress Dupress asked innocently.

The color drained from Evangeline's face.

''Tut, tut, my girl. Don't be afraid. I am not one to carry tales. I expect the same of you, however, and insist that you forget any association you may have had with ANYONE for the past three days. Do we have an agreement?''

''Yes, Ma'am,'' Evangeline answered meekly.

''Now that the matter is settled, I shall ask one more favor. My wish is for the both of you to remain here for one month. By then, my dear little Biddy should be well and on her feet again. Never having given birth to a baby myself, and knowing nothing about being a mother, I want you, Sissy, to teach me what I should know.''

''Yes, Ma'am,'' she answered. ''At Fair Oaks Plantation, I helped Old Clara with the babies. I'll pass my learning on to you.''

Mistress Dupre smiled. "One more thing, Sissy. I notice that when you speak to white people, you speak white English, but when you speak to Biddy and Ezra, you speak colored talk. How did that happen?"

Sissy gasped, stunned by the question. She thought a few minutes before she replied. "I have read many books. All of them are written in white English. Books taught me their language. My slave family taught me colored talk. There are no books, not a single one, written in colored talk."

Mistress Dupre smiled and nodded her head, impressed with the intelligence of the young colored woman sitting on the other side of the tea table. Evangeline looked puzzled. Ezra came in to clear away the tea. Biddy, still a little shaky, followed her papa, walked slowly across the room, and carefully put the infant child in Mistress Dupre's arms.

"Thank you, Biddy," Mistress said softly. "You know I shall love and care for this child as my own, and you shall be like a sister to her. I shall name her Arabella, Arabella Gabrielle Dupre. I like the sound of it. My mother named me Gabrielle and her older sister was called Arabella. The two names go together, don't you think?"

"Yes'um. Dey do. Da names be beautiful, like you, Mistress," Biddy answered.

Sissy stood up and put her arm around Biddy. "Come into the kitchen with me. I've made you some special soup to help your body heal. Then, I want you back in bed to rest for a little while."

Biddy did as she was told but looked askance at the colored body slave who talked white. She glanced at Mistress Dupre for reassurance and permission to leave.

None of them knew that Alexander, retracing his family's route downriver, had discovered Evangeline's belongings in the tool shed on the dock and was disheartened by the thought that his sister and her body servant had either been kidnapped or were already dead.

* * *

Sissy was worried. Biddy's milk had not come, and Arabella's tiny cry was weak. "Mistress Dupre, your baby must have a wet nurse and have one today!" Sissy reported.

"Ezra! Get the carriage!" the lady called and seemed to hand Arabella to Evangeline, put on her bonnet and shawl, and burst out the front door in one flowing motion.

Sissy and Evangeline heard the carriage leave. "What shall I do with the baby?" Evangeline asked helplessly.

"Do what all women since Eve has done!" Sissy answered crossly. "I'm sorry, Miss Evangeline. I should not have spoken to you like that. Sit here in the rocker. Hold the baby in your arms like this or on your shoulder like this. Rock her gently and sing softly like your mammy did to you when you were a baby. You can do it. I've got to tend to Biddy."

Sissy sat beside the bed and held her patient's hand. She thought of the many times before when she had done just that at Fair Oaks and how much she had learned from Old Clara. The memory brought tears, and Sissy let them run freely down her cheeks. She wondered what Luther and the other old slaves left behind were doing and felt pangs of homesickness. *Leaving Fair Oaks was a bad thing for everyone,* she thought.

An hour later, her patient was sitting up in bed and Sissy was spooning soup into Biddy's mouth when they heard the carriage arrive. Mistress Dupre burst into the kitchen door then through to Ezra's room. She had a large red-headed white woman with her. "Where's my baby?" Mistress demanded.

"Evangeline has her in the parlor," Sissy answered as she fluffed Biddy's pillow and helped her lie down again. She returned to the kitchen with the empty bowl and spoon and went on to the parlor.

Sissy was moved by the sight. The wet nurse's bulk overflowed the arms of the rocking chair, but Arabella's tiny mouth hid the pink nipple on the woman's huge white breast. Mistress Dupre had pulled up a straight chair and sat facing the tender scene. Evangeline simply stood staring, having never seen a white wet nurse before much less a breast so much heftier than her own small and dainty ones. Sissy was about to speak when she heard the commotion on the front porch.

"Help me, somebody! I needs some help out here! Somebody come an' help me! I be about to drop 'em!" Ezra called frantically.

Sissy rushed to open the front door. Ezra stood there with a squirming baby in each arm. Sissy reached out to catch the one wiggling out of his grasp. "Dey be Missus Johnson's," Ezra said and pushed his way through the open door. He stood in the front hall and yelled again, "I needs help!"

Evangeline came through the parlor door and found herself holding a squirming red-headed baby boy as Ezra ran out the front door. He reappeared with two toddlers and sat each one in a chair next to the narrow table. "Y'all stays sittin' right here, or ole Ezra, he be back to skin yo' alive! One more," he said as he passed Sissy on his way back to the carriage.

Ezra had the hand of a sullen little girl, closed the door behind them, then dragged her over to the staircase, and sat her down hard on the bottom step. His glare dared her to move. "Dat be all of 'em. Da older ones still be at home, der pa off huntin', and der ma won't come widout da little ones," Ezra explained to those close enough to hear him.

"Now, he addressed the children, "I is gonna get myself a cup of coffee, an' when I come back, I brings a molassas cookie to the chilluns who is still where I puts 'em." Ezra disappeared. The children stayed put.

"I think we're holding twin boys," Sissy whispered to Evangeline.

"And mine is getting squirmy," Evangeline answered. She glanced by accident at the sullen little girl still staying put on the bottom stair. The child suddenly smiled and shook her heard in the affirmative.

"Sugar tit! Follow me!" Sissy said to Evangeline.

As they both started for the kitchen, Evangeline called over her shoulder, "Remember! Molassas cookies for everyone who stays put!"

Ezra was just pouring his coffee in a cup when the two arrived with the squirming twins. He frowned and was about to banish them from his domain when Sissy reassured him. "Sugar tit," she said. He pointed to the sugar bowl and a loaf of freshly baked white bread.

Sissy put her twin in Evangeline's other arm and expertly tore two squares of cloth from a clean dish towel and spread the pieces out flat on the table. She cut the crusts from a slice of bread, tore it in half, and shaped each piece into a small ball. Ezra held the sugar bowl steady while she rolled the balls in it until both were coated with fine white sugar. Sissy carefully placed a sugar ball in the center of each square, pulled up the four points, and expertly twisted the cloth to secure the sugar ball inside. She grasped the rough edge of the dish towel with her teeth and tore off two thin strips of cloth, which she used to tie the sweet bread pieces inside and ready the homemade contraptions for use.

Sissy put a sugar tit in the mouth of each baby and lifted one child back into her arms. Both of the little ones sucked, happy and satisfied. The other occupants of the house sighed with relief and were grateful for the quiet.

"One of 'em is Billy Bob and da other be called Willie Rob, but I cain't tell which one is which," Ezra said as he poured the two women some coffee. "You is gonna need dis. I can tell da two babies done have plenty of der mama's fine milk 'cause dey be so strong an' yell so loud." All three of the grownups burst into laughter.

When he went back into the front hall with his molasses cookies, Ezra found that all of the Johnson children had stayed put. He was surprised but pleased when each one said, "Thank you," when he passed out his cookies.

* * *

Mrs. Johnson thought she had died and gone to heaven. Ezra brought down a bigger rocking chair from the attic, and all she had to do was sit in it and nurse Arabella, Willie Rob, and Billy Bob. Once she fed Willie Rob twice because she said she couldn't tell them apart either. She found her second greatest pleasure, after Ezra's scrumptious meals, to be the peace and quiet away from her other children and romantic husband.

From time to time, Mrs. Johnson, between feedings, would visit the school set up for her other children in the front hall. Mistress Dupre insisted that the Johnson children learn to read and write and called upon both Evangeline and Sissy to teach them. Ezra and Biddy, not yet completely recovered, made up the other members of the student body. A third adult was added when Mrs. Johnson had Ezra carry in her rocker and found nursing to be no impediment to learning.

Mistress Dupre, with the zeal of a Methodist missionary, had organized each person's day and had written the duties and chores as well as bedtimes under the names of all of the children who took pleasure in reading the words even if they didn't particularly like what the words said. They were unaccustomed to such an orderly life but knew better than to complain with Ezra keeping such close watch over them.

The sullen girl, whose name was Mary Beth, was transformed into a child with a delightful personality when she read a simple story in a small book for the first time in her life. "When I grow up, I want to be a teacher like you, Miss Evangeline," she said.

Evangeline admitted to Mistress Dupre that she enjoyed her role as teacher even though she had never associated with lower class people before. "I appreciate your many kindnesses to me, but I am anxious to get back to my family, my own people."

Her words hurt Mistress Dupre although she gave no outward evidence of it. The new mother sat in the parlor with Arabella resting comfortably over her shoulder and gently patted the baby's back until she burped. "I told you, I believe, that I sent a letter to your mother in Brownsville to tell her you were safe with me. I sent it with one of the packet boat captains to give to the Captain of the *Texas Star*. Captain Cunningham was a dear friend of my father and is a loyal friend of mine. I have no doubt your mother has received the letter. A copy is in my desk over there. You may read it."

My dear Mrs. Randolph,

The purpose of this letter is to assuage your fears as to the whereabouts of your lovely daughter Evangeline and her body servant, Sissy. They are safe with me in my home. Captain Cunningham, who has kindly delivered this letter into your hands, can vouch for my character as well as my means.

The story, which we have pieced together is as follows: When your boats stopped for refueling at the company (owned by myself, incidentally), Evangeline and Sissy left their packet boat in search of you. While walking on the dock, someone, unknown and unseen, forced them into a small tool shed and locked the door. They were found later that same day by a person who had connections with my company at that time and brought to my home. Although I was not here at the time, my servants welcomed them graciously and attended to your daughter's every need. I returned a short time later but by then, it was too late to catch up with your party.

I am a new mother. My first child, a daughter named Arabella, was born about that time. With the war on, I was unable to find someone to help and guide me through the joyful but daunting task of motherhood, and your daughter Evangeline with her body servant has been gracious enough to agree to stay with me for several weeks.

I must congratulate you for having reared such a delightful, beautiful, and compassionate young woman, and know how anxious you are to have her safely in your arms once again.

Please know that I can personally assure you that she will be delivered safely to you in a few weeks. Captain Cunningham has sent word to me that he will send his first mate to fetch her and Sissy the next time he sails for Port Isobel and that he will personally deliver her to your door.

In gratitude for her generous assistance here, I plan to present Evangeline with a lovely cameo and diamond brooch given to me by my late Aunt Arabella.

Yours,
Gabrielle Antoinette Dupre

Evangeline put down the letter. "It was very kind of you to write it. I confess being here is much better than being on that packet boat. It was horrible."

"The first mate on the *Texas Star* will be coming for you in three days. He will be in a small launch, not a packet boat, and it should not stink," Mistress Dupree said and smiled.

The following morning, Ezra wondered what had become of Miss Evangeline. An imperial Southern Belle appeared in her place. She expected him to serve her coffee in china cups in the parlor and meals in the dining room. Whenever Mrs. Johnson was ready for feeding time, Evangeline was nowhere to be found and left it to Sissy and Biddy to bring in the babies to nurse.

Evangeline spent her time walking near the river or on her bed resting. She avoided the schoolroom, and the children were puzzled by her absence. What bothered Ezra most was the way Evangeline treated Sissy. "Like a slave," he said to Biddy.

Mistress Dupre missed nothing, held her peace, and adjusted the daily schedule to accommodate the loss of one teacher.

The day before the first mate was to arrive, Mary Beth came running in from the berry patch. Her chore that day was to pick blackberries. "Mama! Mama! Pa's coming!"

Mrs. Johnson, got herself up out of her rocker and went out on the porch. Arabella was still attatched to her nipple. "Lordy! Jacob, what you doing here?" she called to her husband who drove up in a wagon.

"Come to fetch you, my girl," he said with a wink. "Time for you an' the young-'uns to come back home. I brought you a four-legged milker," he said as Mistress Dupre came out the front door. Sissy was close behind.

Mistress Dupre frowned when she saw the nanny goat Mr. Johnson was lifting down from the wagon.

Sissy put her hand lightly on the woman's shoulder. "It's all right. Goat's milk is nearly as good as mother's milk, and Ezra can fix a bottle and some sort of nipple on it. Arabella is healthy and strong now. Mrs. Johnson and her brood can't stay here forever, even though I shall miss them."

The children were delighted to see their pa, and he lifted each one and kissed them all. Sissy thought it a loving family.

It was as much of a whirlwind when they left as when they came, Ezra thought as he led the nanny goat to the barn. He was glad he had just baked a batch of molassas cookies which he sent along with the crowd. *Dey be gone before dey gets home,* I wager.

Mistress Dupre made Mrs. Johnson promise not to open the large package she gave her before arriving back at her own home. When they got there, all of the Johnsons gathered round and declared it a better day than Christmas. There were toys for all the children and a goodly supply of paper along with dozens of pencils and a whole shelf of school books. Mrs. Johnson opened a small box and found a note in it.

Mary Beth proudly read what it said.

> These pearls are as beautiful as you. Thank you for saving the life of my baby. I shall tell her what you did when she is older. If you ever need help, I am here to help you. All you need to do is ask.
>
> Your friend,
> Gabrielle Antoinette Dupre.

"Look!" Mary Beth exclaimed. "Here are three gold pieces for you, Papa!"

* * *

Ezra didn't like the quiet in the Dupre house the next day. "Don't seem normal," he complained to Biddy.

His daughter nodded. "So quiet I can hear a small boat comin'. Must be for Miss Evangeline."

Evangeline had scant luggage. She wore the dress she was found in, and though Mistress Dupre offered her some of her own clothes her guest had been wearing these past weeks, the young woman refused them.

"Perhaps I'll have time to shop in New Orleans," she said.

The First Mate was solicitous and charming as he helped Miss Evangeline into the launch. "Have you more luggage?" he asked.

"No, but where's my body servant?" she replied crossly. "Ezra, do you know where Sissy is? You haven't hidden her away, have you? You know she's been with me since we were children, and it isn't like her not to be here when I need her."

Mistress Dupre stood quietly on the dock. "Evangeline, you will miss your boat, again, if you tarry. I or none of my servants know where Sissy is. When we see her, we will tell her to go on to Brownsville and make the same arrangements for her passage there as we have made for you."

Evangeline, suddenly remembering the responsibility of a Southern belle to be charming, smiled. "Of course, how rude of me. I can't begin to thank you for your hospitality. I shall tell my mother how kind you have been and that my safety was never at risk under your roof. Good-bye."

With that, Evangeline Randolph took the arm of the First Mate and stepped gracefully into the boat. As it left the dock, she waved her dainty handkerchief, then turned her face into the wind and never looked back.

Mistress Dupre held Arabella in her arms, turned, and walked back to the house. The cameo and diamond brooch remained in her pocket. Ezra and Biddy followed her. "Where's Sissy?" she asked.

"Don't know," Biddy said.

"Me neither. Ain't seen her since supper," Ezra added.

Chapter Eighteen

January 1, 1863

Captain Robert Cunningham stepped from the launch to the small pier and met Gabrielle Dupre on the path halfway between the river and her house. "Robert!" she called. "It is you! What a wonderful surprise. Look what I have. Tomorrow she will be baptised, my darling little Arabella Gabrielle Dupre."

The Captain extended his arms and took Arabella who looked into his eyes and pulled on his beard. "She is a beauty, just like her mother," he replied. "The Southernmost Belle of the South, as the crew called Miss Evangeline Randolph behind her back, told me the news. I'm so happy for you."

"Tell me everything about the trip to Brownsville. Was the girl's family there to meet her at Port Isobel? What are they like? And her mother, what about her mother?" Gabrielle pressed.

"I'll tell you what you want to know for a price," he said as he handed Arabella back to her mother. "Can you afford to pay me with tea and Ezra's molassas cookies?"

"The cookies are still warm from the oven, but you'll have to drink chicory coffee with the rest of us. We haven't had a leaf of China tea for some time now, but we still eat better than most of our neighbors."

Biddy alerted Ezra to the arrival of Captain Cunningham, and they found the tea table set when they arrived at the house. "He's a good fellow, that Ezra," Cunningham remarked as he sat in a comfortable chair and spread a linen napkin across his lap. "What will you do when the slaves are freed? The law goes into effect the first of the year. Of course, that doesn't mean the Southerners will follow it, living in a new country all their own. I hear that hundreds of slaves are high-tailing it to the North now anyway without fear of being returned to their owners."

"I assume Ezra and Biddy will stay here with Arabella and me and do what they have always been doing," Gabrielle Dupre said. "Although I inherited them from my father, when I joined the Methodist church and gave my life to the Lord God I came home and told Ezra and his daughter that they were free and could leave my home without fear. I gave them papers to prove it.

"Neither of them wanted to go, although that option is still available to them. Now I regard them as my hired servants and pay each a small wage, plus their food and the roof over their heads. They are free to go to town, visit friends, most of whom are still bound by slavery, and I give them Sunday off to worship how and where they please. They have voiced no complaints to me, and I certainly am satisfied with the arrangement.

"The three of us have agreed that no others will know of their freedom. Free blacks are often kidnapped by scoundrels and sold into slavery. As long as these terrible people view Ezra and Biddy as my property, they would not dare to do such a thing.

"I did not care for Mr. Lincoln and still feel some resentment toward the man for sticking his nose into our Southern affairs, but I am shocked over the loss of life and destruction of families and property because of this dreadful war.

"My dear father, God rest his soul, surely is turning in his grave. His fortune did not rest solely on the shoulders of King Cotton, although his ships and firewood depots did aid in the transportation of the fiber. Father was wise when he invested in packet boats with regular schedules. He found the passenger trade to be as profitable as freight."

"I agree with much of what you have said, my dear friend," Cunningham answered. "The Yankee blockade has hurt my business considerably, although their captains allow me the New Orleans to Port Isobel/Brownsville run. Pitiful as it may be, the money is enough to feed the crew and gives each member a valid excuse not to volunteer for military duty. What's more, no Northern general has ever come across a Confederate cannon forged in South Texas!

"Your father understood, as did I and many others, that the industrial strength of its factories and the overwhelming number of citizens in the North could outlast, if not outfight, a long war with the South. And that is what's happening. This long war has ground down the South to a nubbin, I fear, and it isn't over yet," he sighed.

Gabrielle continued to rock Arabella who had fallen asleep. Biddy came into the room, carefully took the baby from her mother's arms, and carried the little one upstairs to her cradle next to Gabrielle's bed.

"Now, to the other business," Cunningham said as he stood up, put his napkin back on the tray, and stretched his long body before he sat back down again. "I promised Evangeline Randolph that I would come and retrieve her body slave. Sissy, isn't it?"

"Yes. Did Evangeline tell you she could read? In fact, both Evangeline and Sissy are very good teachers and led some of my little, uh, house guests in their lessons while they were visiting here. I'm sorry to tell you that we have not seen hide nor hair of Sissy since your First Mate came for Evangeline. I have worried about her."

"You'll forgive me, Gabrielle. I know you are as honest as the day is long, taught that by your father, but I promised Miss Evangeline I would search the house and property for the slave."

"Of course, I would expect as much from Miss Evangeline."

"Brownsville is some miles inland from Port Isobel, but her mother, two brothers, and the Ellis men had come by carriage to meet Miss Evangeline. All of them thanked me profusely except for one. That younger brother, Raleigh is his name, is an odd one. There's something about him. I can't put my finger on it, but just something about him doesn't seem quite right.

"The ladies left us to take tea in the home of a minister, a friend of Ellis, an acceptable place in a port town. The brothers disappeared somewhere, and I went with the Ellises when they invited me for a drink. I once believed a mint julep was beyond the reach of a saloon keeper in Texas, but the fellow produced one that could pass muster on any plantation in the South.

"I was glad to have a private conversation with Theodore Ellis and his son Teddy Junior. I've known them for years and watched the boy grow up and follow his father into surveying. Of course, he went on every job with his father, learned from him, and probably just absorbed everything else he needed to know as they went along. They've done right by their clients and even better for themselves. The two bought government land for a few cents an acre and must own half of Texas. I exaggerate, of course.

"The Randolphs are land rich themselves, but I doubt their land is suitable to grow the kind of cotton they were known for.

They have enough acreage to run cattle. If it were mine, that's what I'd do."

Gabrielle laughed. "Somehow, dear Robert, I can't see you as a cattleman. The role does not have the dignity of a Captain on an seagoing steamship! What of the Randolphs' slaves?"

"I only saw the body slaves with the family. Theodore Ellis told me the rest are out on the land, some building a big house for the Randolph family, some trying to plow for a crop, what, I don't know, and several of the slaves are busy repairing the few tumbledown shacks already on the property. Those are supposed to serve as slave quarters. For the moment, the slaves are living in old torn army tents they got from somewhere. No one has complained aloud, to my knowledge, but I imagine it's hard-scrabble living compared to what I have heard about Fair Oaks Plantation.

"Now, my dear Gabrielle, I must get back to my ship. I'll walk through your home quickly, carry my greetings to the livestock in the barn, and inquire of the four-footed beasts and the chickens as to whether or not they are hiding the slave Sissy, and then be on my way."

Captain Cunningham stood and kissed Mistress Dupre's hand. He walked quickly up the stairs, and Gabrielle heard him walking in and out of all of the rooms before he came down to the first floor and did the same. He left the house by the kitchen so he could compliment Ezra on his molasses cookies.

Gabrielle Dupre felt she could use a nap herself and went upstairs to her bed. She looked into the cradle to see Arabella sleeping soundly and then settled her head on her own pillow. Before the lady drifted off to sleep, she thanked God for not knowing where Sissy had gone so she wouldn't have had to lie about it.

* * *

When Sissy heard the news that Captain Cunningham's First Mate would be coming for Miss Evangeline, she could not sleep. Sissy knew the joy and excitement of teaching the Johnsons could never be recaptured. Her own skill as a teacher was equal to that of Miss Evangeline's even though Sissy understood that as a slave, she was born inferior to her owner.

Sissy felt a small part of her leave with them when Mr. Johnson came to reclaim his family. Her feeling of loss was magnified in the dark even though she turned over on her stomach, her most comfortable position, kept her eyes tightly closed, and prayed to God that he would give sleep and rest to her tired body and forgive her bad feelings toward her Mistress.

She suddenly opened her eyes, threw off the bed clothes, and sat upright. *Thank you, God, for Your guidance,* Sissy thought. She quietly got up, dressed, tip-toed down the stairs, and walked out the front door. She found her way to the barn in the dark and waited for first light when she saw the wagon tracks.

Sissy left the barn, walked at a steady pace, and followed two sets of ruts left by one wagon. The old, nearly erased tracks must be from the wagon Ezra drove when he went to fetch the wet nurse, she reasoned. The fresh ones had to come from the Johnsons'. She figured their farm to be about sixteen miles away, based on the time it took Mistress Dupre to fetch Mrs. Johnson and her children.

Sissy heard the Johnsons before she saw them. She walked over a little rise on the road and looked down on the small farm. Three big boys she had never met were pitching hay into the barn loft. Two others were fighting each other and rolling on the ground. Mrs. Johnson, with a twin in each arm, stood on the back porch of the farm house and yelled at the fighters to stop or they'd get no breakfast.

Mary Beth, who saw Sissy first, was bringing in the milk cows when she jumped up and down and called out to the others. "Sissy! Sissy! It's Sissy! Come see, Mama!"

Sissy found herself surrounded by a happy mob of Johnsons. Mary Beth took her hand and led her to the house. Mr. Johnson came out of the barn, took off his hat, and scratched his head in wonder at the sight of his children taking turns and going politely through the door.

Mrs. Johnson sat her guest in the best chair, put a cup of weak coffee in her hand, and waited for her to speak. Sissy was overcome by the crowd and was beginning to regret her rash move.

"Well, so you're the teacher!" Mr. Johnson said as he pulled up a chair for his wife and one for himself. The children sat right down on the floor. The ones who knew her were all smiles, and those who did not viewed Sissy with suspicion. "What are you doing here?" Johnson continued.

"I ran away, and I didn't know anywhere else to go. I followed your wagon tracks here." Sissy bowed her head. "I'm sorry. It was cruel of me to put you at risk. It's against the law to help a runaway slave." She got up to leave.

"Sit," Mr. Johnson commanded. "You the one who teached my children to read?"

Sissy nodded. "There were two of us. The other teacher is Mistress Evangeline Randolph. I am her body slave."

"Can you teach me?" Mr. Johnson went on.

"What?"

"Can you teach me? You taught my wife some."

"If you want to learn, I can teach you and your other children too."

"Good. You can stay. I think people cheat me when I do business with them 'cause they know I cain't read." Johnson looked around the room. "All of you children do what Miss Sissy tells you. Don't anybody dare tell another livin' soul we have a runaway slave here with us or I'll take the strap to you afore they takes me off to jail."

He reached over and shook Sissy's hand. " 'Tis a bargain, then! Everybody get back to work."

The kitchen emptied except for the children washing the dishes. Mrs. Johnson handed Sissy one of the twins and led her to a storage shed by the barn. "I'll get the big 'ens to clean this out and we'll use it for a schoolroom. Mistress Dupre sent us paper and pencils and some books. You can sleep out here too. We don't have any more room in the house."

Mrs. Johnson's smile made Sissy feel warm inside. The slave felt welcomed in this place and delighted in the fact that someone had called her "Miss Sissy" for the first time in her life.

*   *   *

All of the Johnsons, except for two, proved to be quick and able learners. Leonard was a bit slow at reading but outshown his siblings at numbers. The speed with which he could figure sums in his head discouraged any others who thought of teasing him when he struggled over words.

Their father made slow progress during his private lessons with Sissy by lamplight at the kitchen table. After months of struggle and determination, marks on a page emerged as words with meaning for Mr. Johnson, and the taciturn man was jubilant.

He sometimes worked as a cutter for a sawmill and one day returned from work triumphant. "Dang!" he reported to his family. "The foreman cheated me on the hours I worked, the number of trees I felled, and the kinds of trees they were. I said he was wrong, and he said he was right and showed me the paper he wrote it all on that goes to the paymaster. Danged if I didn't read that paper out loud and in front of everybody. He wrote it wrong, I told him, and the other men agreed with me. That foreman! He turned red in the face, tore up that paper, and wrote out another one with me lookin' over his shoulder!

"Lookee here! I brought a bag of candy. Two pieces for ever' body," he proudly announced as his family gathered 'round.

* * *

Sissy had been with the Johnsons nearly a year when Leonard called out, "Somebody's comin'!" and ran into the schoolroom to tell Sissy to hide. She had dismissed the children early to catch up with their farm chores, something Sissy did every Friday afternoon.

"No one will look in here," she reassured Leonard. "You all should go on with your work and let your mother meet strangers. Don't tell anyone I'm here."

Sissy sat quietly behind her small table and went over her students' morning lessons. Her concentration was poor, and she could feel the beating of her heart. She heard footsteps and was rising from her chair when someone pushed open the door. It was Mistress Dupre with her daughter in her arms!

She put Arabella down and said, "Go see Sissy. Show Sissy how you can walk. Go see Sissy, Arabella."

Sissy came out from behind the table, knelt down, and extended her arms. "Come, Arabella. Come see Sissy," she said softly and quickly extended one arm as the child wobbled a bit. She held the toddler's hand a few more steps and than scooped the child up into her arms. "Good girl, Arabella, good girl!" she said, danced her around once then returned the toddler to her mother when the child made little noises and held out her arms to Mistress Dupre. "How did you know where to find me?" Sissy asked.

"When I heard that Mr. Johnson could read, I knew that Mary Beth, as good a little student as she is, was not the one who taught him. It had to be you, Sissy. Mr. Johnson caused quite a stir when he challenged his foreman's honesty. I heard the manager required him to read a notice posted in his office before he believed the man could read. He told everyone that his daughter Mary Beth taught him.

"The news that some part-time workers may have been cheated by my foreman disturbed me greatly. My solicitor sent his investigator to weed out any skulduggery that he might find. Based on his report, I let the foreman and one other man go. After the first of the year, I may consider Mr. Johnson for a promotion to foreman now that he can read and write. People at the sawmill seem to like him. I think his older boys can run this small farm now. Do you think he is able to do the job?"

"I am not familiar with the duties of a foreman, but I can assure you that Mr. Johnson can read and write very well and that he is a hard and determined worker," Sissy replied.

Mistress Dupre considered Sissy's words, then changed the subject. "Let's talk about you, Sissy. I believe you must stay right here with the Johnsons where the Randolphs cannot find you. I understand they continue their search from time to time. Ezra, Biddy, and I will say nothing about your whereabouts. Which reminds me. Ezra!" she called. "Get the Johnsons to help bring the boxes into the schoolroom here. We can all help unpack them."

Sissy was amazed when Ezra and six of the children brought in armloads of school supplies—paper, pencils, ink wells and pens, arithmetic, geography and reading books. Teacher's books for Sissy and even watercolors and brushes.

"Come, Sissy. Mrs. Johnson has made us tea with blackberry leaves and Ezra's molassas cookies. He brought some for the children too. You and I shall continue our talk later," the lady said.

Mrs. Johnson was thrilled to entertain Mistress Dupre. The twins sat on the floor playing with old wooden spoons and empty pans. Mistress Dupre sat Arabella down on the floor with the boys and watched Willie Rob, or perhaps it was Billy Bob, happily share his spoon and pan and show Arabella how to make noise by hitting them together.

Both mothers knew noise was a natural part of childhood. It was when things were quiet that mothers needed to go see what the children were up to. Mrs. Johnson and Mistress Dupre carried on a conversation as if the din was no louder than a hymn softly sung in church. The two women clearly understood each other's words, but Sissy had to strain to hear them.

When tea was over, Mistress Dupre graciously thanked her hostess, picked Arabella up off the floor, and asked Sissy to walk along with them as they returned to the carriage. Arabella protested when separated from her two new playmates but calmed down and waved to Ezra waiting by the horses.

Her mother put the toddler down and held one hand as Sissy held the other. Arabella walked slowly and carefully toward the carriage and Ezra while the grownups continued their conversation.

"Mrs. Johnson is delighted that you will stay here with them until after the first of the year. On January 1, 1863, a new United States law will go into effect that frees all slaves in the Confederate States. Mister Lincoln calls it The Emancipation Proclamation. If you can teach your students how to spell it as well as say it, they will be educated, indeed.

"I don't know what effect the law will have on the Confederacy. Our politicians, most of whom own slaves, will simply ignore it. The war goes on even though intelligent people, and some who are not so smart, know in their bones that the South is losing and the North is winning. It would take a miracle to change its course as things now stand.

"Some of us Southerners have joined with our fellow Christians in the North to debate the future of millions of slaves who may suddenly find themselves freed. Where will they go? What will they do? How will they survive?"

Sissy gasped. "I never thought of that. What will happen to the old slaves left behind at Fair Oaks? None of them can read and write."

"I don't mean to be harsh, Sissy, but much of our concern has to do with younger slaves like you. You have seen how Mr. Johnson was taken advantage of because he could not read and write and he is a white man. It is not the same with slaves who cannot read and write. The color of their skin and illiteracy will combine to steal the sweetness from freedom when it comes.

"There is an association organized by Methodists and others for the sole purpose of establishing a college where selected young coloreds could go for teacher training. Then they would spread out through the South to teach others. Sissy, when it comes to pass, I want to take you with me to that college in Tennessee. You have the skills to be in our first group of teacher trainers there."

Sissy was so dumbfounded she could not speak. She simply smiled and watched as Ezra helped Mistress Dupre into the carriage. Sissy handed up Arabella to her and stood watching until the carriage was out of sight. *How strange it would be if I went back to Tennessee and Evangeline stayed in Texas,* she thought. *I do miss her and hope she is well and happy to be with her family again and that things are going well for them in Texas.*

* * *

Overseer Bailey blamed the loss of slaves on the lack of a well-established plantation system in Texas. There wasn't a week that went by but what he had to report to Mistress Randolph and Alexander that the slave count was lower by one or two than the count the previous week.

Raleigh insisted that he be the one to lead the search party. He seldom came back with an escaped slave and even lost a colored member of the search party from time to time. Bailey suspected that Raleigh himself may have hanged the runaways he caught instead of returning them to the plantation for hanging.

After one such search when Raleigh came back without two runaway slaves, a member of the search party, Elijah by name, came to Bailey's tent after dark. The overseer recognized him as one of the young slaves Old Clara referred to as "cream" and had noticed how he stood out among those brought to Texas.

"Mister Bailey, sir," Elijah began, "Ah knows you to be a fair white man. Da slaves, dey not runs away. Der's no place dey can run to. 'Tis Master Raleigh, sir. He done steal em an' sell em. I ax ya not to say nothing'. Master Raleigh, he hang me iff'n he know ah tells."

Bailey shook with anger. He composed himself long enough to reply, "Thank you for telling me, Elijah. I will keep what you told me a secret and will try to figure out a way to stop it."

The next morning, Bailey found his wife in a dour mood. "I hate this place! Look at these awful red spots on my skin! This dry air sucks the moisture from it and makes me look a hundred years old," she complained. She sat on a chair at a small table beneath a large tarp her husband had the slaves erect under one of the few big trees in the area. It was cooler there than in the tent they called home. Theirs was larger than any tent housing the slaves, but it was nothing but a tent, nonetheless. "Just look at Betty making our breakfast outside like we're common white trash!"

Betty had struggled to learn how to cook over an open fire until a young Texas slave taught her how to use a Dutch oven to bake biscuits. While serving them breakfast under the tree, Betty heard the Baileys' conversation.

"Ellis told me the other day that our sons' cattle ranch is only a five days' ride from here. We're waiting for lumber not due to be delivered here for another three weeks, and we've had to stop work on the big house. This would be a good time to go for a visit to see them and meet their families. We could take two wagons with the furniture and things you wanted to bring them from Tennessee. What do you think?" her husband asked.

"I would love it! It will do us both worlds of good to see the boys and meet their wives, at last." She knew her husband was discouraged because of the difficulties he faced in trying to get the new plantation up and running. He still held to the notion that leaving Tennessee for Texas was a mistake. She guessed that when the Randolphs started docking his salary every time a slave escaped, it was humiliating to him. They wanted to pay him with Confederate money but he insisted on gold instead.

The next day Bailey rode to Brownsville and called at the home of Mr. Ellis, Sr. who was hosting Rebecca Randolph and her daughter until their home was built. Alexander and Raleigh stayed next door in the smaller house belonging to Teddy Ellis.

When the house servant answered the door, Bailey asked for Mistress Randolph. He could hear her laughter coming from the dining room. The servant returned promptly. "Mistress says come."

"Mr. Bailey, how nice to see you," Mistress Randolph greeted him warmly. "Do sit down and have coffee with us, or perhaps you might like breakfast."

"Coffee will do nicely," he replied. "I've had breakfast."

"I hope that you have come with a favorable report as to the progress of construction on our new home. Mr. Ellis has been so kind to us, I almost regret the thought of us moving so far out to our new plantation."

He evaded a direct answer and said, "We are still waiting for the rest of the lumber to be delivered, and I'm told it will be several more weeks. As you know, Mistress Randolph, my sons run cattle in Texas some miles north of here. All four have married, and my wife and I have never met their wives. Mrs. Bailey and I would be in your debt if we could have a few days to make the trip by wagon to visit them."

Before she could answer, Mr. Ellis broke in. "Pity it will not be for another year. By then, the train should be running. It would have been up and crossing the entire continent were it not for this damned war, if you ladies will excuse my English."

Evangeline spoke up. "I'd let them go, Mother, provided they look for Sissy along the way."

"Then you have my permission to go. Enjoy your visit, but don't be gone too long. I'm sure Alexander and Raleigh will see that no time is wasted out at the plantation. We are still debating the name for it," Mistress Randolph added.

"I suggested calling it Fair Oaks Plantation Texas Style," Mr. Ellis laughed, "but the Randolphs have vetoed it."

Mr. Bailey smiled at the joke, bowed slightly, and left.

* * *

Early Sunday morning, Mrs. Bailey, wearing a sunbonnet on her head and gloves on her hands, sat next to her husband on the seat as he drove the team of four horses north to meet the Butterfield Overland Mail Trail an old Texan had told him about.

Because his wife couldn't handle a team, Bailey chose Elijah to drive the second wagon with furniture destined for the ranch. Elijah had spaced his load in such a way as to provide places where four slaves could hide from suspicious patrolers, if necessary. Bailey agreed to the plan. He knew that eight people would travel in greater safety than four in this strange land.

Raleigh volunteered to go alone to check on things at the plantation the next day, Monday. Alexander was agreeable because he had a card game scheduled then. He made it a habit never to gamble on a Sunday although he saw no harm in practicing his sleight of hand on the Lord's Day.

When Raleigh arrived at the plantation site Monday afternoon, he was less interested in progress made by the Randolph slaves than in dallying with one of the young slave girls. He did not bother to look for the Baileys in their tent or under the tarp where their chairs sat empty in the shade.

The second day out, Bailey found the trail he was looking for. They traveled north, stopped at mid-day to eat a cold meal, then continued until near sundown when they pulled off to the side of the well worn trail and set up camp for the night.

Elijah proved to have excellent aim with a slingshot, and all members of their party enjoyed fresh killed spit-roasted rabbit for supper. The Baileys ate apart from the slaves.

The next morning the travelers awoke to the smell of frizzled fatback, Dutch oven biscuits, and chicory coffee. Betty served the Baileys who ate in their wagon. The slaves served themselves, gathered in a small group, and sat on the ground to eat. "Betty, you is a good cook," Elijah said.

The two other slave women, Pearl and Esther, cleaned up after the meal. By the time they had sand-washed and dipped the dishes in the precious water used for that purpose over and over again, the men had hitched up the horses and were ready to leave. Betty handed up the clean dishes and pans to Mrs. Bailey who packed them back in boxes.

Caro and Benjamin drove the heavily loaded wagons, and everyone else walked. The only other living things any of them saw were birds and unidentified wild animals, none of which appeared to pose a threat to the small caravan. Except for changing drivers each morning, the routine continued as on their first day out.

When the small party stopped and set up camp late in the afternoon on the fourth day of their journey, they saw campfires in the distance. "I expect they see ours, as well," Bailey remarked.

"I hope they're not wild Indians," Mrs. Bailey said with concern.

"Double the watch tonight," Bailey said to Elijah.

"Dey not be Indians," Elijah said as he shaded his eyes with his hands and watched the approach of a wagon train early the next morning.

"I think you're right, Elijah," Bailey agreed. "Looks like about a dozen wagons. To be safe, I think you and the others should get in the wagons and stay out of sight. Mrs. Bailey and Betty can sit here in your place." Five slaves disappeared into the back of the wagon as Bailey directed his wife and Betty to sit on its seat. "I'll wager Betty can drive this team."

Betty's face was impassive. She climbed up to the seat, took the reins in her hands, and started the team off with authority. She hoped the five slaves hidden behind her would not be discovered. Her wagon fell in behind the one driven by Mr. Bailey.

The leader of the wagon train called out when he was still some distance away. "Hello the wagons! My name is Raines, and we are bound for West Texas. Who may you be?"

"Bailey from Tennessee, bound to join our sons on a ranch not far off this trail!" *I hope!* Bailey said to himself.

"Bailey?" another voice broke in. "It's Sowell! Lord Almighty! To think we should meet in this God-forsaken Texas!"

Bailey stopped his wagon and watched the approach of the wagon train. Finally, he made out the person of Mr. Sowell driving a covered wagon and when the two met up, they embraced each other like long-lost brothers.

"Save your talk," Raines called back. "Your friends can join our train if they want. We're not stopping until eatin' time again."

"Bailey, have your two wagons fall in behind the last one," Sowell yelled as he started up his team. "We'll talk later."

Mr. Bailey jumped at the chance to join up with the train and followed Sowell's instructions. As the wagon carrying the slaves was last in line, Elijah quietly took over the reins from Betty and Mrs. Bailey went forward to walk beside her husband. Both drivers were careful to keep up with the train and not fall behind.

The wagon train continued at a steady pace until the sun was high in the sky. The travelers stopped just long enough for the walkers to rest, the drivers change, and all members of the group to have time for a cold meal and a quick trip behind the bushes. Raines disallowed any campfires at midday. After speaking with Sowell, Bailey told the slaves it was safe to come out of hiding.

The wagon master rode back to speak to Mr. Bailey. "I'm Raines," he said. "Sowell tells me you're on your way to visit your sons."

"Yes, sir, we are," Bailey replied as he extended his hand to shake the callused one offered to him. "They don't know we're coming. I hope we're going the right way. Most of what I've seen of Texas looks just the same to me."

"It's your good fortune we came along when we did," Raines said. "You could easily miss the turnoff to their ranch. We should pass by it tomorrow, possibly before noon. I'm acquainted with the Bailey brothers, good cattlemen from what I've heard. The four families live close together but in separate houses. They share the big barn, the bunkhouses, and the corrals.

"I'll point out the turnoff when we pass by tomorrow. It's a rough wagon trail that leads right up to the ranch houses. If your boys are out with their cattle, their wives will be home. Between the four of them, they have five children now, so I'm told."

Raines tipped his hat to Mrs. Bailey as he reined his horse to go. "Appreciate it!" Bailey called after him and was surprised when the wagon master turned his horse and came back.

"There's a free black family with the train. Their wagon is between Sowell's and Riley's. You might want to tell your colored folk about them," Raines said as he rode by.

Bailey was tired of driving his wagon. He went back and told Benjamin to drive for him and told Caro to give Elijah a rest. When the wagon train was on the move a short time later, Mr. and Mrs. Bailey walked together, and Elijah walked between Pearl and Esther who followed behind Betty. "I's glad to be outta dat wagon. Ma bones near got shaked ta pieces!" Pearl exclaimed, and Esther nodded her head in agreement.

By late afternoon, two campsite scouts rode back to lead the group to the spot where the train would stop for the night. "The stream nearby is small, but the water is sweet," one said. "The grass is only about six inches high and there are many scrubby bushes for forage. There's plenty for our stock now but would never have been enough for the animals if our wagon train hadn't split up at Lone Elm. Although I truly miss the other people, I don't see how this hot and sparse land could support a forty-two-wagon train."

Raines looked solemnly at the scout. "It supported thousands of Indians once," he said. "How long before we camp?"

"About two hours from now," the scout answered. The information went quickly from one wagon to the next, and the travelers looked forward to stopping for the night. The animals smelled water long before the small stream was sighted, and the milk cows strained at their rope restraints.

When Raines and the site scouts directed the drivers to position their wagons for the night, the walkers knew to untie the cattle, lead them to water, and then return to help unharness the teams of draft horses, mules, and oxen and then get out of their way as the animals headed to water.

Members of the wagon train, having gone through the procedure many times before, performed the tasks almost automatically. Members of the Bailey party were confused as to what they should do until Ned, the free black, and Nate came to their aid. The helpers were quick giving directions and calm so as not to confuse the people and the animals. In a very few minutes the stock was where it should be, the two Bailey wagons were in their assigned spaces in the circle, and neighbors on either side of them came to offer wood for the newcomers' campfire.

After supper, Elizabeth called on the Baileys and gave them a list of the Sowell Tennessee Wagon Train rules. "My brother says he knows you," she said. "Please read these rules and make sure everyone in your wagons understands them. When you finish, I need the copy back. Paper is scarce."

"You said your brother knows me?" Bailey asked. "What's his name?"

"Nate. Nate Riley," Elizabeth answered. "My mother and Nate doctored a slave called Hercules a long time ago."

Mr. Bailey gasped, "And Nate's here? I thought something was familiar about the young fellow who helped us get settled for the night. And your mother? Is your mother here too?"

"Mama's dead. We had to leave her buried under her favorite pear tree in the orchard on our farm back home. Papa's arm is buried with her too. But Ben and Caleb are buried under a pine tree near Shiloh Church. They were in the army with Matthew and

Papa, but they didn't get killed by bullets. They died from the measles.'' Elizabeth paused for breath. ''I hear Emma calling me. Remember to give me back the paper when you're through,'' the girl called back over her shoulder as she hurried away.

It took a few minutes for Bailey to digest the information about the Riley family. He found his wife in the wagon and told her what he had learned. ''How did Catherine Riley die? She was really a nice woman for a plain farmer's wife.'' Bailey simply shrugged his shoulders and marveled at the coincidence of their meeting again on the Texas plains.

After supper that evening, Mr. Sowell came to call on the Baileys at their wagon. He brought Ned with him. ''Ned, here, is a free black and my employee when I had my store. I hope to open another one when we settle somewhere. With your permission, Ned would like to visit with the coloreds traveling with you.''

Bailey nodded his assent and pointed toward Caro, who was bringing another chair from the wagon for Mr. and Mrs. Bailey's guest. Although Sowell had not met Mrs. Bailey before, he inquired how she liked the shawl her husband purchased as a gift for her at his store years ago.

Mrs. Bailey thought for a moment. ''It's quite lovely and I still have it in the small trunk we brought with us.''

''And the lovely Japanese fan for your daughter, Patsy, isn't it? How did Patsy like her fan? Is she traveling with you?'' Sowell went on, much to the surprise of Mr. Bailey.

''As I remember, I gave it to Patsy when she was home that summer. She lived with my wife's relatives in Memphis and attended a girls' school there,'' Bailey answered.

His wife chimed in. ''When she finished her schooling, Patsy stayed on with my sister and her family and became part owner of a ladies' hat shop. We haven't heard from any of them for ages and tried to see Patsy and the family when we left Fair Oaks, but the packet boat Captain refused to stop in Memphis.''

''I learned just today that Catherine Riley is dead. What's the story?'' Bailey asked.

''It was terrible, just terrible,'' Sowell answered. ''The kind woman was murdered by Confederate marauders, the scum! They would have killed the rest of the family if not for the slave Hercules, who happened by. Did you know that the biggest slave on Fair Oaks Plantation is a Yankee soldier now?''

Overseer Bailey was speechless. Mrs. Bailey felt faint, excused herself, and disappeared into the wagon.

''I do rattle on,'' Sowell said hastily. ''We make early starts on this wagon train and are on our way exactly one hour after Raines rings his cowbell.'' He rose from the chair and hurried away. ''Ned!'' he called. ''Come along.''

Ned, who had been talking with the Randolph slaves, clasped Elijah's hand then turned and followed Sowell. Betty had been storing the supper dishes in the Bailey wagon and missed hearing the conversation in the other wagon. She didn't mind because, as a house slave, she felt superior to those who worked in the fields and at other less refined tasks.

The Bailey party was ready to leave camp when the wagon master gave the signal to move out. Mrs. Bailey was especially eager to get to the Bailey Ranch and meet the grandchildren she had learned about recently. She was just as eager to meet their mothers.

The wagon train had been moving for an hour when Sowell, on a riding horse, came back to speak to Bailey again. He rode alongside the wagon the overseer was driving and his mount kept to the rhythm of the moving caravan. ''I have been thinking,'' Sowell said. ''Ned tells me the colored with you are runaway slaves, and we both know what that means.''

''Lincoln says slaves are to be freed the first of the year,'' Bailey answered defensively.

''Until the war is over, that means absolutely nothing here in Texas and the rest of the South,'' Sowell countered. ''Hear me out. I'm not a slave owner, never have been, but I will need hired hands who aren't afraid to work to help me start up my business again.''

''Go on,'' Bailey said. ''I'm listening.''

''I'll trade you three hams, a crock of apple butter, and a sack of white rice for the wagon you're driving. But I won't trade you anything for the slaves you stole from the Randolphs. I will, though, take them off your hands, and you won't need to feed them. Anyhow, the time's coming soon when slaves can just walk away and nobody will be much of a mind to chase them. What will you do if you wake up one morning on the Texas plantation and find no slaves there for you to oversee?''

Bailey mulled over the man's words for a time before he spoke. "Mrs. Bailey is walking beside the wagon behind us. Tell her what you've just told me."

Sowell rode back to where the lady was, got off his horse and walked along with her while he explained his offer. He tipped his hat to her, mounted his horse and rode back to give the report to her husband.

"She said she wants to keep Betty and Caro. The other slaves can go. She accepts my offer of trade for one of your wagons and, in addition, wants me to give her some ribbons, lengths of cloth, and any baubles I might have that her grandchildren would like. I agreed to her terms. Mrs. Bailey drives a hard bargain." Sowell meant it as a compliment and laughed as he rode away.

As Raines had predicted, the wagon train arrived at the turn off to the Bailey Ranch before noon. The transfer of goods to the single wagon was completed under the watchful eye of Mrs. Bailey who joined her husband in thanking Raines, Sowell, and the other travelers for their help and kindness. As Bailey turned his team and started down the rough road, they saw a horseman riding toward them. When he came close, the rider got down from his horse. "Papa? Mama?" he called in disbelief and ran toward them to embrace them both.

Sowell, who had stopped to watch, knew the rider was one of the Bailey boys. As Captain of the wagon train, he had talked with Raines the night before and had the wagon master's permission to add another wagon to the train. Sowell motioned Elijah to drive his wagon up to take its place behind Ned's.

As the wagon of Randolph slaves passed him on the way to their spot in line, Mr. Sowell wondered if he had lost his mind.

* * *

During the six months the wagon train was on the trail, Christmas Day was the only time they stopped for the entire twenty-four hours. They made Christmas Eve festive by building a bigger bonfire than usual, and the travelers gathered around it to sing carols. One man brought out his Bible and read the Christmas story. The slaves sat together a short distance away from the others, but everyone listened when the small group lifted their voices to the heavens and sang beautiful but unfamiliar melodies.

Parents surprised their children with little gifts they had made in secret during the months of travel. There were cornhusk dolls and rag-stuffed cloth animals, hard clay marbles made round by grownups rolling soft clay in their hands for hours, sling shots of hand-carved and polished wood, and ribbons from somewhere to braid in ladies' hair. Men were surprised to get leather pouches to hold tobacco or other things they held dear.

When the festivities were over, the Riley family gathered near the yellow wagon for a silent remembrance of those no longer with them. The stars glimmered in the black sky, and the night air was cool and refreshing.

After a few minutes of quiet thought, Nathan Riley spoke aloud. "Thank you, Lord, for seeing us through bad times and leading us to a new place. Thank you for the lives of Catherine and Ben and Caleb. We know they are with you in heaven. Thank you for Matthew and John and Nate and Elizabeth and Grace and Elle. And thank you for Emma, who has come into our lives."

No one else spoke for several minutes and then Emma softly said, "And thank You, Lord, for my gift." She paused, then went on, "I'm in the family way."

Elizabeth's eyes opened wide and she shouted, "Amen!"

* * *

Young children overflowed from the laps of Grandpa and Grandma Bailey who declared it the best Christmas they had ever had. After the initial shock of meeting their in-laws for the first time, the young Bailey wives opened their arms and their loving hearts to the newcomers.

All four sons begged their parents to stay and start life over on the ranch with them. "We need you, Papa. You're so good at organizing things. We can sell all of the cattle we raise if we can just get them to market. We drive our cattle to the railhead in Kansas, and it's a long, hard ride. It will be easier if the war ever ends and the railroad gets built through Texas."

Bailey talked it over with his wife, and they both decided to take their sons up on their offer. "But to be fair," she suggested, "it seems to me that you need to go back to Brownsville and tell Mistress Randolph that you are leaving her employ. I hope she has the courtesy to pay you the back wages she owes."

"It will be hard to give up the job I have had for twenty years," her husband replied, "but the way things are changing so fast, we'll be better off to stay here with our family."

Before the end of January, two of the Bailey sons rode with their father back to Brownsville. They went on horseback, and Mr. Bailey noticed vast changes in the town when he arrived at the Ellis home. A servant he did not recognize answered the door. "Please tell Mistress Randolph that Mr. Bailey is here to see her," he said.

"Mistress Randolph not be here. She be Missus Ellis now and dey both gone on a trip. Don't know where. Dey say dey be back in 'bout a month."

He took a few seconds to regain his composure. "And Miss Evangeline Randolph?"

"She be gone wid Master Alexander. Dey gone to New Orleans. Don't know when dey be back."

"Master Raleigh?" Bailey asked.

"Don't rightly know. He be in some trouble, ah thinks."

"By any chance, did Mistress Rand . . eer, Mrs. Ellis leave an envelope or anything for Mr. Bailey, her overseer?"

"Not dat I knows about," the servant said and closed the door in his face.

Mr. Bailey stopped by the bank to withdraw his own funds. He hoped the Randolphs might have put the money owed him into his account and spoke to the bank manager about it.

The manager expressed his condolences for what he expected to be wrongful practices by the Randolphs. "I'm so sorry they left without paying you the well-earned money. I understand fully. Mrs. Randolph Ellis cheated you, but her dastardly son Raleigh robbed my bank!" The manager held up a WANTED poster for Bailey to see.

"The artist drew a perfect likeness of him," Bailey said meekly. It was all he could think of to say.

Their father said nothing to his sons when he came out of the bank. They followed him into a saloon, and they sat down at a table. "Whiskey," was the first and only word out of Bailey's mouth. His sons ordered the same.

"I think we'd best eat something," the youngest one said finally and ordered steaks for all of them. When the food came, the three ate in silence. When they had finished, Bailey spoke.

"Everybody's gone, and they still owe me six months' wages. I want to ride on out to the plantation before we go back to your ranch." The older son paid for their meal, and the three mounted their horses and Bailey led the way.

After what he had learned in Brownsville, Bailey wasn't surprised to find the plantation site deserted. The slaves were gone. Everything they had worked so hard to bring to this place was gone—tents, wagons, mules, furniture, tools. The unfinished big house was in shambles. "Let's go home," he said to his sons.

Chapter Nineteen

Big Sky

Elizabeth was disappointed. After months of travel with the wagon train through Texas, her family and Mr. Sowell had yet to choose a place for their new home. They had camped on the outskirts of several small communities, and the monotony of travel was broken by trips into the towns. Although the people there were friendly and the travelers enjoyed the feeling of civilization once more, Mr. Sowell rejected all of them as likely places to start his business again.

Mr. Riley was surprised to find little farm land available for sale at any price. Wealthy land owners claimed thousands of acres, much of the land devoted to the single purpose of raising cattle. Most business was conducted in the town's saloons, and the few ranchers who agreed to talk with Nathan Riley regarded the best farmer in western Tennessee as nothing more than just another piece of Southern white trash.

Had the Texans known Riley and Sowell carried a fair amount of gold in their nondescript clothing, they might have paid the two travelers more attention. Texans had watched steady streams of down-and-out Southerners fleeing their homeland and were relieved when many poor ones continued west and spilled on over into New Mexico Territory.

There was a barbershop in every town, no matter its size, and Elizabeth enjoyed walking past the open door and smelling the sweet aromas of hair dressing and astringent. The familiar odors reminded her of Mr. Hall's barbershop and the many times she, her mother, and sisters had enjoyed the tea Mr. Hall served them when he did business with Mrs. Riley.

Now Elizabeth was put out over the fact that girls were not allowed to even step inside barbershops in Texas towns. Matthew explained it was because men wanted to enjoy their baths there in private and without the distractions females would cause. But Elizabeth didn't believe him because she saw with her own eyes painted women going in the back doors of barbershops in some of the towns where they had stopped.

Nate, now taller than Matthew and regarded to be a full-grown man, did gain entrance and sold some of his medicinal herbs and salves to the barber. Once in a while, a barber might try to pay him with Confederate money, but Nate held out for U.S.A. dollars and coins or gold and silver. Sometimes he would trade for bars of soap.

Elizabeth hated leaving any town because it meant more days traveling in the wagon train. She was tired of the journey and prayed Papa and Mr. Sowell soon would find a place to their liking. Guilt made her keep silent about her complaints. *Emma never complains,* she thought, *and she is as big as a house. If the baby doesn't come soon, I'm afraid she'll burst. I'm surprised Emma couldn't just float across the Pecos River when we crossed over.* Elizabeth was ashamed of her unkind thoughts and felt her face flush with embarrassment.

* * *

As the Sowell West Tennessee Wagon Train traveled through Texas, one group after another reached its chosen destination and left the train to settle in that part of Texas. Many of them had made the long trip to join family members who had gone on before and urged others to come to start life anew in that slave state.

It was hard for those remaining each time a wagon dropped out of the train. The travelers had become as one family after having lived and worked so closely together for many months. The women, especially, were mindful of Emma's condition and left her with all kinds of advice as to what to do when the baby came.

"We should reach El Paso in two days," Raines said early one evening at supper. "It's close to the New Mexico border. I have to say this has been a good trip. Since it's my last, I'm happy with the way things have gone."

"Your last trip?" Nate asked, surprised.

"Why would any sane person travel by wagon train when he can travel on an iron horse?" Raines replied.

"I didn't know there were iron horses," Elle interjected.

Raines laughed. "That's another name for a train, Elle. I think that's what the Indians call it, either that or the loudest evil spirit on earth. Tribes are fighting tooth and nail to keep the noisy things out of their territory." He was sorry to have put his thoughts in those words because the little girl looked more confused than ever.

"You know what trains are, Elle. Well, by the time you've grown as tall as Grace, I think there will be trains running on tracks clear across the country. Wouldn't you rather ride on a train than walk beside a wagon? You could get to where you wanted to go a lot quicker and your feet wouldn't hurt."

"I would if you'll come on the train with me," Elle replied.

Raines was taken aback with the little girl's answer. "I'll do that very thing some day," he said.

Nathan Riley broke into the conversation. "What are you going to do with yourself when you stop guiding wagon trains, Raines, go to work for the railroad?"

"I'm ready to stay in one place for a while. I plan to do a little ranching, a little farming. I have me a spread in Arizona on the Salt River, pretty place, plenty of water. I'd have been there already if it weren't for the Apaches. It looks like they're the last of the Indian tribes still fighting the white man. They seem to object to our taking their land, killing off their game, burning their villages, and murdering their women and children," Raines announced grimly.

"What about you and Sowell? We've just about run out of Texas. I imagine you'll be settling here here around El Paso. You'll need to start learning Spanish before the week is out," he said only half in jest.

"No! I don't want to live there! I hate Texas!" Elizabeth blurted out. She surprised everyone with her vehement words. Flustered and embarrassed by what spewed out of her mouth, she turned and ran from the group.

"Elizabeth's just mad because she thinks it's not her turn to wash the supper dishes, but it is," offered Grace as an attempt to explain her sister's behavior. "I'll take her turn tonight." The sister began collecting the supper dishes in a tin tub. *I want to live any old place as long as there's enough water there to wash the dishes and take real baths,* Grace thought to herself as she went about the job.

A short time later, Raines found Elizabeth sitting alone on a rock some twenty yards outside the wagons' circle. Her body was scrunched up like a ball, and her head rested on both arms crossed over her knees. Raines could hear her sobbing. Crying females made the guide uneasy and embarrassed.

"What's the matter, Elizabeth? Did I say something to offend you?"

She shook her head but didn't look up.

Raines sat down beside her and tossed small pebbles at a stunted juniper tree. It gave him something to do until he decided whether he should stay where he was or just get up and leave Elizabeth alone. Finally, she spoke.

"It's too much," Elizabeth said. Her head was still down, and she wiped her nose on the sleeve of her dress.

"What's too much?"

"Texas. Texas is too much. Too much sand. Too much dirt. Too much space. Too many stickery sorry little sickly-green plants. Too many muddy creeks. Too many dried-up rivers. Just too much Texas! I hate it!"

"Elizabeth, I don't understand what you're talking about."

She raised her head and looked at Raines as if he were the dumbest man she ever saw. "THERE'S TOO MUCH TEXAS!" she said slowly and deliberately, "and most of all, THERE'S TOO MUCH SKY IN TEXAS!"

Raines sat back on his heels and looked at this girl as he waited for a better explanation.

Elizabeth took a deep breath. "Back home the sky is pale blue, the color of my real mother's eyes. The sky over our farm starts behind the woods edging the orchard and then it goes up high all the way over the top our house and barn and corrals and fields and all of the animals. Then the sky ends at the edge of the woods where our lane meets the road to town. Back home, sometimes I would even forget the sky was there, except on some nights when the moon was full and the sky was a friendly darker blue color." She stopped talking and put her head back down on her knees.

"Go on," Raines encouraged.

"The Texas sky is huge and covers the whole world like a heavy bright blue blanket. The blue is so bright it hurts my eyes. Even when it catches clouds, the heavy sky is still there waiting to fall down and smother everybody in Texas. The sky is like a huge blue tarp. Even the sun and the moon can't escape from the sky. They just take turns trying to get away from it. I hate Texas. I hate the Texas sky."

Raines's amusement changed to a feeling of great interest in the girl, rather young woman, sitting beside him. She was unlike any farm girl he had ever met.

"There are too many stars in the sky in Texas," Elizabeth continued between sobs. "There are hundreds, even millions of them, and they are too bright and too big. I'm afraid some might be too heavy to stay in the sky and they might fall on me when I'm asleep. With my very own eyes, I saw three stars fall out of the Texas sky. Sometimes at night, even if I'm tired, I can't go to sleep at all. It helps me finally go to sleep when I imagine that the stars are only fireflies like the ones on our farm in Tennessee. I want to go back home."

Raines cleared his throat. "Sometimes I think of stars as lanterns showing the way so I won't get lost." He paused and saw from the corner of his eye that Elizabeth had stopped crying.

"Lanterns?" she said. "That's crazy."

"Lanterns. You see fireflies; I see lanterns. See that bright star up there? The one right there," Raines said as he pointed. "It's called the North Star because it's always shining in the northern sky. It's a dependable star that helps travelers and seamen find their ways. To me, the night sky is friendly and helpful, filled with all shapes and sizes of, well, of lanterns. I don't know a better word to describe them.

"Elizabeth, I'm sure you have a well on your farm. When you draw a bucket of water at the well, what do you use if you want a drink?"

"A dipper. We hang up dippers by our well," she answered.

"Big or little?"

"I drink out of a big dipper, but Elle likes the little dipper best."

"Like those of up there." Raines pointed to the sky. "It's not quite dark enough yet to see them, but two groups of stars arranged in the sky look like the shapes of your dippers. When it gets darker I can point them out to you."

Elizabeth used the hem of her skirt to wipe her eyes dry and looked solemnly at Raines. "Do you really like the Texas sky?"

"I do," he answered, "and if you want me to, I can teach you more about the stars. You might even come to like the Texas sky, at least, the Texas night sky."

"Ummmm. I'm not too sure about that, but I am sorry I've been such a complainer." She wiped her hands dry on her skirt and extended one to Raines so he could help her stand up from the rock on which she was sitting.

Raines stood first and then pulled her up beside him. Her closeness sent a pleasant shiver through his body, and he wondered if he dared hold her closer.

"Elizabeth! Elizabeth! Come quick!" Grace called from the wagon. "Emma needs you right NOW!"

Raines held empty air where Elizabeth had been a moment before and watched her disappear behind the wagons.

She ran past Ned and his wife who were heating pails of water over the campfire. Pearl and Esther were tending to Emma. Both had helped deliver babies before but only under the watchful eyes of midwives.

"Take you' mama's hand," Esther said to Elizabeth as she scrambled up into the wagon. "Hold her hand tight wid yo' one hand and wid you' other, wipe her forehead wid dis wet cloth."

Elizabeth was excited and trying to catch her breath but did as she was instructed by the colored woman who was not much older than she was. The moans, groans, and facial contortions coming from Emma were frightening and then it seemed as if the three assisting her and Emma herself all began hollering at the same time. During one last mighty groaning heave, Emma squeezed Elizabeth's hand so hard the girl thought her fingers had been broken.

Suddenly, Emma relaxed her grip, and the cries of a newborn filled the wagon. The sound spilled over into the outside air. "It be a girl," Esther announced as she held the slippery baby in her two large dark hands.

Elizabeth watched Pearl use Papa's hunting knife to carefully cut the umbilical cord, leaving two inches hanging from the baby's navel. She tied it with a piece of yarn from Emma's sewing basket.

" 'Lizbet, get me dat clean feed sack," Pearl ordered and held it ready when Esther carefully put the newborn in the cloth's center. Pearl wrapped the baby tightly in the improvised blanket and then put the wet bundle into Elizabeth's hands. "Well, girl, take dis chile to her mama's arms. She best see what sweetness caused her so much sufferin'. "

Trembling, Elilzabeth did just that. Ned's wife passed up pans of warm water and the women in the wagon began cleaning up Emma and the afterbirth. Elizabeth jumped down from the wagon, ran outside the wagon circle, and vomited. Still shaking, she went back to find her father, sisters, and brothers waiting near the bonfire.

"Emma had a girl," Elizabeth said.

"We know," Papa answered. "We've all decided to name her Catherine." The Riley children nodded their approval. Nate brought up a stool for Elizabeth to sit on. She thanked him, sat down, and silently vowed to herself that she would remain an unmarried maiden lady starting today and for the rest of her entire life.

The Rileys said little more and sat quietly staring into the dying fire. Esther appeared at the back of the wagon and called out, "Mister Riley, suh, we is ready for you ta come in an see yo' wife an' chile."

Nathan Riley climbed into the wagon and sat beside Emma. She looked to him like an angel and he took her hand in his. He gazed next at the unexpected shock of fine red hair crowning the head of the tiny baby lying next to her. "Are you all right?" he asked.

Emma squeezed his hand with the energy she had left. "Fine. We're both fine now, Nathan. I've just had the most painful and yet the most beautiful experience in my entire life. Look at her; just look at our sweet precious Catherine. I'm so happy, Nathan, so happy. Thank you, Nathan." Tears streamed from her eyes. Not knowing what else to do, Nathan kissed them both and left.

"Y'all can go in and see the baby and Emma now if you've a mind," he said all within earshot. The Rileys accepted their father's invitation, but Sowell felt it best that he wait for another day.

* * *

Instead of two days, the wagon train took four to arrive at the outskirts of El Paso. Emma, though still in bed, insisted that their trip continue. It did, but at a much slower pace as Raines insisted. Elizabeth appointed herself head nurse and soon her bustling about and bossy ways became more of an annoyance than a help.

Mr. Riley appealed to Raines for help. The two discussed a plan. They knew Elizabeth would agree to accompany Raines into El Paso for a day and give the family a rest.

"What are you doing?" she asked as Raines saddled two horses. "I thought we were going to stay here for another day."

"We are, but I'm going to ride into El Paso to do some business and thought someone might like to go along with me. It's been a long time since we've been near a town as big as El Paso."

"I want to go!" Elizabeth said forcefully and without hesitation. She stopped, lowered her head, and sweetly asked, "Can, I mean, MAY I go with you please, Raines?"

"Well, I thought I'd ask Grace, but if you really . . ."

"Grace doesn't ride horses very well. I don't think she'd want to ride that far," Elizabeth cut in.

"Well, maybe so. You'd better ask your father."

Elizabeth disappeared into the wagon and came out moments later wearing Emma's sun bonnet. "Papa said I could go," she said as Raines helped her up into the saddle. He noted the comfortable way she sat the horse and held both reins in her left hand leaving her right hand free to pull the horse's head around if it started to move before she was ready. Raines mounted his own horse called Red, and the two of them started for the town they could see in the distance.

As she used to do when her family lived in Tennessee, she watched what was going on in the road. Elizabeth knew they were getting close to town when she noted the increase in horse, mule, and wagon traffic. Some people were riding a small animal she hadn't seen before. "What kind of little horse is that?" she asked Raines.

"It's a burro. Some folks call it a donkey. Whatever you want to call it, the animal is as stubborn as you are."

Elizabeth turned in the saddle and glared at him.

"Burros are good transportation in this part of the country. They're tough and don't eat as much as horses and mules. Some time ago, you might have seen a camel here, but their hooves were used to sandy deserts, not like our deserts here filled with cactus, coyotes, and rattlesnakes."

Elizabeth made a face and shuddered just a little.

"There are a lot of different kinds of things out here. It wouldn't be interesting if every part of the country looked the same as every other part.

"You'll see Mexicans here. Some live in Mexico, some on this side of the border. An invisible line that's supposed to separate Texas from Mexico doesn't mean much around here. Most of the time, everybody gets along."

The people do look different, Elizabeth thought. She noted that their clothing definitely was not sewn in the South. The women wore dresses and skirts that looked more comfortable than what she was wearing. Her ears picked up the sounds of a strange language, and she guessed it was the Spanish. She remembered Raines telling the family they would need to learn Spanish if they decided to settle around here.

Elizabeth grew more excited the closer they came to the town of El Paso, and she was beside herself with joy at seeing the flower sellers and colorful carts of food vendors along the main street. She followed Raines to the front of a two-story hotel and watched as a young man came out the door to help her down from her horse. Then he took the reins of both horses and tied them to the rail.

Raines took her by the arm and guided her into the lobby. Elizabeth was wide-eyed at its elegance. He sat her down in a large upholstered chair and walked to the desk where he was greeted warmly by the clerk. "Ah, Señor Raines! I am so happy to see you again. Have you traveled far?"

Elizabeth could not hear his reply. Raines continued his business at the desk, and Elizabeth entertained herself by watching the well dressed men and women as they came and went in the lobby. She was admiring the large yellow flowered hat one of the ladies was wearing when Raines took her arm and startled her.

"Come with me," he said, and led her up a wide circular staircase and down a carpeted hallway. He stopped in front of a door numbered 12, inserted a key to open it, and led her into a beautiful room with a bed, settee, two chairs, wash stand, and wardrobe.

"Your papa and Sowell thought everyone is ready to spend a week in real beds. They asked me to make arrangements, and I'm going back to get the rest of them now. You, Miss Elizabeth, are to stay right here while I'm gone. This is the room you will share with Grace. I'm going to have the maid come in and help you with a bath. I don't want you to leave the hotel until we return, but you can get something to eat in the dining room. They'll just charge it to the room. Remember to do what I told you, and the family will be here before you know it.'' Raines closed the door behind him, and Elizabeth just stood there wondering if she had died and gone to heaven.

* * *

Elizabeth followed Raines's instructions to the letter. The maid brought her a clean wrapper which she put on after her bath in a porcelain bathtub down the hall. The tub was as big but more slippery than the galvanized tin one they left at home on the farm.

The maid also suggested she have her dinner brought up to the room because she said ladies don't often dine alone. Elizabeth was thrilled someone considered her to be a lady and even more thrilled when a waiter wheeled in her dinner on a small table and uncovered the dishes of steak, potatoes, corn, and butterscotch pudding. He poured her coffee in a china cup before he left. She knew the food portions were too large for someone coming off a year on a wagon train, and Elizabeth carefully set aside some of the food on a plate to save for her sister.

Elizabeth was napping on the bed when Grace and the other travelers arrived. Grace was as enchanted with the room as Elizabeth had been and thanked her sister for saving her food to share.

While Grace was eating, Elizabeth got up from her chair to answer a soft tap on the door. Papa stood in the hallway. He spoke quietly. Elizabeth knew he was tired. ''Emma, the baby, and I are across the hall in room nine. Sowell and Raines are in room ten. Your brothers have a big room, number eleven. Raines found a place in town for Ned and the other coloreds. The horses and mules are in the livery stable, and the oxen and cattle are in a corral about a half-mile out of town and the wagons are at the same ranch. Raines knows the rancher and says everything will be safe there.

''I see you've eaten. If you want anything more, meet us in the dining room in a half hour. I reckon I can have her supper brought up to Emma like you did, Elizabeth. I've never been in a fancy place like this in my whole life. Sowell tells me we can stay here for a week. He says we deserve it and can afford it. Once we get the Texas dust out of our eyes, ears, and heads, maybe we can decided where to light. I'm getting mighty tired of traveling myself.'' With that, their father closed the door.

Elizabeth called the maid to help Grace with her bath. The two girls didn't go down to the dining room for supper. Both of their stomachs were more full than they had been in months. For entertainment, the girls delighted in jumping on a real bed with springs until they felt worn out. They giggled as they pattered down the hall to the indoor privy then came back to their elegant room, smoothed out the mussed bed, and went to sleep.

* * *

Early the next morning, Raines, Sowell, and Nathan Riley met at breakfast in the dining room before any of the others were awake. They were on their third cup of real coffee before the waiter brought their steak, eggs, and tortillas. "That's Mexican bread," Raines explained.

The men ate quietly and cleaned their plates. Raines had asked for more tortillas and was amused to see his breakfast companions devour the second plateful.

"Well, gentlemen," he said after he had picked his teeth with a real toothpick from the holder in the middle of the table, "there isn't any more Texas that I can show you unless you want to go a hundred miles north of here and start back toward the east."

The two groaned, shook their heads, and reached for the toothpicks themselves.

"I understand that to be a 'NO!' So tell me. Is El Paso your choice?" Raines continued.

The two chewed on their toothpicks. Riley kicked Sowell under the table.

"How much would you charge if we went along with you to where was it? Arizona? I thought it was part of New Mexico Territory," Sowell said.

"It was once but isn't now," Raines answered. "I don't think both of you together have enough money to pay me to lead you on into Arizona."

Sowell's face fell, and Nathan Riley looked as if someone had kicked him in the stomach.

"Sorry I asked," Sowell stammered after an embarrassed pause.

"We've been together so long, I've come to view you all almost like family." Rained grinned. "Sometimes you're hard to put up with, but I'm no angel, either. I'll take you with me for nothing as long as you restock the larder here and feed me as well as you did during all those months we spent crossing Texas."

It took a minute for Raines's words to soak in before the two other men began to laugh and extended their hands to shake his. They were still smiling when they left the dining room and entered the lobby.

The desk clerk was white as a sheet and his hand holding the telegram trembled. The few other guests in the lobby seemed to have been turned to stone. "What is it?" Raines asked, alarmed.

"Mr. Raines, sir. I have bad news. The worst kind of news," the desk clerk stammered.

"Well, tell us, man!" Raines demanded.

"General Robert E. Lee surrendered to Grant at Appomattox in Virginia on the ninth day of April. God help us all!" The desk clerk had tears in his eyes and fumbled in his pocket for his handkerchief.

The stunned silence in the hotel lobby was broken by the sound of a baby's cry. Elizabeth carefully held crying Catherine in her arms and walked slowly down the stairs. "Papa," she said when she reached her father, "Mama wants her breakfast now. You hold Catherine, and I'll find the waiter." She put the crying baby in Nathan Rilcy's arms and disappeared into the dining room.

Catherine suddenly quieted as her father, not knowing anything else to do, bounced her in his arms.

Raines gazed at the two of them. "Life goes on," he said to no one in particular.

* * *

In the many months of travel, whenever Nathan Riley and his son Matthew had been in a town, whatever its size, they had recognized the men and boys who had been in the war from the pieces of uniforms they once proudly wore. One man might wear a belt buckle stamped CSA, another a slouch hat with unit insignia still attached, army-issue boots, a Sharps rifle. Some, especially those missing an arm or leg, wore uniforms more complete than their own bodies.

The farther west their wagon train had come, the more likely it was for them to spot parts of as many blue uniforms as grey. Even Nathan Riley wore the slouch hat of his artillery battery of the Army of West Tennessee, and Matthew carried in his pocket the buttons he had cut off his dead brothers' Confederate uniforms.

When Elizabeth came back from the kitchen after ordering Emma's breakfast, she took Catherine, now sleeping, from her father's arms.

Her father said, "Tell Emma that I will be gone for a spell." Then he turned to Sowell and Raines. "There is something Matthew and I must do. No need to wait for us." He glanced at his eldest son, and they walked together out into the street.

Word of Lee's surrender had spread like a brush fire, and although there were far more saloons than churches in El Paso, it was not hard to find the one they were looking for. The two Riley war veterans followed the men wearing bits and pieces of grey or blue through the doors of a nearby saloon.

It took a few minutes for their eyes to adjust to the dim light inside. Their noses accepted the stale smells of liquor, sweat, tobacco, urine, and fear. The clinking of glass on glass was the loudest sound they heard except for the muted sounds of grown men crying.

They saw no evidence of celebration or even regret on the faces of the men sitting at tables or standing at the long bar. Matthew and his father each placed a coin on its polished wood surface and then carried their drinks to a table where there were two empty seats. The other men already seated there acknowledged the newcomers' presence with their sorrowful eyes.

The eerie quiet in the room caused the barkeeper to break out in a sweat, and he kept wiping the damp palms of his hands on the apron around his middle each time he had poured liquor from a bottle into a glass. The thought of profit from such a brisk business never entered the man's head. The barkeeper had not gone to war, but knew he was in the presence of heroes, as ragged and torn as many of the veterans looked.

After some time, liquor loosened their tongues, and the men spoke softly as they identified themselves by naming their commanding officers at the time in the battles in which they had fought. A former preacher among them thought to himself that the veterans' brief conversations sounded like a litany of war.

For the first time since he deserted and brought Papa home, Matthew felt he was among people who understood his actions, people who didn't need an explanation for what any of them did when caught in war's hell. He wondered if the others in the room were of the same mind. Gradually, he felt the guilt he had carried all this time seep out of his body as if it were nothing more than hot coffee dripping out of a hole in the bottom of a tin cup.

It was dark outside when Matthew and his father left the saloon. On their way out, they hugged and whispered words of encouragement to men who, once strangers, now shared the fellowship of ordinary people who answered duty's call, did extraordinary things, and survived to lift a glass to life.

Raines and Sowell were waiting for them in the hotel lobby. The two helped the veterans, one at a time, into the bathtub, dried, and dressed them in clean nightshirts, and then put them into bed in the room the guide and former storekeeper shared.

Raines and Sowell slept in chairs in the lobby.

Chapter Twenty
Buffalo Soldiers

The hotel cook agreed to serve an early breakfast to the Raines party the day the travelers resumed their journey. The night before, Sowell had settled all bills with the hotel, livery stable, and rancher who agreed to have his hired hands bring the wagons and livestock to the edge of El Paso where Ned and the other coloreds would meet and ready them for travel.

Emma was on her feet and gaining strength daily. Catherine was the joy of her life. Nathan Riley was proud to know he still had the means to be a father again even though he would have preferred a boy. After witnessing so much death during the war, he paid more attention to this baby than he did to his other children when they were born. He used his whole arm to hold her and the stump of the other to balance the little girl as he held her close up to his shoulder. He silently rejoiced in the feel of soft new life.

Matthew, John, and Nate carried their few belongings from all of the rooms and loaded them in Ned's wagon waiting on the street in front of the hotel. The boys joined the other members of their group in the dining room for a breakfast they would not see again. It was a repeat of the steak and eggs feast they had eaten every morning of their stay. They assured the cook no one would ever tire of such a repast.

All of the Rileys rode with Ned to where their wagons were waiting and prepared to begin the next part of their journey. Raines and Sowell met the owner of the General Store who had arrived at his place of business at dawn and was just finishing directing the loading of the supplies Sowell had ordered on the storekeeper's own wagon.

As Raines watched the man and his hired hand load it, he could tell from the boxes that he would eat well once again as Sowell promised. The storekeeper himself drove the delivery wagon, with Raines and Sowell aboard, out to meet the others and was happy with the fine profit he had made. He wished them a safe journey. As he seldom was paid in gold coins, while driving his empty wagon back to El Paso, he took a coin from his pocket, bit it, and was reassured that Mr. Sowell was an honest man.

Esther and Pearl were anxious to see the baby and her mama and expressed amazement at how the wee one had grown in just a few days. Esther examined the newborn's navel and asked Emma for a strip of cloth. "Da baby, she need a belly band," the colored woman said as she wrapped the cloth around Catherine's middle. "We leave dis on 'bout ten days, maybe more."

Emma nodded. She felt foolish because in her pain, joy, and excitement of the birth, she, a midwife, had forgotten about the belly band. To cover her mistake, she changed the subject. "Esther, I want to thank you and Pearl here for delivering my baby. My milk came on time. It's good. Can't you tell? See how much Catherine has grown already."

"An' both of you gets to ride 'stead of walk for a while," Pearl said."Come 'long, Esther. Dis wagon train be on da move again." The two of them jumped easily from the wagon down to the ground, then turned to look back once more at El Paso which was fading in the distance. Esther wished they had stayed longer.

* * *

Raines was almost sorry Sowell and the Rileys hadn't settled in Texas. Familiar landmarks signaled the wagon train's entry into Arizona Territory. A single rider usually attracted little attention here in Indian country, especially one who knew the trails and signs of what might be in the area. He knew the trails well enough but felt his tracking skills could be better even though they had not failed him in the past.

A professional guide. Raines prided himself on being objective and never getting close to his customers. *This trip has taken too long already,* he thought. *The week in El Paso was a mistake, for me anyway. I should have stayed out at the ranch with the stock and wagons. There are too many women in this train. There should be more than twice as many men as women on any wagon train. No wonder everything is so messed up with this one. The sky over New Mexico does look different from the Texas sky. Danged if it doesn't!*

Lost in thought, Raines carelessly guided Red too close to a prickly pear cactus at the edge of the trail. When a spine pierced his pant leg and punctured his skin, the sudden pain alerted him to the surroundings and he became aware of smoke rising from a distant mountain. He said nothing but wondered if anyone else had noticed it.

"Anyone hungry?" he called out. "Looks like a dry creek bed over there and some shade under those trees."

"How do you know the creek's dry?" Nate asked as he walked up beside the guide.

"The stock would have let us know five miles back if there was water. By tonight, we'll be at a river that's wet, I hope."

The group was grateful for the shade. Even though the land was more varied and interesting to look at since they had left Texas, the sun was as bright. Elizabeth swore the sky was more friendly in New Mexico than the sky in Texas was. "Whatever that means," sighed her father, who had given up trying to understand his oldest daughter and her peculiar ways.

The respite gave Raines a chance to move away from the group. He climbed a small hill and studied the sky. He saw a thunderhead forming in the far northwest but the wind's direction was blowing the clouds away from the train's route. Lesser clouds on the periphery came close to the ground and held lightening that flashed now and then. He decided the smoke he saw was not a signal but a lightening-caused fire of no danger to the travelers.

As he turned to return to camp, he jumped to see Elizabeth standing nearby. "I didn't hear you!" he exclaimed.

"What if I'd been a bear?" she teased.

He decided not to tell her that an Indian would have been as likely.

"Tell me about what's happening here in the sky," she asked.

Raines explained the formation of the thunderhead and how to recognize it by the anvil shape at the top. She thought the word "cumulus" was a funny name for a cloud and preferred to call it a cotton cloud because it reminded her of fluffy Tennessee cotton. She knew about lightning but was amazed that the strikes she saw this day were so far away she couldn't hear the thunder. Both of them heard Sowell ring the cowbell. "Time to go," he said.

Early the next afternoon, Nate noticed the animals' sudden change in their manner and quickness of their steps. About two hours before sunset, the cattle nearly broke into a stampede when they came over a small knoll and saw a river down below. The stock got to the water without running over anyone and the drivers held back their teams until the wagons were safely at the water's edge.

The Riley women bathed upstream. Esther waited under a tree and held Catherine. The Riley men, Raines, and Sowell bathed some distance away. Ned and the colored men bathed out of sight, and when Emma returned to take Catherine, Esther and the other colored women took their turns at bathing away from the others.

The travelers were refreshed and rested. Emma took out her carpetbag and finished the crochet edging on a doily she was making from the last scraps of the wedding dress she wore twenty years ago. Ned, Elijah, and Will went fishing and supplied trout for supper. The four Riley men, each with one bullet for his rifle, returned from hunting with a turkey, a rabbit, and two quail.

Elizabeth sat in the wagon and wrote in her journal. Grace listened to Elle recite her numbers. Everyone else, except for Raines, found a quiet shady place near the water and napped. Raines moved far away but stayed in sight of the camp. He sat on the ground with his back resting against a trunk of a cottonwood tree. He cut off a small branch and used his pocket knife to whittle a turkey call from the wood. At supper, everyone agreed that it had been a lovely day.

* * *

Whenever it looked to Sowell as if their wagons could never get over mountains blocking their way, the Butterfield Overland Trail they still followed wound its way through passes between or clung to the lower sides of the rugged western mountains. Some parts of the train went through passes so steep as to require the travelers to use more than one team to pull a wagon up the grade and then restrain the wagon from going too fast down the other side. Hitching and unhitching teams left the people and the animals exhausted. On those days, Raines let them make camp early.

Their party had seen no other human being for more than a month. Every day Raines assured them that they were one day closer to outposts of civilization in Arizona than they were the day before. After a particularly difficult descent down a steep part of the trail, the emigrants were cheered to see a vast desert plain stretching out before of them.

They set up camp quickly and ate a cold supper because it was getting dark. Emma thought she saw a glimmer of light far off to the west but hesitated telling anyone about it. She was relieved to know her eyes were not playing tricks on her when Raines said, "Fort Bowie is over to the right, about a day's ride from here. If it's not dusty, sometimes you can see their fires."

There were no laggards the next morning, and the women packed up breakfast dishes so fast that Raines had to finish drinking his coffee on horseback as he led the group down the gentle grade to flat land. All of the wagons made the transition smoothly. Raines turned Red and rode back to return his coffee cup to Elizabeth who was driving the yellow wagon.

"Thank you, my girl," he said cheerfully. "What do you think of the Arizona sky?"

"I like it. I like the mountains that hold the sky up there in the air where it belongs. The mountains do such a good job that God rewarded them by giving them beautiful colors—purple and pink, and even a friendly blue," she replied.

"Just you wait until you see an Arizona rainbow," Raines said with a smile that hid the concern he felt. He had been watching five riders following them from a distance ever since they started across the desert.

He turned his horse around and rode ahead. He gave the same message to each of the men, no matter the color of his skin. "Don't look back. Five riders are following us, Apaches, I'm sure. They haven't closed the distance, so far. I want you to have your guns ready. Riley, Sowell, arm the coloreds. Do it slowly and easily. If you hear me blow my turkey call here, fall back to the wagons and be ready to take the reins and whip those teams to run! Don't say anything to the women yet."

The wagon train continued traveling at its usual pace for the next hour. Raines watched for the Indians to move up, but the small group of riders maintained the same distance from the wagons. He barely heard the bugle call but did see a column of dust and sunlight bouncing off what he hoped were military rifles. He turned around in his saddle and watched them as the Apaches turned their horses and disappeared behind an outcropping of rock. "Thank God for the Army," he said softly to himself.

Raines did not stop the wagon train which continued at its normal pace. He did ride up to tell the men that the Indians were gone. They had seen the dust themselves, and Matthew had guessed correctly that soldiers were coming.

A scouting party comprised of a dozen soldiers from the Tenth Regiment Cavalry United States Colored Troops reached the wagon train less than a half hour later. Raines called the train to stop, and as he rode up to meet the soldiers, he was impressed by the spit and polish of their uniforms and the large size of their magnificent horses.

The insignia on the soldiers' uniforms caught his eye. The patch was shaped like a shield divided into four sections, each one of a different design. The ribbon unfurled across the bottom of the patch identified the military unit. What was unique about the patch was the magnificent buffalo pictured above the shield.

He knew the Indians had named Negroes Buffalo Soldiers because of their perception that the troopers' dark curly hair was similar to that of the buffalo. All who heard the name knew it was a sign of respect for the soldiers' uncommon bravery and courage, qualities exemplified by the revered buffalo.

Raines took off his hat, held it in his hand, and said, "We are mighty glad to see you! I am very much attached to my scalp, and there are ladies and children with us. We have been followed by five braves on horseback. Am I correct in thinking the Apaches are warring again?"

"You are," replied a huge cavalryman. "Your life may be at risk, but your hair is safe. Apaches don't scalp people. Where are you bound?"

"Through Apache Pass and on to the Salt River south of the Sierra Anches Mountains where I have a cabin and some land."

"You'll find a Chiricahua Apache behind every rock if you go that way. I'll be an old man before we finish herding all of the Apaches up to their reservation at San Carlos. It's not a job I like, but it's my duty. Y'all might want to think about settling someplace where the Indians are friendlier."

The Negro cavalryman's manner puzzled Raines. His curiosity emboldened him and he asked, "You're a colored soldier, once a slave, I would guess. How is it that you speak like a white man?" Raines regretted asking the question and was surprised when the soldier threw back his head and laughed.

"I'll wager I can read and write better than you. I learned white talk from reading books and from listening to the speech of the white officers of my regiment. I haven't read a single book written in colored talk, but I can still talk colored. Dis big ole hoase I be ridin' on, he be da hoase dat belong ta ma massa who done got hisself killed in da war an' . . ."

"Hercules?"

The big trooper was startled by the sound and turned to see Nate who had walked up to the group. He dismounted his horse and extended his hand in greeting to the young man. "It's Nate Riley all grown! What are you doing out here in this lonely place?"

"We left our farm more than a year ago. The whole South has gone to ruin. What are YOU doing here?"

"I found my home in the Cavalry. We're out here fighting Indians and trying to move them to places they don't want to go. I feel sorry about it, but I'm a soldier and those are my orders. They call me Jim now, Jim Randolph." Nate thought he saw a wicked gleam in the trooper's eye. "I don't know my real family name. Who do I see coming?" the trooper continued as he watched John and the Riley girls running out to meet him.

Nate introduced Hercules, rather Trooper Jim Randolph, to his father and Emma and reminded them how the former slave saved their lives. Nate didn't mention anything about the death of his mother out of respect for Emma, but everyone knew the story anyway.

The troopers assured Raines that the wagon train could continue the trip without fear of attack by Apaches as far as Fort Bowie, which was within sight, but that they should wait there until other Buffalo Soldiers were available to accompany them through the rest of Apache country.

Raines thanked the troopers for their help and said he would seriously consider their suggestion to settle in a part of Arizona where the Indians were likely to be more friendly.

Trooper Jim Randolph agreed with him that the central part of the Territory where the Gila River joined the Salt River would be a likely place to consider. "The Gila flows southwest clear to the edge of the California Arizona border, then dips down though a little bit of Mexico before it empties into Gulf of California. There may be some Mexican bandits along the way, but no Apaches."

The soldiers and the emigrants parted, the troopers again assuring Raines they would be in no danger during the remainder of their short journey to the fort. The wagon drivers urged their teams to go a little faster when they saw the buildings in the distance.

There was no stockade around Fort Bowie. The white Commanding Officer made them feel welcome and suggested they camp on the opposite side of the fort from the horse corrals. He was generous in allowing the train's horses and mules to use an empty corral, which relieved one night watch. Nate and John drew night watch for the oxen and cattle. There was plenty of grass for the stock, and both young men dozed on their watch.

The next morning, Elizabeth and Grace carried a basket filled with ham biscuits to the Commanding Officer's quarters. Although he was born and reared in Boston, the Colonel expressed his appreciation for their thoughtfulness and the gift of such a prized Southern delicacy.

The Raines party camped at Fort Bowie for the best part of a week. Nate was disappointed that Trooper Jim Randolph and the other cavalrymen with him had not returned by the time the wagon train, accompanied by a small contingent of Buffalo Soldiers, left Fort Bowie for Tucson, a three days' drive from the fort unless unexpected trouble slowed them down.

Before they left, the Commanding Officer had suggested to Raines that he and the other men at least twenty-one years of age inquire of the lands being offered to emigrants by the Federal Government. "President Lincoln and the Congress wanted to get the West settled. If you'd be willing to homestead, live there, and farm the land for five years, the government will practically give you the one-hundred and sixty acres. It's enough land to grow food for several families, and if relatives homestead together, they might make a good-sized farm of it."

The officer agreed that the confluence of the Gila and Salt rivers would be a possible site for homesteading and was far enough away to be fairly safe from warring Indians. He decided not to add that Apaches have been accustomed to raiding and killing members of other Indian tribes as well as whites many miles away from their ancestral Apache lands.

The wagon train was on the trail three days before the emigrants passed small farms on the outskirts of Tucson. Nate turned back to thank the Buffalo Soldiers who had been following some distance behind the wagons, but the troopers had already turned back and were too far away to hear Nate's call. He was going to miss them. While on their way to Tucson, Nate played a solitary game of "I Spy" looking to spot the Buffalo Soldier outriders on the wagon train's flanks. Their very presence had been exciting as well as a comfort to him.

Once Matthew had gone out himself to ride beside one of the outriders for almost half a day. "What did you talk about?" Nate asked when his brother came back in.

"We didn't talk much," he answered. "I just wanted to get close to a soldier from the other side. I wanted to see if I would be afraid again even though I knew he wouldn't shoot me."

"Were you afraid?" Nate asked.

Matthew didn't answer. Even though the Buffalo Soldiers had set up their own night camp a distance away from the emigrants and posted guards at the wagon train's camp as well as their own, Matthew couldn't sleep. Each time he dozed off, he woke with a start and reached for his rifle thinking the campfires he saw were those of the enemy.

Matthew was relieved now that the wagon train had arrived safely at Tucson, but at the same time, he wasn't sorry that the bluebellies were gone.

"Matthew!" his father called. "Raines wants you to come with us to find that Government office. The rest of you stay here and set up camp for the night. We'll be back well before sundown."

Those left behind automatically went about their tasks. Elizabeth had hoped her father would treat them to another night in a hotel but then felt somewhat ashamed for being greedy. Nate couldn't get Hercules, now Trooper Jim Randolph of the Tenth Regiment Cavalry United States Colored Troops, off his mind.

The men were true to their word. They returned to camp before sundown and brought back with them fresh corn, tomatoes, and spare ribs for supper as well as documents relating to homesteading near the confluence of the Gila and Salt rivers.

After supper, Mr. Riley saw Nate reading one of the documents by the light of the campfire. The father was proud that everyone in his family could read and write, even though Elle still struggled over some big words. *Learning is a gift given to her children by their mother,* he thought, *God rest her soul.*

That night when he slipped into bed with Emma, baby Catherine between them, Riley surprised himself with an uncommon thought: *I'll wager Ned knows how to read. I wonder if he's teaching the other coloreds on this trip. Wouldn't be a bit surprised. I'll ask Sowell tomorrow.*

After breakfast the next morning, Sowell and Ned rode away. "Where are you going?" Riley called out after them.

"Tucson," Sowell called back over his shoulder. "We'll be back by the time you break camp."

Elizabeth suspected the men purposely stayed away until the rest of them had everything ready to travel again. Even so, she couldn't help but share in the excitement Sowell and Ned showed as they rode back to where the wagon train was waiting for them.

"I talked again with the man at the Government Office," Sowell said. "If Riley, Matthew, John, Raines, and myself homestead next to each other, we would have eight hundred acres altogether. When Nate comes of age, he could add one hundred and sixty acres more. I could set up my store again if you all would help me with the planting and harvest.

"And that's not all. Colored folks have the right to homestead same as whites. If Ned, Elijah, and Benjamin homestead too, and Ned's boy follows when he comes of age, they would own six hundred and forty acres if my calculations are right. What do you think of that!"

The former slaves thought Mr. Sowell had been in the hot desert sun too long without his hat.

* * *

When the troopers guarding the wagon train approached Fort Bowie, their stoic faces masked the fear they felt at the sight of a fresh grave. Against all Army regulations, a broken arrow piercing an Apache scalp was stuck in the dirt in place of a headstone. One of the troopers dismounted, pulled up the gruesome symbol, and threw it out of sight under a mesquite tree bordering a dry wash. He remounted and led the quiet group into the corral where they unsaddled their horses and put them out to pasture.

The troopers walked as a group to meet the Commanding Officer coming toward them. "Who?" one asked.

"Jefferson," he replied. "It was an Apache ambush. The men came in two days ago. Four are in the infirmary. William, arrow in the right shoulder; Logan, arrow, left leg; Edward, two arrows, one in his right arm, one in the right leg. And Jim . . . Jim's right leg was shattered by a stolen Sharpes rifle, government issue."

They went in a group to the infirmary to comfort their comrades. The troopers' cheery greetings and well wishes belied the sadness and fury they held in their hearts. The doctor tending Trooper Jim Randolph's severe wounds was surprised at their lighthearted greetings but he understood that when they had been slaves, these men had learned to hide their true emotions.

When the doctor finished changing Trooper Jim Randolph's bandages after his comrades had left, he saw tears in the big man's eyes. Both of them knew his days as a soldier were over. He didn't know that the last time the cavalryman had cried was when he had been a small boy and was torn from his mother's arms at a slave auction near the Tennessee–Mississippi border.

Chapter Twenty-one
Railroad

It took Raines only one growing season to know that God never intended him to be a farmer. Yet, he understood that if he gave up, he would lose the homestead and cause a huge hole in the properties the emigrants had come to view as one farm.

The solution to his problem came on a Sunday in October after their first joint harvest, a harvest which proved to be less than good but better than fair and terribly disappointing to Nathan Riley and his son Nate.

Elle, now old enough to read parts of the Bible by herself although she still skipped over the biggest words, told them God had punished them with a sorry harvest because no one in the family had been to church since they had settled here.

Grace thought her little sister got that idea from a circuit riding preacher who had stopped by the farm and invited the family to attend church. The service was held every other Sunday at nine o'clock in the morning in the barn belonging to one of the homesteaders who lived on the other side of the river. Both Preacher and the homesteader encouraged worshipers to bring food to share at the picnic following the preaching as was the custom.

Emma told her husband that Elle might be at least half right about the Good Lord's displeasure of their neglect of church attendance. "Besides," she added, "our family should think about socializing more now that Catherine is walking and has been potty-trained for more than a month."

Nathan Riley, head down and watching his left boot kick a clod of mud until it broke into small pieces, finally agreed that everyone could attend church the following Sunday if it didn't take all day for everybody to get there. "Emma, there are only two ways to get to the other side of that river. One is to ride over in that piddlin' little rowboat, the only fishing boat we have between the lot of us. The other way is to swim. Which way do you want to go?''

Emma, as stubborn as her husband, crossed her arms, stamped her foot, and held her ground.

When Sunday came, she decided not to ask her husband the method he and the other men used to select Raines as the only one among them to row the boat. Mr. and Mrs. Riley, Catherine, and Elle were his first passengers, and they heard no complaints from him.

During his fifth trip rowing three more worshipers at one time across the water, Raines had a revelation and chided himself for not thinking of it before. *If the Rileys will farm for me, I'll build a ferryboat,* he thought. *My land will be kept in the family when I marry Elizabeth. This might be a good day to ask her even if the roof isn't on my house yet.*

Raines was lost in thought when the bow of the boat bumped up hard against the river bank. He helped his passengers step gingerly from the unsteady rowboat and on to the land and watched them walk down the path leading to the barn. Raines tied the boat to a tree branch overhanging the riverbank, found himself a shady spot under a willow tree growing a short distance away from the shore, and went to sleep.

The robust sounds of worshipers singing the closing hymn woke him, and he mingled with the churchgoers as they filed out of the building. Everyone, except Elizabeth and Preacher, thought he had attended the service and had been sitting on one of the hay bales in the back. For months Elizabeth had made it her business to keep an eye on Raines and enjoyed the feeling of butterflies in her stomach when she caught his eye.

Matthew volunteered to row on the trip back to his family's side of the river, an offer for which Raines said he would be eternally grateful. Elizabeth held back from getting in the boat until only Raines and she were left waiting on the river's bank. When they saw the rowboat reach the far shore and the passengers carefully step out, Raines took both of Elizabeth's hands in his.

''Elizabeth, I think I've loved you since the day you renamed cumulus clouds for Tennessee cotton. I've seen enough of this land to last me a lifetime, and I'm ready to settle in one place so long as you are there. I love you and ask you to be my wife. I'm no farmer, but I think I can make a good living for us right here with your family. Will you marry me?''

Elizabeth hadn't expected to be so choked up when she heard his words so softly spoken. She simply nodded and lifted her face to be kissed.

*   *   *

Preacher married Raines and Elizabeth in the Rileys' modest parlor the day before Thanksgiving. It was the first wedding the circuit rider had ever performed. Emma invited him to stay over for Thanksgiving Day dinner, an invitation he gladly accepted, and Nate generously give up his own bed in the loft to the guest and slept that night in the barn.

The next day Preacher was amazed to see a large gathering of people who had come from miles around to share the bountiful Thanksgiving meal served under the cottonwood trees growing between the farm house and the river. The sight gave him hope that a church with its own building might be possible before too long.

The tables were set for turkey, roast beef, ham and parsnip casserole, sweet potatoes, cornbread dressing, brown gravy, egg and tomato bake, fresh greens dotted with sweet butter, Sally Lunn bread, sweet potato pie, bread pudding with cream, apple pie, rum raisin cake, chicory coffee, and genuine China tea.

Preacher had not seen the likes of such a meal in his entire life, nor had he ever seen whites and coloreds sitting at the same table and apparently enjoying one another's company. He didn't really relax until the end of the meal when Sowell passed around a bottle of whiskey and the men lifted their glasses to salute the couple and wish Elizabeth and Raines long life and happiness.

When the women had cleared away the last of the communal meal, Esther and Pearl shared the news with Emma that both of them were in the family way. "I'm thrilled for you!" Emma replied. "I'm a midwife too, and now I can return the help you offered me when you delivered Catherine."

Nate overheard their conversation and congratulated Elijah and Benjamin on their approaching fatherhood. Then he asked, "How did your crops do?" to change the subject as he still was not comfortable to be around women in the family way.

"Fair," answered Elijah, "but Mr. Sowell, he help an' keep us busy buildin' da new store. Ned, he be a good boss, an' his boy learnin' to be a real fine carpenter. But we is doin' jest fine. Neber thought I own my own land.'' Benjamin nodded his head in agreement.

''Raines told me he's going to build a ferryboat to get people and goods across the river. Did you know that?'' Nate continued. ''I guess he'd have work for you this winter too. He's hired me, but he jokes that I should work for free now that he's part of our family.

''Raines has a good head on his shoulders. He says when the railroad comes through near here, there will be more farmers who'll want to get their crops across the river and to the train for shipment to folks who live back in the East.

''Raines even told Elizabeth he'd take her on a wedding trip to California on the train some day and show her the ocean. He's seen it himself and says it's way bigger than the Mississippi River.

''Sowell can get big things like cooking stoves and bathtubs a lot quicker by train than by wagon. Maybe that's why he wants his store building bigger than the one in Tennessee.

''Matthew and I are helping Raines work on his house. Elizabeth told him he'd better get it done before he starts building a ferryboat. Of course, it will just be a flatboat, not like the sternwheelers that took us across the Mississippi. Matthew told me when the house is done, he's thinking about working laying track for the railroad this winter. But don't say anything about it. He hasn't told Papa yet.''

The group enjoyed the mild November day on the desert and sat under the trees to visit with one another until late in the afternoon. Preacher thanked the Rileys for their hospitality. Before he left for the next farm where he was to spend the night, he said that he would be looking forward to seeing them at worship service in the weeks to come.

Sowell bid his farewell, and Ned left his friends who wanted to get home before dark. ''Esther, you must show me how to make your ham and parsnip casserole. It was delicious!'' Emma called her as she was climbing into Elijah's wagon.

''I'll do that. It sho' saves on ham,'' Esther called back.

It was twilight when Nathan and Emma took Catherine with them and made their bed in the barn. They had given their room in the farm house to Raines and Elizabeth for a few nights until the family helped the bride and groom stuff a new mattress with goose feathers for use on their own marriage bed.

* * *

Three weeks before Christmas, Preacher brought the Rileys a copy of a Tucson newspaper. In it was an advertisement for hard-working men—white, colored, Chinese, Mexican, almost anyone with a strong back and an empty stomach—to lay track and other work for the railroad now less than twenty miles east of Tucson.

The next morning, Matthew, Nate, and Ned's boy Will hitched a ride to Tucson with Preacher in his old wagon pulled by two older mules, a gift from an even older rancher who was a member of one of his small congregations. "Never look a gift horse, er, mule in the mouth," Preacher said to the young men as he urged his mules to go a little faster.

* * *

The three young men signed their names on the employment roster the day they arrived in Tucson. The railroad company fed them and put them up for the night in a rundown hotel. Early the next morning, they joined twenty others who climbed into wagons hired to drive them to the railhead.

At mid-day, one of the wagon drivers pointed and called out, "See down there. That's the work train. Ain't she a beauty!"

Matthew didn't see much beauty in the scene even though he was impressed with the organized activity. It reminded him of the precision of a military drill. As his wagon grew closer to the workers, the driver proudly explained what was going on and gave silent thanks that he wasn't one of them. *Work's too hard even if the pay is good,* he thought.

"See those flatcars up there in front?" he explained. "They carry all the tools, and that there's the blacksmith shop sittin' on the last one. Those next three boxcars have bunks in 'em for y'all. Beats sleepin on the ground, I'd say.

"And the car after them is the kitchen and where you wash up and eat. Folks tell me the workers get plenty of food, but the cook isn't as good as the last one, who had a fight with one of the Chinamen. It made the others madder than old wet hens, and when all of the Chinamen were gonna leave the job, the boss fired the cook instead. They say Chinamen are just about the best workers they have, but you wouldn't know it to look at the skinny little fellers.

"Look ahead there! See that horse hauling rails down to the section where the railroad ties have been set. Listen and you can hear the singing. The beat of the music helps those gandy dancers, lift, carry, and lay down those heavy rails all together at the same time. It makes the work easier and gets the track laid faster."

Nate watched the smooth flow of actions as the second rail fell into place and the rail setters moved forward as a body to place the next section. At the same time a worker behind them used a wooden gauge to make sure that the two rails just set were exactly four feet, eight and a half inches apart, or so their driver said.

"Watch now; watch careful now," the wagon driver continued. "There! See the gauger jump out of the way so as not to get hit in the head when the spike man's hammer comes down to set the spike. "See?" The action happened so fast, Matthew missed it and paid closer attention the next time.

"Well, gentlemen, here we are," the driver said as he drove past the boxcar housing the carpenter shop and pulled his wagon up behind the others. "The project engineer's office is in this car. Y'all are s'posed to line up out here, and the boss will call you in a few at a time. Don't work too hard!" the driver called out as he turned his team and drove away with the other wagons.

The new hires, many of them with prior military experience, lined up quickly and were standing at attention when an office worker came and called the names from a list he held in his hand.

"Good. You're all here. We'll call you six at a time to come in and the foreman will assign your jobs. Laying track is our major focus at this time, although we do have a few jobs open for men with some special skills. As you can see, this work train is set up like the small towns some of you may have just left. You will work, eat, and sleep here. As for entertainment, well, there are tents a mile or so behind us that are set up for that purpose on Sunday, your day off. The railroad does not officially condone camp followers.

"As you can see, our locomotive is located behind the cars instead of in front. This is a work train and the engine pushes instead of pulls the cars. The engineer can uncouple the engine and return to our storage depot some miles back and bring up supplies and equipment when needed.

"When you were driven alongside the tracks in the wagons, I hope you could see how important teamwork is in building a railroad. It is hard work, but railroaders can take pride in the knowledge that they have brought the country together in a way that will benefit everyone."

Matthew, Nate and Will were in the last group to be interviewed. Out of the six, the three of them were the only ones who said they knew how to read and write.

The interviewer gave each of them a different page of print to read aloud and asked each one to write out on paper his full name and the state in which he had been born. The foreman was surprised that the young colored boy was literate.

"My pa taught me," Will explained. "He taught me how to build things, too."

"That's right," Nate spoke up. "Where we come from, Will and his pa are the best carpenters around."

Literacy was not a requirement for the jobs of laying track even though teamwork, following directions and strong backs were. It happened that the carpenter was short handed, and the foreman sent Will down to see him. When the young man didn't return after half an hour, the foreman knew at least one apprentice position had been filled.

"Matthew Riley, you were a soldier?" the foreman asked.

"Yes, sir. Army of West Tennessee." Matthew answered.

"Do you know anything about the telegraph?"

"Not much, sir. The only thing I know is how to climb up the pole and cut the lines when ordered to."

"Well, if you can shinny up the pole, I guess you're smart enough to learn how to work a telegraph key. Our telegrapher here has been ordered back to Silver City when we can find somebody to take his place." The foreman took Matthew to the back of the car where the telegrapher and his equipment were in a small office.

"George, this young fella has climbed up telegraph poles and cut the wires. Do you think you could teach him how things are supposed to work at this end? He can read and write, and he survived the Battle of Shiloh."

Matthew winced. "My brothers died near there, sir."

"Sorry," the telegrapher said.

He rose from his seat and offered his hand to Matthew. "Sorry," he said again. "There were no winners there. I fought on the other side. Now, let me show you how this works. Sit down here. This is an important job, and one you'll need to learn quickly."

That settled, the foreman turned to Nate. "Well, young man, you're another Riley, eh? What do you do best?"

"Farm," Nate answered.

The foreman looked up from the list he still held in his hand. "Farm? I'm afraid we don't do much farming along the tracks here. Can you cook?"

"Yes, sir, but I came to lay track, to help build a railroad."

"My boy, do you know how soldiers win wars, captains sail ships, and tough men build railroads? Not with guns, not with sextants, not with steel, but with the food in their stomachs! Yes, sir! Empires are built on stomachs! You said you cook, lad. Do you cook well?"

"As well as my mother did. She taught us all, her sons as well as her daughters, to cook and everything else we would need to know to take care of ourselves. She's dead now," Nate answered quietly, his eyes downcast.

"Bless your mother. I'll take you myself to the kitchen. Come along."

When the two climbed up into the railroad car, the foreman led Nate past the washroom and into the kitchen. "If you were the cook, what would you do first?" he asked.

"I'd clean it up, if you don't mind me saying so. And I'd throw out that meat with the bad smell. Don't you have anyone here who can hunt? On our wagon train, the best shots were our designated hunters."

The former cook was relieved of his duty and expected to be back laying track. Nate asked the foreman to let the man stay. "He just didn't know what to do here, but I'll tell him. If he can't learn, I'll let you know. Cooking is something everybody needs to learn to take care of himself. He can start learning by taking out the spoiled food, burying it, and then scrubbing the sinks, the drainboards, the cupboards, and the floors."

Nate gave a long list of food staples to the engineer the next time the locomotive went back to the depot for supplies. Both Riley brothers and two of the gandy dancers hunted for game early in the mornings before reporting to their regular jobs. The former cook made progress in the kitchen, and although he was something of a stumblebum, he made the most improvment in washing and drying the dishes.

The railroad workers, to a man, noticed and were grateful for much better food and told the foreman so. They especially liked the freshly killed game and the sides of beef Nate managed to buy from a rancher who would accept nothing but gold or silver for payment. The size of their helpings and the quality improved dramatically when the engineer returned from the supply depot with the items on Nate's grocery list.

The blacksmith was among the workers who went back to the kitchen to seek out the new cook and thank him for improving their stomachs as well as the dispositions. He limped back and found the cook stirring a big pot of venison stew over the cook stove. "Is it Nate? Left farming for cooking, did you?" Jim Randolph said. Nate, surprised, let go of his spoon which slid slowly down the side of the pan and disappeared in the steaming stew. The two men embraced each other like brothers.

* * *

More than one hundred miles of track had been completed and the railroad opened to freight and passenger service about the time spring planting was to begin. The hiring agent offered Matthew, who had excelled as a telegrapher, a permanent job at the train depot in Tucson. When the young man said he would lose his rights as a homesteader if he took the job, the agent suggested he go home and think about it. "We'll hold the job open for a month," he offered.

Nate, who rightly believed he had cooked thousands of meals, was ready to get out of the kitchen. Before he left it for the last time, he made sure the kitchen was clean enough to please his mother if she were looking down from heaven. He thanked his cook's helper and the foremen and then went back to the car with the blacksmith shop to talk to Jim. "What are you going to do now?" he asked the big man.

"I could stay with the railroad, but I'm tired of living on a train. I want to stop someplace and go fishing. Then after I catch a whale," he smiled, "I think I'll get myself a smithy someplace where there's no fighting."

"There's no fighting where we are," Nate offered. "We're where the Salt River flows into the Gila. Raines was going to build a ferryboat to carry people and freight across it, but I don't know if it's done yet. Mr. Sowell's new store should be finished by now. There isn't any blacksmith anywhere around, as far as I know. Why don't you build a smithy there?"

"Ummm, it's something to think about, I guess," Jim answered, "but right now, I'm going back to San Carlos and pick up my wife and babies. They must be half grown by now."

"I didn't know you had a wife. How many babies?" Nate asked.

"She's an Apache woman. Imagine that. We kill 'em; we marry 'em. We have two babies, two boys. I guess they're about the size of Elle and Grace when I first saw you back on your farm in Tennessee. That was a bad time for y'all. I'm glad to see your family got through all the sadness. You say you're farming now in Arizona. What's it like?"

"It's different from back home. The land is different, but the growing season is longer. We can't depend on the rain here. Somebody told Papa he would have to irrigate the fields, dig little ditches from the river for water to flow through to the crops. Seems Indians did it that way years and years ago.

"Matthew's calling me. I've got to go. Remember what I said about coming up where we are." Nate started to leave, then stopped and said, "Do you know something? I was just a boy when I first saw you at the slave auction in Tennessee and they called you Hercules."

"I'm Jim Randolph now."

Nate walked on to the carpenter shop car and called for Will to come along. The carpenter was reluctant to see him go. "You're a good man, young Will," he said. "Your pa can be proud of you. Tell him I said that. And here, this is for you." He handed Will a handsome block plane with a well-sharpened blade.

"Thank you, sir. You taught me a lot." He extended his hand to shake that of the carpenter, whom he considered a friend, and then jumped to the ground and ran to catch the flat car coupled to the engine just beginning to move on the trip taking the workers back to Tucson.

* * *

While they worked for the railroad, the three of them avoided visiting the entertainment camps that followed a mile behind the railroad workers every time the railhead moved. Matthew, Nate, and Will, who held on to their wages, had more than enough money to buy saddle horses in Tucson. "Let Nate choose for you, Will," Matthew suggested. "He's the best judge of horses in our family. I want him to choose mine."

* * *

Because he was outside working to repair a broken step on Nathan Riley's house instead of in the fields with the farmers, Raines was the first to see the three approaching riders. He had looked up when he heard the horses, and his lack of attention to the job at hand caused him to hit the thumb instead of the nail with his hammer. After sucking his wound, he called to Emma. "They're coming back! Grace, Elle, run down to the store and get Will's mama and papa."

By the time the riders dismounted, Ned, Birdy, Sowell, Grace, Elle, Emma, Catherine, and Raines were there to welcome them with cheers, hugs, and kisses.

"Who dis big man? Not my little boy Willie!" Ned said and embraced his son. His tall and muscular son kissed his mother and lifted his surprised father off his feet.

"I'm big enough now to lead your horses to the barn," Elle announced proudly as she and Grace took the reins and led the animals to hay and water.

"Matthew, Nate, your father will be so glad to see you!" Emma exclaimed as Nate took Catherine into his arms. The toddler wasn't sure she liked the stranger and puckered up to cry. He handed her back to her mother.

Raines stood back watching. He felt proud to know the three young men and took some credit for their upbringing during those many months they worked and lived together and were intelligent enough to follow the rules necessary to survive on the trail.

When they came in from the fields, Nathan Riley and John were overjoyed to see Matthew and Nate and listened to their stories until way past the farmers' bedtime.

Nathan Riley, at Emma's urging, allowed his sons to rest a whole day before he got them up early for breakfast and out to the fields. "Papa, is it a little early for spring planting?" Matthew asked. Nate thought the fields looked poorly but didn't say a word about it.

"Would be in Tennessee. Isn't here," their father answered and handed each of them a hoe.

John was already in the field and nodded to his brothers and father without missing a beat and continued to chop away at the dry and dusty dirt with his hoe.

"Keep that row straight!" Riley yelled at him.

Nate thought the sound of the dinner bell was the sweetest music he had ever heard. The four of them walked to the lone cottonwood tree halfway between the house and the field. Grace was waiting for them there with their dinner carefully packed in a basket. She waited until they had finished eating. Then Grace took the empty basket home, and the farmers walked back to the field. They passed Ned and Will on the way.

As Sowell was not very busy in his store during the first days of the week, Ned spent Monday, Tuesday, and Wednesday working his own homestead and was glad to have his son's help. When Raines approached them and asked for Will's help to build his ferryboat and promised to pay him a good wage, Ned relinquished his claim on his son's labor on Monday, Tuesday, and Wednesday if he tended the fields Thursday, Friday, and Saturday.

"Our family don't work on Sunday. It be da Lord's Day an' a day of rest," Will explained.

Raines had come to the conclusion some weeks ago that God never intended him to be a boat builder either, but he kept that revelation to himself. It had taken him several months to work out the design for his ferryboat on paper and another month before the lumber wagons arrived from the sawmill. He hoped it would be enough. Lumber was scarce on the desert, and forested areas on mountains were some distance away. The extra long square-headed brass nails had already arrived from San Francisco. Sowell ordered them for him, and even though they were expensive, the brass would not rust away like iron nails.

Early one Monday morning Will met him by the lumber stacked near the river. Raines showed him the sketches he had drawn of the boat he planned to build. "I haven't done much thinking about the docks we'll needed to build on each side of the river," he added.

Will studied the drawings carefully. "What ya gonna do when da river flood?" he asked. "Docks does ya no good when dey be underwater. How deep da river now?" Raines shrugged his shoulders.

Will picked up a long stick nearby, walked barefoot and fully clothed into the water until he got to the middle of the river. He pushed the stick straight down through the water until its point hit bottom. " 'Bout five feet deep here," Will called back to Raines, who stood on the bank. "Water might be two, maybe up ta five feet higher when da river flood."

"Ya needs a pole boat," Will said as he climbed dripping back up the bank. He squatted down and drew a design in the dirt with a small stick. "Ya nails yo' boards together 'til dey makes one big bottom fo' da boat. Needs ta be 'bout twelve feet wide, eighteen feet long.

"Den ya builds sides all 'round lak ya be makin' a box. Sides be 'bout two, two an' a half feet high. Now we be ready fo' da top a da box, but it be bigger than da bottom. Da tops sticks out 'bout three feet beyond da sides. When we nails da top on, we has ta mark where da sides be or da nails miss 'em when we hammers 'em all da ways through da wood."

Raines, having no better idea, took a leap of faith, and by quitting time the following Wednesday, he and Will had finished the boat's bottom and had two sides nailed firmly to its perimeter. "I'll finish nailing the sides," Raines told him, "and start nailing boards to make the top of the box." The former professional wagon train guide felt foolish as he heard childish wordings coming out of his own mouth and looked around to see if anyone was near enough to hear him.

Will was pleased when he returned to boat building Monday. He wished he could build boats all week instead of farm. He noted that the sides were in place and the angles were square. Raines proudly showed off the box top that he had nearly finished. "Good work!" Will said. "When it be finished, best we get all da men to lift it up on da sides. Den da box top be called da deck when it be sittin' three feet wider den the bottom a da boat. Da bottom's da part dat gets wet in da water. Da deck sits up outa da water an' keeps people and everythin' dry."

On Friday evening after work in the fields but when it was still light enough to see, all the men from miles around came out of neighborliness and curiosity to help lift the deck and nail it securely to the wooden sides. Most of them agreed that its shape did resemble a boat although some of the women spectators thought it looked more like a dance floor.

On Monday, Will and Raines started work on the railing that would encircle the deck. They built it high enough to prevent a person or animal from falling off into the water. On the short side of the deck, they built a hinged gate wide enough for a wagon to get through and another gate directly opposite on the boat's other side so the drivers could guide their wagons straight ahead to get off when the ferryboat reached the other side of the river.

"Da next thing we gotta do is take dese here boards an' nail 'em from da edge of da deck ta da edge of da bottom. Dat way der's a wedge on all sides of da boat. Lets ya come right up a little ways onto da shore. Lak I tells ya, dat way you don't needs a dock," Will patiently explained. "Now, ya writes dis down. We needs some mo' things, an' ya has ta go ta Tucson ta gets 'em."

Raines promised Ned that he himself would work the fields for three days if his father allowed Will to come to Tucson with him and help choose exactly the right things needed to get the ferryboat in the water.

Ned agreed to Raines's request but with one stipulation: "I wants my son home by Sunday."

* * *

It was nearly dark when Raines drove the wagon into his barn late Saturday. "We'll unload on Monday," he told Will. "Thank you for going along. I wouldn't have gotten the right things if you hadn't been with me. On the other hand, if we were building a prairie wagon, I could have shown you how to do it." Raines was too tired to eat. He kissed Elizabeth and went straight to bed.

Will regaled his parents with descriptions of the goings-on in the big city of Tucson. "I still talk colored in public, like you told me," their son added.

Raines and Will, with some help from others in their families, finished the boat on Wednesday. He named it *Elizabeth.* Raines carefully painted the word on two smooth flat boards attached to each gate. The men worked as a team to secure the end of the thick rope to a stout post on the near shore and threaded the other end of the rope through two pulleys fastened on posts at each end of one side of the boat then on to the far shore where the rope was pulled taut and secured to the stout post on the far side of the river. The rope rested in a straight line high above the water from one side of the river to the other. The ferryboat sat still. Three feet of its stern gently rested on top of the muddy bank on the near shore.

Grace and Elle had watched the entire event. "Emma," Grace said, "I don't see how the rope can pull the boat unless the men untie one end of it."

Emma, like several women, had brought out a stool to sit on and her mending basket so her hands would not be idle while watching the men at work. She broke off a long piece of thread from the spool and threaded a needle. "Here, Grace, you hold this end of the thread, and you hold the other end, Elle. Pretend this needle is the ferryboat and your thread is the rope. The eye of the needle is the pulley. Hold the thread taut, and I'll push the needle back and forth like this, see? The needle moves through the air just like the boat will move through the water."

"Are you going to jump in the water and push the ferryboat through the water like you pushed the needle through the air?" Elle asked.

"No, you silly girl!" Grace smirked. She paused and asked, "Who is going to push the boat?"

"Some very strong men called 'polers' who stand on the same side of the deck but outside of the railing. They push long poles down through the water until their poles touch the river bottom. Then they push the ferryboat forward and pull up the poles, then push them down again. Down, push, up! Down, push, up! Like that."

Raines gave Will, Nate, and Matthew the honor of being the polers for the first trial run of the ferryboat *Elizabeth.* They worked together in a rhythm that reminded the three of the gandy dancers on the railroad. The crossing was a success, and any man, young or old, who wanted to try poling had the chance to try his hand. All of them had at least one try by the time the sun went down.

The participants and observers were impressed. Grace and Elle were equally impressed with the gleaming brass bells hanging from a post on each side of the river. "See," Grace explained, "if you want to go to the other side of the river, you just ring the bell like this, and the polers bring the boat over to get you. Ring the bell, Elle, but not too loud."

The Raines Ferry Service made its first official crossing the next day. The first passengers were his friends and family who came across country on the wagon train together. They laughed and marveled at the convenience of it all. Raines gave free passage to everyone the first week of operation. The only trouble he had was keeping track of who had taken turns at poling the boat across the river. Everyone—men, women, and children—wanted to have a turn as a poler. He knew their enthusiasm wouldn't last.

Chapter Twenty-two

Going Home

Nathan Riley had not been this discouraged since the losses of his sons and wife during the War. His companions from the wagon train were prospering. Sowell's store and bank did a brisk business. Elizabeth was even helping Raines run the ferry until he could find a competent hired hand. Ned and Will had all the business they could manage in the carpenter shop, much of it ordered by the newcomer Jacobson who was building a mill a half mile down river.

Riley had to admit to himself that he thought it unfair for Sowell, Raines, and even Ned to hire and pay Mexican laborers to take their places in the fields. He knew there was no rule that homesteaders couldn't hire help to farm their land so long as they lived on the property. Mexican labor was cheap and available, but Riley blamed them for what he considered to be poor harvests. All of the Rileys worked in the fields. Even little Catherine dropped seeds from her small bucket into the trench rows.

John held the family's attention at supper one evening after a long hot day of work in the fields. "Papa," he began, "ever since we got here, I've stayed and worked the fields with you every day except Sunday. What do you think about putting in fruit orchards instead of vegetable and corn crops we have to plant every spring? An old Mexican told me oranges grow well here. They don't spoil fast like peaches. We could ship them to markets on the railroad.

"We'd have to plant the trees and tend them. I don't know how long it takes for an orange tree to set fruit, but we wouldn't have to plant every year. I'd rather pick standing up than pick bending over. What do you think, Papa?"

Nathan Riley, who had been chewing on the end of his toothpick while listening to his quiet son talk, nodded his head in the affirmative. "John, you've got a right good idea. Tomorrow, let's go find that old Mexican. I'd like to talk to him."

Within a week the Riley family, Benjamin, Elijah, and the hired Mexican workers dug irrigation ditches and tilled the land to be ready to receive several hundred orange trees seedlings Sowell had ordered from a citrus grower in California.

Matthew and Nate picked up the crates when they arrived at the Tucson Southern Pacific Train Depot Freight Office. The farmers eagerly awaited the return of the two wagons and were relieved to find the burlap bags wrapped around the roots still damp and the seedlings in perfect condition.

At the end of the two weeks it took to plant, most of the farmers walked with their backs bent over. "Well, now we know trees are harder to plant in the ground than seeds are to sow on top of it," John said. Nate distributed bottles of his liniment, and the farmers took turns rubbing one another's backs.

"Either liniment helps or joy heals all pain," Emma remarked two weeks later when her husband came in from the orchard and did his best to dance a little jig.

"Every dadburned seedling is showing new growth!" he crowed, grabbed his wife's hands, and twirled her around the kitchen.

The family's feeling of jubilation lasted through supper. Although he didn't want to dampen their spirits, Nate felt he could wait no longer. "Papa, Emma, everybody, I'm going back to our farm in Tennessee. I don't want to wait until I turn twenty-one to get a homestead and then farm five more years before I can own the land. I have a railroad pass. The foreman gave it to me. I can ride the train for free."

Emma finally broke the stunned silence permeating the room. She rose from her chair, walked around to Nate's side of the table, and put her hands gently on his shoulders. "Your family will miss you," she said softly. "As for me, I won't let you go unless you promise to buy me a Sunday hat with lavender flowers on it in New Orleans and send it back to me by rail!"

The gloom broken, Grace chimed in, "I want one too! And send one to Elle or she'll always borrow mine!"

By the time supper dishes were washed, dried, and put away, Nate had a long list of requests by others in his family. He knew Raines and Elizabeth would add theirs when Elizabeth heard the news.

*　　*　　*

Too emotional to say good-bye, Nate was up before the sun and followed the lantern light to the barn where his brothers had hitched up the wagon and were ready to go. They had planned his departure the night before when they laughed and cried together as the three told stories of their childhood and remembered their mother and Ben and Caleb.

"We'll stop on the way for breakfast," John said while pointing to the basket already loaded in the wagon's bed. Nate threw his canvas satchel, a gift from Emma, in beside it then climbed up into the wagon bed where the youngest Riley always rode if the wagon seat beside the driver was occupied.

"Not today." Matthew grinned. "You get to sit beside me. John will be the youngest now. Let's give him a head start in knowing how it feels!"

Matthew drove the wagon at a steady pace for about an hour before they saw a likely place to stop and eat. It was a small grove of trees with good shade. As the Riley brothers grew closer, they noticed another wagon stopped there. Matthew reined in his team a short distance way, and John grabbed the basket and jumped down to the ground before Matthew even set the brake. "Howdy!" he called to the other travelers.

"Let's eat!" Nate said as he scooped up the food basket.

"Look!" John said and pointed. Both brothers approached the man and were caught up together in Jim Randolph's huge arms. Matthew was close behind them and finding no more room within the embrace, simply put his hand on the big man's arm.

"What are you doing here?" Nate asked after he caught his breath.

"What you said. I'll be setting up a smithy by the river. Come meet my family." He led them around to the other side of his wagon where a young Apache woman was stirring a pot of stew over a small campfire. Her hair was long, straight, and shiny black. Matthew was struck by the contrast between it and the short tightly curled black hair of her husband. He had never been that close to an Apache woman before and thought her to be quite beautiful.

"What's your name?" he asked.

The woman looked at her husband. He nodded his permission that told her she was in no danger from these particular white men.

"One four three," she answered with downcast eyes.

Jim Randolph enjoyed the quizzical looks on the Riley brothers' faces. "Apache names are too hard for whites to pronounce and even harder to spell, so the government assigned them numbers. One four three is her father's number and his unmarried daughters carry the same until they marry; then they take their husband's number.

"See?" He held up the metal tag she wore on a leather thong around her neck. "It's stamped S C for 'San Carlos Apache' and 143. I don't have a number but I have this." He turned the tag over and showed them the picture of a buffalo carefully incised in the metal. The huge man threw back his head and laughed.

"And what do YOU call her, one four three or buffalo wife?" Nate asked getting in the lighthearted spirit.

"Bright Moon," he answered and gently caressed his wife's face with two fingers of his huge right hand. "I saw her first on the night of a full moon."

Giggles coming from behind spokes of a wagon wheel broke the tenderness of the moment. Jim reached his long arms under the wagon and pulled out two squirming, laughing little boys. "My sons," he announced proudly and lifted each with one arm high into the air. "The big one answers to the name of Luther and the young one to the name of Noah." He put them down and they scampered away to hide behind the tree until their mother called in Apache for them to come and eat.

The Rileys accepted the invitation to share their meal and offered the food from their own basket. When all had finished eating, Nate rose from the ground and said, "I'll miss the train if we don't get on. I'm going back to our farm in Tennessee, but the rest of the family is staying here. Like I told you, there's no blacksmith where we settled and there's great need for one. My family and Sowell will be glad to see you and help you set up."

"Look," Jim replied as he pulled off the canvas covering the wagon's load. Nate gasped at the sight of a blacksmith shop on wheels. Everything was there, the anvil, the hammers, the tongs, the tools. "All I need is a piece of land and I can start before I have the walls and roof up."

Jim and Bright Moon watched until the Riley wagon was out of sight. Luther and Noah tugged at their mother's bright calico skirt.

Its hem brushed the tops of her high soft leather moccasins. The soles of hard leather swept forward beyond the ends of her toes and curled up to a point as defense against cactus thorns. "Get in the wagon," she said softly in Apache. "We are going to a new home."

* * *

Nate arrived at the Train Depot with little time to spare. He showed his railroad pass to the ticket agent who urged him to hurry. Nate hugged Matthew and John then jumped on to the step, held tight to the rail, and waved to them until his brothers became nothing more than tiny specks in the distance.

Nate had never been on a train that had been built and furnished to carry paying passengers. The elegance caught his breath. Cushioned seats were upholstered in red velvet and could be moved to face backwards or forwards. Short draperies were tied back at the sparkling clean windows, and the crystal wall vases between them held fresh flowers.

The largest earthenware crock Nate had ever seen sat at one end of the car. It provided the passengers with ice water, and Nate couldn't decide which he liked best, the chill on his tongue when he drank from a clean glass or the workings of the shiny brass spigot that never dripped independently at the bottom of the crock.

The conductor walked from car to car to collect tickets, point out interesting sights as the train went along, and assure one woman passenger that it was not at all likely that the train would be attacked by Indians, as least here in this part of Texas. He neglected to tell her that the engineer's greatest fears were cattle on the tracks or meeting up with train robbers. From time to time the conductor walked through and passed out small linen towels to the passengers for their use in the washroom. Nate leaned back in his seat and enjoyed the luxury. He fell asleep and woke much later when a man shook his shoulder.

"We're stopping for dinner," he said. "I doubt a young man like yourself would want to miss a meal."

Nate opened his eyes and saw the fellow who had been sitting across the aisle. "Excuse me? What did you say?"

"Dinner. I said we're stopping for dinner," the fellow wearing a city suit repeated with a smile. "This dining room has the best food on the line, and you'll be sorry if you miss it. My name is O'Brien," he added.

"Riley, Nate Riley," he said and extended his hand before he got out of his seat and followed the man out onto the platform and the Texas Dining Room, "where travelers eat best." The two shared a table with several others, most of whom ordered the daily special—chili beans, cornbread, apple sauce, pecan pie, and coffee.

Nate thanked O'Brien for waking him, and the two left the eating establishment soon enough to have a little time to stretch their legs walking on the station platform before boarding the train again. Nate stopped to read the wanted posters tacked to the side of the building's wall. One large poster announced a five hundred dollar reward for the capture of any of the four train robbers pictured below.

"Someone you know?" O'Brien asked, half joking.

"I know the name. This one, Raleigh Randolph. I spent some time on his family's plantation once," Nate answered and then added. "In the slave quarters, not the big plantation house." He was about to say more when the telegrapher walked out the door to his small office and used his pocket knife to cut away the picture of Raleigh Randolph and one other man from the poster.

"Just got the message about a train hold-up this side of San Antonio. The express car was carrying a shipment of gold bars, and the express clerk took the precaution of hiring extra guards. Train robberies are on the rise in these parts.

"And wouldn't you know, it happened again. The extra guards earned their pay. These two, shot dead!" the telegrapher said as he waved the cut-out pictures in the air. "The others got away. The four, bold as brass, boarded as passengers, then shot their way into the express car. Can you believe that? One of the guards was slightly wounded, but I'd say the day was better for the railroad than for these two!"

Nate and O'Brien ran to catch their train. Nate was quiet for several more hours as he relived in his mind's eye the events long ago at Fair Oaks Plantation. He wondered if he had made the right decision in coming back to Tennessee.

The novelty of train travel wore off for Nate. He had already seen more than enough of Texas. His body was sore from sitting so much, and he remarked to O'Brien that he hadn't expected the ride to be so rough in places. "The track layers should have done a better job," he said. "The ones on our work train were better. It's probably because they had a better cook."

"Who was the cook?" O'Brien asked.

"I was!" Nate exclaimed proudly and went on to explain how he made three meals a day for two hundred people and kept hot coffee in the pot available all of the time for anyone who wanted to bring his own cup and fill it. O'Brien was duly impressed and filed the story away in his memory to regale his business partners when he returned to Los Angeles.

* * *

"You're not taking the train on to Tennessee?" O'Brien said as the two collected their bags and left the train in New Orleans.

"I could," Nate answered, "but I want to get better acquainted with the Mississippi River." He realized immediately how foolish that sounded and went on to explain. "A long time ago when the war was nearly over, my family was part of a wagon train heading west. I had never even seen a river like the Mississippi. There were so many wagons in our train, it took three days to ferry them to the other side of the river. In the year we were on the trail, our wagons crossed over rivers and streams and creeks, some of them dry as a bone. I never thought I'd see the Mississippi River again. Now that I'm here, I want to get to know her better."

O'Brien looked more closely at the young man. "I found you to be an interesting traveling companion, but I didn't know you had the soul of a poet."

Nate didn't know whether to regard the remark as an insult or a compliment.

"Come along. My business requires travel and I know the river well. It's best seen from the decks of side-wheelers. Let's go to the docks and see what passage is available," O'Brien said and led the way to the Steamboat Ticket Windows located not far from the Railroad Depot.

The ticket lines were long, and O'Brien had Nate sit at a table nearby and order breakfast for two while he went to stand in line. "Go ahead and eat," he called over his shoulder. "I won't be too long.

"My young friend," O'Brien said as he returned to the table and signaled the waiter for more coffee. "There was only one ticket available on the *Evangeline,* my steamer of choice. However, the ticket seller, who is a friend, told me the chef on the same is in dire need of another cook. It seems that the baker apprentice's appetite for rum was the man's undoing. Too many bottles were found to be missing from the locker where spirits are stored. The unfortunate soul was stripped of his short white cap and exiled from the *Evangeline* until he can prove sobriety of at least thirty days.

"Upon my recommendation, the chef will accept you on a temporary basis until the next port of call and then make his decision as to whether or not your talents in the kitchen are up to the standards of the most elegant steamer plying the waters of the Mississippi. Although you would receive no wage—the boat's owner is quite frugal in some ways—your passage would be free."

That afternoon Nate was invited aboard and reported to the galley where the Head Chef asked him to prepare a strawberry torte, black walnut cake, and any bread of his choice. Before the sun went down, both Nate and the Head Chef were disappointed in his strawberry torte and black walnut cake. The buttermilk biscuits, however, were acceptable. "You will have to do. No one else applied for the position," the Head Chef remarked and dismissed him with a wave of his hand. "Be here tomorrow morning at five A.M. We leave the dock promptly at ten."

Because he was a frequent passenger on the *Evangeline,* the steward extended O'Brien the courtesy of access to his stateroom the night before departure. He waited on the main deck for Nate to leave the galley and was pleased he had been hired.

"Come with me," O'Brien said and led Nate up the stairs to the second floor. "This is the cabin deck where the central saloon is located. The staterooms are built around it and face out to the river. Here we are." He opened the door. Nate followed him in and rejoiced at the sight of two real beds. "It would be wise if you didn't leave these quarters until after dark," O'Brien continued. "The steward would not be pleased to know a galley cook is sharing my luxurious stateroom even though I'm sure he has seen stranger sights."

"I have no time to shop in New Orleans," Nate complained. "I promised the women in my family to buy them Sunday hats here and send them back to Tucson by train."

"There are millinery shops in Memphis," O'Brien replied, "and I'll see that the ladies' hats get back to Tucson myself on my return trip west."

Nate was careful not be seen when he left O'Brien's first class stateroom and arrived in the large galley promptly at five o'clock the next morning. He was not the only cook at work and walked past others preparing chickens, hams, duck, and several different cuts of beef, more meats than Nate had ever seen at one time. The butcher told him most of it would be served at dinner or evening supper.

"Over here," the Head Chef called impatiently and motioned to a flour board sitting on a counter top near several large bake ovens. "The owners and their party will have breakfast in an hour. I want you to bake your buttermilk biscuits and help serve in the Gentlemen's Cabin." The Head Chef left quickly and shouted orders to the others who were working at top speed.

"Where's the Gentlemen's Cabin?" Nate asked a cook as he took his biscuits, perfectly browned, out of the oven.

The cook took the biscuits from Nate's hands and put the pan next to other covered dishes sitting in the dumbwaiter. He grasped the rope and slowly pulled as the breakfast meal disappeared from sight on its way up to a server waiting for it in the saloon on the deck above. The cook laughed at the surprise on Nate's face. "You have to walk," he said. "Up the stairs there," and he pointed to a narrow passageway leading to the saloon. "The Gentleman's Cabin is in the saloon. It's for gentlemen only, as you could guess, except at mealtime, when women and children are allowed."

Nate came out of the passageway and found a waiter wearing a white jacket seating two woman at a table set for breakfast. Two men then took their seats as the waiter motioned Nate to take the food out of the dumbwaiter and set it on the serving table.

Although he was not allowed to serve, the waiter quietly relayed instructions to Nate to keep the coffee hot, replenish the food in the serving dishes, and keep the dining ritual running smoothly. "And make sure these flowers are fresh before you put them in these crystal vases. Put one in the center of every table in the dining room, except theirs," the waiter said.

Aware of his lowly status, Nate did not look directly at the diners. He could not help overhearing their conversation.

"How could you do such a thing! I'm ashamed of you both!" the older lady said between bites of buttered biscuit.

"Why? Papa would be proud if he were alive," the young woman replied. "It's a profitable business. Our status has not changed. We're still well-born and well-bred. And you should know the food on our table here is a match for any that graced our table on the plantation. Mama, you just don't realize how many of our friends have lost their slaves, their homes to flames, and may be starving! Why can't you understand that?"

"Delicate Southern women like your mama shouldn't have to understand things like that, Evangeline. I thank God every day that He has given me the means to offer my wife the comforts to which she is accustomed," the older man replied.

Nate dropped a flower vase on the floor. The waiter threw him a look that would kill. The fine heavy crystal didn't break, and Nate wiped up the water on the floor with the sleeve of his shirt. He replaced the flowers and set the vase on the table.

"Brownsville, Texas, is not exactly what my mother has been accustomed to," the younger man said with sarcasm that seemed to drip from his tongue. "Mama, Evangeline and I can't go back to Fair Oaks. There's nothing left. The Federals burned almost everything, and you took the slaves to Texas. And where are they now? Scattered to the winds! At least you know where to find Evangeline and me." He pushed back from the table and crossed his arms while pacing back and forth across the large room.

Mrs. Rebecca Randolph Ellis dabbed at her moist eyes with a dainty lace handkerchief. "Alexander, your father would have had you whipped if he ever heard you speak to me in that tone of voice! And Raleigh! My precious baby boy! What has happened to Raleigh? You know, don't you! What are you keeping from me?"

Nate knew but sucked in his breath and went on about his task as if he were deaf.

"They're not keeping anything from you, my dear," Ellis said as he patted his wife's free hand. "I think one thing your mother wants to know is where you got the money to purchase a packet steamer of this size and quality," he quietly said to her offspring.

"From my petticoat," Evangeline answered. "Remember? Sissy sewed so many gold coins in my petticoat the cloth still has bloodstains from the needle pricks in her fingers."

"Mama," Alexander went on to explain, "Evangeline bought this boat when it was little more than a shell. The Union Navy had used it as a war vessel, and it was rotting away at a broken-down wharf when we saw it. My gambling winnings paid for its repair.

"Evangeline bought many of the furnishings from private parties right here in New Orleans. They needed money to buy food more than they needed elegant chairs to sit on. Some of the other things came out of a ferryboat warehouse full of things passengers used for payment. Won't you try to understand? Your approval would mean so much to both of us."

Mrs. Ellis rose from her chair and walked to the door.

"Mama?" Evangeline said softly.

Their mother turned sobbing, opened her arms wide, and offered her two grown children a warm embrace.

* * *

Nate's duties aboard the *Evangeline* prevented him from forming a close friendship with the Mississippi River, and he vowed next time he would travel the waters as a paying passenger. His duties as a baker ended when the Head Waiter suggest to the Head Chef that the diners were getting tired of buttermilk biscuits. He wondered if passengers might be better served if Nate could be assigned to serve late night refreshments to the men playing cards until the early morning hours.

"He lacks in ability when it comes to preparing tortes and cakes, but the young man does as he is told, and I have never seen dirt under his fingernails," the Head Chef replied.

When told of his new duties, Nate went to find O'Brien and ask what this meant.

"I would call it an advancement of sorts," O'Brien said. "You have advanced from one nonpaying position to another nonpaying position. However, now you may have better opportunities. If a man gambles and wins, he is more likely to leave his server a small gratuity than if he loses. From what I have observed on the *Evangeline,* it is a foolish man who thinks he can win at Alexander Randolph's table. Even so, the beautiful Evangeline lavishes attention with such charm on the losers as well as the winners, she keeps them coming back to spread their money around. Nate, my boy, I don't think the only reason why they return to the *Evangeline* time after time is to consume the food and drink."

After dinner and again after supper, Nate helped close the handsome doors separating the Gentlemen's Cabin from the Ladies' Cabin which was off limits to men unless they were husbands, male relatives, or men of the cloth. Then he got out the brass cuspidores, emptied, cleaned and polished them twice a day before setting them out around the room. He served drinks and light refreshments to gamblers and sometimes received a coin for his service from a winner. He never got a penny from any gambler sitting at Alexander Randolph's table.

Early one morning, the steamer stopped to take on wood and a few day passengers who were fortunate if they found chairs to sit on among the boxes and freight carried on the main deck. It was the *Evangeline's* last stop before Memphis and when the steamer approached that city, Nate carried his satchel in one hand while he thanked and shook the hands of the Head Chef and Head Waiter with the other. He paused just long enough for a Memphis dock worker to secure the gangplank and was first in line to disembark.

He waited on the dock for O'Brien and waved to attract his attention in the crowd. "Ah, Nate, I suggest we find a room with beds that don't sway before we go shopping for your Sunday hats. I have two days' business in Memphis. Each of us can take a room at the Jackson Hotel. Incidentally, I'm quite certain the boat's steward knew you shared my stateroom but said nothing about it., That's one reason I'm loyal to the *Evangeline.*"

Nate groaned. "I've had my fill of the *Evangeline* and prefer cleaning out pig sties to cuspidores." The two hurried to the hotel.

Among the last passengers to disembark were Madam Dupre, who held tightly to Arabella's hand, and Sissy who walked beside them and directed the dock worker to put their trunk in the carriage waiting for them on the street.

* * *

Nate had never before in his life been to a big city. Even though Memphis still carried the scars of war, he found it exciting and quite impressive. On many streets, especially those near the river, some buildings stood proudly while others beside them had been reduced to rubble.

O'Brien led him through the streets of the city in search of a millinery shop. They passed two that had been closed and then found one that looked to be open. The two men went inside, and Nate explained his needs to a comely young lady who appeared to be the owner.

When none of the hats in the small showroom caught their fancy, the young lady disappeared and brought out from the back room several more. She made suggestions as to which ones were suitable for younger children, which ones for young ladies, and which styles seemed appropriate for more mature women. Nate chose a pink bonnet with ribbons for Elle, a soft yellow straw sailor with a brown grosgrain ribbon encircling the crown for Grace, and a wide-brimmed navy straw festooned with white daisies with yellow centers for Elizabeth.

"Those are for my sisters," Nate said. "Now I need a Sunday hat with lavender flowers for Emma."

"Is she your wife?" the shopkeeper inquired.

"No. She's my father's wife. My real mother is dead, but I like Emma a lot. She's been good to all of us, and she wants a Sunday hat with lavender flowers on it."

The young milliner admired his taste, and although she searched again in the back room, she couldn't find any kind of hat with lavender flowers. "I'm sorry," she said. "I don't have as many hats as I had before the war. Ladies aren't buying many these days. There are only a few shops still open in Memphis, and I am closing mine soon. I suggest you try the shop six blocks up this same street. Ask for Helen Ann and tell her Patsy Bailey sent you."

Nate reached for the door knob as he turned to go then stopped and asked, "You wouldn't, by any chance, be related to the Baileys who lived on Fair Oaks Plantation, would you?"

"My father was the plantation overseer, but he and my mother have gone to Texas. They're with my brothers on their ranch now. They want me to come out, now that there's a train, and told me to go back to their house at Fair Oaks to see if there was anything there I wanted to bring with me."

Nate stood as still as a post, his hand still on the door nob. It was O'Brien who spoke first.

"My dear young lady, you have been most generous with your time and very helpful. My friend here and I have recently traveled by train across Texas. It was something of an adventure but quite comfortable. It might be of value to you to know something about our trip so as to make wise decisions concerning your own.

"We would be pleased to entertain you at supper this evening in the dining room of the Jackson Hotel," O'Brien said as he handed her his card. "I can assure you that both of us are honorable men, and the desk clerk at the Jackson, who knows me well, would be happy to vouch for my character."

"Thank you," Patsy Bailey said quietly as she took O'Brien's card. "I shall be happy to accept. I'll wrap and bring the hats with me." She did not tell him how long it had been since she had a truly full stomach.

"Seven o'clock, then," O'Brien said as he tipped his hat, peeled Nate's fingers from the door knob, took the still silent young man by the arm, and walked him back to the Jackson Hotel without stopping to shop at any other store.

* * *

Miss Bailey arrived on time with the hats, and O'Brien tipped the bellboy to carry the boxes up to Nate's room. "I shall order for us," he said after they were seated at the table. The scuppernong wine relaxed them and conversation became less stilted as the evening went on.

"The wine was quite nice and the fish delicious, but the vegetables were not up to your usual standards," O'Brien said to the maître d' when the man inquired as to the diners' enjoyment of their meal.

"I am so sorry, Mr. O'Brien, but since the war it has been impossible to find produce of excellent quality. It seems the best farmers disappeared. To where I cannot say." The head waiter sighed.

"You are fortunate, my good friend, to have sitting at this very table the best farmer in all of Tennessee, or so he tells me. This young man is coming back from the West to reclaim his family farm. The cook would be wise to speak with him. With the trains running once again, I would think his products could be on your tables the day they are picked once he has his first harvest."

Miss Bailey was wide-eyed and insisted on Nate's telling his story. They were the last diners in the room by the time he had finished. As the three finally rose to leave, Nate said, "Tomorrow after I find a hat with lavender flowers, I plan to buy a wagon and team of horses. I'm going back to our farm. If you like, I can take you on to Fair Oaks Plantation. It's not that much out of the way, but to tell you the truth, I'm not sure what you'll find here. There appears to be as much damage in the country as in the cities. I'm sorry to say."

"I'd like to go with you. It was kind of you to ask me. But don't shop for another hat. I'm sure I have lavender flowers somewhere in my attic. I'll make the hat tonight and deliver it here in the morning," Miss Bailey said and extended her hand first to O'Brien and then to Nate. Her touch made him tingle.

* * *

If Patsy Bailey had not directed him, Nate would never have been able to find Fair Oaks Plantation. Nothing looked familiar to him. They passed miles and miles of dead, fallow fields even the crows avoided. Both were relieved to hear human sounds that clarified as spoken words and singing voices as they drew nearer to the slave quarters. Nate noticed their garden plots were flourishing and seemed to be much larger than when he was here years ago.

A large number of children ran out of a gunbarrel house and startled Nate's team of horses, but he quickly got them under control. "Let's stop here," he said and got down to tie the reins to a post. "We'll walk the rest of the way." He helped Patsy Bailey down to the ground and held her hand as they walked together up the lane. She gasped and stood stock still at the sight of the charred remain of what once had been her home.

"Who dat?"

They stopped and turned to see a stooped old colored woman walking toward them. They stood waiting and when she got closer Patsy recognized Old Clara. "It's Patsy Bailey. I've come from Memphis. This here is Nate Riley, who brought me."

"Nate Riley, you say? Da same as da one who come wid his mama to nurse da big ole slave Hercules?"

"The same," Nate answered and felt a lump in his throat.

"Glory be! Luther! Luther! Come see! The boy Nate all grown to a man be here! An' young Mistress Bailey be wid 'em! Come all da way from Memphis!"

Luther had a big stirring spoon in his hand when he came out the open door of a gunbarrel house number four. A dozen or so young children whose skin varied in hue from warm chocolate to fresh cream, followed behind him as he walked slowly toward the visitors. "Lord, Lord! What y'all doin' back here?" Luther asked.

Before they could answer, a group of children walked two by two and holding hands in a long line. They followed a young woman who called, "Luther, are we too early?"

"No, Miss Sissy, I's jest too slow. My li'l cooks here helps me gets da food on da table right quick. Come 'long," he said and his little helpers scampered behind him.

"Where did all the children come from?" Nate asked.

"Let's jest sit down on dis fence ober here an' I tells ya." Old Clara said. "When da bluebellies come, de burn da big house an yo' house." She nodded to Patsy. "And da fields but not the slave houses or da slave gardens. An' dey didn't burn da Compound 'cause dey don't know it be der." Old Clara stopped to laugh.

"I tell ya somepin', dose mixed-blood chilluns an' dey mamas be good folks. Some of 'em even be cream. We gets along fine. Den Sissy comes wid da white woman and starts up a school right here on Fair Oaks Plantation. Eben some ole slaves, we be learnin' to read an' write some, but der be no books in colored."

"Where did Sissy come from?" Nate asked.

"Why, chile! Don't you 'member? Sissy be da chile dat come wid da big Hercules. She be da one Master Randolph buy at da slave auction fo' a present fo' Evangeline."

"Excuse me, please," a young boy interrupted. "Luther asked us to come and invite the two of you for dinner."

"And if you kindly accept, he said to tell you to come in ten minutes," the second boy added.

"Thank you," answered Nate. "We will be pleased to accept his kind invitation. What is your name, young man?" he added.

"My name is Hercules," he answered. "H-e-r-c-u-l-e-s."

"And what your name?" Nate asked of the other.

"My name is Jim. J-i-m."

Jim took Hercules's hand and the two ran back to tell Luther the visitors had kindly accepted his invitation.

It was then when Nate and Patsy noticed the woman with the little girl watching them. The two approached and the woman said,

"I am Gabriella Antoinette Dupre and this is my daughter Arabella." The lady extended her hand in greeting.

"What do you think of our little school here? We have taken the empty slave quarters and turned them into classrooms and dormitories former slaves can use while they are getting their education. We have three teachers in addition to Sissy. We don't charge for the schooling but do ask our students, even the youngest ones, to work the vegetable gardens, tend to the chickens and hogs, and help in the kitchen. We hope to get another milk cow soon.

"Things seem to be going well enough now for me to return to my home on the Mississippi River. I have several businesses there that need my attention. I plan to be on the *Evangeline* when it starts back downriver."

"My friend and I came from New Orleans to Memphis on the *Evangeline,*" Nate replied, "I expect you know the steamboat well."

"Very well," Madam Dupre replied with a smile. "Evangeline, the person, not the boat, was a wonderful teacher. However, she was born and bred to be a Southern Belle and that is exactly what she is. She is expert at playing her role—beautiful, gracious, charming, seductive—and keeps well hidden that steel fist in her velvet glove. I can appreciate her. Think of a world bereft of Southern Belles. What a dull place it would be!

"Oh, and one more thing. I understand you are returning to your family farm. You can see the extensive vegetable gardens here. The new owners of Fair Oaks Plantation are selling seed. You might like to buy some before you leave."

The lady turned to Patsy Bailey. "If I were you, my dear, I would avoid Texas. The air there is as dry as a bone and sucks the beauty right out of a woman's face."

"I have a question," Nate called as the lady was walking away. "You said the NEW owners of Fair Oaks Plantation. Surely you don't mean the former slaves own it."

Madam Dupre threw back her head and laughed loudly. "It's a legal matter. Have you any idea how many of these children of varying hues were sired by Randolph men? Not that it matters in most of the South. I seriously doubt that the former occupants of the big house will banish these people from their lands, at least not in this generation." Her mother took Arabella's small hand, and the child waved back as they walked away.

"Patsy, may I call you Patsy," Nate said, "would you object if we stayed here a few days so I can buy seeds for the farm. My mother and I stayed in gunbarrel house number four long ago. We were perfectly safe and treated with courtesy. Old Clara will find you a bed on the women's side, I'm sure, and I'll sleep on the men's side. And the food is wonderful. Luther is the best cook next to Bessie, or so she says."

When Patsy and Nate entered the room for supper. Gabrel greeted them and sat them at the head and foot of one of the old wooden tables. The children sat among the adults and displayed their perfect table manners throughout the meal. Sissy and a few older children served the food. "You'll enjoy this, I believe," Sissy whispered to their guests. "Both Luther and Bessie prepared this meal and are still arguing which one is the better cook. Don't dare tell them which dish you liked best!" she cautioned them with a wink.

Nate put his hand on Sissy's arm. "I need to talk to you. Will after supper be all right?"

Sissy nodded her head and wondered why.

When supper was over some of the older folks walked with Sissy and Nate down to where they held Sunday church under the trees. Patsy Bailey said she would stay behind and help with the dishes but felt uneasy in the company of so many colored faces and hurried to join Nate and the others.

They sat in a circle and listened as Nate began to speak, "When I was a young boy and went to town with my family, I followed some town boys who climbed up on the roof of a shed to watch a slave auction. I had never seen a slave auction in my life. It was exciting. A planter bid three thousand dollars for a huge slave he called Hercules. The town boys left, but I stayed on the roof. I saw a little girl torn away from her mama because the buyer wanted the mama but not the child. The little girl was sold to the planter. That little girl was you, Sissy."

There were tears in the eyes of Nate's listeners, but not one person moved or made a sound.

"Not long after that, my mama and I came here to Fair Oaks and doctored Hercules. The little girl was there too.

"Then the war came and Papa and three of my brothers left to fight. One day some marauders came to our farm. They killed my mother and would have killed my sisters and brother and me if this big bluebelly hadn't come out of the woods and saved us. Sissy, it was Hercules."

"I remember when the Confederates came and took him off to bury the battlefield dead. Mistress Randolph had a hissy fit," Sissy added. "I never knew what happened to him after that."

"Hercules told us when he helped us bury our mama that he ran away and a Union Cavalry Troop made him blacksmith," Nate said. "Then Papa and only one of my brothers came back to our farm. After he got well, Papa gathered up what was left of his family and headed west with a wagon train. We saw Hercules in Arizona Territory. He was a Buffalo Soldier, one of the best. You can be proud, Sissy. He calls himself Jim Randolph now.

"Anyway, I saw him not too long ago. He's out of the Army now. He's married to a beautiful Apache women he calls Bright Moon, and they have two little boys. One son is named Luther and they call the other son Noah. By this time, I expect Jim has set up his blacksmith shop. It's where my family finally settled on the Gila River in Arizona Territory."

It was quiet, each person reliving in memory events of the past. Finally, Sissy spoke: "He's my pa, you know. I'll send him a letter. I taught him to read and write."

"Send it to him at Raines Ferry, Arizona." Nate said.

* * *

Patsy Bailey learned to cook from Luther and Bessie but not at the same time. The old cooks alternated days and shared with the daughter of their former overseer their secrets to good eating. Patsy overcame her fear of living with colored folks and expressed reluctance when it was time to leave.

Nate and the farmers carefully selected vegetable seeds from their supply. They encouraged him to get them in the ground right away even though it was a little late for spring planting. Nate paid them in gold and suggested they might like to spend it on a cast-iron stove because there was so much cooking to do for the boarding school students.

"Best not to let Bessie hear dat," Luther said quietly to Nate. "Dey be a stove like dat in da Compound house. Master Randolph, he bought it fo' Bessie, but would dat ole woman have da shiny new thing? No! Bessie, she sits herself down, crosses her arms over dat big belly o' hers, an' won't cook another meal 'til Master got that stove outta her kitchen. Well, Master, he say no slave gonna boss him. Jest the same, dey took dat fancy iron stove out to da Compound where Master's Sunday women an' der chilluns lived. Bessie says dey neber had a good meal out der after dat."

Nate thanked Luther for the information and vowed to keep his mouth shut when it came to advising other people as to how they should spend their own money.

* * *

Patsy wept as the school children, standing in straight rows, sang "Yankee Doodle" and "Swing Low, Sweet Chariot" as a tribute to them as Nate drove his wagon past the gunbarrel houses and vegetable gardens. They didn't know that Madam Dupre and Sissy had suggested the importance of being nice to customers of the fledging seed business. "Serenades are nice," they said.

By the time Nate passed the hogs in pens awaiting shipment to market by rail, he had asked Patsy if she really wanted to live in Texas. When he drove past the newly re-opened General Store that once belonged to Sowell, he asked Patsy if she would marry him. He waved to Mr. Hall and stopped his wagon in front of the barbershop.

Mr. Hall invited the two of them in and served them wild blackberry tea. "We still can't get China tea," he apologized. "It was the kind of blend your dear mother liked best." The barber listened with rapt attention as Nate told the story of Sowell and his family's adventures and settlement in the West. Mr. Hall was relieved to hear about it. He had worried that all of them might be dead.

"I've come back to farm again," Nate continued. "I'd like you to be a customer of mine like you were for my mother. Is there still a preacher in town?"

"Yes, indeed!" Mr. Hall answered both questions at the same time. "I look forward to being your customer and the Methodist minister is in the little church at the end of the street. As I recall, he is the same one who married your father and the Widow Morris."

"They have a baby now. They named her Catherine," Nate said. "Patsy and I want to get married today."

"Excellent!" Mr. Hall exclaimed. "You fetch the preacher and I'll do the bride's hair."

By the time Nate returned with the preacher, several joyous spectators lined the walls of Mr. Hall's shop. Patsy, looking beautiful with flowers entwined in her hair, blushed as she repeated her vows.

"A ring! A ring! Does anyone have a ring?" Mr. Hall asked the assembled guests.

There was a pause in the barbershop. "Well," an old blacksmith spoke up, "you can have this. It isn't much. I made it out of a brass button I found." He handed the small brass circle to Mr. Hall who passed it to Nate. When he slipped the ring on his bride's finger, both of them could clearly see part of an eagle and the letters CSA incised in the metal.

Although it had been a long day, Nate pointed out landmarks and told stories of his boyhood on their way to the Riley farm. They stopped at the usual place to water the horses and eat the meal both Luther and Bessie had packed for them in a basket. Nate told his new wife about the time the deer darted in front of the wagon the first time he drove it to town.

When they passed the small crossroads store serving the simple needs of the farmers nearby, Nate told her they were getting close to home. He pointed out Emma's place and noticed that no one seemed to be living there. Nate held his breath as the horses neared the Riley farm house. They found the barn intact but the house roof sagging. "Maybe we should sleep in the barn tonight. It's not too dark for a roll in the hay."

The next morning Nate took his bride on a tour of the farm. They went first to his mother's grave and spent a few minutes there in silence. The pear tree looked healthy although it needed pruning like most of the trees in the orchard.

"It's not as bad inside as it looks from the outside," he said of the house. "Come with me back to the little store. We need some groceries, and I need some tools. We took all we owned with us when we left for Texas."

Nate was proud to introduce his new wife to the storekeeper, his wife, and the old man. "You're still here, I see," Nate joked. "I thought sure you would have worn out that old chair by this time."

"If you help me up out of this chair, young Riley, I'm so glad to see you I'll hug you good and proper. There's been no other farmer in a hundred miles who could best a Riley!'' Nate hugged him back and felt the old man's thin bones through his papery skin.

* * *

Even though they were a little late, Nate and Patsy got in their spring planting. They repaired the farm house room by room and it was finished by harvest time. Although Nate took some of his produce to the General Store in town and his herbs and medicines to Mr. Hall, the Rileys regularly shipped large quantities of their fresh produce by rail to the Jackson Hotel in Memphis and an equal amount to be picked up on the dock by the galley crew of the *Evangeline.*

As a surprise for Patsy on their third wedding anniversary, Nate had ordered a walnut wardrobe built for his wife. It would stand in their bedroom where his mother's had been.

The cabinet maker carefully loaded the handsome piece into his wagon and set out to deliver it. He stopped at the little crossroads store to ask directions to the Riley Farm. The storekeeper, his wife, and the few customers there listened closely and clenched their teeth to keep from smiling.

An old man sitting in an old wooden Douglas chair tipped back against the wall pointed and said, ''Well, you go down this here road about four miles. You'll come to a sorry old rock wall. It marks the boundry of the farm that used to belong to Riley's neighbor. The Riley Farm starts on the other side of that sorry old rock wall. Now, the Rileys don't build rock walls, never did. Riley men always plant their rocks. Only farmers I ever knew who could plant a rock and watch it sprout in less than a week. I hear tell there's a new Riley just born. Wouldn't be at all surprised if Nate Riley didn't teach that baby how to plant pebbles before the young'n learns to walk.''